AN EXPLOSIVE ENDING

HAUNTING AVERY WINTERS
BOOK VII

DIONNE LISTER

ISBN 978-1-922407-71-9

Paperback edition

Cover art by Melinda Chapman

Content Editing by Hot Tree Editing

Proofreading L. Brodey

Created with Vellum

To Joanne Forsstrom Smith, for all your encouragement and support. Your love of Avery is much appreciated, and your gentle prods helped get me over the line with this one.

CHAPTER 1

"I'd like to thank you all for coming." Julian peered around at the well-dressed crowd in his living room. "Congratulations to my team, and in particular Avery. I can say that hiring the new kid from Australia is one of the best decisions I've ever made. You've become such an integral part of our team, and you have a great nose for sniffing out murders. Our articles have certainly benefitted from that."

Everyone laughed. I smiled awkwardly—was that such a great thing to bring to the table? I supposed it was, considering this was a news outlet. The only person who didn't seem to agree was Joyless's sister, who stood on the other side of the group, a look of distaste warping her face. Even though a truce existed between her sister and me after I helped get her out of a murder charge, Bethany wanted to keep the flame of intense dislike burning.

"Please raise your glasses." We did, the champagne flutes glinting in the light of the small chandelier. "Cheers, team!"

"Cheers!" we said as one. Carina, Finn, and I grinned at each other, then swigged our champagne.

Meg, who stood next to me, put her arm around my waist, squeezed, then let me go. "I'm so proud of you, Aves."

The awards night had been last night in London, and since it was such a long way from Manesbury, we'd stayed the night, then made our way back for another party at Julian's for tonight so our friends and family could celebrate with us. Not that I had any family here, but that was actually a good thing.

"Thanks, lovely. And thanks for helping me when I first got here. You saved my bum when I had nowhere to stay." The day I'd opened the door to the dead body in my new apartment seemed like a lifetime ago. So much had happened since then, yet it was only a few months ago.

"I could tell we were going to be friends from the moment I met you. I've got a good nose for those things." She smiled.

"Cheers to that." I took another large sip, almost emptying my glass. This was my third of the night and should probably be my last for a while. A light buzz vibrated through me, and my gaze was straying to Finn too often. The last thing I wanted was for anyone, especially him, thinking I had some kind of crush. I just liked to look.

That was all.

Yep. That was it.

"Congratulations again, Avery."

I turned. A smile lit the rounded face of Julian's old friend and mentor, Morris. His grey hair was neatly parted on one side and smoothed with product. With his tailored suit but no tie, he was the epitome of a sophisticated older man.

His wife, Meredith, dressed in a floor-length black gown, held his arm. "It gives us such pleasure to see Julian mentoring a new group of talented journalists." She smiled lovingly at her husband. "It's good to know that Morris's protégé is taking that knowledge and using it, not letting Morris's legacy disappear."

Julian had worked under Morris for fifteen years, from when he first started in the family company to when he took over running the *Manesbury Daily*. Apparently, Julian and his own father didn't get along so well, so Morris had the job of teaching Julian everything he knew.

Morris held his hand out to me, and we shook. "If you ever want any foreign correspondence work, let me know. I've reported on four wars and two coups."

Blood drained from my face, and I knew this because my cheeks became clammy, and the sudden dizzy spell wasn't from the alcohol. Imagine all the ghosts… likely angry and sad ones, I'd have to talk to. How many would want me to contact their families and give them some last words? If there was anything more traumatizing, I couldn't think of it.

Meredith's eyes widened. She gave me a gentle smile and patted my arm. "Don't worry, darling. Reporting from a war zone isn't for everyone. Goodness knows, each time Morris went, I fretted that he wouldn't return whole and healthy, if at all. Thankfully, he did."

Julian had mentioned that Morris received two prestigious awards for his war reporting, but that was a path I wasn't following. Dealing with the dead in and around Manesbury was more than enough for me.

"Ah, thanks for the offer, but I'll pass. It's noble work, but I like where I'm at." Dealing with the crazies around here and the occasional murder were my preferences, but I couldn't say that out loud.

He chuckled. "Well, the offer stands if you ever change your mind. Congratulations again, Avery, on a job well done."

"Keep in touch, darling." Meredith gave me a quick hug. "We have a forty-minute drive and a trip to prepare for. We're off to Spain for three months."

Morris took his wife's hand. His eyes sparkled as he said, "I've been promising her this trip for ten years, and with my recent retirement, we can finally be off."

"That sounds amazing," Meg said. "Have fun."

"We will." Meredith gave a wave; then, the couple made their way to Julian and his wife for goodbye hugs.

Carina and Finn joined Meg and me. Carina handed me a full champagne flute. "Drink up, superstar. The night is young."

I looked across the room at the walnut grandfather clock. "It's almost midnight." I lowered my voice. "The night is about as young as Morris." Not that there was anything wrong with being in your late sixties.

Carina chuckled. "You're naughty."

I held up the full glass and my empty one. "I'm blaming these."

Finn laughed. "You look pretty undrunk to me, Lightning. One more won't hurt."

I narrowed my eyes. "You just want me to say more inappropriate things. Not happening." I placed my empty glass on a table and held the other one. I'd wait a bit before drinking it—it was the sensible thing to do. If I wasn't careful, I'd be throwing myself at Finn, and that was never going to end well. "Let's take a selfie! We haven't done that yet." Yes, I was changing the subject. So sue me. I went to my clutch that was on a nearby table and took my phone out. I put it on camera mode and gathered Carina, Meg, and Finn.

Finn held his hand out. "Here, give the phone to me."

I was standing at one end of our group, but my arm still wasn't long enough to get a great angle, plus I hadn't put my drink down. Priorities. "Fine." I handed the phone to him. We all grinned, and he took a shot.

"Funny faces, everyone!" Carina called.

I stuck my tongue out and crossed my eyes. Who knew what the others were doing, but I couldn't wait to see. "Okay, done." Finn handed the phone back, but before I could check his handiwork, it was as if a cloud passed in front of the sun, even though it was night-time and we were inside.

Bethany sidled up to Finn and batted her lashes. That explained it. "I was wondering if you could give me a lift to Jensen's. A few friends are partying, and I'm going to meet them."

He cocked his head to the side, considering. As he opened his mouth to answer, a huge crack deafened us, the house shaking and rumbling, the windows at the front smashing in by the sounds of things. A hissing whoosh seemed to suck the air away. Two people fell over, and I stumbled backwards, my eyes bugging out, champagne drenching my arm.

"What the hell?" I clunked my crystal flute on the table, my heart racing.

Typical journalists, we all ran for the front door, Finn leading the way.

"I'll call de police." Carina was dialling as we jogged, which wasn't easy in heels.

"I'll call an ambulance." Meg put her phone to her ear.

We reached the front door, which seemed to be intact. Finn opened it, revealing a scene of flaming horror in the street. Julian pushed through our staring throng from behind. He ran down the front steps. I was right behind him. Someone might need our help—unfortunately, whoever had been in that car explosion was likely beyond it.

My fears were confirmed when Morris and Meredith stepped out of the car. Clothes unsinged, skin white and untouched, hair coiffed to perfection as it had been ten minutes ago. Their ghosts glowed faintly against the blackened, burning hulk of their Range Rover.

Julian sprinted over. I called out, "It's too late. I'm sorry." The message was for Julian and his newly deceased friends.

Meg stopped next to me and grabbed my hand. "Are you sure?"

I wrenched my gaze from the gruesome, twisted metal that used to be a car and other things that were glistening on Julian's lawn in the muted beam of streetlights—some of it was glass, but not all. "No one could've survived that blast and the fire." The red and orange flames reflected off the black road and backlit Julian, who stood near the wreck, slowly shaking his head over and over.

Meg placed a hand on her mouth, her voice straining through her fingers. "Of course not. What was I thinking?"

Neighbours had come outside, converging on the scene like zombies sniffing a good meal. Most were in their pjs, dressing gowns, and slippers. Which reminded me that it was the middle of winter, and I was out here in a halter-neck evening gown. I shivered. But instead of going inside, I watched Morris hug his wife. "Are you all right, love?"

She looked around, spied the car, and gasped. "Is that me?"

Silence met her question. It seemed that being an award-winning war journalist didn't equip you to handle your wife's demise in a similar way. It took everything in me not to hurry down to talk to them and ask them what happened before the explosion. I was going to miss my chance. *No no no*!

Light engulfed the couple.

Morris found his voice. "Is that what I think it is?"

"I do believe we're off to the next place. It's not Spain, but hopefully, it will be just as good." She was handling it remarkably well. Maybe she was in shock?

Morris tried to pull her into a hug, but his arms went right through her. His forehead wrinkled. "What is this?"

Meredith's chest rose with a deep breath, her voice steady. "We're dead, obviously. Very bad timing." She patted her arms. "I feel real." She reached out and tried, unsuccessfully, to touch her husband. "But you… don't." Her head lifted as if she was gathering her strength. "At least we'll be together. Neither of us went first. That's what we always wanted, wasn't it?" Her eyes focussed on the expanding brightness. "I feel a pull."

Morris reached up to touch her hair. When his fingers disappeared into her head, he flinched and snatched them back. "I'm not going. I'm sorry, love, but I need to stay here and figure this out. Whoever did this needs to be brought to justice. Wait for me?"

"Please don't do this, Morris. Haven't I waited long enough for you to be finished with work? I put up with you never being home for so many years. This was meant to be our time. I can't go without you."

My heart broke for her. They were finally going to enjoy his retirement, and then this. Why was life so unfair?

"I love you, Meredith. Please. I just need more time. I promise I won't be long. I can't let someone murder the love of my life and get away with it. And the children. What if they're in danger? Please understand." They'd mentioned their three adult children in passing during the night—two sons and a daughter.

Her eyes shone. "I won't wait forever, Morris. I've waited too long already." Pain radiated from her eyes as the hissing sound that always accompanied these events rose in a crescendo, and the light sucked her away. Morris gritted his teeth and strained to move backwards, resisting the other-worldly pull. He grunted and fisted his hands. I held my breath—if he managed to stay, he'd be a big help to me in solving this thing.

Because this was all about me. Yes, I know.

The loud rushing stopped. The searing light extinguished, leaving the street illuminated by the dim overhead lamps, twinkling, coloured Christmas lights, and whatever brightness escaped from nearby houses, whose occupants were standing around shaking their heads and conversing in murmurs. This had to be the most shocking thing that had ever happened in their street, I would've imagined. It was only a few weeks till Christmas. Somehow, that made it worse.

Morris was still here, among the shattered glass, forlorn, shoulders sagging, face slack, as if he was only just now realising what he'd done—abandoned his wife at the end. I guessed "'til death do us part" was apt in this case, even though it was his decision and not fate. As sad as I was for him and Meredith, I was here to help him solve this ASAP. Hopefully, I'd be able to reunite him with Meredith way faster than if he had to go it alone. That was if the light took him after his refusal. Did the universe just know when he was ready? Would it come back for him?

Finn rubbed his arms, trying to get warm. His shirt and jacket weren't enough to stave off the biting cold. He looked at me and Meg. "Maybe you should go inside. There's nothing you can do." He gazed at our boss, who'd fallen to his knees. "I'll go and see if Julian needs anything." At his reminder of the cold, I shivered and flexed my numbing fingers. I'd been so engrossed in the scene that I'd tuned out.

Loud sobbing came from behind us. Carina held Julian's wife in her arms—the woman devastated about her friends. She'd known them almost as long as Julian had. They'd holidayed together many times, and Morris's daughter used to babysit Julian's three children. They were practically family.

I hugged myself because I couldn't ignore the cold now, but I wasn't ready to go inside. "I'll go inside in a couple of minutes. I just want to check the street out."

"You don't have to cover this one, Lightning. Julian will understand."

"I know." I wasn't going to argue, and I didn't feel like a lecture. "The quicker I check it out, the quicker I can get inside and stop freezing."

He huffed loudly. "Fine. Stubborn woman." He reefed his jacket off and threw it at me, so I had no choice but to catch it or let it drop and get dirty. "At least wear that so you don't die of hypothermia."

I was so bloody freezing that instead of insisting I didn't need to wear a piece of clothing that smelled like his subtle, masculine aftershave, I put it on and turned to Meg. "Can you go inside? This isn't pretty, and I'll just be five minutes. Okay? You're not a journalist, and you don't need to see this."

Meg wasn't a china doll, but she was a sweetheart and not used to what I was, and even I had nightmares. I wanted to spare her as much as I could.

"Okay. Let me know if you need anything." She gave me a

quick hug, then collected Carina and Julian's wife on the way inside. Four of the other guests I'd met tonight joined them.

I peered around at the crowd—a few of whom, having seen the carnage, were hurrying back inside. The only ghost was Morris. And it was time to talk to him.

I recorded video on my phone—as tragic as the scene was, there might be a clue in this later. I filmed the car and surrounding carnage, then walked up and down the street, filming one side, then the other. Sirens caterwauled, becoming louder with every one of my misted breaths. Hopefully Bellamy would be on duty tonight, so I didn't have to repeat everything to him tomorrow. Whoever showed up would want my version of events.

Standing a little away from Finn, who was comforting Julian, I stared at Morris, waiting for him to notice. The ghost was standing next to his grieving friend. "I'm sorry, old chap. Don't cry on my account." Morris folded his arms. "We need to catch the bastards who did this." He frowned and peered up and down the street, his concerned gaze finally landing back on Julian. "It would be easier if you could hear me. But then again, I trust you to find them. I have a feeling you'll do your best. But you don't even realise what I've given you." When Julian didn't so much as glance Morris's way, the older man sighed. "Is it too much to ask that someone could hear me? What's the point of being a spirit if I'm on mute?"

He had a point. I put my phone to my ear. "That's where I come in," I said, loud enough to carry. Finn gave me a weird look, but when he figured I was on the phone, he gave an understanding chin tip and tried to coax Julian inside, but our boss wasn't having it.

Morris jerked his head towards me, and I gave a small smile and a nod. His eyes widened. "You can see me?"

"Yes, that's right."

"Hmm, you could just be on the phone, and that was a coincidence. Say journalists eat sharks for breakfast."

My brow furrowed. "I don't repeat everything I hear, especially when I'm in a crowd." Would he get the idea that I didn't want anyone within hearing distance—aka Finn and Julian—to think I'd lost the plot? I was still meeting his gaze.

"Fine. Say, yes, no, yes."

"Yes, no, yes." Luckily, he was a quick study, which shouldn't be surprising given he was an award-winning journalist.

"Well, Avery, it looks as if you're keeping secrets."

"Yes, but doesn't everyone have them?" Unless this explosion was an accident or some bad guys targeted the wrong person, Morris might very well have secrets of his own. And what did he mean by saying to Julian that he doesn't realise what he gave him? "Anyway, I'm here to help. Whatever you need."

The sirens homed in on us, stopping our conversation, the flashing lights painting the streetscape red. The colour of blood. Why did I have to think of these things? The wailing stopped as the three cars parked in the middle of the street, blocking it off. The other end of the road was a cul-de-sac, so they didn't drive further than Julian's house. The police jumped out. Two of them immediately cordoned off the road and set up barriers, another two cordoned off the other side of the scene, and the last two approached the crowd.

A relieved sigh left my lips when I recognised Bellamy. He quickly assessed the disaster and gestured for his offsider to approach Finn. Bellamy made a beeline straight for me, glass crunching under his feet. He dodged a small lump of... something. I took a steadying breath and put my phone in my pocket. Because Morris had come to stand right next to me, I was able to whisper, "He knows my secret."

Morris gave me an appraising look, and I might've been mistaken, but I thought I saw hope in his eyes.

"Winters." Bellamy nodded in greeting, his expression grim. "It's quite the scene." His gaze roved over the blackened metal, and he took his notebook and pen out. "Care to give me a rundown of what happened?"

More wailing cut off our conversation as two fire engines flew down the street, jerking to a stop just outside the barriers. The cavalry had arrived, but the fire was more of a smoulder now, so there wasn't much they could do, except maybe start their own investigation.

"Yes, Sergeant. I can do that." I looked at Finn and Julian. They were occupied by the policeman Bellamy had sent to them. I lowered my voice. "I have one of the victims here… Morris. He and his wife were in the car."

Bellamy's eyes widened. "Well, that's good news." He cleared his throat. "Ah, not good in that they're deceased, but good that we'll get some firsthand information."

Morris nodded, his expression carefully neutral. "Tell him I'm not sure who did this, but I can give him several names." I glanced at the ghost, surprise hijacking my common sense. He held his palms face up and floated them outward in a "whatever" gesture. "Don't look so surprised. You've exposed far fewer people than I have, and from what Julian tells me, you've made enemies. I've had a long career, and I've pulverised more than a few sets of toes." He folded his arms and gave what looked like a satisfied nod.

Fair enough. He had me there. Still, why was he suddenly so… detached? Was that his journalism skills kicking in? One of the first things we learned was to gather facts and, even if we had an opinion, wait till we could prove it one way or the other. Okay, not all journos worked to that standard, but I tried.

I looked at Bellamy. "Morris said he's made many enemies —he's an award-winning journalist with decades of experience. He was Julian's mentor, and from what I learned at the party tonight, not afraid to tell it like it is and expose those who deserve it. His investigations have sent more than one person to jail."

Before Bellamy could answer, two firefighters hurried over. The taller of the two, a broad-shouldered guy in his thirties, spoke. "What's the situation?"

Bellamy gave him a quick rundown of what he knew, which wasn't much but the obvious. "I'll get my guys to clear the area, and you can get to work."

"Thanks." As quickly as they'd arrived, they left, heading for their truck.

One of the police who'd set up the roadblock joined us. "Sergeant, we're all done."

"Great. Can you clear the area and start interviewing everyone? Get them into their houses, and then ask questions."

He gave a nod. "Can do." He turned to look back at his partner, who was having a conversation with one of the firemen. "Bobby, let's get to it."

His colleague waved once. "Right you are."

Once we were alone again, Bellamy made notes. "If anyone asks, you questioned Morris about how to deal with disgruntled subjects at the party because you've had some issues, and you knew he had experience with it."

"Okay, Sergeant. I can do that."

"Can I give you those names now?" Morris glanced at the

car. "I'd like to get this all squared away so I can get to my wife. She's not too happy with me."

I repeated Morris's request. If only I could find a way for Bellamy to see and hear what I could. There must be something I could do.

Bellamy's gaze travelled to my right, where he'd seen me look when talking to Morris. "Sorry, but before we get into that, I'd like you to describe what happened. It will help us build a case and get to the bottom of what caused the explosion. You could have information we'd never find otherwise."

Without looking at the ghost, I said, "Morris, can you stand next to the sergeant so I can look at you when I talk?" It was weird peering at supposedly nothing whilst talking. There was much chaos and movement around us, but someone might notice. Okay, not just someone. Vinegar.

Morris stood next to Bellamy. "Tell the sergeant that when we exited the party, there was nothing unusual. I unlocked the car with my fob, opened my wife's door, then went around and got into the driver's side." He rubbed his chin as he pondered, and I repeated everything to Bellamy. "Come to think of it, there was a car further up the street, across the road with its brake lights on. I didn't pay much attention to it. I remember seeing the red lights when I looked in my mirrors before I started the car. It could be nothing."

I told Bellamy. Before he could ask anything, I jumped in. It was an obvious question anyway. "Do you remember anything else about the car? Could you tell if it was a sedan, a sportscar, or an SUV? Was it dark- or light-coloured?"

He shut his eyes for a moment, then opened them. "Possibly an SUV. The lights were higher than a sedan… I think. Colour-wise, I have no idea. It's night, and like I said, I wasn't paying close attention."

Bellamy cleared his throat. "Why am I even here, Winters?"

I bit my bottom lip. *Oops*. "Sorry, Sergeant. It was just easier than going back and forth. Anyway, he said it could've been an SUV because of the height of the brake lights, but he's not sure of anything else."

"Right." He turned to his left, knowing that's where I'd been looking at the deceased journalist. "Sorry to have to ask this, and I'm not sure of etiquette here, but what happened next?" I tried not to laugh because the moment was so inappropriate, but Bellamy had a point. Not that I'd ever worried about that before. Hmm, did that make me heartless or rude? Argh, this was totally going to bother me in the middle of the night. Instead of sleeping, I was going to feel guilty.

Morris's wispy smile held sadness. "I put my foot on the brake and pushed the ignition button. There was a flash, and I had a sense of being pushed upwards for a millisecond, but nothing after that. It was instantaneous. Thank the Lord for small mercies Meredith didn't suffer." He swallowed and turned again to stare at what was left of him and his car. "I need a moment." He walked away. Maybe reality was setting in?

Holding Finn's jacket tightly closed against the frosty air and trying not to shiver, I looked at Bellamy and told him everything. "Now what?"

"I take it, the victim needs time to process. Before you leave here tonight, figure out a way to talk to him later. He wants to catch his killer, so I'm assuming he'll make it easy for you. In the meantime, the blast needs to be investigated, evidence gathered, etcetera. I'll be in touch in the next couple of days unless you hear something first. I want to start questioning people ASAP." He pointed his pen at me. "Now, get inside before you catch your death."

"Yes, sir!" I saluted him and half smiled. "See you later. And good luck with all this." I gestured to the disaster. "I'll have a quick word with Morris first, and I'll let you know when I have more info. Bye."

"Night, Winters. Oh, and congratulations on the award."

I turned and was about to ask how he knew, but he was already walking away.

CHAPTER 2

Sunday morning, I rolled out of bed at eleven thirty-five, bleary-eyed and hungry. Carina, Meg, Finn, and I had stayed at Julian's until three in the morning, making sure he and his wife were okay. Eventually, they shooed us out, claiming they needed to try and sleep. To be fair, they both looked the worse for wear and were still trying to process. Such a wonderful night had ended so horribly. It was a night none of us would ever forget, and for the wrong reasons.

When I went into the kitchen to make my coffee, my award sat on the table, shiny and proud, as if nothing untoward had happened. Sometimes I wished my heart could be as inanimate.... Okay, not physically, but you know. I wasn't ready to join my ghostly friends. Speaking of which....

"Hey."

Thankfully, I'd been facing the table and saw Everly as soon as she appeared. No heart attack for me today. Ha! "Hey, yourself. What's up?"

"I need to talk to you." She fiddled with the locket around her neck—the same one I'd given to police a few weeks ago. This was an interesting turn of events. She'd been avoiding me since I'd found it because I'd wanted to know who killed her. Was she ready to tell me?

I abandoned coffee making—I could do that when we were finished. I wasn't risking fobbing her off for even a minute in case she chickened out and changed her mind. Sitting at the kitchen table, I pulled out the seat next to me and beckoned her over. "Sit." Not that she needed the chair to hover in a sitting position, but it made me feel better. I adjusted the seat so it was back a bit—I hated when the table cut them in half.

Everly wrung her hands together. "Hang on a minute." She disappeared. That had to be record time for changing your mind. I sighed and sank back into the chair.

"That's cruel," I called out to the empty apartment. *So close, yet so far.* I pushed my chair back—might as well get myself a coffee after all.

She materialised next to me, and I jumped in my seat. "Jeez! Did you have to?"

A half-hearted smirk graced her face. "Sorry." This time, she sat where I'd asked. "I don't want to have this conversation, but I need to." It was her turn to sigh.

I tilted my chair to face her, my forehead wrinkling in concern. "I'm sorry, but you know this is important… both for your mother and any other victims." We didn't know if there were any others, but if the person who did this to her hadn't done it by accident, chances were, she wasn't the only person they'd murdered.

She swallowed and licked her lips. "That's why I'm going

to talk." Her wavering gaze met mine. "I… I just had a session with a woman a few years older than me—Jenny Frankel. She was twenty-six when she died." Her gaze drifted to the window overlooking the street, not that we could see anything except the grey sky from where we sat.

When she didn't speak for a while, I prodded a finger into her shoulder. I shuddered when it went straight through. *When would I learn*? "And?"

She looked at me, squaring her shoulders. "He killed her."

I froze.

"Don't look at me like that. I'm sorry, okay? I should've said something when you originally asked. But I didn't know…. I didn't know." Her head fell forward, and her eyes closed.

This was the news I didn't want to hear. "When? Did they catch him afterwards?" Maybe she was okay with telling me who he was because he was already in jail, and it wouldn't be her fault he ended up in prison.

Her head snapped up. "No, they didn't. That's why I'm telling you. He's still out there, and he could do it again. I mean, he's a serial killer, right?"

I scratched my head. "Um… I don't know. Two murders might just make him evil. But realistically, yes. There are probably more victims." That was the conclusion I was making, and it wouldn't hurt if it got her to finish telling me who it was. "So, when did this happen? You haven't said."

"He killed Jenny eight years ago."

"Right, so it's not your fault." Her reason for telling me meant she felt guilty, which was terrible because she had enough pain heaped on her without this. "Who could you have told before I came along?"

"Um...." She looked at the window again, then finally at me. "No one. Absolutely no one. There was a young boy once, but...." She rubbed her locket between her thumb and forefinger. "But he ran away when I spoke to him."

My forehead furrowed. I'd file that away for later. Was it a young boy recently or one twenty years ago? It would be hard for her to tell me because of ghosts' inability to accurately measure the passing of time, and where had she been when this happened? A needle in a haystack, for sure. It wasn't worth worrying about. I'd have to be content with being one of the only people I knew with this affliction... talent? I wasn't sure which one it was—my mind changed daily.

"That's just one reason it's not your fault. Not that I'm happy you didn't tell me straight away, but before me, you couldn't talk to anyone. And I know you didn't want to upset your mum, but that point is moot—she's already thinking about it."

She sighed. "And with Christmas coming up, she's sadder than usual. She had the photo albums out last night... or was that the night before?" Her head quickly shook like a dog rejecting water. "In any case, I'm still scared, but it's time to bring him to justice." Fire ignited in her eyes. She was serious. *Finally*!

"But what have you got to be scared of? He can't hurt you any more."

A melancholic smile lifted her lips. She stood and went to the window. After a minute, she turned and looked at me. "So, do you want to know who he is?"

The fact she'd ignored my question wasn't lost on me, but I'd let it slide because she was going to spill on the important stuff. Besides, trying to get something out of her that she didn't want to explain was an impossible task—she was one of the most stubborn people, ah, ghosts I'd met.

"Yes." I pulled up the Notes app on my phone. My thumbs hovered over the keypad as I waited.

She turned back to stare out the window, resting her hands on the wide sill. They went through, but I didn't think she noticed. "He was my boyfriend of a few months. Mum had introduced us. He was her friend from church's son."

Things clicked into place. "You didn't want her to feel guilty when she found out he'd killed you?"

Everly turned. Her eyes held such pain that my nose tingled with impending tears. I swallowed them. "Yes. That's one reason." She came back to the table, slipped through the chair, and "sat" on it. "I told myself that it was too late to do anything about me dying, so why add to her grief? She'd blame herself. As it was, she's hated herself for not being able to protect me. She's questioned if she was too lenient, letting a boy take me out. But I was eighteen, practically an adult. She couldn't have said no."

"What's his name?"

"Andrew Crumps." She stared at the table, drawing circles on it with a finger.

I typed on my phone. "How old was he when it happened?"

"Twenty-one. And I thought I was so cool, going out with an older 'man.' He was good-looking, too, opened my car door every time, bought me flowers, and paid when we went out." Her self-deprecating smile bared some teeth.

"I'm getting the vibe that you blame yourself. This isn't your fault." The journalist in me warred with the friend—I wanted to give her comfort, but there were things I needed to ask. "Do you know when his birthday is?" I could probably find out quite easily since she knew who his family were, but the more information I had from the get-go, the better.

"January twenty-third. When I dated him, he was studying to be a dentist. Jenny, the woman he killed, was an ex-patient he'd tried to date. She rejected him, and he… didn't take it well."

"Do you know where he worked?"

"He works out of London…. At least he was when he killed her. I don't know where he lives or works now. Mum still speaks to his mother every now and then… well, at least she used to. She doesn't much speak to anyone any more, so, yeah, I don't know if she's talked to her lately."

My thumbs tapped double time, inputting the information. "Did she say how he killed her? Did someone find her body?" If he was a serial killer doing what he did with Everly's body, chances were that they wouldn't have found her body either. But with a bit of luck, they had, and that would be one less thing I'd have to untangle.

"She lived alone and said that she got home one evening after work, and when she checked the doors before bed, she noticed the back door was unlocked. She had no idea how because she was sure she'd checked it that morning. But she put it down to being tired and went to bed. The next morning, after drinking her tea, she felt unwell and groggy. Just before she passed out on the kitchen floor, he walked in, smiling. She said she'd never forget what he said, even though she was half out of it. 'Good morning, Jenny. Are you ready for our date?"

I shivered. That was so creepy. What a psycho. "That poor woman."

"I know." She hung her head.

"I hate repeating myself, but I'm going to. This. Is. Not. Your. Fault. Now, I have more questions, but about what happened to you?" I didn't ask if she was okay to answer them—the less room I gave her for bowing out, the better. "So, he took you on a date and killed you that night. Wasn't anyone suspicious when he didn't bring you home?"

Her lips pinched as if she were trying to crush coal into a diamond. Where had she been hiding this anger? Whenever we'd touched on this subject up till now, she'd been cool, calm, and collected, as if it had happened so long ago that the horror and anger had faded. Apparently not. "The next morning, he told my mother that he left me in the laneway. Back then, there were no street cameras, no mobile phones. One of our neighbours said they heard a car coming and going at about the time he said he dropped me, but that was it. He supposedly dropped me back around one in the morning."

"A convenient time that everyone would be asleep."

"Yep."

"Do you know if the police searched his car or home?"

She shook her head. "He was living with his parents during the university breaks and living in London during study times. He'd come home to Devon for the Easter break and wanted to take me out—they lived in Salcombe. It's a posh seaside area. I think after my mother vouched for him, and with his hysteria or supposed grief, they questioned him, had a quick look around his parents' house, and left. His dad was a top surgeon. His family *knew* people."

Now the truth came out. Special rules for special people. He'd gotten away with it so easily. "That's depressing. Scumbag. And a pox on those bloody police for not doing their job properly. Argh."

"I know, Avery. I know." She sighed, and I added to my notes.

"What do you remember about that night?"

She rubbed her breastbone as her eyes focussed past me to a reality that had long since faded into nothingness. "We went to a classy restaurant near his house in Salcombe—Mrs Fisher's. It was expensive, and he paid. He was a gentleman the whole dinner, pulling my chair out for me, giving me flowers, paying. He was the sweetest all night."

She frowned, maybe attempting to work out how the two parts of his personality could gel—the suave romancer and the cold-blooded killer. Her eyes watered, and she wrenched herself away from whatever world she'd been in to stare hauntingly into my eyes.

"We left just after ten. He said he had something to give me." Everly's fists balled, the muscles in her forearms tensing and shifting under her skin as she squeezed.

Even though I knew Everly, and she'd been dead the whole time I'd known her, my body broke out in goosebumps. A chill settled in the air—as if we sat in a graveyard, not my… our cosy kitchen. I didn't want to ask the next question because I had a feeling it would lead to the inevitable conclusion of my friend's life, but I needed to. I tried to put my journalist's hat on, but it wasn't easy when a friend was involved. "What happene—"

My phone vibrated loudly on the table, and I jumped. We stared at it.

"You should get that."

My eyes widened, and I focussed on her. "No. This is way more important. We're not done. I need more information. We have to make him pay and stop him from doing it to others." I was losing her. This wasn't good.

Everly kept her eyes downcast on my phone. It stopped ringing. "You should call them back. It might be about Zeus." Finally, she slowly lifted her head. "This has been a lot… much more than I thought I'd get out. I'll come back. Promise." After she disappeared, I wondered if that look in her eyes was grief for what she'd lost… what he'd stolen from her.

Before I picked up my phone to call Josie, my neighbour looking after Zeus, back, I made a promise I'd do everything to keep. "I'll bring him to justice, Everly. And he'll never hurt anyone ever again."

CHAPTER 3

I stood in Josie's lounge room, still in the black, puffy winter coat I'd donned to cross the laneway. She handed his cat carrier to me. "I'm so sorry, Avery, but I don't want to drive in this weather, and he really needs to see a vet. My eyesight isn't what it used to be."

Holding the carrier up, I peered inside. Zeus gazed up at me forlornly, head resting on his paws. "Don't be silly, Josie. You've done so much for me just by looking after him. I'm sorry I haven't found anyone who can take him yet."

"I know, sweetie, but I can only have him for three more days. I'm visiting my cousin for a week. I'll be back for Christmas, but I don't want to leave him with my Freddie while I'm gone. They don't get along. I truly am sorry."

I sighed. "I know. So, how long has he not eaten for?"

"He went off his food two days ago, but I thought it might just be him being picky. I tried all his favourites—baked chicken, cheese, those fishy treat things. He wants none of it." We all knew that cheese wasn't great for cats, but as a treat, it was okay. If he was refusing all those things, there was definitely something wrong, and his demeanour was very un-Zeus-like. He was usually very vocal, energetic, and affectionate.

Please be okay. "I'm sure the vet can sort him out. I'll let you know as soon as I find out what's wrong. And thanks again for everything. You really have been a lifesaver." I hid my worry behind a soft smile. She'd done everything she could for him and had looked after him longer than we originally agreed. I didn't want to make her life difficult. She'd been kind and welcoming ever since I arrived, and I didn't want to ruin things. Relying on others was new for me, but guilt wasn't, and it was turning my stomach. "You've done so much, and I'll make sure he doesn't have to come back here. You're officially Zeus free." Maybe Finn would agree to have him for a few days? Maybe the vet could arrange something?

"Thank you, Avery, and I am sorry. If I didn't have my Freddie, I would love to adopt Zeus. He's a gorgeous boy." She bent to look into the cat carrier and made kissy noises at him. "Bye, darling one."

I waved and headed for my car. There was an emergency vet about two miles out of the village. They were open seven days, thank goodness. This weekend had wasted no time turning into one of the most stressful I'd ever had. First the explosion, then Everly coming to me, and now this.

Zeus whined a couple of times. "I'm sorry, buddy. We'll fix this. I'm sorry you're not feeling well."

I didn't let myself think that the vet couldn't fix what was wrong. Maybe Zeus had a cold or something? Although there were serious cat viruses. What if he had feline leukemia? *Oh my God, Avery, just stop.* I turned the radio onto a pop station. Spiralling right now wasn't productive. Before I drove off, I called the vet's and let them know I was coming.

It started raining as I drove. *Perfect.* By the time I reached the vet's, I was sour-faced. Christmas was shaping up to be positively awesome. If anything happened to Zeus, there was no way I would enjoy the holiday season, not to mention all the other things. Although, if I could at least solve Everly's case, at least Mrs Crabby might have an okay Christmas.

The scent of cleaning fluid trying to cover the animal excrement odour greeted me in the white-floored waiting room. I went to the desk, told them who I was, and then took a seat four down from a young woman with a cockatoo in a cage. The bird's feathers were half plucked out. Someone needed Valium. Did they have that for birds?

I placed the cat carrier on the floor, and Zeus hissed. Sitting opposite was a middle-aged man, the Dalmatian at his feet, wearing a cast on one front leg. I turned the cat carrier around so Zeus couldn't see the dog. "It's okay, buddy. I won't let anyone hurt you."

The bird squawked. "Stupid cat! Bad cat!"

I chuckled. "Don't listen to him, Zeus."

His owner frowned at me and turned to her bird. "Who's a good boy, Dundee."

"Dundee's a good boy. *Squawk*!"

"Yes, you are. And you're right"—she glared at me this time—"cats are bad." Wow, she was taking passive-aggressive into the more aggressive route.

I didn't have the spoons to deal today.

I smiled at her. "I beg to differ. He got best-behaved at day care last week."

"He did not. You're lying. No one would give a cat best-behaved. Unless it was a cats-only day care."

For a minute there, I thought she'd realise I was kidding. Meh, might as well run with it. "No, there are dogs and guinea pigs too. They used to allow ferrets, but they were too cranky and started lots of fights." I took my phone out of my pocket—in my rush, I hadn't gone back to the apartment, and I'd only brought keys and my phone. At least my debit card and Aussie driver's licence were on my phone. Yay for technology. "Would you like to see some photos? It was Vomit's birthday two weeks ago, and they had a meaty cake."

Her chin doubled as she reared back. Who knew she wouldn't be a fan of meaty cakes… or maybe it was the word "vomit." "No, thank you."

"Where's the cake? No cake. Dundee's a good boy." The parrot followed that up with three shrieks of the eff word. The man sitting opposite snorted, and his dog raised his head to gawk at the bird.

I couldn't help but smirk. "I hate to point this out, but good boys don't swear."

The woman gave me a dirty look. She opened her mouth, but whatever she was going to spout was cut off by a vet who entered the waiting room. His gaze fixed on my combative neighbours. "Dundee Perkins, please come this way."

Thankfully, the woman, and the bird, managed to leave without any more insults. The dog owner and I gave each other the look strangers exchange when the public drama of a less-than-pleasant person has ended. We were survivors of an idiot attack. There was camaraderie in that.

After a ten-minute wait, it was my turn. A middle-aged woman with a greying ponytail and a kind, tanned face took us into her exam room. "Please place the carrier on the table."

I placed it on the stainless-steel bench, and she opened it, cooing to Zeus as she did.

"He's an affectionate cat. He shouldn't be a problem."

She brought him out and placed the carrier on the floor. "What seems to be the problem?"

I told her everything Josie had told me and explained how I'd ended up with him. "He's usually very curious and active." Zeus lay placidly on the table and wasn't even purring—a very bad sign. As the vet poked and prodded him, her expression giving nothing away, worry grew in my gut. I knew she probably couldn't tell me anything without doing blood tests, but I had to ask. "Do you have any idea what it could be? Will he be okay?"

Her serene smile was obviously meant to put me at ease, but it didn't. "I'll take his temperature first, and we need to do further testing. Just a moment." She took out the thermometer, lubed it up with some KY Jelly—I was glad I wasn't Zeus at this point—and stuck the thermometer where it was likely to cause the most embarrassment. I winced, but my poor cat didn't even flinch. It reminded me of the time I went on a cruise for schoolies week—the end-of-school trip that most Aussie teens did. I was so seasick that when the ship's doctor told me to lie on my stomach and pull my pants down so he could stick a needle in my cheek, I didn't care. I was all for it, if only the nausea would go away.

The longer she examined him without saying anything, the more I wanted to beg her to tell me what she thought. Finally, she looked at me. "His temperature is elevated, and his glands are swollen. It can mean anything. Unfortunately, it could be something serious, so I'd like to take bloods and keep him overnight. Is that okay?"

Thank goodness for the journalism prize I'd just won—I could afford whatever these tests and vet stay were going to cost. I stroked Zeus's head. "Yes, that's fine. Whatever you need to do to figure it out." Zeus managed a small purr under my ministrations. "Get better, little guy. You'll just be here for one night, and then I'll come get you. I'll do whatever it takes to sneak you in. If you're quiet, I bet Mrs Crabby won't notice." I didn't believe that, but I was going to try. If she caught me, I'd say I was minding him for the afternoon. Surely I couldn't be evicted for that.

"If you need someone to foster him till you find him a home, I'll ask around and see what I can come up with. Who knows, I might be able to find him a new forever family."

My throat tightened against impending tears. In the short time I'd known him, Zeus had curled his way around my heart, and I couldn't imagine never seeing him again. "I've signed a twelve-month lease. If I could find somewhere else near Manesbury to rent, I guess I could try and get kicked out." That wasn't a bad plan, actually. The only problem was that there were limited listings within a twenty-minute drive of work, and any further, and the transport costs would become too high. Rental prices were also a problem. At least 50 per cent more than what I was paying. As annoying as Mrs Crabby was, her rent was more than fair. Not to mention that if I got evicted, it would be on my tenant record and would make it harder, if not impossible, to find another place.

The vet gave me a sympathetic look. "Say goodbye to Zeus, and I'll get started on his tests. One of our staff will call you later to tell you how he's getting on. We'll bill you when you pick him up, hopefully tomorrow."

"Thanks." I gathered Zeus in my arms and snuggled my face into his fur. "I'm sorry, sweetie. I have to leave you here, but I'll be back tomorrow. This lovely lady is going to make you all better. Okay?" I kissed the top of his head, and he licked my chin. "Love you, buddy."

The vet held her hands out, and I passed him over. *Please get better.*

She must've recognised the stressed look on my face. "We'll take good care of him. Don't worry."

I held in my impending breakdown until I was safely in my car. I wasn't ready to say goodbye to my baby, but it wasn't up to me. When I turned the ignition on, the radio filled the car with happy music, the sound all sharp edges grating against my raw heart. Before I pulled into the street, I switched the radio off. If only I could switch my heart off as well.

CHAPTER 4

Sunday afternoon passed by in a depressing heap on my bed. One of the vet nurses called me to say that Zeus's condition hadn't changed. Afterwards, I checked in with Carina, Meg, and Finn to see how they were after last night. They were coping as well as could be expected and didn't want company, so I had a "nap," which lasted until the next morning. Waking up for dinner was too much effort and would mean more thinking time, so I rolled over and went back to sleep.

Monday morning came, bringing with it the hope of a new day and new information, as well as the hope that Zeus would be okay. I was taking the fact that the vet hadn't called before I'd left home at nine as a positive. My sweet boy mustn't be any worse, at least. If the vet's hadn't phoned by the time I finished my first interview, I was going to contact them—I couldn't wait. Not ringing them as soon as I got up had been a challenge.

My first appointment was with a seventy-year-old lady—Mrs Agnus Fernhouse. She lived in an apartment in a three-storey walk-up in Cramptonbury. After I saw her, I was going to pass by and see Bellamy. He'd messaged last night when I was asleep and asked me to come in.

Up on the first floor, I knocked on her door. A slim, short woman, her shoulders rolled forward so that when she looked up at me, it was as if her neck and spine did a zigzag, opened the door. She squinted at me. "Oh, you must be from the paper for my interview about the charity drive."

I smiled. "Yes, Mrs Fernhouse. It's lovely to meet you. I'm Avery." I held out my hand for her to shake. She placed her hand half a foot from mine and waited. I closed the gap and shook. Strange, but if her rounded spine was anything to go by, she probably had a sore back.

"Please, call me Agnus. Come in. The living room is through there."

I went through the door from the entry area into a neat and tidy room. A pink, floral-patterned three-seat sofa faced a large TV on a faux-wood entertainment unit, and a single brown recliner snuggled up to it on one side. Knitting needles and sky-blue wool sat on the recliner. A colourful pile of knitted jumpers sprawled on two of the three couch cushions. They must be the items she'd made for her charity drive.

"Sit, sit." She gestured to the couch, then picked up her knitting and lowered herself into the recliner.

I sat on the vacant couch cushion and took out my notebook and pen. "Did you make all those?" I nodded towards the woollen garments.

She smiled, the wrinkles at the side of her eyes deepening. "Yes. It's taken me a whole year, but there are twenty. This is twenty-one." She held up her current piece. "Feel free to go through them. You might want to describe them for your article. The more you can write about my work, the better. We're auctioning these at the Cramptonbury Christmas Fair."

Manesbury was having its own Christmas thing, and it didn't include a charity knitwear auction. The board might be upset if they found out that they'd not thought of it, and I wasn't going to be the one to tell them. I reached over and picked one off the pile. The body of it was lime green and the sleeves dark green. Was it just my imagination, or was one sleeve slightly shorter than the other? I surreptitiously folded it in half and lined the sleeves up while I stroked it. "The wool is so soft. This is lovely." Yep, the left sleeve was about two centimetres shorter than the right. I placed that one to the side and picked up a red jumper. The colour was gorgeous, like freshly applied scarlet lipstick, but as I turned it around, I saw a hole about the size of a peanut in the back. I placed it down and looked at Agnus. "Which one is your favourite?"

"The turquoise one. I think it's in the middle of the pile."

Hope dangled a cookie in front of me as I reached into the cosy pile of potential disappointment. "Such a lovely colour."

I was perusing it for the fault I knew must be there when she leaned towards me, her eyes narrowed. "Are you sure you have the right one? That looks more like the peacock blue."

"I… ah…. I thought this was turquoise. Maybe I'm wrong. I'm definitely not an artist, so I probably got my colours mixed up. Just a sec." I reached in again, feeling like I was drawing lotto numbers. I pulled out the peacock-blue one. "Is this the turquoise one?"

She placed a finger on her closed mouth. "Hmm…. I'm not sure. Maybe the other one is." Her head fell back, and she laughed. "My eyesight has given me a bit of trouble lately, but not enough to need glasses. I think it's the low light in here, makes it hard. You had trouble picking the colours out, didn't you?"

"Yes. I'm not sure which is which." I chuckled. I wasn't here to make her feel bad, although she probably should get her eyes checked and invest in some glasses. The jumper in my lap had two threads hanging off the bottom, and they weren't short. I held it up. The shape was trapezoid-like. I wasn't a fashion major, but I was pretty sure that jumpers weren't supposed to look like that. Also, who knew I'd ever need to know that shape? My primary school maths teacher had been right—weird-shapes knowledge had come in handy one day. I owed him a huge apology. "So, how long have you been knitting?"

"Too many years to count. My grandmother taught me when I was about eleven." A wistful smile erased years from her face, and her eyes shone as I imagined her eleven-year-old self's had. "She was such a wonderful woman. My time with her was some of the happiest of my life. Unfortunately, she died when I was twenty-two."

"I'm sorry."

She waved my comment away. "It's been so long, I'm surprised I still remember her. It's funny how our loved ones can leave us, but their lessons live on. I taught my two daughters and son how to knit when they were young too. So her knowledge survives for another generation." Her fingers cascaded gently over the yarn in her lap.

I asked a few more questions, and in the middle of answering one, she jerked forward and threw the knitting onto the chair arm. "Oh my! I'm late feeding Cyril."

"Who's Cyril? Do you need any help?"

"Cyril's the hedgehog I saved last night. He didn't look too well on the footpath outside. I grabbed a cardboard box from the bin area and gently prodded him into it. I put a small towel in there, and he seemed to want to hide, so I added a dish of water and a bit of cat food that I borrowed from Tilly in unit three. When I checked on Cyril early this morning, he hadn't moved, and I didn't want to scare him. I wonder if I should take him to the vet?"

"Had he been run over?" I wasn't going to say it, but maybe Cyril had died. Which made me think of Zeus. I took a deep breath and tried to force the slithering dread from squeezing my heart. *They would've called if he'd died. He has to be okay*. I pulled my phone from my bag and checked it. No missed calls. Of course there weren't—I would've heard it ring.

"No. I don't think so. I couldn't see any blood."

"But it was dark?" *And your eyesight is worse than a mole's.*

"Yes. I didn't touch him. I kind of pushed him in with my shoe." She gasped. "You don't think I killed him by doing that, do you?"

"No! Of course not." Yikes. I was going to make her feel bad without even trying. "Why don't we check on him? If he needs to go to the vet, I'll take him. I'm going later today to pick up my cat." Yes, I was crossing my fingers.

"Oh, would you? I'd be ever so grateful."

"Of course. Why don't I take a couple of photos now, and then I'll help you with him."

She clasped her hands in front of her chest and beamed. "You're an angel. Thank you."

I got her to sit in her chair with a few of the jumpers strewn all over her. Her wide smile and kind eyes would attract buyers for sure. What they'd make of their spoils when they received them was anyone's guess, but at the end of the day, I was betting they'd still be happy they were contributing to a worthy cause. Some might even wear them as a silly Christmas jumper, so it wasn't a total loss.

"Okay, let's see this hedgehog." I loved hedgehogs—they were so cute. I'd only seen two since I'd been here, and we didn't have them in Australia. The closest we got was an echidna, which was a monotreme. I was rather proud that Australia was the only place with monotremes, not that I had anything to do with that.

She emerged from under her pile and led me into the kitchen. A round table and two chairs huddled next to the wall. A closed box sat on the table. She whispered, "He's in there. Be careful not to scare him."

"I'll do my best." I crept to the box, then realised how ridiculous I was being. It wasn't as if normal footsteps were going to scare him to death. Agnus had her hands over her mouth as she leaned in while I carefully opened the flaps.

"Has he had any of the food?"

Ew, the stench of fishy cat food suddenly let free wafted in my face. I could almost taste it. "He hasn't." But I couldn't blame him. He was used to eating fresh bugs or ants. Is that what hedgehogs ate? I'd have to look it up later.

"Can you see him?"

Oh. My. Word. I pressed my lips together and tried not to laugh. A few of Cyril's spikes showed from underneath the towel Agnus had placed in there. I lifted the towel out to reveal the hedgehog, reached in, and yanked him out.

"Oh no, be careful!" She flapped her hands in panic.

I couldn't help it, and I was so going to hell for this—okay, so it could just get added to the list of the many reasons I was headed down there—but I snorted in laughter. Holding up the grey and black ball, I said, "This is a pompom. It probably fell off someone's beanie."

She froze and stared at it, then reached out and touched it. "Really?"

"Yes. I think maybe you should think about going to get your eyes tested and maybe buy some glasses."

Agnus gathered Cyril into her hands and started laughing. Before I knew it, we were both guffawing. She managed to say between breaths, "I think I'm going to wet myself." At least she was taking this well.

"Please don't. But if you do, I guess you can mop it up with Cyril." I snorted again. Agnus placed a hand on her stomach, tears streaming down her face, and doubled over. I had to admit, I needed this laugh. Remembering all the reasons why sobered me. Why did real life have to get in the way of a good time?

Agnus straightened and took a few deep breaths. "There's only one thing to do now."

"What's that?"

"I'm going to knit a beanie and pop Cyril on top."

I gave her a thumbs-up. "Brilliant!"

When I hopped back in the car, I called the vet. They were still awaiting results, but Zeus was a tad better. They'd put him on a drip and given him some medicine, and if he wasn't well enough to come home, they were okay with me visiting this arvo. After the call, I drove to Cramptonbury Station, which was only five minutes from Agnus's.

PC Adams manned the front desk, her normal, cheery self.

She always seemed happy to see me. "Avery! Long time, no see." She laughed.

"Yes, it's been about five days." These days, I tended to pop in if I was in the area, whether there was a crime to solve or not. The dead sergeant, Fox, liked me to update Bellamy on what he'd found out in the ghostly realm. If there was a way to make Bellamy see the dead, I really needed to find it. So far, we'd tried holding hands, but that hadn't worked and had almost ended in PC Patel walking in on us. If we'd been busted, it wouldn't have looked good. Bellamy was way too old for me, and he was happily married. The last thing I wanted was for people to think we were getting it on. Not to mention that Finn was a family friend, and if he found out, there'd be no explaining it away—telling Finn I could see ghosts was the *last* of last resorts.

"Sorry to hear about what happened on Saturday night. Was your boss's mate, wasn't it?"

"Yes, unfortunately. He was a top journalist and a nice guy."

"Well, if anyone can get to the bottom of it, you and the Sergeant can. You've been a real help around here. I daresay, you two make a good team."

I had my ghosts to thank for that, but I supposed I had to be brave to listen to them in the first place. The credit was more theirs than mine, but I was happy to admit to myself that I'd been doing good things over here. "Thanks, Lizzie. I appreciate it. I like helping, and of course, I get all the good articles out of it." I winked. Plus the consultant's fees I received. It really was a good deal.

"Oh, I saw you won that award. Congratulations!"

"Thank you." I smiled, but all I could think about was what happened at Julian's. A reminder of my prize was a reminder of Morris's and his wife's deaths. Before I knew it, I was frowning.

"Oh, sorry. The murders happened the night you were celebrating at your boss's, didn't they. You probably want to get working on it ASAP. I'll buzz you in."

"Thanks, Lizzie."

I went through into the hallway that led to the open-plan desk area where PC Adams's colleagues sat. I waved hello to everyone and continued to Bellamy's office. The door was shut, so I knocked.

"Come in!"

Inside, the whole crew was there—Bellamy sat in his chair, Fox in his usual spot standing next to him, and Charles in one of the guest chairs. I shut the door and looked at them one by one, finishing on Bellamy. "Hello, everyone."

The sergeant slow nodded. "I thought they were here. The chilly air gives it away every time."

I sat and placed my bag on the floor. "I wish I could give you more than that. It would be awesome if you could chat to each other face to face." And less work for me.

"I can't think of anything new to help." Sergeant Fox glanced at Bellamy, then me. "Can you tell him that the lads I've had spying on Ironfist's gang haven't got anything for us yet?"

"Okay." I shifted my gaze a bit to the left, to Bellamy, and repeated what Fox had said. The gang had gotten away with murder, and their leader had vowed to make trouble for us, so we were keeping an eye on them.

At least we'd gotten to the stage where Bellamy spoke directly to Fox by looking approximately where he thought the ghost was. Unfortunately, today, he was looking at his crotch. "Thanks, Sergeant. I appreciate the update."

Charles shook with laughter. "Are you going to tell him?"

I pressed my lips together, trying not to smile.

Bellamy frowned at me. "What is it, Winters? I don't see anything funny in this room. You didn't make up that he was there, did you?"

"Definitely not, Sergeant. Um.... Sergeant Fox never sits down. He always stands next to your chair."

The moment he understood was clear by the blooming roses on his cheeks. He cleared his throat. "Righty-ho, then."

"Sorry, Sergeant."

He sighed and, without looking in Fox's direction, asked, "Any other news?"

Fox shook his head, and I relayed it. Argh, there had to be some way to make this communication easier. Hmm.... Up till now, I'd only tried to link with Bellamy but not the ghosts. Maybe there was a way but trying from the ghost end. I'd have to mull on that and attempt something next time I was here. "So, have you got any information about Saturday night? Any clues?"

"We're still working on it. As far as evidence goes, we've confirmed it was a man-made explosion and not a freak accident. Chemical residue was found on the wreckage. They're still gathering evidence from the bodies—it's an involved process. It took a while to... ah... thoroughly go through the scene and collect everything." He linked his hands on his desk. "Have you spoken to the victim again?"

"Not yet. I'll try to get in touch with him this afternoon. I have some work to do in the office this morning."

"I'll need that list he promised."

"Of course. I'll get it as soon as I can." I wasn't sure if I had to go back to the scene of the crime, visit Morris's house, or just sing out from my apartment. My ghost friends came when I called, but they knew me well. Was Morris capable? Did he have to be tuned in to me in some way?

A knock sounded at the door. Bellamy huffed. "I can't go ten minutes without someone adding something to my day." He cocked his head to the side while looking at the door. "Come in."

PC Patel stuck his black-haired head in. "Julian MacPherson's here to see you. He doesn't have an appointment."

Bellamy and I shared a look before he swung his attention back to the constable. "Send him in."

Patel didn't give me a second look as he ducked out to get Julian. I wasn't an unusual sight around here any more, thank goodness.

I whispered to Charles, "Get off the chair, or you're going to get sat on."

The ghost smirked. "I don't mind."

I narrowed my eyes at him—he knew how much I hated when weird things happened to them, like sliding through solid doors and chairs cutting them in half. "Cheeky."

"What do you expect? I'm just a kid."

"Just a kid my—" My eyes found the door as Julian walked through it. Yeah, it would've looked weird, talking to the "empty" space to my right.

Julian did a double take when he saw me in the chair. "Oh, hi, Winters. Am I interrupting your statement?"

"No. I'm just here to see if the sergeant had any information he can pass on for my article."

"Ah, okay." Dark circles had taken up residence under his eyes, and instead of his usual brightly coloured shirt, he wore a black T-shirt, which was very un-Julian-like. He carried a caramel-coloured leather computer bag, the strap over his shoulder.

Bellamy gestured to the chair. "Please sit. What can I do for you?"

Just before my boss sat, Charles poked his tongue out at me and jumped up to stand near the door. Julian dropped into the chair, and settling the bag on his lap, he glanced at me, then Bellamy. Julian frowned. After a moment, he shrugged. "I suppose you can sit in on this, Winters. But don't put any of it in your article, and don't tell anyone. I think I have some information that might help."

"Of course not. Everything said in this room is confidential unless it's cleared by Sergeant Bellamy and, of course now, yourself." Sometimes, all a journalist had was their word, and once you'd shown yourself to be untrustworthy, your name would quickly be stinky swamp mud. I had no desire to work for publications who would hire someone like that, so Julian knew I'd keep my mouth shut.

"So, what do you have for me?"

Julian opened the computer bag and pulled out a blue folder. He opened that and emptied it of a pile of papers, which he placed on the desk. "Morris's son gave me those when I went to see him yesterday. Apparently, Morris said if anything happened to him, to give these to me." Looked like Bellamy didn't need me to chat with the dead journalist—he'd thought ahead.

"Have you looked through them all?" Bellamy asked.

"Does a squirrel hoard nuts for the winter?" Julian placed his palm on the pile and slid them towards him.

Bellamy looked at the first page. Silence stretched as he read, Fox leaning over his shoulder and reading too. I was curious, but I needn't worry because Bellamy would fill me in later… or Fox.

I turned to Julian. "How are you and Kim holding up?" It

was an awkward conversation to have because I didn't want to upset him in public, but then again, it would be impolite not to ask. Plus, I actually cared.

He gazed at the ceiling for a moment; then his eyes met mine. "It's been tough. It's hard to believe it happened. You know, we cover the news, have covered it for many years, yet I've always been at arm's length. Somehow, you don't think about it happening to someone you're close to. Not that we think we're immune, but he's covered some of the most dangerous stories you can imagine, and to die like this… in Devon…." His lips pressed together, and his fists balled in his lap. "It's bloody ridiculous." His pupils dilated. Bellamy was the recipient of the manic stare. "I want these animals found and dealt with. I'll do anything to help. I'm thinking of taking some time off so I can assist… make things go faster."

That got Bellamy's attention. He jerked his head up, concern lining his forehead. "I appreciate the offer, but that's not necessary at this stage."

"One journalist pretending to be a police officer is enough." Fox's stern countenance was aimed at Julian, but it was obviously a dig at me. I'd be lying if I said I wasn't hurt by that. If it wasn't for me, he wouldn't be able to communicate with Bellamy. Hadn't I been doing good things here?

"But I want to help. I can't sit and do nothing." He punctuated that by standing and waving his hands, palms up.

Bellamy sat back. "I understand you want to help catch the killers, but the last thing we need is for something to happen to you—some of these names are well-connected, dangerous men. I don't think your wife would appreciate it if you went the way of your colleague. If we need you for anything, I'll be the first one to call. Okay?"

Julian ran a hand through his hair, dishevelling it so it

matched the slightly unhinged glint in his eyes. He gulped in a huge breath and huffed it out, looked to his left and right—at what, I wasn't sure—then sat. He rubbed his thighs. "I just feel so helpless. There should be something I can do."

"At this stage, staying out of trouble would be a huge help." Bellamy gave him a wry smile. "In fact, Winters can update you as things move along. I'll be keeping her in the loop for her article, and it will save me time if she can pass things on to you. So, you'll be helping by sharing some of her work time with me." I had to hand it to the man—he made some questionable logic sound like he was doing him a favour. Julian was smart enough to get the silliness of it, but if he disagreed, he'd look like the difficult party.

Julian threw me a raised-eyebrow look. The defeat in his gaze was obvious, but there was also hope. "Well, you are our best crime reporter, and you've helped solve a few since you've gotten here, but I want you to stay safe. And make sure you let me know where you are when you're investigating this. I won't have anything happening to you on my watch." His serious expression relaxed into a small smile, one that made him look tired more than happy. "I'd never hear the end of it from your colleagues if you got yourself killed or injured."

I chuckled. "I understand. I'd hate to get you in trouble with them."

"Exactly." He stood and leaned forward, offering Bellamy his hand. "Thank you, Sergeant. I'll look forward to hearing about things via Winters." They shook hands. Julian gave me a nod. "See you later."

"Bye."

Once the door closed, Bellamy kept reading.

"Care to fill me in?" There were quite a few pages to get

through, and I wasn't in the mood to sit for thirty minutes while he went through it all.

"Give me five. Why don't you make yourself a coffee?" He raised his brows. "I'll tell you all the relevant information. I'm doing you a favour by weeding out what doesn't matter. Besides, you can ask the victim yourself if you don't trust me." His face was playing it straight, but his eyes sparkled with amusement.

I rolled my eyes because I was mature like that. "Fine. I'll be back."

"Can you get me one too?" Charles asked.

I stood. "Oka— Argh! I can't with you today. What's with the extra annoyingness?"

He giggled. "No reason."

Fox shook his head. "He's in a 'mood.' Better you than me, I say."

Bellamy looked from me to the space next to me. "What's going on?" He held his hand up. "No, actually, don't tell me. I don't have time for nonsense."

"Right you are." I saluted him, opened the door, and made my way to the break room, Charles's giggles following me out.

After making my coffee, I returned to Bellamy's office. Hopefully Bellamy would have some clues for me to chase, and I needed to chat to Morris.

As soon as I walked in the door, Bellamy looked up. "Ah, Winters. Glad you're back. I've got a job for you. How would you feel about going undercover?"

I smiled. "They don't call me Undercover Avery for nothing."

He blinked. "They do? I've never heard anyone call you that."

I chuckled. "Just kidding. It seemed like the thing to say." I sat in the chair I'd been in before. "So, what do you need me to do?"

He shook his head and gave me a withering look before leaning back and folding his hands over his stomach. "So, it goes like this…."

By the time we finished our conversation, I wasn't chuckling. There were no jokes. Have you ever had the feeling you were in too deep? I did, and we hadn't even left the shallows.

CHAPTER 5

After receiving my assignment from Bellamy, I headed to the office. I had an article to write and a hot reporter to talk into minding Zeus for a few days. Finn had catsat him once and insisted that was the one and only time, but surely he'd be okay with him for three or four more days… or even a week. If not, maybe he could help me sneak the cat into my apartment. He could play decoy with Mrs Crabby.

Unfortunately, Finn wasn't there when I went in. Carina looked up from her laptop when I entered. "Hey, Aves. How are you?"

"I'm okay. How are you?" She at least didn't look like she'd had a traumatic Saturday night. Her hair was vivid pink, her eyes were bright, and the tunic dress she wore over green stockings had little watermelons all over it.

"That's a summery outfit for winter."

She grinned. "I t'ought we could all use d'e cheering up. I

took Julian his tea early d'is morning, and he's not doing too well."

"I know. I ran into him at the police station. He's miserable." I pushed out my bottom lip in a sad pout.

Her shoulders rose and fell with a deep sigh. "Are you working on the case?"

"Yes. Sergeant Bellamy met with me, but he didn't have much to tell, unfortunately. They're still waiting on lab results and autopsies." I didn't have that much info, but what I did have and the fact that Julian had potential clues were things I wasn't allowed to divulge. I imagined that if I had a significant other, maybe I could share some of the intel, but since I didn't, I'd have to keep it to myself. A thought taunted me—Finn would make a good significant other. I ignored it because it was bad advice. Very bad advice. Come to think of it, I could discuss things with any of my ghost friends. At least I had that outlet.

"Yeah, d'at was a chaotic scene. I can't imagine how long t'ings are going to take." She stared at me. "I've had nightmares ever since."

"I'm so sorry. Do you want to talk about it?" I'd had nightmares the first night but not last night. Was there something wrong with me? Maybe my brain wasn't super shocked because I'd seen so much since I'd come here, or maybe it was because I knew that flesh was just that and the important part—the essence of who we were—made it out alive, so to speak. Whatever it was, I was compartmentalising with the best of them.

She waved the comment away. "I'll be okay. If I'm still having nightmares in a week, I'll see someone. Julian offered to pay for counselling when we had a quick chat d'is morning."

"That was nice of him. Make sure you take it up if you

need it." What I didn't add was that when I was in hospital for mental illness—care of my parents—the doctors made me have a few counselling sessions. We didn't talk about the apparitions I saw but about my relationships with Brad and my parents. To untangle everything I'd suffered would've taken months, but just in those five sessions, my eyes were opened to how they controlled and abused me. The seed was planted to leave and only grew once I got out and had to live with my family. Was I going to say any of that to my friend? Not a chance.

"I will. Maybe we should have a t'erapy session at the pub tonight, say around six?"

I laughed. "Sounds good to me." With everything I had going on, maybe a dinner with my friend was just what I needed. "Should I text Meg and see if she can get the night off?"

"Yes! And I'll text Finny."

"Excellent. I suppose I should get this article done. I've got a bit of running around this arvo." I couldn't tell her about my undercover thing, and I didn't want to say anything about Zeus because talking about it would just upset me. Besides, it was silly to overreact because he would probably be fine. That's what I told myself, anyway.

Carina smiled, and I texted Meg, then got to work. This afternoon, I was going to see my beautiful boy, and then I had a ghost to contact.

I stood at the front counter at the vet's, the blonde vet nurse smiling up at me, her light-blue shirt plastered with cartoon dogs and cats. "The vet said to show you through. They're still awaiting the test results, but Zeus has been stable. We should have the results tomorrow, but we do want to keep him for observation for another night or two."

"That's fine, thanks."

She led me through a door and down a corridor. We ended up in a large room with many cages stacked two high. Most were occupied. She crouched and opened the door to one of them, reached in, and brought out Zeus. He saw me and started purring. I smiled and pretty much snatched him from her, pulled him to my chest, and squished him in a hug. "How are you, sweetie?" A tiny meow escaped through the purrs. "I know, baby boy. I'm sorry you're sick."

"He's had some water and one mouthful of food, which is a good start. We'll need to see him eat more and use the litter tray before we let him go, but if things go well, that might be tomorrow."

"Okay, thanks." So I had potentially another day to find somewhere or plan sneaking him into my apartment. If Finn knocked back Carina's invitation to dinner, I'd have to accost him at home. I'd put on the waterworks if I had to. Desperate times called for desperate measures. "Did you hear that, Zeus? I might be able to bust you out of here tomorrow. The faster you get better, the faster you'll be out of here." He nudged under my chin and meowed again. I was pretending he understood.

After ten minutes of sitting and cuddling, the vet nurse came back and put him in his cage. I hated leaving him there, and the look he gave said he wasn't impressed, either, and how could I possibly do this to him? It was clear I'd have some making up to do. I'd go past the supermarket later and buy some chicken thigh fillets. He could have a treat when he came out.

Next on my list was getting in touch with Morris. The list we'd wanted the other night was what his son had given Julian, but there was only brief information on each person—a basic rundown of who they were, how and when he met them, and also why they were angry…. Specifically, he'd included the articles he'd written about them. Out of the nine people he'd told us about, three were in jail thanks to his investigations and what he'd handed to police over the last ten years. Another of them had been jailed twenty years ago but was released after eighteen months.

One of the disgruntled people was another journalist, someone Morris had fired when he'd been an editor at one of the newspapers. The guy went from full-time investigative journalism to working as a freelance copywriter. Not that there was anything wrong with being a freelance copywriter, but it didn't have the same prestige, and if you had a massive ego, it would be a kick in the proverbials. Someone like Brad, my ex, would be ropable if someone fired him. Maybe karma would do the job one day. I'd love to witness his downfall. Forgiveness was beyond me, and I was too nice to take revenge, so I had to rely on karma. Hopefully one day I'd see him get his dues.

I stopped by the village supermarket and then went home. As much as I didn't want every ghost in England to have access to my flat, it was the most private place I could meet him. So I'd try that first. If that failed, when it got dark, I'd drive to Julian's and wait outside in my car. He'd died there, so he'd be linked to the place.

As I walked across the laneway, Josie hurried out of her front door and waved. She must've been waiting for me because she was wearing pink wellies and a scarf. "Avery! How's Zeus?"

"He's getting better. I just saw him and had a cuddle. He says hello."

"I'm so glad! I love that little guy. Sorry again that I can't take him. Anyway, let me know how he goes."

"I will, and thank you again. You really saved both of us. I'll figure something out."

She patted my arm. "I know you will. Maybe there'll be a Christmas miracle, and Marge will let you keep him."

I laughed. "More like it would signal the apocalypse. But whatever, I'm not ready to give up yet." I smiled. "Have a good afternoon."

"You too, love."

I was careful to make as little noise as possible when opening and closing the front door. As I was tiptoeing to the stairs, Mrs Crabby's door opened. She narrowed her eyes. "Why are you sneaking around?"

"I'm not sneaking… just trying to be quiet so I don't disturb you." Or bring down your wrath.

She sniffed, could find nothing else to argue about, then pulled her head back through the doorway like a turtle and shut it.

Good riddance. I didn't dare whisper that because she would've heard. She had the hearing of a greater wax moth, the animal with the best hearing in the world. Unfortunately, she didn't have the temperament of one.

All pretence at silence gone, I hurriedly thumped up the stairs, being free with my noise. *Let it out, feet. Let it out.*

Once my door was closed, I placed my handbag and laptop bag on the couch. "Morris, can you come here? Hello, Morris? It's Avery." My eyes tracked the room so I wouldn't be surprised by his appearance. Nada. "Morris. Calling Morris." I waited a minute, then tried again. Nope. Looked like I was taking a drive to Julian's tonight after dinner at the pub.

It was time to research the killer dentist.

I set up my laptop on the kitchen table. I hadn't mentioned anything to Bellamy because he had his hands full with Morris's investigation. The more information I could gather before going to the police, the better. Hopefully, there would be lots of evidence if the ghosts would give up their secrets, and the arrest would be easy. Maybe there were other victims of his who hadn't passed over. It seemed that ghosts with traumatic passings or lives were more likely to stay around. At least in my experience with them. Obviously not all of them did—Morris's wife was keen to move on. Did it depend on the individual ghost, or was there a higher power who decided these things? I shook my head. Argh, I was time-wasting.

I typed "Andrew Crumps dentist" into Google.

Looked like he was still in London. An entry for his practice came up, as did two other things. One was an article on the latest information on dental implants, and he was quoted in it. The other was for a conference he spoke at a year ago. When I clicked on his website and navigated to his bio, his photo made me shudder. This balding man with the piercing and creepy blue eyes was a serial killer. It was a head-and-shoulders shot. A white dentist's coat hung on his broad shoulders. It looked like he'd kept in relatively good shape, although his face was rounded, his chin having a small twin sitting under it. I downloaded that photo and another one showing him shaking someone's hand at the conference. I started a file called "Killer Dentist" and slipped them in. I also put in the links to everything and then the notes I'd taken whilst chatting to Everly.

After that, I looked up Andrew Crumps's surgeon father.

Harris Crumps came up, something about him retiring a couple of years ago and how Mrs Crumps and their son were proud of him. No obituary. So, he was likely still alive.

"Everly, are you around?"

After a moment, she materialised. "Hi. What's happening?" She smiled, acting as if we hadn't spoken about her murder the last time we were together.

"Seriously?"

She shrugged one shoulder. "You called me. How am I supposed to know what you want?"

"I'll give you a pass since you don't really want to talk about it. I'm doing research into Andrew. What's his mother's name, and do you have their old address?"

She sat, then stared at me for a moment. Was she warring with herself over whether to stay and dig deeper or leave and avoid the discomfort? Her eyes shut before springing open and pinning me with a haunted look. "I can do this," fluttered softly from her lips.

"You can. I got you." I wanted so much to comfort her physically, and even though I knew my hand would go straight through, I reached out and laid my palm on her forearm. The sear of ice speared through my hand, but solidity met my touch. I gasped. Tears burned my eyes. No way. Oh. My. God.

Everly's mouth dropped open, and she stared at me, slack-jawed.

The freezing cold dulled the longer I kept my hand there. I pressed my fingertips into her skin. It was spongy, like a living being. My breath came faster. This was incredible.

"I can feel that. It's like it was when I was alive. You… you could try a hug." She shut her eyes and breathed deeply as if she was savouring the sensation. And I wasn't surprised. She'd lived for so many years without the touch of another. So lonely. Humans needed touch, and dying didn't stop you being human.

I hesitated. "It might break the spell, or whatever it is." I didn't mean an actual spell, but you never knew. This was freaky. Unless I'd died in that moment. Was I still alive? I looked around, and there wasn't my body on the floor or slumped over the table, so I must still be alive.

She opened her eyes. "Well, we can't stay like this forever, so why not? And if it doesn't work this time, it might the next—you did it once, Avery. You'll be able to do it again, whether that's now or later."

"Hmm, good point." I gave her one last squeeze, and she smiled. Slowly, reluctantly, I lifted my hand from her arm. I leaned over to hug her, but all I got was the normal, creepy temperature drop as I went right through her and fell into the chair. I slammed my hand down through her body to the chair bottom to stabilise myself. Disappointment hit me. I lowered my head and tried to banish it.

"Don't worry. Like I said, maybe next time."

I lifted my head and settled back into my chair. "You're smiling."

"Yep. Do you know how long it's been since I've felt someone's warm skin? You've just given me the best gift I could ever ask for. Thank you. I'd hug you, but…." Her mouth lifted on one side in an "oh well" smile.

"Yes, but maybe next time." *Let the disappointment go, Avery. You'll get another chance.*

She placed her hands in her lap and straightened her back, ready to go into battle. "Right, so the monster's mother's name is Eve, and they lived on about two acres at Falcon's Nest, East Portlemouth."

I made notes on my computer, then googled that. "There's no Falcon's Nest there."

She looked at me as if I was stupid. She wasn't too far off. "That's the house name, dummy." She leaned towards me and looked at the laptop screen. "Hmm…." Can you move the thingy that way?" She pointed to the right, and I did as asked. "That's the road there."

I zoomed in a bit. "There's no street name. What's with that?"

She shrugged. "I have no answer for you. I didn't create the system—I just live by it."

"Big help… not." I changed it to an aerial Google Maps view, then brought it into street view.

She pointed. "That's it there. See how there aren't any houses close by, and there's land and trees at the back. That looks pretty similar to how it was back then, only the house colour's changed. It used to be pink, and now it's white."

The white Georgian house with its slate roof was only half visible from the street, obscured by large, green hedges. Not unusual for England. "I wonder if they still live there."

"You can find that out, can't you?"

"Yep." I bit my lip in thought before turning to Everly. "Um, this is a lot to ask, and I'll understand if you say no, but would it be possible for you to see if you can find any other ghosts of the women he killed… if they're still around?"

"You're assuming he's killed more women than me and Jenny?"

"Yes, but chances are…."

She sighed. "I know. The problem is, I won't be able to get into his house or his workplace, and then where else would I wander? It's like looking for a needle in a haystack."

"His workplace is public. Could you go in there?"

Red stained her pale cheeks. "Not any more. I got in once, but then tried a few times after that, and I've been blocked. I don't know if it's because he doesn't want me and it's automatic or if he's had someone come in and banish ghosts. I tried to haunt him that one time, and I'm pretty sure he felt me… the cold… and I pleaded with him and begged to know why he killed me. I don't think he heard me, but maybe he could feel my distress. Ever since then, I can't get in. I haven't tried lately, though."

Possum poo. "Don't worry. I doubt he's reversed whatever it was that he did. Maybe he's had more hauntings than just you. I'll figure something out. So, what does Jenny look like?" Maybe he had a type?

She cocked her head to the side, and her brow furrowed. "She kind of looks like me. Slim, pale skin, longish, straight, light-brown hair, but her eyes are brown, not hazel. She's about an inch taller than me."

Two people who looked similar weren't exactly a type, but it was a possibility. "Do you know where she lived when she was killed?"

"I don't have her address, but I can ask. I've told her you want to help make sure he's punished, and she was happy about that. Maybe I could get her to chat to you? She is a bit messed up, though. I don't think you should invite her here."

Yikes. I wasn't going to ignore that warning. "Where could I meet her? I'm assuming I can't come to where you counsel ghosts." I hadn't thought about it, really, but I assumed it was in their ghostly plane somewhere.

"I meet them in Manesbury Town Hall. In one of the offices. It helps my clients relax, and it's as if we're still alive."

"Oh." Breaking into there wasn't on my top ten list of things I wanted to do. It wasn't even top twenty. In fact, it was on my list of things I never wanted to do. Besides, I was pretty sure they had a security camera outside. I had no idea if there were any inside as I'd never taken notice, but I wasn't taking any chances. They probably had an alarm of some sort too. "Is there anywhere else?"

"What about after-hours at your work? She could get in there anyway."

I grimaced. "Yes, but if I upset her or she wants to nag me, she'd know where I worked and could show up at any time."

"So? You can just ignore her, can't you?"

I rested my elbow on the table, leaned my head into my hand, and rubbed my forehead. "It's not ideal, but okay. Actually, could we meet in Sergeant Bellamy's office? He can't see ghosts, so he won't be bothered if she shows up unexpectedly." It would mean coming clean to him a bit earlier than I'd like about Everly's case, but it probably made no difference. He wouldn't take his focus off Morris's case until it was solved.

"I suppose so. I'll have a chat and let you know." She stood. "Do you have any other questions?"

"That's it for now. Thanks."

She grinned. "No. Thank *you*. I'll never forget today, Avery. It's changed things for me. I have more… hope. Maybe we can figure out why you could touch me, and then I can see if we can help ghosts do the same. Imagine if being dead could become just like being alive?"

I blinked, trying to get my panic under control. Why was it that with a good thing, there was a bad one to balance it out? "Ah, yeah, that would be cool." That would be just what the world needed—ghosts who could be poltergeists and touch people whenever they wanted, maybe even hurt them. And it would open ghosts like Charles up to being hurt—he had the body of a boy. And what if someone tried to hurt Everly again? Not that they could kill her twice, but imagine living your nightmare over and over. The evil ones who managed to avoid hell would be out to continue their depraved ways. I wasn't going to chuck dirt on her ice cream, but I wasn't going to let that happen. We could discuss it later, after I got evil Andrew arrested.

"I'm so excited! This is going to be a game-changer! Bye, Avery."

I waved, but she was already gone.

Game changer indeed.

CHAPTER 6

The pub was busy for a Monday night, the animated hum of happy diners filling the warm space with even more cheer than the hearty fire in the fireplace. It was eight thirty-six. Carina, Finn, and I had finished dinner, and now that the serving rush was over, Meg finally slid into the last seat at the table. "How was it?"

I grinned. "Yum. The food here is always top-notch."

Carina chuckled. "As if we'd tell you it was terrible anyway." Meg gave her a horrified look. "Oh no, love, it was delicious. I wasn't insinuating anyt'ing."

Finn placed his hand on her forearm. "Stop digging. The hole's big enough."

"Just as well." Meg raised a brow. "I was about to call Bailey over here to kick you lot out. Terrible, indeed." She narrowed her eyes and mock-glared at Carina.

Now would be as good a time as any to hit Finn up for Zeus. My girls would help convince him. Mrs Crabby had been a bit nicer… um, maybe not that. Maybe more, she'd been less cantankerous and more subdued since I found her daughter's locket. Today, she was back to her old self, so any leeway I'd had was gone. Sneaking Zeus in had to be a last, last, last resort.

I can do this.

I looked into Finn's gorgeous baby blues and gave him my most disarming smile. He replied with a suspicious look. Hmm, maybe it wasn't so disarming.

"Spit it out, Lightning. I know that look." He folded his arms. This wasn't going well.

"Okay, so you know how I love you guys, and I'd do anything for you." My gaze floated over all my friends and landed back with Finn. I was laying it on thick, but I needed him to say yes.

"We know you would, hon. Whatever you need, I'm sure Finn would love to help. He's a good guy like d'at." Carina smiled kindly, then turned to Finn and gave him a look that suggested he would definitely love to help, and God help him if he didn't. This is why I wanted to do this with my girls here. I wasn't totally stupid.

He side-eyed Carina and leaned away from her before turning back to me. His face was carefully arranged into a neutral expression. "What do you need?"

"Well, um… Zeus is at the vet because he hasn't been well, poor puss."

Meg stared at me. "Oh no! You didn't tell me. Is he okay?"

"I think he'll be okay. He's been there since yesterday. They're keeping him in tonight as well. But when he comes out, Josie can't take him as she'll be away for a few days, and her cat doesn't like Zeus. I could take him home and sneak him upstairs, but I risk Mrs Crabby evicting me. If that happens, I'll have to move out of the village, which isn't ideal."

"You got that place cheap too. You'd likely end up paying more somewhere else." Meg fixed her gaze on Finn as she said that. God, I loved her and Carina.

"Exactly. Anyway, I'm still looking to place him in a loving home, but this close to Christmas, it's hard. Maybe the vet can find someone, but if she doesn't, could you pretty, pretty please have him for a week or two? I can give you all his supplies. I don't expect you to pay for anything. Please, Vinegar. It would be the best Christmas present you could get me."

"Who said I was going to give you a present?"

Carina slapped his arm. "Bad Finny."

Meg's voice held a warning note. "Do I need to call Bailey over? Hmm, maybe I need to message Ariana and tell her you said she was gorgeous." Ooh, she was bringing out the big guns. I didn't know who Ariana was, but by the way Finn's eyes bugged out and his lips pinched together, she was someone he didn't want to see.

"Jesus, Meg. Fine. No need to ruin my life." With a defeated hunch to his shoulders, he turned to me. "I'll look after Zeus, but only until a couple of days before Christmas. I'm going away."

"Can't he stay there, and I'll come feed him?"

"No. I don't want him tearing anything up with those sharp claws or vomiting on my expensive rugs. My uncle's cat once ruined a five-thousand-pound antique rug with orange vomit. They couldn't get it out and had to put it in my cousin's bedroom so her bed could cover the gross part."

Carina gave him an assessing look. "You don't own any expensive rugs."

"How do you know? That one in my living area cost me a fair amount, but I won't say how much because a gentleman doesn't brag."

I snorted. "Umm, okay."

"Hey, don't push it, lady. I'm doing you a favour." His lips twitched at the corners as he tried to hold in a smile. Why was he so gorgeous? His dimples were threatening to appear. Damn man. At least he'd succumbed under the pressure. It had taken three of us, though. If I'd approached him by myself, he never would've said yes.

"Okay, I concede. Thank you so much. I'd give you a hug, but you have new rules." I rolled my eyes.

The look he gave me suggested he had regrets about the no-hugging thing. Interesting. But he didn't cave because whatever the reasons he had—and there were likely many good ones—we were better off friends than trying something that didn't work out. Or maybe I couldn't really read him, and he wasn't interested in me like that, which made sense. He had the pick of the litter around here. But now I had a bit more time to figure this Zeus thing out, I could deal with not hugging him.

"You can bring him around when you break him out of the vet's. Just message me."

"Will do. You have no idea how happy you've made me." My grin was close to breaking my face. I likely looked like a maniac, but the relief was massive.

Carina gave him a thumbs-up. "Nice work, Finny. I knew you'd do d'e right t'ing."

"Anything for you ladies." He waggled his brows. Meg and I looked at each other and rolled our eyes. But we shouldn't be too hard on him. He agreed, and even with all the ridiculous threats, he could've said no. "Now, what are we having for dessert?"

After dinner, I pretended to go home because I didn't want to answer any questions from Finn about where I was going at this time of night on a Monday. He unlocked his door and went in while I was still at my front door. As soon as his door shut, I hurried back down the steps and out the front gate. At least there wasn't much traffic at night, and I made good time to Julian's place. I parked a few houses away to avoid being seen. Not that he'd recognise my car, but you never knew. He'd be extra suspicious after what had happened, and I wouldn't be surprised if he'd installed a camera or something outside his house. Being a journalist, he might even approach a car that had parked and that no one had exited.

I got out my pad and pen and kept the lights off. The streetlights gave enough illumination to scribble a few things. "Morris, are you around? Morris, it's Avery. I need to speak to you."

He appeared in my front passenger seat, still in his suit from the other night. Thankfully, he didn't hold onto the gore or stains. It was as if he'd made it safely home. Sadness swamped me, and I blinked back tears. Dammit.

"Avery, hello. What day is it? I feel like it's been a week since I saw you. Any progress?"

"Um, it's been two days. It's Monday. I hear from other ghosts that time is weird where you are. Nothing like it is for those of us still *here* here."

"Yes, it seems that way. If only I could come back to life and write a piece on the afterlife. It's wild. I thought that was it when you passed, lights out, sayonara. It's been a revelation. Maybe you should write one. I can co-author."

I laughed. "Um, no. Maybe you could write one, and I'll get it published under M. Parkinson. Wouldn't want to upset anyone who thinks it's a sick joke."

He tapped his chin with his forefinger. "Hmm, you've given me an idea."

"Ah, can we not have ideas right now? I've got enough on my plate. Can we talk about who wanted you dead? I've seen the list you gave Julian. I want to narrow it down to most likely and start my investigations there."

"Far be it for me to tell you how to do your job, but I used to find that getting rid of the least likely was a good way to narrow things. It clears your head to think only about the others. But sometimes it becomes evident that who you thought was least likely is most likely. And then you rejig the list."

Yes, far be it for him to not tell me how to suck eggs. I barely avoided an eyeroll. I pretended I was the CEO of my own company. It helped to put on "the voice that could not be ignored." "Either way, I have to look into everyone, and I prefer this way, so let's continue."

His laugh was a tad uncomfortable, but he said, "Alrighty then. What questions do you have?"

I should cut him a break—he was old school, and he'd just had the most shocking experience anyone could have. He'd been super nice at the party. Although I'd never worked with him. Maybe he was a bit territorial and bossy at work, and he had every right to be with his experience and what he'd endured to reveal hard truths to the world.

"The ones who went to jail because of your investigations, which one or ones are most likely to kill someone? As well as that, I need a bit more background on your relationships with the other names on the list. How much do they hate you, and why? I'm going to gather as much information as possible, give it to Sergeant Bellamy, and he and his team are going to do the rest." He'd given some basic answers to those questions, but there was a lot left out, and now I had the opportunity to delve deeper. On a curious level—because all of us journalists loved getting to the bottom of things—this was going to be very interesting.

"Hmm, where to start? This could take all night."

"Actually, can we do this at my place? It's too cold in here." I wasn't going to last long without the heater on, and a car idling for hours was going to attract attention. "All you have to do is stay in my car while I drive, and then I'll invite you in, and it'll be fine."

"Okay. Let's go."

I did a U-ey and headed back towards my place. "How are you?"

He chuckled. "Dead."

"Ha ha, very funny. You know what I mean."

He turned his head and stared out his window, his voice thick with emotion. "I'm as well as can be expected. I hope I didn't do the wrong thing, staying for justice. It's what's kept me going all these years—a sense that we must speak out when we see people hurting others, doing the wrong thing. But should I have left the human dilemmas on this earth and gone with my wife?" He turned to look at me. "I might have just made the biggest mistake of my life. Meredith always said I didn't know when to call it quits. That I was like a dog with a bone. I used to take it as a compliment." He sighed a shuddering breath. "What if I can't leave when it's all done?"

His fear buried itself in the shadows at our feet, its eager fingers creeping a trail to my chest. I couldn't give him the answer he wanted. Thinking of him and his wife spending eternity without each other broke my heart. Could the powers that be really be so cruel? I knew the answer to that, unfortunately.

I gave him the best answer I could. "When it's your time to leave, you'll leave. Whoever runs this whole show probably let you stay. I've seen ghosts who wanted to stay, and they got pulled in, so maybe this is meant to go this way. In any case, we can't change it now. I'm going to focus on solving this as quickly as possible. I can't promise you'll find your way to Meredith, but I can promise I'll do my best to give you that opportunity."

He cleared his throat. "Thank you, Avery. You're doing this despite the danger you'll be courting. Julian said you were a good egg. He's rarely wrong."

"I'll do my best to live up to those expectations." *And do my best to stay alive, unlike you.* I smiled through the chill that skipped down my spine. I had a feeling this was going to be the trickiest case I'd worked on yet—there were numerous shady characters, and many knew people in high places. It was likely one of them had already shown what they did to people who crossed them. If only I'd thought about this properly before I promised to make it right.

But it was too late to pull out now. I had a job to do, and I'd better do it well because if I failed, I'd be failing a good man and his patient wife. I had enough issues without carrying that guilt for the rest of my life.

"I'm sure you will."

That remained to be seen.

CHAPTER 7

I yawned as I drove to my first appointment the next morning. Morris had stayed till about half one (look at me, speaking like a true Brit), and it took me a while to fall asleep as my brain ordered things so I had a direction today. Before I'd left home, I'd called my first target for that investigation—the least dangerous of the lot. A man called Danny who'd been caught up in a drug ring. He did five years for dealing and supplying commercial quantities of heroin and cocaine. His sentence had been reduced because he'd spilled the beans on his bosses, both of whom were dead, which was why he was out in the open and not in hiding. I was meeting with him in Exeter this afternoon for a coffee and chat under the guise of reporting on the story.

But right now, I was on the way to a house halfway between Manesbury and Cramtonbury to interview Abby Evans, a twenty-eight-year-old author who'd won a coveted Devon writing prize for her biography on a locally born businessman who'd become internationally successful with his pet food business. She sounded nice enough on the phone, so there was hope that I would have a pleasant and "normal" experience. My brain was already overloaded with everything I had cooking, and I could do without a "unique" experience for once.

I turned off the main road into a winding street that took me down a hill, where I turned into a laneway that wasn't much wider than a python, undulating green fields spreading out on both sides. Okay, the python thing might be an exaggeration, but not by much. There was no room for anyone coming the other way. I hated these roads. *Please no one come the other way.* I drove a bit faster to reduce the odds of an oncoming car and me duelling it out for who had to reverse until there was another road, a convenient driveway, or a return.

Thankfully, a minute up the road, there was the property I was looking for. I drove into the short gravel driveway and parked in front of a white, rendered cottage that had a thickly thatched roof and pretty blue-framed windows. The garden wasn't much to look at since it was winter, but the slightly raised, sandstone-framed garden beds hinted at a gorgeous summer garden, and there were a handful of naked trees, their bony fingers pointing to the sky, which would be lush and elegant when cloaked in summer greenery.

I grabbed my bag and got out, the slap of winter air making me regret forgetting my scarf. I hurried to the front door and knocked. It was only when I released the red knocker that I realised it was a devil's face, horns and all. Interesting stylistic choice for a character country cottage. Try saying that quickly five times.

The woman who answered the door wore a purple coat, yellow woollen gloves, a pink skirt that finished mid-thigh, and black stockings. Her curly red hair sprouted out of the confines of a mauve beanie. I might suggest she buy one of hedgehog lady's jumpers. She'd probably wear it on purpose. "You must be Avery." She smiled, her freckled face lighting up.

I returned her smile. "Yes. Lovely to meet you, Abby." Saying her name made me think of Abyssinian cats and, of course, Zeus. I'd have to ring the vet to see if I could break him out of there today.

"Please come in." She stood aside, and I went in. "Keep going down the hallway. The living area's through the door at the end."

The home was colder than a tomb, and stepping into the living area didn't help. We could've just held the interview outside.

The living area featured exposed stone walls and a fireplace with a large timber mantle. Three lifelike heads sat on it. Normal people had candles or family photos, but not this woman. Of course she didn't. And why did those heads—two men and one woman—look like they were staring at me? They even had hair, with one of the men sporting a moustache as well as curly red hair. Was that her dad or something? Surely not. You couldn't embalm heads and have them at home, could you?

"Please sit." She gestured to an emerald-green two-seater lounge, and I started, so engrossed as I was in the disturbing decorations. I carefully sat on one end as I eyed the silent crowd. Abby sat next to me. Hmm, this was cosy. There were two chairs opposite, and I resisted the urge to get up and sit in one. Maybe she wanted the heat from my body? Could she not afford heating? I shivered.

"Oh, I'm sorry, Avery. I don't heat the place because I like to feel closer to the dead."

Say what? "What?" *Oops*. That was meant to be an internal comment only. And here I was thinking this was going to be a fun, weirdo-free zone. I only just managed to hold in my sigh.

She giggled. "It's not as bad as you think. I can't talk to ghosts or anything, but I like cemeteries, and death fascinates me. I know there's ghosts, but I've only ever felt the cold as they pass by." She crossed her legs and placed her hands on her knee. "So, feel free to ask what you want about my book prize. It's been exciting, but the man I wrote the book about was so annoying. I earned every penny of the two-thousand-pound prize."

I took out my notebook and scribbled. "Yes, well, I won't put that he's annoying. Congratulations on the prize. There aren't many out there these days. How many other entries were there?"

"I'm not quite sure, but it was over two hundred. And they were shortlisted from a lot more entries." She folded her arms and settled back into the chair. "I tasted some of the pet food, specifically the dog food. They make it with all fresh ingredients."

I raised my brows. It was near impossible to keep my feelings to myself. I wasn't being very professional. "What kind of ingredients?"

"Chicken, beef, or fish, but they mix it with the entrails, rice, and some vegetables, but it's just like eating a sausage, right?"

I might as well ask. "What did it taste like?"

"The entrails kind of overtook the flavour, but it wasn't too bad."

"Maybe you could do an ad for them, vouching for the quality? 'Fit for human consumption' or something."

"Hmm, you might be onto something. I could ask—the extra money would be great."

After using almost all the rest of my restraint in not slapping my forehead, I despaired leaving here without offending her. Although, she missed that I was making a joke, so maybe I'd get away with it. "How long did it take you to research and write the book?"

"Eighteen months. It's a back-and-forth process with the subject."

We chatted for another ten minutes without incident until she randomly turned to look at her friends on the mantle. She stood and walked over to them, then caressed each one's hair one by one. "This is my family." She pointed to the ginger-haired man. "This is my Uncle Patrick, and this"—she stroked the cheek of the dark-haired woman who looked to be in her late teens—"is my sister, Maeve. She was hit by a car while training on her bike. She was thrown onto a fence post, so her face was preserved."

My eyes widened. Horror seeped through me. "That's her *real* face?"

She laughed. "Not her *real* real face. It's a ceramic rendering taken from a mould, and then textured rubber is laid over it and painted. Pretty lifelike, no?"

"Totally. And the hair. What's that made of?"

She rubbed her "sister's" strands between her fingers. "Oh, that's their real hair. I got permission from my family to get their hair." She moved on to the next man, who had thinning grey hair and rosy cheeks. "That's my da. He died of cancer, so the skin colour is more like before he was sick. I had the artist take some liberties."

"But why?" I wasn't sure if she knew, which was why I was asking, but it was just a general why. *Seriously. Why?*

"Their ashes are inside and some nail clippings."

I threw up a little in my mouth. Ghosts were less icky than this lady. It was time to change the subject. "I'd like to get a photo of you with your book." I stood and peered around. "What about over there, in front of that lovely painting of the beach?"

"Could we do it here, in front of my family? And could you mention the artist? They do these urns for anyone who wants them. They're local."

Of course they were. Every weirdo must live around here within easy driving distance of my place because I was cursed to interview every one of them. I gave up. "Yeah, sure. Why the hell not."

"That's the spirit." She snickered. "Get it—spirit."

"Hmm, yes. Great pun." I didn't often ask "why me," but I was asking it now. Over and over. And over again. When I'd first gotten this assignment, I'd had the brief thought that we would've gotten along well because we were both writers and that we could have an interesting chat.

Nope. I was wrong.

At least our readers would be entertained by the normal part of the article. What they'd make of the creepy heads was another thing. I supposed it would get reactions—whether they were good or bad, Julian probably didn't care since it was all attention. It had the potential to go viral. Not the kind of reporting I'd studied for, but it paid the bills.

"I'll just grab a copy of the book. Be back in two shakes."

Abby left, and I went to the mantle and took a few close-ups of the morgue.

"My niece is a strange one, no?"

I turned. Right behind me, admiring his own bust, was Abby's uncle. "Yes," I whispered.

"She's harmless, though. Can you ask her to put my head in the garden sometimes? If I come here, I'm tied to the inside of this house because of the ashes. I do love the garden, though. I was a horticulturalist back in the day. Tell her I want to be among the daffodils. They're out in a few months. I heard her mention to her mother on the phone that Christmas was coming soon."

"I'm not sure if I—"

"Avery, who are you talking to?"

Ah, possum poo. Did I reveal my secret? What if she complained to Julian? But then again, she thought death was interesting, and she had these heads in her lounge room. I could always tell Julian she was off her rocker, and he'd believe me once he saw the photos. I took a deep breath and smiled like nothing was wrong. "You like death." She nodded. "I'm about to tell you something that if you repeat to anyone, I'll deny."

Her eyebrows rose into her red fringe. "Oh, interesting. Do tell."

Her uncle smiled and nodded encouragingly. I glanced at him before meeting her gaze. "Um…. I can see ghosts. Your uncle is here and has asked to be placed in the garden when the daffodils are blooming. He said he loves it out there, but he can't leave your house when he visits because his ashes are"—I side-eyed his bust—"there."

She placed her fingers over her mouth. "Oh, wow. He planted those bulbs three years ago when I moved in. In fact, he designed the garden as a housewarming present." She placed a hand out and felt the air in front of her. "Where is he?"

"Just here." I pointed to where he stood next to me.

She felt the air. "Ooh, it's cold."

Her uncle chuckled. "That tickles."

I looked at him. "It does not."

"All right, it doesn't. Party pooper." He stuck his tongue out at me.

"This is way off track. Is there anything you want to say to each other—I have to get going soon?"

"Yes. Something I should've told her when I was alive, but I was too much of a chicken." Oh, God. Did I really want to know? What was he about to unleash?

"He wants to come clean about something, apparently."

She raised an eyebrow. "Yes? I'm listening."

He stared at the ceiling for a bit before gazing at his niece. "Your mum and I had an affair, and I'm your real father. It only lasted a few weeks. When we found out Mary was pregnant, we stopped. She brought you up as hers and your dad's. No one else knew."

My mouth dropped open. I placed my hands on my hips. "I'm supposed to drop that bombshell? Seriously?" How did I get myself into these situations?

"What? What is it?" Abby had wandered into the space where her dad stood, and they were blurring together.

"Can you step that way a bit?" I gestured to the left. "It's creeping me out. You're merging with the ghost."

"Oops, sorry. Now, what did he say?"

"Don't shoot the messenger, and before you get angry at me for making it up, go get a DNA test." This could be about to go horribly wrong.

She held her breath before blurting, "I know."

"You know he's your dad?"

"Yes. I got a DNA test after my sister died, and it showed that we weren't full siblings. Neither my mum nor my da have red hair. I thought it was a throwback, which is possible, but I look more like my uncle than Dad."

I might as well tell her the rest of it, then. "Your mum and uncle… dad… whatever, had an affair that lasted a few weeks, so he says, and when they found out she was pregnant, they stopped it."

"I didn't want to tear their family apart."

"How noble of you," I said dryly.

"What did he say?"

I repeated it to Abby. "So, there you go. I'm sorry to have dropped that on you, but let's take those photos. I've got a long drive to Exeter." Even I thought I was being a cold meanie, but if I offered myself as a conduit for their conversation, I could be here for days. She probably had millions of questions, but I wasn't going to be the one to answer them. "Maybe you could talk to your mum about it?"

"I don't want to upset my da, but maybe Mum will talk to me quietly and leave him out of it. Still, can I ask a question?"

"Just one."

"Did he love me as if I was his daughter?"

Her dad smiled. "I loved you… love you more than anything, which is why I wanted you to have the parents you did. They could give you so many things I couldn't. It's why I stayed in your life, found you your first car, planted your garden. I'm sorry I wasn't in your life all the time, but you're my girl forever and always. I still love your mum, too, which is why I never got married and had kids of my own. I figured they could never live up to you and Mary. It's why I travelled a lot." Despite his sacrifices, he didn't look broken—love shone from his grey eyes.

Well, if that wasn't one of the saddest things I'd ever

heard. When I told Abby, she teared up. "I'm so sorry, Uncle Patrick… Dad."

The ghost smiled. "I can be Dad, and your da is still your da."

When I told her, she grinned through her tears. "That sounds good to me. Love you, Dad."

"I love you, too, Abbs."

Now that I'd facilitated a family reunion, I took the photos of her with the book and her "family" in the background, made her promise not to tell anyone about what happened, and left.

It was time to head to Exeter and hopefully take a step towards finding out who killed Morris and his wife.

CHAPTER 8

I was early to the meeting with Danny, so I ordered a cappuccino, wrote my article on Abby, and did more research into Everly's killer. The police were doing much better than I was in their investigation on Morris, so they probably didn't need me digging on the internet for limited information. I could just interview people for them, and I still had that one undercover thing to do.

Danny arrived five minutes early. In his late twenties, his lanky build was topped with short, caramel-coloured hair. A smattering of freckles dotted his face in a random pattern, and a scar slashed through his left eyebrow. He was dressed in pale, ripped jeans and a black, puffy jacket. I only recognised him because I'd seen his mugshot. I held up my hand, and he gave me a chin tip and wandered over, his face giving nothing away.

I stood and held out my hand. "I'm Avery. Nice to meet you."

"Hi, Avery. I'm Danny… obviously." He shook my hand

limply. Ew, I hated when people did that. Also, I hoped he'd washed his hands the last time he went to the toilet. We sat, and he rubbed the back of his head. "Not trying to be rude, but can I get my money now?"

Yes, I'd had to bribe him to get him here, which wasn't a surprise—he wasn't obligated to talk to me. The police had called him to get his alibi (which had checked out) and I mentioned that if he spoke to me, they likely wouldn't need to see him in person. This had been enough to get him here. Whether he'd say much was another thing. I handed him fifty pounds, provided to me by Bellamy. I wasn't sure if the police had a budget for stuff like this or whether it had come out of the sergeant's pocket.

"Thanks."

"No problem." I closed my laptop and took out my pen and pad. "Do you want anything?"

He looked around. "Nah. Want to get this over and done with." Had I made a mistake giving him the money upfront? I figured that showing some trust would help him relax a little and speak more freely. Maybe not.

"Fair enough. But don't forget—if you don't answer the questions well enough, the police will still want to haul you in for a chat." It was sad that threats worked better than bribery.

He pulled an unimpressed face and folded his arms. "Right. So, ask your questions."

"Are you glad Morris is dead?" Throwing that out there first for shock value would hopefully get me a real reaction. I stared at him.

His forehead furrowed, and he shook his head. "No. I won't lie—I was pretty pissed when his information was the nail that sealed my fate, but really, I often thought about thanking him. Now I won't get the chance."

"Thanking him?"

He leaned forwards and rested his elbows on the table, clasping his hands together. "If it wasn't for his intervention, I might have ended up dead. I was heading so far down the wrong path that I couldn't get out. My parents were on at me, but if I'd left, they woulda killed me. Being arrested was the best thing that coulda happened." His dark-eyed gaze fearlessly met mine. "I owe him my life. Yeah, jail was shite, but it's better than a grave. And I'm out now. Making an honest go of things."

My BS radar wasn't going off. He was, as far as I could tell, genuine. I wrote it all down—including my take on it in the moment. "I bet your parents are happy."

"Yeah, I guess. I'm working my way up at my dad's landscaping business and saving to move out with my girlfriend. Been clean since my second year of lock-up too. I don't want to jinx it, but things are going well." He licked his lips. "I wouldn't wanna stuff it up now, if you know what I mean."

In other words—why would he kill Morris when his life was finally going well? He made a good point.

He sighed. "My dad wouldn't talk to me when I was in jail, and he stopped my mum from coming to see me. I don't blame them, though—that place is nowhere I wanted my mum to be. The last thing I want is to put them through that again, 'specially Mum. She's been through enough."

"You mean you going to jail?"

He scratched the side of his head. "Yeah. Anyway, is that all the questions you have?"

"Well, I'm writing an article about Morris's life, too, so I might quote you that he was a help and that you appreciated it. Would that be a fair comment?"

He tapped the table with his fingers, thinking. Finally, he

looked at me. "Yep, that would be a fair comment. I didn't appreciate it at the time, but I'm glad he did what he did."

"What's your girlfriend's name?"

"Jessica. Why?"

"I just want to wish you and Jessica good luck in the future. Was she your girlfriend before… as in when you weren't on the straight and narrow?"

"Nah. Met her after I got out. She moved next door to my parents when I was inside. Lives there with her mum and sister. She's a good egg… too good for me, but I got lucky." He gave me his first smile of the interview. So far, I couldn't see him being guilty of blowing up Morris and his wife. But I still suspected I hadn't gotten to the bottom of what he knew.

"I get the feeling you're not telling me everything. I'd hate to inform the police you weren't as cooperative as you could've been." My journalistic sixth sense nagged me, and if I'd learned anything since I started this job, it was that if my gut talked, I needed to listen.

He screwed up his face, shut his eyes, and breathed loudly out of his nose. When his eyes opened, there was a shiny pebble of warning in his dark irises. "Can I trust you to keep quiet?"

"Yes. A journalist has nothing without their integrity. Informants have a right to their privacy. As long as the police get the intel they need, they won't care where it came from, provided it's the truth." Obviously they'd be hankering to know who told me, but I'd keep mum, unless there was a ridiculously good reason not to.

"I'm relying on you to keep quiet. I don't want them coming after me. I've got a good life now, and if anything happens to Jessica, I won't be in my right mind." The look he gave me left no doubt as to what he was capable of if he wasn't in his right mind.

"I appreciate the risk you're taking, but threatening me isn't going to make me want to keep the secret. Either you trust me or you don't. And I could easily tell the police you threatened me." If someone found out he spilled the beans, I was going to cop the blame. Might as well take a stand so he didn't think I was easily cowed. "Now, what can you tell me?"

He eyed me for a good sixty seconds. I held my ground and didn't flinch. Finally, he made up his mind. "One of the guys in my cellblock was another con that Morris helped put away, but the proof of this guy's guilt mainly came from Morris. A couple of times he told me what he'd like to do to the guy. He said, and I quote, 'I'll wipe him off the face of the earth.' He used to be in the army and still has a couple of mates there."

Wiping someone off the face of the earth certainly sounded like blowing someone up. You wouldn't say that and shoot someone or stab them. At least I wouldn't.

"Why would he confide in you?"

He gave me an "are you stupid?" look. "He knew Morris had a hand in my situation too. Thought I'd be a sympathetic ear, which I was. It took a while to forgive the man."

I wrote it all down. "What's his name? Is he still in jail?"

"Yeah. Carl Brown. He's got four years to go. But he's got contacts outside who could"— he looked around before meeting my gaze again —"arrange what happened to Morris. Carl's a violent man." He rubbed the scar on his eyebrow. "He gave me this memento when I wouldn't give him my bangers and mash one lunchtime."

Yikes. Carl was one of the names on my list. I hadn't discussed the plan regarding him with Bellamy. Maybe I should sit that one out. We were weeding out the unlikelies, and Bellamy had hinted that the police would deal with the probables. I didn't fancy going to jail to interview some creep who was getting out in four years.

Ghosts I could handle. Flesh and blood psychos, I could not.

And if I interviewed Carl, he'd know who I was. He could easily find the article I wrote where I quoted Danny and connect the dots. "Right. I'll pass that information on, but I'll give it a few days, interview a few others, if you know what I mean." I had a duty of care not to hand the information to Bellamy about who gave me this intel, so I'd do the bare minimum to at least put doubts in his mind. If I gave him this information today or tomorrow, he'd know I'd only spoken to one suspect. He wasn't stupid—he'd figure it out.

"I'd appreciate it, and so will my family and Jessica." He stood. "I hope that's all. I have to get back to work."

With that information, as well as his alibi, I could cross him off the probably list. Bellamy was still doing background enquiries and making sure he had no ties to extremists or bomb makers, but I had a feeling he'd find nothing. This guy was actually as clean as he professed, which was a nice surprise. Jessica and he had been at his cousin's engagement party that night, and there were photos and videos to prove it. Not that he couldn't have organised someone else to do it, but he didn't give me that vibe. No doubt, Bellamy had gotten phone records on the sly. Well, not *sly* sly… legally, but so Danny didn't know. If he'd been communicating with any undesirables capable of the murder, the police would discover it.

Were we already close to solving this thing? Morris would be ecstatic if we were. But things rarely worked that way.

I packed my laptop away and stood. At least I could check off one name and put another on the probable list. Now I "only" had eight to go. Well, I had to start somewhere, and I was certainly off and running. With a bit of luck, this would be a sprint, not a marathon.

I just had to be careful not to trip.

CHAPTER 9

I had no other appointments after speaking to Danny, so I ventured down to the seaside village where Andrew's parents lived. It took over an hour, and the cloudy day had turned to rain. Only part of the house was visible through the hedges. It was set back and down a slight hill, with the ocean vista smudged in the distance through the drizzle.

I parked the car a couple of hundred metres away and got out with my umbrella. It was a crappy afternoon for a walk, but parking outside the property would be more obvious than strolling by. I wasn't sure what I wanted to achieve by being here, but getting the lay of the land would help me understand things better, especially if Everly wanted to explain anything. With a bit of luck, talking about her murder would help her remember details.

A car sped past through a puddle and splashed my legs. *Thanks, jerkface.* Wet jeans over bare skin was gross. At least it wasn't thundering. If it had been, there was no way I'd be out here. Getting struck by lightning twice was not on my to-do list.

I reached the property and stopped. Glancing around, I confirmed there wasn't anyone watching. I turned back to the property. Smoke drifted from the chimney poking through the grey slate roof. It hung lazily in the air until a small gust puffed it towards me. The setting was idyllic. How had this place nurtured a serial killer? Were his parents to blame, or had he come out that way?

A young woman in red and black running gear walked out from the driveway and stopped a few feet from me. The amulet around my neck helped me see the glow that confirmed she was a ghost.

I swallowed. Was this one of his victims? Her brown hair and slim build could be Jenny, but she could be anyone too. I hated to think how many millions of women had brown hair and a slim build. Had he buried her here or killed her here? It had to be one or the other… unless he had a dead sister, I knew nothing about.

The ghost hesitantly came towards me. "Can you see me?"

"Yes. I'm Avery. Who are you?" If he'd buried this woman on his land, there would be proof for the police. If he'd killed her here and moved the body, I'd be back to square one.

"Petra Flinders. How come you can see me?"

Across the road, a horse walked up to the timber fence and hung its white head over. Horses were awesome. Maybe I should go pat it so it didn't look like I was talking to myself in the middle of the street. "I was struck by lightning once, and ever since then, I've been able to." I glanced towards the driveway and back up the road. "I'm going to pat the horse. Other people don't know I can see ghosts, and I'd prefer they didn't find out. Come with me?"

"Sure." Her running shoes made no sound as she followed me.

I reached the horse, lifted my hand, and stroked its nose. "Hey, big fella. Aren't you gorgeous?" He pushed into my palm. "How did you end up here, Petra?"

Her pale cheeks glowed with colour. "It's stupid, really." She gazed at the horse, lifted her hand to pat it, then dropped her arm to her side. The slap didn't come. Nope, still not used to the weirdness that were ghosts. If I could hear their voices, why couldn't I hear any other sounds they made?

"I bet it's not. I also bet that your family would like to know what happened. How long have you been dead?" Was that cruel of me? Yes, but it was true.

"Four winters. I realised early on that time was weird here, so I counted every time Christmas came around… including now because their tree is up. I was killed in September two thousand and nineteen." Her hand slammed onto her mouth. Was she shocked at her admission that she was killed?

"Don't be ashamed. It's not your fault, and I had a feeling because of where you came from." I turned my head and stared at the Crumpses' driveway before sliding my gaze back to her. She was staring at the driveway and biting her lip.

Another car drove past, the shhhhhh of tyres on the wet road overpowering the timid pitter-patter of rain against my umbrella. The gentle eddies of air stirred the tang of brine, wet grass, and mild manure around us—it would be a refreshing time in nature if it wasn't for me standing here talking to a murdered woman.

"If you can get past how you feel and let me know what happened, I can help others. I know another two ghosts who Andrew killed. I can stop him hurting anyone else."

Her eye widened, and if it were possible, her white skin

turned fluorescent. "Oh, God... this... um.... Andrew didn't kill me."

"What do you mean?" Had she died of natural causes or been run over outside here or something? Talk about a coincidence.

"Andrew didn't kill me. He brought me to the house—we met at a café the day before. He mentioned he was a dentist and that his dad was a surgeon, and when I found that out, I asked if he could recommend any surgeon for a nose job." She ran a finger down her nose. "I hate the bump, but I wanted to make sure someone good did it."

"Right." I wasn't sure how this was going to tie in, but I was eager to find out. I stopped patting the horse, pulled out my phone, put it to my ear, and gave her my full attention. "Tell me everything."

"What's the phone for?"

"I don't want to look weird, standing here talking to myself."

She gave an understanding smile. "That makes sense. I forget I'm dead sometimes." Sadness dulled her eyes. "Those are the best times."

What the heck could I say to that? Nothing. That's what. A tornado of devastation and fury twisted inside me. I gritted my molars together. If only I could wish evil people dead and it would happen. Would be nice if there were superheroes in real life.

Unfortunately, I was all these ghosts had.

"I'm sorry, Petra. I can do something if you tell me who did this to you. Or was it an accident?"

"Andrew introduced me to his dad, a surgeon... but he wasn't a plastic surgeon. He told me to come into his study, that he had a number. While I was in there, his wife brought me a cup of tea. After I drank it, that was it. I was out. I woke up like this. Andrew's dad was… using my body, and I don't want to say how." What the actual? My stomach plummeted. This was worse than I could've imagined. So much worse. "They buried my body on the property. I'm out there, under a woodpile near the incinerator."

I blinked, trying to absorb what she'd said. A father, mother, and son murdering team? Chills assaulted my body, and I couldn't speak for a moment.

"Are you all right?"

I cleared my throat. "Ah, yeah. Um… that's a lot." Look at me almost falling apart when she was the one who went through everything. I needed to toughen up. "You're the one who suffered. I have no right to freak out, and that's not what you need from me right now. I'm sorry to ask, but I need to know—how many women…?" Evidence was key, something to tie the Crumpses to her disappearance; otherwise, there was no way Bellamy could investigate this or go on the property.

Petra stared across the road. "I'm friends with two other ghosts, but that's all—Emmy and Lila. We get together in the house. The other two come and go—they visit their families and old workplaces. We like to keep each other company, and we can vent because, well, we can all relate. It's… it's a sick club, and we're the pathetic members."

My voice was strong and hopefully convincing when I said, "Don't you dare say you're pathetic. None of you are. Victim blaming is the worst. You were all just trusting women. Who could've thought that these supposedly upstanding members of the community could do what they did? It's crazy what they've done. Crazy and horrific. Never ever be ashamed or blame yourself."

The horse whinnied, tossing his head before leaning further over the fence for more pats. I obliged.

"I have a friend, another ghost, and Andrew killed her many years ago. She might've been his first, but I don't know." I shied away from thinking about the repercussions of this new information. I'd dissect it later. "In any case, she's a smart, funny, amazing young woman, and I know she wasn't to blame for liking Andrew and dating him. You wouldn't blame any of the other victims for their own demise, would you?"

Fire came into her eyes. "No! Never!"

I gave her a sad smile. "So, why would you blame yourself?"

Her head dropped, and I had to strain to hear her whispered, "My parents always told me to be wary of strangers. I knew." Her head lifted, and her teary eyes met mine. "Why didn't I listen? Why was I so stupid? I went into a stranger's house without hesitation. I'm an idiot. A stupid, stupid girl. I've ruined my parents' lives, and my brother's. I know they're still not over it. They probably never will be."

I inhaled a shuddering breath and straightened my back against the sorrow. "If I could hug you, I would. But this is not your fault. And maybe we can get a message to your family somehow, but after these monsters are in jail. I think your family would do much better if they had answers. Let's give those to them. What do you think?"

For the first time during our talk, hope shone from her face, like the sun after a long winter's night. "I'd like that. I'd like that a lot."

"Can you remember the details of the day you disappeared? The date and time you met Andrew, the name of the coffee shop, the time you went to his house, anything at all."

"I remember everything. I can't ever forget that day—I

relive it over and over again, always beating myself up for how dumb I was, looking for any warnings I didn't heed."

"They're good at what they do. They've been doing this for decades—at least Andrew has. Let's make it stop."

"Yes. Let's."

CHAPTER 10

By the time I finished with Petra, it was mid-afternoon, so I passed by the vet on my way home to pick up Zeus. The vet nurse brought him out in his carrier. As I settled the account, the vet came to the counter. She smiled. "He was a model patient. He's a very smart cat, and we all fell in love with him."

These compliments should've filled me with pride, but all they did was bring on a wave of nausea. I gave her my best fake smile. "That's great." Did they notice how high-pitched my voice was?

"One of the vets here fell in particular love—Antony. He left this morning for a break in Spain. He'll be back in time for New Year's, and he's keen on picking up Zeus and becoming his new family. What do you think?"

I swallowed the cat-sized lump in my throat and pretended I wasn't about to cry. "Ah… that's… great. Thank you. I guess if he has to go to another home, you can't get better than a vet."

She beamed at me. "No, you can't. I've passed on your number. I hope you don't mind."

"No, of course not. This is… good. So, I'll be hearing from him when he returns?"

"That's the plan. Have a good Christmas, Avery."

"Yeah, you too. Thanks." If my thanks sounded sour, I was sorry, but it was the best I could do. My throat and eyes burned. This was terrible. What a crappy Christmas I was going to have. The time would overlap where Finn and Antony would be away at the same time. Maybe Finn would let me live at his place for a couple of days so I could say a proper goodbye to my sweetie.

As soon as I strapped his carrier onto the back seat and hopped in the car, I let go. My tears burnt my freezing cheeks as they waterfalled down my face. Zeus would get a loving and safe home. I should be happy. It's what I wanted.

No, it wasn't.

I wanted to keep him.

But life was unfair more often than not, at least in my experience.

Get a grip, Avery. Think of Mrs Crabby losing her daughter. Think of all the families of the women who the Crumpses murdered. They have a reason to cry. You don't. Get over it.

I could hear my father's voice when my cousin's cat got run over. *Stop crying. It's just a cat.*

But Zeus wasn't *just* a cat. No cat was. They were smart, gorgeous, warm, soft, loving beings, and I loved Zeus, even though I hadn't known him long. He'd made me realise how much I missed having a fur baby and company, someone (yes, just like a person) who didn't judge me, except when he wasn't fed on time or played with enough.

When I returned home, I parked in the laneway and called Finn to check where he was. He was home, and it was time.

I didn't even have to knock on the door—Finn was waiting when I reached his house, cat carrier and bag of bits and pieces in my hands. "Thank you so much for doing this. You'll be happy to know someone from the vet wants him. He's going to get him just before New Year's." I had to stop my voice from wobbling at the end. I pretended I wasn't blinking back tears. *How embarrassing.*

Finn looked at me for a beat before reaching out to take the bag of food, litter, and plastic litter tray. "I hate to ask, but what about the time between Christmas and New Year when I'm away?"

"Um… I was hoping it would be okay if I just came to your place to look after him. Maybe I could crash here for a couple of days… you know… to say goodbye." I pressed my lips together and tried to blink away the tears, but they kept coming. *Dammit*! Who was I kidding in pretending? I took a deep breath and wiped the tears away.

Finn gave me a sad smile. "That would be fine, Lightning. You can sleep in the spare room, and even while I'm here, you can pop in any time. Just text me first, so I know it's you and not a burglar." He chuckled. I already had his spare key, and he had mine—in case of emergencies since we lived next door to each other.

"Thank you. You have no idea how much I appreciate it."

"Anyway, come in before we all freeze half to death." He was only in a T-shirt and trackpants since his house was heated. And we were letting all the warm air out too. Not very environmentally friendly.

He stepped back, and I hurried through the door, shutting it behind me. I let Zeus out straight away and followed Finn to his laundry, where I placed the cat carrier on a bench and got to work setting up his litter. Finn grabbed the bowls. "I'll put these in the kitchen. Do you want a tea or coffee?"

"Yeah, sure. A tea would be lovely. Thanks."

By the time Finn brought me a tea in the lounge room, Zeus had finished sniffing around and reacquainting himself with the place. He jumped into my lap, kneaded my leg, then sat, curling himself into a warm, purring ball of adorableness. I stroked his back as I sipped my tea. A fire crackled in the fireplace, my skin soaking up its heat. A more perfect evening, I couldn't imagine. Even if Finn and I weren't together.

I had to remind myself it was a good thing. *Hmm, yeah, right. Shut up, needy Avery. You have a great life right now. Keep it that way.*

I had to admit, there was something freeing about not worrying if there would be heartbreak down the line. And I didn't have to answer to anyone. My life was my own. I could come and go as I pleased, spend my money on stupid stuff if I wanted—not that I wanted, but still.

Finn settled into the other end of the three-seater couch. "So, someone's taking him, huh."

"Yep." I didn't have the energy to not sound despondent. Besides, if you couldn't be yourself in front of your friends, who could you be yourself in front of? I had a moment of gratitude that I didn't have to pretend here. "He's a vet, and I have no doubt he's going to take great care of Zeus." Best leave it at that, or I was going to cry again. "So, how are you going after the other night?"

"Generally okay. What about you?"

I swallowed my mouthful of tea. "I'm okay. Had a couple of nightmares, but not too bad. I'm putting my energy into helping Sergeant Bellamy solve it. That always helps."

He smiled. "He's a tough nut to crack. I'm surprised he took to you so quickly."

I chuckled, remembering how they both treated me when I first arrived. Finn tried to one-up me on information, and Bellamy froze me out. "What can I say? I'm obviously adorable, and people have a hard time saying no to me."

His lips stretched into a cheeky smile. "Is that so?"

I gave him a smug look. "You know it."

His gaze softened, his smile retreating. He mumbled something, the last word the only one I could make out. "Well."

Something, something well? "What was that?"

His cheeky grin returned. "Nothing. How's your tea?"

I rolled my eyes. "Just fine, Vinegar. Thanks." I wasn't getting anything else out of him, and to be honest, I probably didn't want to know. If it was him agreeing, it wouldn't do anything to help since even if he liked me, he had no intention of getting tied down.

"So, you've been helping Bellamy. What's the latest?"

We were past competing for stories, so I could tell him what I wanted, within the scope of what I was allowed to tell. "We have more than a few potential suspects. We're in the process of narrowing the list."

"Being a journalist is a dangerous business."

"You can say that again." All the cases I'd solved recently came to mind. I'd even plonked him into a dodgy situation or two.

"Being a journalist is—"

I held up my hand and laughed. "Stop! You're such a dag."

His forehead wrinkled. "How is that eccentric?"

"Ha, no. A dag, as in the crap that hangs all tangled in the wool at a sheep's bum. It kind of means you're a bit of a silly nong. Kind of a loser, but affectionately so. As in, that was such a bad joke, but what can I expect from Vinegar?"

"I can revoke key privileges."

I gasped. "You wouldn't!"

He waggled his brows. "Nah, but it's fun messing with you."

I picked up a cushion and threw it at his head. He blocked it and made to throw it back, but I pointed at Zeus on my lap and raised an eyebrow.

He rolled his eyes. "No fair, Lightning."

"Sometimes I play dirty. There's nothing wrong with that."

His lips moved as if he was going to say something, but he placed the cushion next to him instead. "So, what else are you working on?"

"Everly's murder. I've been doing quite a bit of research."

"I can't imagine how hard it is to investigate a cold case."

I sipped my tea. "Well, the sergeant has been very helpful. He's pulled the files from back in the day, and he's let me look through them." It was true he'd ordered them, but they hadn't come through yet. We were hoping they'd arrive any day. The more links we could draw between the Crumpses and Everly, the better. It would also give the police—really me—a reason to look up other missing persons from the area or others linked to this guy. We had so many more things at our disposal now, not to mention hindsight.

From what I'd seen so far, Everly was the first woman Andrew had murdered. But I couldn't be sure. And how many women had his parents killed before he even got involved? I finished my tea to cover the shudder ripping through me. The horror of the situation hit me. Being out there, interviewing Petra, I hadn't had time to think about it. And talking to her made it seem not as bad since it was almost as if she were alive. As I drove back, the facts bounced around my brain, but more about where to take things next, and then, of course, there was Zeus and the fact that I'd gone straight to pick him up.

Finn's face tightened in concern. "And…? What aren't you telling me?"

I couldn't tell him too much, but… the truth was, I needed to tell someone as nausea's slimy fingers tightened around my abdomen. "We think there's more than one victim. He might be a serial killer."

He blinked. "He? How do you know it's a he?"

"We're assuming. She went missing after a date with her boyfriend. The police did the bare minimum where he was concerned. His dad was a respected surgeon. You know how it is."

"What makes you think he's a serial killer?"

Because I've met some of the women he killed. Yep, that would go down well. "It's too early to say. Call it a hunch. We've got a lot more work to do."

"Is the boyfriend still alive?"

"Yes. He's a dentist in London."

He put his empty mug on the table. "Have you spoken to him yet?"

"No. It's too early. We need to go through all the old evidence first. See where it leads."

He nodded and fixed me with a determined stare. "Okay, but be careful. Don't interview anyone dangerous without Bellamy or me there. Promise?"

"Promise." Bellamy would want to be there for sure and probably lead the interview. Besides, if I tried to trip the guy with things only the ghosts would know, I wouldn't be able to explain that to Finn, so better that he not be there.

"How do you find all these dangerous assignments? You're a murder magnet. I should get you a badge."

I laughed. "Funny, not funny. I don't know. Maybe it's my destiny."

And wasn't that the truth.

Whether I wanted it or not, solving murders was the assignment. It wasn't as if many other people could speak to ghosts, so I was pretty much their only hope. Which meant I would never turn them away.

"Well, I'm here to assist with your destiny when needed. I'm always happy to help."

I smiled. If only I could tell him the whole truth; I had no doubt he'd be a massive help, but it could never be. "Thanks. I appreciate it." I rested my hand on Zeus's back and watched the slow rise and fall of his side as he breathed cute little cat breaths.

"Hey, do you want to stay for dinner?"

He was obviously giving me as much time with Zeus as possible. I looked at him and smiled. "I'd like that. Thanks. I know you hate Carina and I telling you this, but underneath your 'lover-boy, don't really care' exterior, you're a good guy, Finnegan Walsh."

I'd never seen him blush before. It was, of course, adorable. "Yeah, well, don't tell anyone because I'll deny it." He stood. "Come on. You can help."

I gently placed Zeus on the couch. He looked up at me and meowed. I dropped a kiss on the top of his head and straightened, ignoring the cramp of grief in my heart. Did life ever get easier? It seemed like there was always some kind of heartbreak around the corner. I met Finn's gaze. "Lead the way, boss."

CHAPTER 11

When I got home last night, I researched the three women from the Crumpses' property. Petra gave me the other two names. One was killed about four years after Everly, so there wasn't anything on the net about it. The other one, however, was killed two years before Petra, so there was some info online, including two articles about her going missing. I tracked her sister and mum on Facebook. They'd written many posts from that time asking for help to find Emmy, a twenty-five-year-old nurse. She'd disappeared after her shift at a London hospital. There was video of her hopping on and off the Tube, but nothing after that. She'd apparently driven to the station, but her car was found at the car park, still locked.

Right now, at five past ten in the morning, I was sitting in Myra Anderson's living room on her stained white couch, my gaze trained on her devil-spawned offspring in case they tried something, like hitting me with the plastic sword, Byron, her five-year-old, held. Why you would pick white furniture when you had two monster children, I could never guess. To be clear, I didn't think all children were monsters, just these two, and I doubted it was their fault.

Myra Anderson had completed a three-month course on child-rearing two years ago. She was trying to launch her own business now the children were a bit older—three and five years, which were "handful" years if you asked me. But good on her for seeking personal growth through helping others. Unfortunately, the longer I spent with her, the less I was inclined to recommend her services.

Byron was smashing his sword against the wall, his berserker mode leaving grey marks on the white surface. But did his mother say anything? Nope. In fact, I was the only one watching him. Myra smiled at me. "Keep your eyes on me. It's best if we ignore bad behaviour. When the child doesn't get the attention they're looking for, they stop."

I dutifully focussed on her. "Okay. Great. Let me write that down." I made a note and didn't look at demon-spawn number one. When I looked back at her, demon-spawn number two caught my eye. She was sticking her small hand into the bottom of a houseplant and throwing clumps of dirt onto the carpet. Maybe Myra couldn't see because her back was to the child? "Um, Myra. Don't look now, but at what point do you stop a child from throwing dirt all over the floor? Do you wait for the whole pot to be emptied?" I doubted she recognised my sarcastic tone or got my "don't look now" reference. This was ridiculous. I made more notes.

Myra ignored my suggestion and didn't take her own advice. She turned and looked over her shoulder at Bessy. Myra blinked, took a deep breath, then turned to me, her smile more teeth than was necessary. Did she have a toothache? Maybe it was postcoital regret a few years too late.

A clump of dirt hit the back of Myra's head, the spray of grit landing in my lap and on my notepad. If she wasn't worried about her kids trashing her place, why should I? I shook my notepad so the dirt fell on the floor. "So, what can parents expect of your course? What methods of discipline do you use?" None, if her kids were anything to judge by.

She eyed the dirt in my lap and briefly closed her eyes, as if she was summoning strength. Her smile was even more strained than before. "They can expect an understanding and non-judgemental environment. All children are precious and need room to test their boundaries."

Byron was testing those boundaries right now. He'd given up banging on the wall, but it wasn't capitulation to better behaviour. Oh, no. He ran to his sister and thwacked her on the head with his sword. Bessy screamed, and one of my eyes scrunched shut at the pitch. Precious my ar—

Myra held up her hand as if she could read my mind. I was sure my face said everything I was thinking because I wasn't trying to hold it in. It was enough that my mouth managed to stay closed. I couldn't ask much more of myself, really. Julian would be proud if he could see me now.

Myra stood and went to her children. She dragged Byron away from his sister while he punched her with his non-sword fist. Once she'd moved him to the other side of the room, she went to Bessy and gave her a cuddle. Once in her mother's arms, the poor kid sobbed and sucked her thumb. If I were Bessy, I'd learn how to fight back because there were no consequences to Byron's behaviour. Speaking of which....

"Are there any consequences for that behaviour?" Yep, we journalists asked the hard questions. Confrontation was our middle name.

Myra stared at me. "He can see he's upset his sister. His guilt should be consequence enough."

Byron's smug face seemed to be missing this guilt she spoke of. Yep, Bessy better take up martial arts and sleep with one eye open. I snapped a picture of Myra hugging her daughter, dirt on the floor in the background. I'd blur out the child's face if we used the photo in the article. I'd also get Myra's permission as well. But seriously, if anyone came to this woman for advice, they might as well ask the neighbourhood fox for their opinion because it was going to be less harmful and free.

What a waste of my morning. Instead of being traumatised by bad parenting, I could've been investigating either of my cases. In fact.... I stood. "Myra, our time is up here. I have everything I need. I'll just show you the photos I've taken"—I'd taken a couple when I arrived—"and you can sign my release form if you're happy for us to use them in the article."

She stood, bringing her daughter with her, and settling her on one hip. "Of course."

We finalised everything, and I left Myra to clean up. I wondered how sane she was going to be in twelve months' time. As I started my car, I hoped Byron didn't turn out to be the next Andrew Crumps. Maybe I was exaggerating, but maybe not.

My next stop was to see Bellamy. Even though I wanted proof of things before I met with him again, he might be able to steer me in a good direction that would save time. As much as I didn't want to bother him when he was already working on a complicated case, whoever killed Morris wasn't as dangerous to the public as Andrew Crumps and his parents. Morris's killer hated Morris specifically and wasn't necessarily going to strike again, whereas Everly's killer was a danger to young women everywhere.

It was time to drop the bomb on the sergeant.

My stomach flipped and went splat. Being the bearer of bad news always ended, well, badly in my previous life. If I had to tell Brad that I'd scratched the car or ruined his favourite white shirt by putting a black one in the wash with it, making it slightly grey, he was never understanding or forgiving. His style was to yell and berate me and then not talk to me for two days.

I shook my head. I would never ever, ever, ever put up with that again. It was embarrassing enough that I'd put up with it for as long as I did, but you couldn't see the disaster when you were in the middle of it. It happened slowly until it seemed normal. Even if my subconscious knew better, my brain and heart didn't want to catch on.

The officer at the front desk was one I barely knew. He buzzed me in, and I went straight through. It must've been a busy morning because all the PCs' desks were empty. I knocked on Bellamy's closed door.

"Come in."

I went in. Fox and Charles weren't there. They'd become super close since I'd introduced them, and now, where one was, the other usually tagged along. If I'd done nothing else in my life, I'd die happy, knowing I'd given each a good friend to see them through this phase of their existences. Charles finally had the father figure he deserved.

"Hi, Sergeant. How's it going?" I sat down without an invitation. The amount of time I spent here, I should probably get a desk in here as well.

He looked up from his screen. "Have you got news?"

My stomach muscles tightened. "Yes, and it's pretty much bad. Although the fact that I have more information is a plus. I have no evidence, though. This is all via the ether."

Bellamy leaned forwards, his gaze intense. "Do you know who killed Morris?"

"Oh, um, no. Sorry! I know who killed Everly, and he's killed others. We're also dealing with a whole family of psychos." I worried my bottom lip between my teeth while I waited for his reaction.

His eyebrows rose. "A whole family? How many are we talking?"

"Three. Mum, dad, and junior. I know of five women they've killed, including Everly. I'm not sure if the parents had a hand in Everly's killing or the other woman she told me about, Jenny. I know the parents killed three women at their house, and two of them were lured there by Andrew Crumps, Everly's boyfriend." Or was that ex-boyfriend? It wasn't like they were dating now, but they'd been dating at the time and never actually broke up. Although killing someone was the ultimate way of breaking up with them, I supposed.

I supposed. Argh, someone save me from my gruesome brain.

"And you're sure?"

I gave him an "are you really asking me that question" look.

He cleared his throat. "It just sounds so…." He sighed. "Who am I kidding? It's not that unbelievable. I don't know why I'm surprised. Just when I think I've seen all there is to see in my career, someone comes along and proves me wrong. I'm too old for this poppycock." He leaned into his chair, dropped his head back, and stared at the ceiling. He might've mouthed a choice phrase. I gave him time to recover. He finally dropped his chin and looked at me. "Tell me everything you know."

"This might take a while."

"It's fine." He waved a hand dismissively in the air as he

spoke. "It's not like I've got another murder case to solve, or other miscellaneous cases and criminals to deal with. Or a whole station full of police to manage. Go right ahead." He finished by folding his arms as if he was settling in for the long haul.

I pressed my lips together to hold in a smile. Poor Bellamy. At least he still had his sense of humour, dry as it was. I pulled out my notebook and told him everything Petra had told me. I had names, dates, all the information about how each of the women had met their demise. Surely this was going to make it easier to pin this on the family. "Two of the three women had been carrying a mobile phone when they went missing. Surely the police would've requested phone tower records."

"We would assume. Although that area doesn't have a lot of towers. It likely won't pinpoint an exact location."

"I was afraid of that. It is fairly remote. Still, we might get lucky. If we study those files, we might find a link the other police missed because we know where these women died and their movements that day. If we could sync anything up with Andrew's phone...."

There were a myriad of things that could've happened—maybe Andrew was smart and didn't carry his phone the day he met Petra, or maybe he turned her phone off later—but we had details no one else had. Now we needed some luck. Not a lot. Just a bit. Life often came down to random luck. Whether you won the lotto, landed the job of a lifetime, or avoided dying in a natural disaster. I was a prime example—if that nurse hadn't been passing by when I was struck, I likely would've died. But then again, if I hadn't had a fight with Brad that morning and run late to work, which meant I ran into Mrs Anderson in the hallway—she loved to chat and held me up for a further ten minutes—then been held up in traffic getting to my interview for my article because the heavens had opened two minutes before I got into my car, I wouldn't have been struck.

So many things had to happen that day for me to be where I was at that exact time. Luck.

Bellamy linked his hands and twiddled his thumbs. "There's only one problem."

"Only one? That's a first." I chuckled.

He gave me a wry smile. "One is all we need to put a stop to everything. We can't request those files without having a reason, a logical link to Everly's disappearance that would hold up in a legal way."

"You mean Everly's murder?"

"As far as the law is concerned, she's missing. The murder is a presumption at this stage. Oh, and I have good news." He turned his chair to the side and bent, then straightened, lifting a cardboard storage box from the floor. He placed it on his table. "Everly's files arrived this morning, but I've been snowed under and haven't had a chance to call you or look through them."

I made an *O* with my mouth and held my hands out. "Give me; give me."

He pushed it across the table. "Go for it. You can stay here and look through. I'd like to go through them, too—I just don't have time today."

I checked my phone. "I've got time to spare before I need to get back to the office. My article isn't due till three. Although, it's going to take some deft skills to make it into something that isn't too insulting to the woman."

"Do I want to know?"

"Probably not, and neither of us have time." I spared a thought for Myra who believed consequences didn't exist and her kids shouldn't be disciplined. Ah, the irony. She was suffering the consequences every day.

He nodded. "I was hoping you'd say that. Let's get to work."

I stood and eagerly pulled the lid off. "I wonder if we could get these scanned—it'll be easier to search through everything that way." Everly died pre-computer era. I picked out one of the many folders and flicked through it. Everything in it was typed or handwritten. Some of the handwriting was scrawly and hard to understand. Great.

Bellamy didn't look away from his screen when he answered, "Feel free. My officers are too busy for that, but no one is stopping you. You know where the scanner is, don't you?"

I gave him a sassy look that he ignored, which was easy for him since he refused to move his gaze from the computer. If only I could ask Charles to do it. He'd been practicing manipulating real-world things, but he was nowhere skilled enough to put a sheet of paper in a printer, let alone close the lid and press a button. "Yes. Fine." I didn't miss the smile he wrestled. "Santa's going to bring you a sack of mouldy potatoes."

"I look forward to it. Besides, it's not as bad as having to scan all those documents."

I sighed as I walked out.

Bellamy one. Avery zero.

CHAPTER 12

After going through a couple of the files, I ran out of time and returned to the office. I'd managed to write the first draft of my article, edit that, and now I wanted feedback before I sent it to Julian. He had enough on his plate to worry about me upsetting a local, but I couldn't in good conscience recommend Myra's services to everyone. Thankfully, Carina came in thirty minutes before I had to submit it.

"Hi, Avery. How's it going?" She crossed the room to her desk and started unpacking.

"I'm good. Do you have time to read something for me? I need some feedback."

She stopped what she was doing and stared at me. "D'is is a first."

I shrugged. "Might not be the last. It seems people are getting nuttier as time goes on. The woman I interviewed—Myra—wants exposure for her business. I can't recommend her."

"Oh? What does she do?"

"She teaches parents how to parent, basically, but her methods are a bit woo-woo and result in disaster, at least from what I've seen. She's anti-discipline, and I'm wondering if she's bringing up a serial killer."

She chuckled. "Is d'at in d'e article?"

I laughed. "Not quite. I could add it if you think it helps."

She flicked her hair over her shoulder. "Mmm, I'm sure Julian wants a lawsuit on top of everyt'ing."

"So, can I send it to you?"

She sat. "Yep. I'm ready." She rubbed her hands together eagerly.

"Ha, ha, thanks. Just let me know if it's shading her without being horrible. She's not a bad person… just misguided." I addressed the email and pressed Send. While Carina read through it, I called a couple more leads for articles. When I was done, my email dinged.

"D'ere you go, love. I t'ink it's fair." She grinned and looked at her screen. "I particularly loved d'e closing line: 'If you choose to work wi'd Myra, be prepared for an eye-opening experience.' You're not lying, so d'at's good. I t'ink most people can read between d'e lines, and you didn't say anyt'ing horrible. Nicely done. D'ere were a couple of typos I fixed."

I slashed the back of my hand across my forehead. "Phew. Pesky mistakes always slip through. Grrrr. Thanks, lovely."

"Any time."

I read over it again and sent it to Julian. I was about to line up my next interview for Morris's case when my phone rang. "Hi, Sergeant. What's up?" I'd summarized the things I'd read on Everly's case and left Post-its on what I felt were crucial pages. Maybe he wanted to discuss some of it?

"Hello, Winters. We can cross one of the names of

Morris's list. We've just found out that one of the gentlemen is in a nursing home with advanced Alzheimer's. Donald Briggs."

I pulled up the file on my computer. "Okay, thanks. That's helpful. Have you had a chance to look at the notes I left?"

"No, sorry. I'll peruse them tonight at home. I would love to put this on hold, but in light of your recent discoveries, we can hardly leave them running free. They're a danger to all young women."

"Agreed. Is that all?"

"Yes. Let me know if you discover anything else about either case."

"Will do."

"Have a good afternoon."

"You too, Sergeant. Bye."

The line dropped out. Poor Bellamy. If only I could find some tangible evidence on one of the cases and make his life easier. He worked hard enough during working hours without having to take stuff home. *But isn't that what you're doing?* a little voice piped up in my brain. Yes, it was, but I didn't have a wife who wanted to spend time with me. It was a good way to fill in time. Especially now that I was losing Zeus. Keeping my mind active and away from that depressing reality was self-care.

"Was d'at about Morris's murder?" Carina stared at me from her desk.

"Yes. One of our long-listed suspects has dementia and is in a home, so at least we can cross one more off the list."

"Good luck wit' d'at." She frowned. "Morris was a good man and a brilliant journalist. D'at night was horrific." She shuddered.

"Thanks." Thankfully, Finn walked in and interrupted our depressing conversation.

"Afternoon, ladies." He went to his desk and sat. "Are you coming over tonight for a visit?"

"You couldn't keep me away." I smiled. He was being such a good friend. I couldn't ask for better.

Carina smirked and waggled her brows. "Ooh, is d'ere somet'ing you're not telling me?"

I rolled my eyes. Finn turned around and gave her a dirty look. "Don't be ridiculous. I've got Zeus, and Lightning's coming over to see him. There's not much time left." He turned his gaze on me, sympathy clear in his eyes. I didn't like feeling like a charity case, but at the moment, I was. Also, calling the thought of us together ridiculous—*ouch.* I might not want to jump into another relationship, but I didn't want to be reminded that I was undesirable. I shook my head quickly to dispel my ridiculous thoughts. Unproductive and stupid. *Act your age, Avery.*

"Aw, d'e poor kitty. I'm sorry, Aves."

I kept my expression neutral. The less we said about this, the better. "It's fine. I mean, I'm upset, but it is what it is."

Charles appeared at the door. "Avery, Morris wants to talk to you. He's waiting outside."

I flicked my gaze to him, then quickly back to my friends.

"Are you okay?" Finn gave me a quizzical look.

"Ah, yeah. I just remembered, I have to make a phone call." I stood and grabbed my phone. "I'll be back." I gave them a wave and made my way downstairs, Charles walking ahead of me. He went clean through the front door, and I stopped just before I hit it. Yikes. I had to remind myself I wasn't a ghost, and I needed to open doors. That was a first—me thinking ghostly behaviours were normal. I'd better watch myself before I broke my face walking into something.

Outside, dark clouds hung low and threatening. It was cold

enough for snow, and idiot me forgot my coat. I wrapped one arm around my middle, held my phone up to my ear with the other hand, and joined Morris on the footpath next to our building. "Hi. What's up?"

Morris's suit from the night he died was spotless, the only markings on his face a couple of age spots and wrinkles. It was as if the explosion never happened. "Thanks for seeing me, Avery. I've got some information, but I also wanted to see if you and Sergeant Bellamy are getting anywhere."

"We've ruled out Donald Briggs. He's in a home because he has advanced Alzheimer's. I spoke to Danny, and we think he's most likely not a suspect. He didn't seem particularly angry at you, and he had a strong alibi. Bellamy let me know that one of the others, Frederick, has an alibi that checks out too. I still have to look into the others. Bellamy might have more info, but he's not telling me anything I don't need to know, and his officers are still making enquiries. I have an undercover gig to sus out Angelo Fortense, that ex-politician you outed for cheating on his wife with a fifteen-year-old. Cheating is probably not the only word we should use. Sicko. Anyway, he's out of jail, divorced, and running a nightclub." I shivered, white clouds fogging the air with every word I spoke. I suddenly needed to do a wee. Stupid freezing weather. "What's your news?"

"Funny you should mention Angelo. I need you to talk to a colleague of mine. There are some notes we shared about the exposé I wrote. There are a couple of names of his more… criminal associates. He might have met others in jail, but those two men are of particular interest. One of them owns a few brothels, and the other is an ex-special services guy who knows how to make bombs."

"Why weren't they in the stuff you wanted Julian to have?"

My nose and fingers were numb, and I needed a coffee to bring them back to life. "Walk with me. I need to warm up." I headed towards Heavenly Brew. Since I'd saved Joyless's bum, she'd been quite cordial. Anna, at Joyless's insistence, now gave me a 20 per cent discount on all beverages. I hadn't wanted to take it because it was coming out of Anna's profits, but she insisted since she had her best barista back.

"An oversight. I didn't know I was going to be blown up. And while I worried I might be attacked by some of the people I'd exposed, I didn't expect to be murdered. Hindsight is a wonderful thing." He sidestepped a dog being walked and went half through my arm.

The iciness of his touch was worse than the zero degrees. "Ouch. That was like being branded with frozen metal."

He put his hand on my arm to pat it better, and I flinched. A guy walking towards us gave me a weird look.

"Sorry, Avery. Old habits."

"I know. It's okay. Um, here we are. Can you wait out here a minute? I'm going to get off my phone because I hate buying things while I'm on it. I'll be back in five."

"Nice to see a young person with manners. I'll be here. Take your time."

I hurried in. Being the afternoon, there was only one person in front of me. When Joyless was finished with them, she smiled at me. It even looked genuine. I wasn't ready to let my guard down, but I smiled back because there was a chance she was being legit. "Hiya, Avery. How are you?"

"I'm good thanks. How are you?" I kept waiting for her to start laughing and say "just joking."

"I'm great. Every time I feel a bit down, I remember I'm not in jail, and it gives me perspective. I've also started an online accounting course. I figured it was time to level up. So, the usual?"

"Yes, please. And congrats. I'm sure you'll kill it." She stared at me. My eyes flew wide, and I whacked a hand over my mouth. "Oh my God, bad choice of words. Sorry." Having hot cheeks and a numb nose was a weird feeling.

She laughed. "I know. It's fine. Besides, I didn't kill anyone, so yay me."

Who would've thought I'd laugh at a joke intentionally made by Joyless. There was hope for the world yet. "I'm glad you can laugh about it."

"Me too." She sprinkled chocolate on the top of my cappuccino, clicked the lid over the top, and slid it across the counter.

I took it and paid her. "Thanks. Have a good afternoon."

"You too. See you next time." She gave me a wave, and I left. Who knew all I had to do to win her over was get her out of jail. Yes, that was sarcasm. Still, beggars couldn't be choosers—what a terrible saying—so I'd take it. If she was going to be nice, it didn't matter why. It was one less stress in my day.

Morris stared at the cup. "Is that a cappuccino?"

I gave him a small nod and walked back towards the office.

"Can you take the lid off so I can smell it?"

I stopped walking, stood to the side so I wasn't blocking the path, and took the lid off. Morris leaned over and sniffed. And sniffed. His face fell in sadness.

"I can't smell anything."

I put the lid back on, slid my phone out of my pocket, and put it to my ear. "I'm sorry. Being where you are sucks." I started walking again.

He hurried after me. “I would kill for a coffee. What’s the point of the afterlife if you can’t drink coffee?”

“I have no idea. If you find out, let me know.” Something about the way he walked made me curious. “I’m assuming you can’t feel pain.”

“No. Why?”

“Because you’re moving like a twenty-year-old.”

His brow furrowed. “You’re right.” He smiled. “I knew there had to be some benefit to being dead.” He jumped up and clicked his heels together like in some famous old movies. “Imagine that—I didn’t break anything.”

I gave him the side eye, then grinned. “Good to hear.” I sipped my coffee and relished the life-giving heat. It didn’t even burn my tongue. Maybe Joyless really was cured of her cattiness. “Should I call your colleague, or should I go and see him in person?”

“You might have to call him. He’s not always around—they send him all over the UK to cover stories. Actually, he might be at my funeral.”

“When is it?”

“I don’t know. They haven’t released my body yet.”

And wasn’t this the most casually gruesome conversation I’d ever had. “Well, we want things to move along, so I’ll call him. What’s his name?” I brought up my note-taking app and pressed Record.

“Duncan Wilson. His number is—”

Pain lanced down my arm. “Ow!” I jerked away from his accidental touch.

“Sorry, love. I didn’t want to tread in the dog poo. People really need to clean up after their dogs.” Most dog owners did the right thing, unless maybe the dog had escaped, and the owner wasn’t tagging along.

"You can't really touch it. You do know that, don't you?" We'd just about reached the office, and I was keen to go upstairs and thaw out.

"It's hard to remember these things. Anyway, his name is Duncan Wilson." He rattled off his number, and I repeated the name and number into my phone, then pressed Stop on the recording.

"Okay. Is that everything?"

"For now, yes. Good luck, Avery, and thank you."

"My pleasure. Apparently, this is my life now." I smiled. "I'll call for you if I discover anything." I was about to put my hand on the door and go inside, but he held his hand up.

Morris's face was set in seriousness. "Will you come to my funeral?"

"Um…." No one had ever asked me that question, and if they had, it wouldn't have been from beyond the grave. It would've been a "in the future, which is probably a long way away, can you come to my funeral?" "I can. I would say I hardly knew you, but I guess I know you now."

"And it would mean a lot to Julian. I want him to have as much support as possible."

"I'll make sure I'm there."

"Thanks again. See you later."

"Bye." I lowered my phone arm stiffly—because it was frozen—and he disappeared. I went back upstairs.

Carina had just finished packing up. "I'll see you two tomorrow. Enjoy your romantic dinner." She winked in a ridiculous, dramatic fashion.

Finn shook his head with an unimpressed look on his face.

I smirked. "Zeus and I will enjoy our time together. Thanks."

"Ha, good one." She grinned as she walked past my desk. "Toodles."

I waved to her and sat. I wanted to call Morris's colleague ASAP, just in case I had to book to see him in advance. I grabbed my pen and notebook and placed my phone on my desk. After going into my recordings, I pressed Play, pen at the ready.

"*. . . is*—"

"*Ow!*"

The blood drained from my face as I pressed Stop.

"Are you okay?"

I looked up. Finn was staring at me. *Possum poo.* I blew out a measured breath, my heart hammering, and tried to sound as unaffected as possible. "Yep. Nothing to see here." I smiled, careful not to make it too wide or weird.

His eyes narrowed slightly. *Please give it up and go back to work.* Was I crossing my still-freezing fingers? Why, yes I was.

"If you say so." He shook his head as if to say he didn't believe me, then went back to his screen.

The voice had been tinny, but I was sure it was Morris. I grabbed my AirPods from my bag with shaking fingers and put them in my ears, then played it again. It was only a second or two—the time he was touching me—and it was fainter than last time, but it was him. I sucked in a breath. Had I just stumbled upon a way that Bellamy could hear Sergeant Fox and any other ghost?

I played it again, but this time, I could barely hear Morris's voice. Was that an anomaly, or did ghosts' voices fade if you recorded them?

Or was I imagining the whole thing?

I glanced at Finn. There was no way I could ask him what he'd heard, and he probably wasn't paying proper attention anyway. There was only one way to figure this out, and that was to test it.

I listened again. Morris's voice was gone. Hopefully it wasn't a one-off. I kept the recording going and jotted down Duncan's number. Once that was done, I called him, and it went to voicemail. I left a message, then packed my stuff up and stood. "Do you mind if I get to yours at four and have some couch time with Zeus?"

"Not at all. Go for it. I'll see you about five."

I smiled. "You're awesome. Thank you."

He smirked. "I know, but don't let it get out."

"I wouldn't dream of it." I put my coat on and hurried out—I couldn't wait to test my theory.

After sneaking through the front door, I made sure to avoid the squeaky stair. Surprisingly, I made it to the top without a Mrs Crabby intervention. It was my lucky afternoon. Maybe she was out or having a nap because she never missed an opportunity to berate me.

Inside, I put the kettle on for a cup of tea. The coffee had been good, but I was still cold after spending too long outside without a coat. Once I'd settled, I took my phone out of my bag and sat on the couch. "Charles, are you around? Charles?"

He appeared in the middle of the lounge room. "Hey. What's up?"

"I wanted to test something out." I explained what I thought had happened this afternoon—there was still the chance I was imagining things, and I didn't want Charles to think I was delusional. That would be a new low point if even the ghosts in my life thought I was nuts.

He stood stock still for a moment, his mouth hanging open as he processed my news, maybe thinking about how this would affect him. I hadn't even thought through the impact.

Finally, he shook himself out of his stupor. "Did you just say what I think you did?"

"Yes. I could've been imagining things, but I don't think so. The voice faded after a couple of listens, and by the third time, it was gone."

He shifted from foot to foot and rubbed his chest with one hand, the excitement pouring off him. "That's amazing. I didn't think anything like this was possible. You could prove to people that ghosts exist, and then no one would think you were crazy.... Well, they still might think you're a bit crazy, but you know what I mean."

I gave him a "thanks very much" look. "Very funny. And I'm not going to try and use it for that. The way technology is, people wouldn't believe me anyway. It would be so easy to fake, and who's to say it wasn't a person speaking into the recording?"

"But it fades away." He'd stopped bopping on the spot. I was killing his happiness. I sucked.

"Again, technology is amazing these days. I'm sure some genius could figure out how to make that happen."

"But you could prove it. You could have a conversation with a ghost in front of someone and record it and play it back straight away. They'd have to believe you then." His voice contained a hint of desperation. If people believed in ghosts, it meant they'd believe in him, and then he'd be a little less dead. I was surmising the heck out of it, but other than that, and being able to talk to Bellamy, he didn't stand to gain anything.

"Maybe. How would it change things for you if people did believe?" He didn't have any living family, so it wasn't as if he wanted to talk to them.

He rubbed the back of his head, then dropped his hand to his side and captured me with a look that shot sadness to the depths of my soul. "I miss being alive. Even though I have ghost friends, before you came along, I hardly ever laughed or enjoyed myself. Something was missing. I didn't realise that it was normal people until I spoke to you, till I got to know you. I've missed being alive… really alive. But you've opened up my afterlife. When I talk to you, I feel like I exist, like I haven't been forgotten about. Do you know how traumatic it is when you walk up to someone and they ignore you because they can't see you? When I first died, I kept trying to get someone to acknowledge me, but it was as if I wasn't there… because for them, I wasn't. I even jumped in front of a few cars but nothing. I screamed at my mother to see me. I cried. But no matter what I did, I was invisible." He took a stuttering breath. "You've given me hope that I won't always be in nothingness, and you've introduced me to Sergeant Fox. It's given me a new lease on the afterlife." A smile broke through the angst, and even though he was cold and dead, I felt warmth wash over me.

I gave him a sad smile. "Well, I don't know that this will ever be something I tell the wider world about, but you'll be able to talk directly to Bellamy if this works. Is that good enough for now?"

He sighed. "I suppose so." His head fell to the side, and he grinned. "Actually, it will be awesome." There was my boyish friend who had the ability to bounce back faster than anyone I'd ever met.

My lips stretched wide in joy. "It will. I can't wait to show Bellamy next time I'm in there. But we need to test if it works. So, let's record. Ready?" I hovered my hand over my phone screen and placed my other one inside his hand. The chill sluiced up my arm. My fingers ached, and I resisted the urge to pull away.

"Yes! Let's do this."

I pressed Record.

"What's your name?"

"Charles. What's yours?"

"Avery." I pressed Stop, took my hand back, and shook it. This was going to be an unpleasant experience if it worked. Every time Bellamy wanted to listen to any ghosts, I was going to have to go through bone-aching torture. "Okay. The moment of truth. Ready?"

He nodded and stared at my phone as if unicorns were about to fly out of it.

My stomach muscles tightened as I turned the volume up and pressed Play.

My voice came through loud and clear. "What's your name?"

"Charles. What's yours?" I placed my hand over my racing heart. I hadn't imagined anything.

"Avery."

Wow.

I sucked in a breath and stopped the recording. Charles and I stared at each other as my heartbeat skipped, raced, and tripped. Yes, it could do all that.

Charles's face screwed up. "Do I really sound like that?"

I laughed. "That's what everyone says when they first hear themselves. Also, that's the first thing that came into your mind?"

"My voice is more high-pitched than I thought."

"Oh my God! This is monumental, and that's all you can say? Boys. Also, it's a bit tinnier than my voice. I guess it's coming from somewhere that might actually be far away." I had no idea how this other dimension stuff worked. Were they light years away, or was there a thin membrane separating everything?

"I'm old enough to be a man, I'll have you know." He folded his arms in emphasis.

"I know. Anyway, moving right along. Let's see if your voice fades, and if it does, how many plays we get out of it."

I played it twice, and his voice faded each time. By the third time, it was gone.

"The sergeants are going to love this." Charles grinned. "Can I tell them, please?"

I sucked in a breath, my open-mouthed smile lifting my cheeks almost into my line of vision. "That's a brilliant idea! Bellamy and Fox are going to lose it." It had been a while since I'd been super excited about something. This was such a breakthrough. If people believed in the spirit world, this might've been a ground-breaking discovery. It still was to me, but I couldn't tell any solid people who weren't Bellamy about it. Story of my life.

"Okay. Let's make a recording now, and then I have to get going. I'm spending time with Zeus tonight."

"I can't wait to see their reactions."

"Neither can I."

CHAPTER 13

At around eight the next morning, my phone rang. It was an unknown number, but considering all the balls I had in the air, I decided it was worth the risk of suffering a scam call to answer it. "Avery speaking."

"Hello, Avery. This is Duncan, Morris's colleague. I'm returning your call. I understand you want to have a chat." With his posh English voice—I imagined he was from a rich family—and smooth tone, he could've been a radio announcer.

"Hi, Duncan. Thanks for getting back to me so quickly. I'm sorry for your loss."

"Thank you, but I imagine that's not why you called."

I hadn't said too much in my message, but he was obviously switched on. A random person wouldn't call him to give their condolences—it wasn't as if he was Morris's immediate family.

"You would be correct. I'm getting things together for an article about him, and since the police don't know who murdered him, I wanted to investigate. Apparently Morris left some notes on who the police should hone in on if he was ever murdered. He mentions one name and said you would have further information on the person."

"I'd prefer not to discuss this on the phone, in light of everything that's happened. I'm having a week off. Everything with Morris has been…. Let's just say, I'm not taking it as well as I imagined I would—not that I ever thought he would go like this. I mean, when he was working abroad and covering war zones, I worried, but then it happens at home." His voice tightened towards the end, an angry edge to it. He cleared his throat, and I felt guilty for bringing it up. But that was part of my job as a journalist, and I'd promised to speak to him. "He was an amazing journalist and mentor. My dad died when I was a teenager, and Morris was like a second father to me. So, if you want to come to St Ives, you're welcome to meet with me. Where are you?"

"I'm in Manesbury."

"That's about a two-hour drive. If you have time today or tomorrow, I'm available."

I didn't have anything newsworthy booked today, and Julian wanted this dealt with ASAP, so today it was. "What if I'm there at eleven? Does that suit?" I was giving myself way more than two hours because who knew what debacle the traffic would be, and I'd never been there before. There was always the chance I'd get stuck behind a tractor for some of it as well. Devon was full of farmland and narrow laneways. The joys of English country roads.

"Yes, that's fine. I'll see you at Crafted Coffee House at eleven. Bye."

"Bye." And that was that. At least he hadn't been difficult about it. I tried not to overthink that he didn't want to discuss anything over the phone. Morris hadn't said anything about their phones being spied on. But with technology, you never knew who was listening in or how.

I was on the road within ten minutes of the call, and it took me an hour and fifteen to reach the top of St Ives. My GPS took me down a long hill, and was that a sign that said not to drive further? Hmm, I wasn't sure. Trying to follow the GPS and navigate unfamiliar, anorexic streets wasn't easy. The closer to sea level I got, the dodgier the thoroughfare—which wasn't thorough or fair.

I had to pull over to allow other cars to pass me as they drove up the hill. I wanted to turn around and go back, but the GPS insisted I could be down here. Well, all righty then. I gave a narrow-eyed glance at my phone screen. "I don't trust you." The cars had stopped coming, so I pulled out and continued into the narrowing street. Stress rose through my body like the pressure in a volcano.

By the time I made it to the town centre, I was travelling down a street only wide enough for one car. Three-storey 1930s, Georgian, and older sandstone buildings crowded in on both sides, and pedestrians ambled in the middle of the road, only getting out of the way at the last moment. The architectural beauty was lost on me—I was ready for a panic attack.

If someone came the other way, what was I supposed to do? There was nowhere to pull over. What if I got stuck down here forever? Was I going to get a ticket, or was some random person going to expect me to reverse for half a mile? I didn't know if I could. How did I even get out of here? Was this a dead end? Did I have to try and do a million-point turn and come back this way?

"Siri, I hate you."

"That's not nice."

"Well, neither is this situation, and it's all your fault." Great. Not only was I dealing with the roads, but my phone was talking back. Tell me again how good technology was?

My heart raced as I made it to a right turn. Thank God no one was driving the other way. I edged the car around the corner, almost scraping my door on the corner of a building. What fresh hell was this? They should have a roadblock so no one could drive down here—it shouldn't just be a suggestion on a sign. Then they should reinstate horse and cart.

I glanced at the time. At least I still had twenty minutes.

I finally made it through the maze of horror to a harbour parking area. Water and at least a mile of sand stretched out in front of me. Timber fishing boats and a few small yachts leaned over on the sandy expanse, stranded and colourful. Blue-grey water sparkled in the distance under an expanse of cloud-smudged, faded-cerulean sky. It was enough to calm the whirlwind of panic spinning in my brain. I'd found somewhere to park.

If you thought it would be that easy from here, you'd be wrong.

No empty spaces existed. Of course they didn't.

I made my way through the parking lot at a crawl, careful to not run over any of the hundreds of tourists that flocked here even on a freezing winter day.

I bravely left the car park and pointed the car up the hill. I wasn't trusting Siri any more. It was time to use logic and gut instinct.

Eventually, I found a parking lot near the top of the massive hill that constituted much of St Ives. A bus service went from there back to nightmare land, so I hopped on. If only I'd known this before. I really should research more before I went places.

By the time I'd returned to the bottom and had time to enjoy the scenery from the bus windows, I'd calmed down. Never again though. From now on, I was going to research the hell out of wherever I was going and ask my friends for their input.

I had time for a ten-minute walk around before meeting Duncan, so I revisited the waterfront and took deep breaths of the fresh, salty air and snapped a few photos. It would be a gorgeous place to live except for the visiting crowds. If this was what it was like in winter, I'd hate to see summer. It must be a madhouse. The residents probably needed holiday houses out of town. The irony.

The Crafted Coffee House was a small café on one of the main streets. It had light-coloured floors and partly exposed-brick walls, although they might have been brickish decorations rather than the real thing. The baristas were busy behind the counter, frothing coffees and making tea. Delicious-looking pastries and scones lay in temping wait for their next victim. My mouth watered. In my haste this morning, I'd forgotten to eat. I'd rushed to finish my coffee after Duncan's call, and then I'd been focussed on getting here.

I went up the few stairs to the higher split level that led to the back of the café. I'd looked Duncan up on the newspaper website, so I knew what he looked like. He sat at a small table, his long-fingered hands elegantly pinching a teacup handle. A teapot and small milk jug sat on the table. "Duncan?"

He'd already been looking at me, maybe wondering if I was me. Yes, that made perfect sense. He stood and towered over me. He was much taller than I expected, and as in his pic, looked to be around forty, his dark, curly hair an inch this side of unruly. "Avery?"

I held out my hand. "Yep. Lovely to meet you."

He shook my hand. "Likewise. Please sit. What can I get you?"

"Thanks. Um, I can get my own. Would you like anything to eat? I haven't had breakfast, so I'm going to get food."

"Nonsense. I've got this. You've driven a long way to see me." He made to step away from the table.

"No, please. You're seeing me to help, so…."

"Morris would have my head if I let you pay. Now, tell me what you want. No more discussion." He stepped away from the table and looked down at me, waiting.

I knew when I was beaten. "A cappuccino and a piece of lemon drizzle cake." I would've gotten a proper meal, but that would've cost more. I'd grab something else after he left.

He smiled. "Coming right up."

I sat and took out my notepad and pen while he ordered at the counter. He returned and managed to elegantly position himself into his seat, even though his long legs were close to hitting the table. He wore a dark-green jumper and blue jeans, a tailored woollen jacket hitched on his seatback. A tuxedo would definitely suit him—he gave off the impression that he'd grown up breathing in the rich, antique-musty air of mansions on country estates. He probably played polo. I'd have to ask Morris later.

I explained my link to the prize-winning journalist. "So, I've seen quite a bit of him in the weeks before he died, and I feel like I got to know him to a degree. Julian could never speak highly enough of him."

"Ah, yes, Julian." His tone was tired, even defeated, but a smile crinkled the skin around his eyes. "We had a bit of a rivalry when we worked together, but he's another good man. I imagine he's taking this rather hard."

"Yes." I didn't want to elaborate because I didn't know

anyone who wanted their private business gossiped about. Not that we were gossiping, but I'd keep the details to myself. "How are you doing?"

His chest rose and fell with a big breath. He gave me a "there's no good way to answer that" look. "So, what did you want to know? Also, before we start, can you turn your phone off?"

I peered at his face, waiting for any tell-tale sign he was kidding. Hmm, apparently not. "Sure." I turned my phone off and put it back in my bag. "Do you have reason to believe you're being spied on?"

"When you cover the kinds of cases Morris and I covered, you soon learn that privacy is a fallacy."

"Did you ever do the spying?" I'd never done anything illegal in the name of journalism, but I did spy. Having ghosts to snoop around and listen in on conversations wasn't exactly going by the book. Not that there was a book for that kind of thing.

"That's not what we're here to talk about. So, what did you want to know?" Hmm, cagey, but then again, I didn't need to know about him and what he did to get to the truth.

"Part of why I'm here is that I'm covering Morris's murder for the *Manesbury Daily*, but I'm also doing a separate piece on his life and accomplishments. Can you tell me a bit about your relationship and what he was like to work with?" Might as well loosen the guy up, get his guard down a bit after the last question.

"Morris was my mentor. Twenty years ago, I started at the same paper he was working at. He took me under his wing. We've covered a few stories together, mainly with me, green as new grass, tagging along to see how the pros did it. I learnt almost everything I know from him." His gaze drifted to the table for a moment. "He was patient and gave me plenty of wonderful advice. He was well-liked in the office, and he had lots of connections with other news outlets and informants. He was the type of guy you wanted to help." Duncan folded his arms and gave a wry smile. "My own father was never that interested in what I was doing, but Morris truly cared about me—he always had my back. He was also generous with praise, and who doesn't want to be on the receiving end of that?"

I knew all too well what it was like to get the opposite. Moving here had come with a healthy dose of positivity. I could admit to doing the best job I could partly because I wanted my boss's praise. There were other reasons, of course, but that was definitely one. "I totally get it. How did you feel when he retired?"

His gaze drifted past me to outside, his face tightening in a way that suggested he was controlling his emotions. This must be so raw for him. Was I pushing too hard? I could see he respected Morris and would miss him.

"Don't worry about answering that. You were obviously sad to see him go."

His eyes met mine. "Yes. It's been a lot quieter around the place now he's gone. I still called him a few times to ask for advice." He shook his head slowly. "I can't believe I'll never talk to him again." He sniffed and blinked, maybe holding back tears.

"Is there anyone else I should talk to from your office to get any stories about him over the years?"

Duncan scratched the back of his neck. "No one in particular. I'm sure anyone would talk to you. But I worked with him the most over the years. When he was in the field, he was one of the bravest journalists I've ever seen. There were a couple of times I thought we'd both be killed, but we got lucky. For him to go like this at home…." His laugh was short and bitter. "The irony, right?"

There was no need for me to draw this out any longer. Time to get to why I was really here. "Terrible irony. Um, why don't I just ask about him from a few others at your work? You've given me enough that I can quote you as his protégé. Can we talk about Angelo and two of his associates?"

He cast a suspicious glance around the café, then leaned towards the table. I was sitting opposite him, but we still had a table in the middle of us. Just as he was about to speak, he jerked back. I frowned and opened my mouth to ask what the matter was when the waitress put my piece of lemon drizzle cake on the table. "Thanks."

She gave a nod and walked off. The café was abuzz with patrons, a steady stream of people walking past providing endless customers. I imagined the workers here were exhausted at the end of the day.

I would've held off eating to give Duncan my full attention, but my stomach grumbled, reminding me I was starving. I put a forkful of deliciously light cake into my mouth. It practically melted. I did my best not to close my eyes in bliss. After a couple of bites, he leaned back in. I put my fork down and picked up my pen because I didn't want to miss anything.

The coffee machine made gravelly hissing noises as someone frothed milk. Duncan spoke quietly, and I had to lean forward to hear. "The two names you're after are Ivan Novikov and Jack Noonan. Ivan's a criminal boss. He owns brothels and runs a drug cartel. He recently got out of a ten-year jail stint. Not that being incarcerated slowed him down." Duncan rolled his eyes, which looked weird on such a distinguished person. "Jack Noonan was discharged from the army on medical grounds. Only, it turns out that wasn't the full story. It's too long to get into here, but look up the two articles Morris did. They're online. I can give you the addresses of a couple of places I know Ivan frequents. I kept tabs on him after he got out seven months ago."

"To get another article or because you were worried?"

"The second one. At least, I was worried for Morris. He didn't seem bothered. Ivan wasn't mentioned in any of his articles, but I have a feeling Morris wanted to keep an eye on him because he'd heard that Ivan and Angelo were going into business together. And any enemy of Angelo's was going to become an enemy of Ivan's. It's how these things work."

"Do you know what Jack's been up to?"

"No."

"What about informants? Are there any that might be willing to talk?" It was rare for a journalist to give up their informants—for their protection, but also, we were a competitive lot. But since Morris was dead, it might not be a problem, unless those informants were now Duncan's.

He frowned. "Sorry. I don't know who they are. As I said, Morris kept this stuff close to his chest. The only reason I have those other two names is because I helped with that part of the investigation. As he got older, Morris developed a terrible memory for names. As much as I didn't want him to retire, it was his time." His gaze left mine, and he gave the room another once-over. "Anyway, I have it all written down somewhere, but I keep a lot up here." He tapped his head. "I hope this doesn't hinder your search for answers."

I comforted myself with another bite of cake. "It is what it is. I'm trying to help the police, but maybe they don't really need me. They might be close to figuring it out. Who knows?" They likely weren't, but there was always that hope.

His eyes studied me intently. "Do you think they're close to solving it?"

"To be honest, I don't know. I hope they are, but just in case they're not, I'm here to try and help."

He nodded slowly. "That's good, Avery. I'm glad you came to me since there's a chance one of these men might be involved. Will you let me know how you get on?"

"Of course. I'm sure Morris would want you to know." The waitress came and took his cup away. When she was gone, I said, "So, do you have those addresses? I'll write them down."

He gave me the information and pushed his chair back. "I hope you don't mind, but I've given you everything I can, and I have a couple of things on this afternoon."

"Ah, not a problem." What was I going to do, say yes, I minded? That shouldn't even be a phrase. It was redundant because no one was going to argue the point.

He stood and grabbed his satchel. "I hope you enjoy St Ives. It really is a lovely place."

He didn't smile, but I gave him a small one anyway. "Thanks. And I appreciate you talking to me."

"It's the least I can do if it means the police can catch Morris's killer ASAP. And don't forget to keep me in the loop. Bye, Avery."

"Bye."

He strode through the cafe, his long, lean legs carrying him through the door and out of sight rather quickly. It was almost as if he was running away from something. But what?

It was time to have another chat with Morris.

CHAPTER 14

I spent half an hour wandering around St Ives before starting the drive back. I wanted to stretch my legs and take a breath. Since the awards night, I hadn't stopped chasing information and stressing—having two murder cases and one soon-to-be-gone Zeus was almost too much for me to deal with. You know when so much is going on that you think just one more thing and you'll lose it? That was me right now.

Once I was sure I was ready to spend over two hours on English roads, I took the bus back up to my car and used the long drive home to sort through everything in my head for Morris's and Everly's cases.

I was no closer to any answers and exhausted by the time I rolled into the police station that afternoon. The excitement of revealing my ghost recording to Bellamy pepped me up a bit, though. PC Falkner, the young male constable who'd only started recently, buzzed me in, and I hurried back to the kitchen to grab a coffee. I made Bellamy one, too, then knocked on his door.

"Come in."

I hadn't thought this through properly, and I had to put one of the cups on the ground to open the door. I picked it up again and went in.

Bellamy eyed my full hands. "You that tired, Winters?"

I grinned. "Yes, but one's for you anyway." I put his on the desk, plonked myself into one of the chairs, and settled my bag in my lap. Fox stood in his usual spot next to Bellamy's chair, but Charles wasn't here.

"So, to what do I owe this visit? Are you going to give me good news?"

"Not in relation to our cases, but I did speak with one of Morris's colleagues today. He's passed on some information that may or may not help. I'll follow it up over the next couple of days and let you know."

He sipped his coffee and relaxed back into his chair. "What's it in relation to, then?"

"Someone's missing. Hang on." I got up and shut the door properly, then sat again. I looked up at the ceiling, which was what I tended to do when calling ghosts, at least when I wasn't at home. When I was home, I was watching all the places they might appear so that I didn't have a heart-stopping surprise. "Charles, can you come to the station?"

After half a minute, Charles appeared in front of the door. He looked at me with hyperaware eyes. "You haven't said anything yet, have you?"

I smiled. "No. I was going to make sure you were here to see it."

He grinned. "Thanks, Ave." He looked at Fox. "We have a surprise for you."

"Just me?" Fox cocked his head to the side.

"No. Sergeant Bellamy too." Charles dropped into the

seat next to me and swung his legs back and forth. His barely contained energy was rubbing off on me, and I grinned.

"Well, get a toddle on. We haven't got all day." Fox's forehead wrinkled. He wasn't a fan of surprises, and who could blame him? When you were a police officer—even a dead one—surprises usually meant bad things.

The only downside of what we were about to do was the chill thing. I shuddered in anticipation.

"Are you all right, Winters?" Bellamy frowned.

"Ah, yes, Sergeant."

"Can you get to it? I hate these conversations when I'm missing half of them." He waved his arm around as if to indicate the room was full of ghosts.

I laughed, put my phone on the table, and pressed Record on my app. "Well, you're about to have your mind blown." I looked at Charles. "Ready?"

He reached out and put his hand in mine… kind of. "Am I ever!"

A deathly stab of ice shot into my palm and up my arm. My stomach clenched. I sucked in a quick breath. Best not to drag this out. "Sergeant Bellamy, can you please ask Charles a question." I hoped this worked.

Bellamy's brows crept together, like two caterpillars slow-mo running to embrace. Okay, it wasn't quite like that, but they were rather thick eyebrows, and they'd almost joined. "What?"

My bones ached. "This is killing me, Sergeant. Not literally, but I'm touching Charles's hand, and it hurts. Please just ask a question. I don't even care what it is."

He looked at my hand. I was holding it out midway between the two guest chairs. Bellamy looked at the chair to my left, assuming Charles was sitting there. At least he was trying. "What day is it?"

"I don't know. Time is weird for ghosts. Also, Sergeant, that's a boring question." Charles looked at me. "He's not even trying."

My fingers cramped. I pulled my hand away and stuck it under my arm to warm it. "I'm sorry, Charles, but it hurts too much." I pressed Stop on the recording with my other hand.

Bellamy peered at my shoulder. "Let me look at your hand." I pulled it out and showed him. My fingers were white, the cold having chased all the blood back into my body. "You weren't kidding."

"No, I wasn't."

"Play him the tape." Charles's big eyes implored me. He was finally going to be heard by a living person other than me for the first time in his life… ah… death.

"Without further ado." I couldn't be bothered talking it up any more. It was time. I pressed Play.

We listened to me saying, "Well, you're about to have your mind blown. Ready?"

I held my breath and watched Bellamy and Fox as I waited for Charles's voice to fill the room.

"Am I ever!"

Bellamy's mouth dropped open, and he leaned forward. Fox blinked in astonishment, his face slack, lips parted.

I grinned while Bellamy and I spoke, and then Charles's voice came through. "I don't know. Time is weird for ghosts. Also, Sergeant, that's a boring question. He's not even trying."

And that was it. I stopped the playback, pressed Record, and grinned. "So, Sergeants, what do you think?" I stood and went to Bellamy's chair. This time, I would get Fox answering so Bellamy could hear it. This was too much fun. "I'm going to touch Sergeant Fox, and his response will be recorded."

Bellamy just nodded. We'd rendered him mute, which was a first. He usually had an opinion on everything. Not that he was big on chatting, but when it came to the important things, he always said what he thought.

I touched Fox's arm and gritted my teeth against the icy sting. "What would you like to say to Sergeant Bellamy?"

He cleared his throat and rubbed his chest before composing himself. "You're doing a bang-up job as sergeant, and I'm just sad our time on the earth didn't coincide. I would've enjoyed working with you directly. I also love how far technology has advanced." He smiled. "Catching and convicting criminals has come a long way. It's good to see them get their comeuppance."

I retrieved my tortured hand, stopped the recording, and played it back. Bellamy stared at the spot next to his chair. "And yet, I still need Avery's and your help. Technology hasn't come far enough for my liking." His eyes crinkled at the corners with his smile. "I have to say that I would've enjoyed working directly with you too. Thanks for always watching over the station."

Fox touched my arm, an indication he wanted me to record. I did as asked. "It's been my pleasure. I don't know why I'm still here, but I am, and my wife is no longer with us, neither are my children, so it's only natural that I'd want to frequent a place that brought me so much fulfilment. My wife often asked me to spend more time with her, but I didn't. And that brings me to another thing.... Don't put off spending time with your family until it's too late. Those were different times, I'll admit, but still.... There are some things I regret."

I was practically panting with the cell-deep ache. "Sorry, Sergeant Fox, but…." I tore my arm away.

"That's okay, lass. You've done so much already, and I've said all I need for today." His moustache twitched with the upturn of his lips.

I played that back, and Bellamy nodded towards Fox. "Thank you. I'll take that under advisement."

I bit my lip against a grin. In other words, he was chucking that advice out the window. He was as addicted to trying to keep people safe as Fox was. Their job was their passion. And the world should be thankful for people like them. I knew I was. I suspected that was partly the reason Bellamy had so readily believed I could talk to ghosts. He would leave no opportunity to solve a crime go unexplored. He was willing to suspend disbelief on the small chance that I could actually talk to ghosts, and it might help him catch a killer.

Bellamy looked at me. "Can we listen to all that again?"

I smiled. "Yep. But it will fade. That's something I haven't worked out—how to keep the voices on there. The more I play it, the fainter it becomes. By the third or fourth play, the voices will be gone."

Fox smoothed his moustache with his fingers. "That's interesting. I wonder why."

Bellamy frowned. "How inconvenient."

"It is rather." I pressed Play, and we all listened as the voices sounded tinny and far away. Before Bellamy could ask, I played it a third time, and we could only just make out their voices, although mine was clear as day. On the fourth play, they were gone, even though I'd turned the sound to max.

"So," Bellamy said, "you have to be touching the ghost you want to record?"

"Yes, unfortunately. It makes it rather awkward. Touching

them for any longer than a couple of seconds feels like standing naked in a snowstorm."

"Argh, did you have to give me that visual?" Charles pulled a face. I rolled my eyes, and Fox chuckled.

Bellamy locked an assessing gaze on my face. "Are you going to do anything with this?"

"What do you mean?"

"You could record messages from the dead to their loved ones."

I shook my head. "No way. I'm not jumping up and down and shouting to the world I'm nuts. People would think that or that I was a charlatan. You've heard of deepfakes?"

He linked his hands together on his desk. "Yes, but the ghosts would know things no one else would. I'm sure some people would believe you."

"I sometimes pass on messages, but I'm selective. I think with these recordings, it makes too much of a drama of it, and it would be less believable. Also, again, I don't want people thinking I'm crazy and deporting me." I had a lot to lose if I attracted the wrong attention, and let's not even think about what Finn would say.

"Suit yourself, Winters, but I think you could do good things with it."

I smirked. "As you did with Sergeant Fox's advice, I'll take it under advisement."

He gave me a respectful nod. "Touché, Winters. Touché."

Sergeant Fox laughed.

"Have you got anything else to tell me?" Bellamy asked.

"Yes, as a matter of fact. I've got two more names to add to our list, and I think it's best if you check them out… at least check if they had an alibi." I still had to go undercover and see if I could find anything out about Angelo, but as far as the two names I'd just been given—Ivan and Jack—they sounded too dangerous for me to approach. Let it be known that I didn't have a death wish. I explained who the men were. "Just don't mention Morris's colleague when you're questioning them."

Bellamy folded his arms and cocked his head to the side. "You must think I'm daft."

"Sorry. Of course I don't. Habit, I guess." My cheeks heated. Bellamy was a police sergeant—as if he needed to be told how to do his job.

"In any case, thanks for the information."

I was lucky that Bellamy was one of those people who could move on quickly. He was too practical to be a grudge holder. "Thanks for not holding my stupidity against me." My smile was sheepish.

He delivered his next line with a straight face. "If I held people's stupidity against them, I wouldn't be talking to anyone. It would be a rather lonely existence, would it not?"

I chuckled. "It would indeed." My phone rang.

He looked at it. "You'd best get that, then, and I'd best get back to work."

"Right." I grabbed it off the table as I stood. So much for basking in the excitement of the revelation. The real world always got in the way. At least Fox and Charles were still grinning at each other—although, was it from my stuff up, or were they enjoying the big revelation? I glanced at the screen before I answered—the number was one I'd called the other day and left a message about doing an interview. "Hello, Avery speaking." My work was never done.

CHAPTER 15

After seeing Bellamy, I went back to the office. I had a couple of other leads to call to make appointments for the usual weirdo interviews. After that, I was going to start a more detailed timeline of Andrew Crumps's life, but before I could get into the office, my plans changed. I was a few steps from the *Manesbury Daily* front door when Morris appeared.

"Avery. Just the person I wanted to see."

I stopped short and stared at him. He was speaking as if he'd just stumbled across me and it was totally normal. It took a moment for me to get my bearings and pull out my phone so I didn't look like a lunatic. I put it to my ear. "Hi. I'm afraid I don't have any news for you yet." Maybe he thought it had been a few days since we last spoke?

"Oh, that's okay. That's not why I'm here." A woman walked straight through him. His eyes bugged wide. He stared after her, an indignant expression animating his face. "I beg your pardon!"

I snickered. He turned and glared at me, so I did my best to neutralise my face. I didn't know how successful I was because when I began talking, he was still giving me a dirty look. "Um… so, what can I do for you?"

"I need you to go to my former workplace and stop one of the journalists from making a terrible mistake."

Huh? "Is it related to your case?"

His forehead wrinkles deepened. "No. But it could ruin their career. One of their informants falsified documents and gave it to them. They're going to run a story on one of the biggest accounting firms in London. If they run this, the paper could get sued."

"But why does it matter to you now? Haven't we got bigger fish to fry?"

"Yes and no. I'm already dead. That can't be changed. Besides, you going there now doesn't mean my case will take longer. Does it?"

"Um, no."

The look on my face, the one that asked "will I, or won't I" likely prompted him to speak again. "This is important. I worked for that news outlet for many years. I have lifelong friends still working there. I don't want the journalist who's made one bad judgement call in the whole of his career to go down now and take the company with him. He's a fantastic investigative reporter." I couldn't help the look I sent his way. "Yes, Avery. Even with this mistake, he's fantastic. He's one of the braver ones. If we lose him to a lawsuit, it will be a sad day for justice. All those frauds he won't be able to uncover. Did you know he's helped put over ten people in jail and been the reason the government has investigated several companies and fined them for breaking the law?"

"Obviously no. I don't even know his name."

"He's a good kid. Well, he's thirty-nine, but to me, he's just a kid. Started with us fresh out of university. He shadowed me in his first couple of years and has lived up to my expectations. I recently put in a word with the CEO. There's a promotion going, and he'd be perfect for it." He put his hands in prayer position. "I'm begging you, Avery. Please."

So many questions came to mind—were the accountants engaging in illegal activity? What was the agenda of the person passing on false information? If they were doing illegal things, how could I help expose them? But I bit my tongue because I didn't have time to jump into another investigation right now. I tipped my head back and gave the heavens a tortured look. *Why me*? I puffed out an angst-filled breath and looked at Morris. "Fine, fine, fine. I'll do it. But what if he doesn't believe me? How am I supposed to have discovered this information? And how did you find it?"

Morris stared at me blankly.

"You're kidding? You haven't thought that far ahead?" *Argh*! I was ready to go inside and claw back some mental health. *Give these ghosts an inch….*

The ghost scratched his head. "You could tell him that I contacted you before I died. That I discovered what was going on and wanted to confirm everything before I went to him. At least he'll look into it before he submits his article. I know this guy, and he'll want to do the right thing… make sure."

"But why would you talk to me about it?" I wanted all my bases covered before I walked into this potential drama.

"Hmm…." He cocked his head to the side, thinking. After a bit, his eyes widened. "I know! You can tell him you were helping me research it because my wife had forbidden me from doing anything journalistic, since I was supposedly retired. I promised her I would stay out of it and had to use you to help.

By the way, I had a funny feeling and went to their office and spied as a ghost." He looked rather pleased with himself.

I sighed. "Of course you did. Also, that's not the best excuse in the history of excuses."

"Can you think of anything better?"

"Not right now. No." My brainpower was spread so thin, there was no room to think of excuses for this. "Fine. I'll use your excuse."

"Righto. Excellent. Also, I have an email address and password to give you. He'll hopefully find something in this informant fellow's emails. So, you'll see David today? This is urgent." He gave me an apologetic smile.

I shut my eyes and attempted to draw in some zen. "Why can't I just call him?"

"People could be listening in. And what if he won't believe you? It will be more convincing if you go there. He won't be able to just hang up on you either."

I rubbed my freezing nose. "Fine. Yes. Give me the address. Although, he'd be likely to believe me when he logs into this person's emails." As annoying as this was, ghosts really did have the best spying abilities. Being invisible was amazing. When he told me where it was, my mouth dropped open. "Are you serious? London's almost four hours away." I'd have to drive to Exeter and catch a train. Not the way I'd envisaged spending the rest of my day and night.

"I'm sorry, Avery."

I rubbed my eyes. This was going to be awful. It would be late afternoon and dark by the time I got there and pretty much bedtime by the time I returned. Unless.... Maybe I could find somewhere cheap and stay the night and visit Andrew Crumps's office? Would there be ghosts I could chat to who would give me crucial information that could break the case? "It is what it is. Just in case I need you for anything while I'm there, can you listen out for me calling?"

He nodded. "Yes, certainly. And here's the email address and password." He rattled it off.

"Okay. I'll see you later. I'd better get going if I don't want to get there after the office is shut. What if he's working from home? Have you got that address?"

"I'll go grab it. Just a moment." He disappeared to who knew where while I shivered in the icy breeze. Top temp was eight degrees Celsius today—not exactly my favourite weather. Just as I was contemplating going inside the office to sweet warmth, he returned and gave me David Cornell's address and mobile number. At least having those things would make me seem more legit… or maybe it would make me look like a stalker. Right.

"See you later, Morris."

"Good luck, Avery."

"Yeah, thanks." Good luck didn't pay the bills, but it was all I was going to get. By the time I paid for a return train ticket and accommodation, this little trip was going to cost a few hundred quid. And I couldn't even ask Sergeant Bellamy to pay for some of it as it wasn't technically about Morris's case. One of these days, I'd learn how to say no to ghosts who needed help.

Today obviously wasn't that day.

CHAPTER 16

I called David's office before I left to confirm whether he was in or not. I was in luck—he was happy to wait for me to come in. I didn't tell him exactly why I was visiting, but I said it had something to do with Morris and it was important. Luckily, that was enough information to keep David there. So far, so good that I didn't have to run around London searching for him—although I wouldn't count my platypuses before they hatched. Things still had a high chance of devolving into a mess.

How unusual….

I had to change from the train to the Tube, and after that, the office was a short walk. The six-level 1960s brick building had modern, black-framed windows and clean bricks, as if it had recently been renovated. A large café on the ground floor faced the street. I went through the tinted-glass front door next to the café and through to the lifts in the polished-concrete-floored foyer. Yep, definitely had a spruce up in the last year or two. According to the directory on the wall, I was headed to the fourth floor, so I pressed the button and waited next to a young man in a charcoal-coloured business suit.

The businessman got off on the third floor, and then the doors opened to Change Media's offices. Wide-board timber floors glowed yellow under track lighting hanging from a steel cable suspended from a concrete ceiling. Very industrial and expensive. A massive, rich mahogany panel was affixed to the wall opposite the lift. Mirrored letters spelling Change Media were stuck on it. At least I was at the right place.

I turned right and approached the receptionist's desk, which was a waterfall-style table made out of terrazzo, the polished stones in different shades of blue and green. It was actually pretty. I'd hate to think what it weighed or what it cost. And here I was, along with millions of others, struggling to pay my rent. Okay, so it wasn't that bad any more, but I still had to watch my pennies.

The gorgeous young woman with long, silky, brown hair looked up at me and smiled. "Welcome to Change Media. Can I help you?"

"Hi. I'm Avery Winters. I'm here to see David Cornell."

She looked at her computer screen and typed something. "Ah, yes. You're in here. Just a moment, and I'll let him know you're waiting." She called him via an internal phone system. While I waited, I perused the framed awards on the wall. Some were for individual journalists, and some were for the organisation. I smiled when I found four for Morris. Impressive. There was one for David for a story on people smuggling. Yikes. He was brave. Investigating something like that was akin to sticking your hand into a death adder's nest.

"Avery?"

I turned. A redheaded man stood there, only a bit taller

than me. He had a slight build and freckles on his pale face. His smile was warm, and I returned it. "David?"

He held out his hand to shake mine. "Welcome. I'm not sure why you wanted to meet with me, but any friend of Morris's is a friend of mine. Come through to my office."

"Thanks. I really appreciate you waiting for me."

He waved his hand in dismissal as he walked. "I've been editing my latest article, so the time was well spent." We went through a black door into a hallway. In a few steps, it revealed an open-plan office area with many desks. Windows ran all along the wall to our right. At the back were a few offices with glass partitions that had frosted tinting to the bottom half, so you couldn't really see in. To our left were doors with toilet symbols on them and a kitchenette/lunchroom. Only a handful of desks had people sitting at them, not unexpected at a news outlet when people were out and about, not to mention that many people worked from home these days whenever they could. "I'm just through here." He continued to the back of the room and to an open door to one of the glass offices. "Please, sit." He walked past a couple of sixties-inspired olive-green padded fabric chairs in front of his desk to his own chair, which was chestnut-brown leather.

I sat and put my bag on the floor, pulling out my notebook and pen. I might as well get a few words from him about Morris for my article. It was hard to ignore an opportunity for information. Once he was settled, I shoved my nerves down and got straight to it. "I'm not sure how to say this and have you believe me, so I'm just going to say it and hope for the best."

He frowned. "That sounds ominous."

My half-laugh was more nervous than anything. "Ah, it kind of is." I licked my bottom lip. *Just get on with it, Avery*. "I spoke to Morris before he died. He was a good friend of my boss, Julian."

He nodded. "I know Julian. We even worked together briefly. He's an upstanding guy."

"He is. Morris was too, which is why I need to tell you this. I know Morris would've wanted me to." David leaned forward while I ploughed on. "You're working on a piece about Bradley and Sons Accounting. Morris was convinced that your informant had passed you false information."

David's green eyes widened. I wasn't sure if they were full of disbelief or the beginnings of anger. "And what brought him to that conclusion?" His voice was unexpectedly calm. Was he really listening to me, or was the explosion and refusal to entertain the idea to come? Also interesting that he wasn't questioning how Morris knew who the informant was. Maybe they'd used the same person, or maybe he'd told him? I should've asked Morris more questions before coming here. Too late now.

"He didn't say, but he had looked into it. He talked to me about it to get my take. He didn't want to speak to anyone else because you all knew each other, and I guess he didn't want to cast aspersions on your skill and professionalism. He said some great things about you. He mentioned that he'd recently recommended you for a promotion. He really respected you." I swallowed. Was I getting through?

David sat back, folded his arms, and stared at me. I relaxed into my chair. Looking stressed was not going to help him believe me. I waited and waited for him to say something. Speaking into the silence would make me seem nervous. And while I was nervous, it wasn't for the reason he'd think. "I'm submitting that article tomorrow. My boss is waiting for it, relying on it for Saturday's paper. Why should I believe you?"

"I don't know. Because I'm telling the truth? Look, I gain no benefit from sabotaging you. Here's my card." I pulled it out of my bag and slid it across his table. "I don't work for the accounting firm, and I'm not exactly your rival. I cover the ridiculous doings of the Manesburians, stuff you wouldn't touch if your life depended on it. I also write articles about local murders, but that's it. It took me almost four hours to get here today. I don't want or need a job for this paper. Seriously. Morris was worried about you. He wants you to succeed. He said that he didn't want your whole career destroyed because of this. He also mentioned your company would likely be sued for publishing false information. Morris confirmed the accounting firm was dodgy but that the information you had was incorrect. The least you could do is check out whether your informant is telling the truth. Oh, and here's an email address and password I found on his study table after he died." I pulled the piece of paper from my bag and handed it over. "Morris mentioned he had it, so I went looking after he passed. It's your informant's work email address and password."

His eyebrows rose as he perused the paper. He raked a hand through his wavy hair and stood. After pushing his chair to the side, he stood behind it and stared out the window to the steel and glass building across the laneway. "I looked over everything. It looked legit." Hands on his hips, his head flopped forward. "Shit." Hands dropping to his sides, he turned, then plonked back down with much angst, his chair making a thunking sound. His gaze met mine. "This is terrible timing."

"Oh. Why?"

"A few days before Morris died, my boss quietly told me that they were giving me the promotion. They're announcing it at a company function in a week. It's a big deal. Head editor. The senior journalists have been waiting five years for this position to become available. It's prestigious and sought after. If you've made it at this firm, you're the best of the best as far as the industry is concerned. I'll be second only to the big boss. Me pulling this article is going to look bad, and after what you've said, even if I don't understand how Morris could've known, I have to dig deeper on this, make sure I'm not bollocksing it all."

I couldn't exactly say that Morris had been spying as a ghost. "From what Julian's told me, Morris had a sixth sense for this kind of thing. I guess that's what made him one of the best at this gig."

His breath rushed out in a huff. "I'll pull the story. With a bit of luck, I can resubmit for next week or the week after, but they're missing a main story now." He pressed his lips together, frustration oozing from him. "It's what Morris would've done."

Relief cascaded through me, and my shoulders relaxed. Mission accomplished. "Speaking of which, mind if I ask you a few questions about the man himself? I'm writing something for our local paper."

"Yeah, sure. It's not like I don't have time to kill now that I have to find something else to submit quick smart." His smile negated the sarcasm. "So, what would you like to know?"

When we finished, I stood and shook his hand. "Thanks again. I hope everything works out. Feel free to let me know how everything goes, and congratulations on your promotion. I know Morris would've been happy and proud."

He smiled. "Thanks, Avery. It was lovely to meet you. I'll drop you a line when I figure this whole thing out. And I appreciate you taking the time to come and see me. It's more than most people would bother to do."

I shrugged. "I'm a people pleaser. What can I say?"

"Lucky for me. Do you mind showing yourself out? I have a bit more work to do, if you know what I mean?"

"Ha, yes. Sorry about that. Good luck." I waved, then wandered out into the hall. Two offices down from David's, raised voices came from inside. The frosting on the glass went to only just over halfway up, so anyone sitting wasn't visible but people standing were. I halted and backed up so I could just see them, but they couldn't see me.

"It's a betrayal. Pure and simple. He promised it to me, back when we were covering the South Sudanese civil war. I almost died for this promotion, for god's sake. And we can't trust David. You know this. You should've let him go before Morris left. He always had a soft spot for that con artist." The voice was familiar, but the tall man's back was to me.

The other man, about six foot tall, wearing a tailored dark suit and gold cufflinks, looked rich and distinguished, even though he was balding and had more than a few wrinkles. He held up a placating hand. "I'm sorry, Duncan, but the decision's been made. I know you've sacrificed a lot for this company, so I'll take your warning under advisement."

My eyes widened. Oh my god. It was Duncan Wilson, Morris's other favourite colleague.

"You're making a huge mistake, Harris. It's on your head if it all goes to hell. Don't say I didn't warn you." Yikes. That sounded like the end of the conversation, and I didn't want to be caught eavesdropping. I ducked and rushed past, making sure none of me was above the frosted line. Although, maybe I should stay and say hello to Duncan. Why didn't he trust David? Had I just warned the wrong person? Did David know that the information on the accountants was false and wanted to go ahead with the article anyway?

Possum poo.

I checked my phone. Nope, it was late, and I had something else to do before I left London. Maybe I could talk to Morris about it later. But the damage was potentially done now. Would David have something against me now? Was I a target? Surely not. He was a journalist, not a criminal.

It was after hours, so the receptionist desk was vacant. I pressed the Down button a few times in a flurry of desperation. Not that it would make the lift come faster, but when in a hurry, we all did it. Maybe it made us feel like we were doing something to speed up the process?

As the lift doors opened, I took a deep breath.

No panicking, Avery. You'll go home later and log in to that email to see if David has been hoodwinked or if he knew and was going to submit the article anyway.

Out of all the things I expected today, this was not it. But I didn't have time to ponder it right now. I had somewhere to be.

It was freezing and dark by the time I left Change Media, yet it was only just after six. I grabbed a burrito for dinner and texted Finn that I wouldn't make it tonight. I'd decided to check out Crumps's surgery now. If I couldn't find any ghosts on the street outside, I'd get a room for the night and visit tomorrow, when people would be there, and I could get inside. As it was, I probably wouldn't get home until eleven tonight, but that might be better than spending two hundred quid on a hotel room. Not to mention that I hadn't packed any clean underwear, so I'd be putting dirty things back on after my shower. No thanks. There was probably a supermarket around here somewhere I could buy underpants and socks, but what a pain in the butt. If I could avoid that side quest, I would.

I looked at the map on my phone. Crumps's surgery was three Tube stops away. Too far for me to walk if I wanted to save time, not to mention how cold it was. So I entered the underground and hopped on a train.

I emerged from the Tube station into drizzling needles of rain. Brilliant. At least I had one of those retractable umbrellas. I pulled it out of my bag and activated it. If only they had built-in heaters like the ones at outdoor eating areas.

I breathed out frosty white and walked quickly, dodging all the other unlucky Londoners who were out at this time of night in winter. Strings of blinking and static Christmas lights glowed in shop windows and from decorated trees inside apartment buildings. I hoped the people living in those places were warm, happy, and safe. It got me thinking about the families of Andrew's and his parents' victims. Mrs Crabby, for instance. Losing her daughter had stripped her of almost all her happiness, if her demeanour was anything to judge by. I imagined those parents and siblings, aunties, uncles, and grandparents and how they must yearn for their missing loved ones even more at this time of year. No celebration would go by without their absence being felt.

Which reminded me of my parents. Did I miss them? No. But I did miss what they should've been to me. The love I always craved that was never given. Why had they even had children if they didn't like them? They'd been slightly nicer to my sister, but even she wasn't treated as she should've been. At least they'd been leaving me alone since the initial few harassing phone calls soon after I'd arrived in England. Okay, so I'd blocked their numbers, and I'd changed my email address, not that they were big on emailing and using computers. But their silence had given me room to breathe.

Would Christmas be a reminder of the things I didn't have? Possibly, but if I could find a way to prove Andrew and his parents killed those women, it would cancel out all the negativity associated with having a disappointing family. I'd also be grateful for my new friends, but they were all going away over the Christmas period, so I'd be home by myself. But I'd have peace, and that was most valuable of all.

I stopped walking. The building to my left was the one.

I turned and peered up at all six stories of 1930s reddish brick building, glittering flecks of light rain drifting past and catching the light, making it seem magical when this moment was anything but. The building façade on the ground floor was clad in maroon granite that appeared almost black in the streetlights.

The main entry door was shut. I pushed it, but it was locked. Fair enough. I hadn't expected it to be open. Looked like I was going to be doing this outside. At least no one was hanging around to listen to what I was going to say. Anyone unlucky enough to be outside was hurrying to rectify the situation. And the sooner I did what I was here to do, the sooner I could be on the train back to my car.

I slid my phone out of my bag with fumblingly freezing hands. A police car sped past, siren blaring, slicing into my eardrums. If only they'd been in time to save all of Andrew's victims.

Huddling under my umbrella, I put the phone to my ear. "I know Andrew Crumps is a bad man. Is there anyone who wants to talk with me and tell their story? I'm trying to bring him to justice. Hello?" I peered up and down the street to confirm no one was about to walk past. People were heading this way but were out of earshot. "Any ghosts want to talk to me. Hello? Has anyone been killed by Andrew Crumps?" I knew one of his victims couldn't access his surgery any more, but from what I knew of the "rules," he couldn't banish ghosts from a public place, which this street surely was. Not that I knew everything there was to know about what was and wasn't possible when it came to ghosts, but hopefully, there was some kind of logic to it.

"Hello? I'm Avery. I'd like to speak to any ghosts around here, if you can hear me."

A man appeared next to me. His puffy brown wool pants stopped at the knees, where cream-coloured tights took over. His taupe shirt had a few dirt spots. The darkness under his watering blue eyes was exaggerated by his paler-than-pale skin. "How fare you, mistress?"

I swallowed and stepped back, which was silly since he was dead, and whatever he died from couldn't be passed to me a few hundred years later. Unless he was dressed in period costume from a play or something when he died, it looked like he'd been alive during the 1600s at some point. "Oh, I'm sorry. I was calling women who've been killed by a dentist who works here. I didn't mean to put a call out to everyone in the vicinity." My bad. I should've been more specific when requesting an audience with local ghosts.

He inclined his head towards the building. "I used to dwell 'ere."

"Oh?"

"'Twasn't like this, though."

"I imagine not. When were you alive?"

"During King Charles II's reign. I died of the Great Plague in sixteen sixty-five."

"I'm so sorry." I looked around. No other ghosts had

appeared, and the cold was seeping through my coat. The fingers holding my phone were numb. That would teach me to go out at night without gloves on.

He shrugged. "It is of no moment now. May I enquire as to why you are asking after these murdered women?"

"The man who killed them is still alive, and I'm trying to help the police catch him." A woman walking past gave me a surprised glance but, thankfully, kept walking. I'd need to keep my voice down. Being "on the phone" didn't counter the impact of my words. "Have you seen anything? Do you ever go inside this building?"

"Yes, and yes." He gazed up at the building. "On the fourth level. I have twice felt the opening of the divide betwixt this world and the next." He licked parched, flaking lips. Ghosts could change the way they looked. Why did he want to appear as a dying plague victim? It wasn't important enough to waste time with, so I didn't ask.

"What happened?"

He cocked his head to the side. Rain fell through him to the ground. "'Twas a pull, a tug. I hurried in to see, and both times, a woman walked into the light." His eyes shone in wonder. "I wish my turn would come. I have suffered greatly, and I am tired."

I didn't know what issues were keeping him here, but I wasn't about to offer to help. *Evil, Avery*. I just didn't have the time or the headspace. "I'm sorry. I can't help you, but I do find that ghosts are usually here because they don't want to go or they have unfinished business. If you can work out what you need to fix or accept, it might help."

"Thank you."

"So, did you know either of the women's names or what they looked like? Was there anyone else in the surgery when they died? Did he do anything with the bodies, or did he call an ambulance?" It wasn't unfathomable that one of them had died from natural causes. Maybe I could identify them from their descriptions. If only his sense of time wasn't skewed. There was no way I'd be able to find out roughly when they died.

"The dentist was alone with them. It was daytime when they died. The other offices were empty."

I frowned. Had he killed them after hours during summer, or was it the weekend? Who would go to a dentist appointment on the weekend? Maybe they were emergency clients and took what they could get? I didn't have enough hands to take notes. "Can you hang on for one moment?"

"Certainly."

I brought up the voice-note app and pressed Record. After repeating what he'd just told me, I put the phone to my ear again, as if I was talking to someone. "What did they look like?"

"Both ladies hadst long, brown hair. One was of a satisfactory childbearing age. I would estimate eight and ten years. The other appeared to be older and nearer to my age—eight and twenty."

Yes, "great" childbearing age… eighteen—said with the utmost sarcasm. Thank God times had changed. Dad would've sold me to the highest bidder at sixteen, and I probably would've had five children by now. Not that there was anything wrong with having children at eighteen if that's what you wanted, but women had choices now, and living a bit of life before getting weighed down with offspring was a grand choice.

"He was…" His face screwed up, and if it was possible, his skin turned a light shade of green. "…Intimate with the bodies, and then he removed a tooth from each, before he placed the bodies in black plastic bags. He referred to one as Jane and the other as Charlie. That is all I can tell you because I left. I had witnessed enough and wished to be free of the pain of it."

I quietly repeated all of that into my phone while my old-time companion watched, his forehead furrowed. Surely he knew what mobile phones were. Maybe he just didn't realise they recorded stuff too. "How old did Andrew look at each time? Was he different, the same?"

The ghost stared after a woman walking her giant poodle. They wore matching blue Tartan coats. "People are much changed since my day." His bemused tone changed when he looked back at me. "I think with Jane, he would be in his thirties. His hair was brown, yet to change colour. He was clean-shaven. With Charlie, he had grey here and here." He touched the hair above his ears, which in his case was still a rich chestnut colour—the natural colour of a young person who shouldn't have died. "His belly was rounder as well." His hand indicated the circumference in front of his own slim stomach.

I gave my phone the information. "Thank you for all your help. I appreciate it. I know it wasn't pleasant to remember."

He smiled. "You would be surprised. I feel lighter, having told you. Mayhap I have helped in some small way."

"Mayhap you have." I returned his smile. "You've given me crucial information, and I'm sure it will help us catch this scoundrel." If I chatted to him long enough, I'd devolve into all archaic language. Although, he seemed to have updated many of his words. It was kind of interesting, actually, and speaking that way was fun.

"Glad to be of service, mistress." He inclined his head. "And now, I must fare thee well."

I smiled. "Bye." He faded away, and I shivered—it would be warmer in a freezer. Just in case they were around, I called out to the women, but no one materialised. At least I had first names, which was better than nothing. The next step would be to sift through reports of missing women with those names. Would there still be patient records for them in storage, or had he destroyed them? Then again, he was cocky and probably didn't worry about getting caught—he'd fooled the police after murdering Everly. Had he ever been a person of interest in any other cases? Hmm. His name could be buried in a box from another police station. All we needed was one link to show up, and then we could request files from the other murders.

I hurried to the train station. I'd had enough of the cold and rain, and the sooner I got home, the sooner I could go to sleep. Because I'd missed seeing Zeus tonight, I wanted to drop in first thing and give him a cuddle. Time was running out, and soon, I wouldn't be able to give him a hug at all. At least he wasn't sick any more. I could be thankful for that. It should've made me happy, but I couldn't find it in me to have joy. As much as I was happy that he was going to a loving home, he might as well be dead to me because I'd never see him again. *Macabre, I know, but….*

I spent the train trip trying not to spiral. All the pain around me—the murdered women, Morris's case, Zeus—the negativity was closing in on me. I had to figure out a way to fix something. Anything. If I could give even one family peace and closure this Christmas, it wouldn't all be for nothing.

When the train clacked out of the tunnel, rain splatted against the windows. I stared at the droplets and my reflection, the dark night beyond cloaking the view.

Don't be sad, Avery. You'll come up with something.

I stared into my eyes, and I knew the truth—I didn't believe myself. Why would I come up with something? The ghosts didn't have enough clues. I was useless without them. Had my luck run out?

Argh, stop.

Instead of taunting myself, I rested my head back on the seat. Folding my arms to keep warm, I shut my eyes and tried to dream of a Christmas where Zeus was mine, all the families of the dead women had answers, and Morris had reunited with his wife.

Dreams, as they said, were free.

It was a shame they weren't also easy.

CHAPTER 17

The next morning, I popped in early to see Zeus. Finn didn't answer my knock, so I used my key. He was probably out for a run. As soon as I shut the door, Zeus came bounding from wherever he'd slept and rubbed against my legs. He meowed, stood on his hind legs, and pawed my thigh. I bent and picked him up. A bombardment of kisses later, I made my way to the lounge and sat. We cuddled for ten minutes. When I was sure he knew I loved him, I checked his food. Looked like Finn had fed him before he left, as there was a bit of fresh food left in the bowl.

"Okay, buddy. I have to go now, but I'll be back tonight. I promise." I gave him one last kiss on the top of his head and left. I had an early start this morning with an interview. Apparently, Peter Peterson—yes, his parents had a questionable sense of humour—had a must-see collection. He wouldn't tell me what it was, which was a red flag, but really, what job wasn't a red flag around here? It was either some weirdo who put seafood in fudge, someone who wanted to marry a tree, or someone who thought they were a horse. And let's not forget how many times I turned up to dead people. I honestly couldn't be shocked any more. If not being shocked was an Olympic sport, I'd win gold.

With the morning traffic, it took me ten minutes to drive to Peter's place. His place was a double-fronted, white bungalow set in a wide block in a semi-rural spot. The houses on either side were some distance away, which made it nice and private. Fields adjoined the back of his block. I parked in his driveway and got out. So far, so good. There wasn't anything rundown or unusual.

His doorknocker was a brass beagle's head. Cute. Barking came from inside, and when the door opened, two beagles stared up at me from under a man's legs. "Avery from the paper?"

"Yes. Mr Peterson?"

"The one and only." He smiled, wrinkles forming at the corners of his eyes. His hair was just this side of white, and his skin was tanned, although I wasn't sure how. Maybe he'd just gotten a spray tan, or he'd recently returned from a trip somewhere warm and summery. "Please, come in."

The beagles sniffed my feet as I followed their master further into the house. We ended up in a kitchen/family room at the back of the house. It overlooked the back garden and fields beyond. Although, at this time of year, they weren't much to look at. Frosted dirt would be a good descriptor. At least his house was warm and neat. Everything appeared to be in its place, except for one thing—his dining room table was covered in a tablecloth with small lumps under it, ready for a big ta-da moment. Did I dare hope for an interesting collection?

I shed my coat and hung it on the back of a dining chair.

As I took my notepad and pen out of my bag, I asked, "So, what is this secret collection you have for me?"

He grinned and looked at the table. "Well, I was a podiatrist—retired now—and I had many interests." His hand fluttered near the edge of the tablecloth. "This isn't my whole collection, mind you. It's about a fifth of it. But I've been collecting for my whole adult life." I stared at the table. Despite the odds of it being something not very interesting, I was curious. He at least had suspense-building skills. His fingers skimmed the edge of the tablecloth.

Not long now.

Were they rocks? The shapes kind of looked like that. Or maybe plates of cookies. He might be a serious baker. I couldn't think of what else it could be.

Since I didn't actually have all day, it was time to get this show on the road. "So, I'm ready when you are." I gave him an encouraging smile, pen poised.

"Ooh, I'm so excited!" He grabbed the tablecloth with both hands. "Prepare to be dazzled." He yanked the fabric upwards, and it snapped over his head and behind him, revealing....

Lots and lots of small, clear jars with screw-on yellow lids.

I blinked and tamped down my disappointment at the lack of cookies.

Sample jars, like when you did a wee for the doctor to test. It wasn't wee, though—there was no yellow liquid. Each lid had a sticker with a date and name. There were small whitish things in the jars, and I had to lean over the table and inspect them closely to discover what treasures they held.

Peter stood next to me, anticipation clear in the wideness of his eyes and the way he stepped from foot to foot. He was practically vibrating.

I frowned and narrowed my eyes as I peered closer. My stomach gurgled, and my throat manned all stations. "Are those…." I swallowed my morning coffee's attempt to reappear. Oh God.

"Yes! Toenail clippings from all my years as a podiatrist."

"Toilet?" I gurgled before clamping my mouth shut to prevent disaster.

"Just around there. There's a sign on it that says Loo."

My closed-mouth grimace was hastily thrown on as I turned and bolted. I only just made it into the toilet and slammed the door before my coffee had its way and gained freedom with a wretched war cry. I was cursed with being a loud thrower-upper. I gagged again, but nothing came out except that godawful sound.

They didn't pay me enough for this. There was no way Julian would put this in the paper, not that I could even last writing a whole article about toenails before throwing up again.

What had I done to deserve this? Hadn't I paid my life dues? Surely everything I'd suffered from my parents, ex, and extreme weather, gave me a pass from future disgustingness?

There was a knock on the door. "Are you okay, Avery?"

I carefully straightened and took stock. Okay, I thought I was done. Thank goodness I hadn't had breakfast yet. I hated wasting food—wasting coffee and milk was bad enough. I rinsed my mouth out and drank a mouthful of water for good measure. I had gum in the car for emergencies. I dried my hands on the guest towel hanging on the wall, wiped my teary eyes, and opened the door. Peter stood there, concern on his face. "Um, I ate leftover sushi for breakfast, and I think I have food poisoning. I'll take a quick pic of you with your collection before I leave."

"Thank you! Also, sorry to hear you're not well. Bad timing, I suppose."

"Very." The bad timing was actually that he hadn't asked the paper to do a story on his collection a year ago, before I was here.

He plucked some jars off the table and held them up around his gargantuan grin. "Cheese," he said. Argh, bad word choice. If only I could close my eyes. As it was, I looked out the back window instead of the sea of nightmare containers.

My stomach roiled as I took two pictures that would never be shown to anyone but my colleagues. If I had to suffer, they had to as well.

I put my phone in my bag and hastily slipped my coat on. "Thank you, Mr Peterson. Good luck. Bye." I didn't wait for any response before hurrying to the front door. I made sure I closed it after me so the dogs wouldn't get out.

Podiatrists were the true unsung heroes in our world. Not that one since he was a psychopath, but I couldn't deal with people's feet all day. Not in a million years. At least someone was willing to.

The morning road was wet and slick, the sun trapped behind dark clouds, so I was extra careful on the drive back to the office. Some annoying person stuck to my behind half the way, but bad luck, buddy. I wasn't going to crash my car because someone had no idea what a safe speed was for the conditions. It was my turn to buy the office beverages, so I walked up to Heavenly Brew. When I finally made it into the office, everyone was there, even Julian. Lucky I'd bought him a tea. His smile seemed genuine and not super despondent this morning.

"Thank you, Winters. How's the investigation going?"

He didn't need to ask which one. I hadn't said much about Everly's case. He knew I was working on it, but we'd only spoken about it when I'd found the locket, and he'd probably forgotten about it. "Slowly. There are quite a few suspects, so the police are doing what they can, and I'm trying to speed it along with my own information. I went to the company he used to work for yesterday and spoke to one of the journalists." Okay, so I wasn't there for the case, but he didn't need to know that. As long as I reassured him that things were moving along, he'd feel less helpless.

"Did they have anything of note to impart?" He sipped his tea and stared at me, hopeful.

"Not really. But there are a couple of suspects who are floating to the top of the list as likelies. I haven't spoken to them yet, though. The police are working on them separately, as far as I know." Well, I did know. They had to figure out everyone's alibis, and in the meantime, I'd have to figure out a way to check them out without angering them. I didn't want to be on anyone's hit list.

"Okay. And would you like any help?" If he kept giving me puppy-dog eyes, I was going to cave. But the last thing I wanted was for him to be on the murderer's radar. This was closer to his heart than mine, and maybe he'd take a risk too far. Also, he didn't have ghosts to help him.

"Not at this stage, but thanks."

He tapped his desk with his pointer finger a few times. "Okay. But please keep me updated."

"I will."

"Oh, and here are a couple of people to chase up for local stories."

He picked up a Post-it Note from his table and handed it over.

"Thanks. Oh, by the way, the story this morning was a bust. The guy had—" I gulped down my nausea. "—a massive toenail-cuttings collection."

Julian's eyes popped wide. "Good heavens. And you had to look at this collection?"

I nodded and let my face display my suffering. "Yes. After which, I threw up in his toilet."

"I'm terribly sorry about that, Winters." He paused and blinked a few times, processing. "No matter. I'll excuse you from an article today, then. We don't want readers leaving us in droves."

"That's what I thought." I chuckled. "I appreciate it. I'll see you later, and I'll make sure to keep you updated on Morris's case." I turned and went to the door.

"Good luck, and thanks again."

"No problemo." I shut the door behind me and went down to the office. Carina and Finn were both in, which I'd checked before I bought the drinks. I went to their desks and handed them over, then went to mine and put all my things on my table and my coat on my chairback. I sat and got my laptop and notebook out, then took a sip of my coffee. Ah, the joy of replacing what was lost.

Finn sat back in his chair and gazed at me. "So, you went into London last night."

"Yep." When I texted, I hadn't explained why I wasn't going to make it to dinner. "I wanted to interview one of Morris's workmates."

"About Morris's enemies?"

"I did ask, but there was no information forthcoming. I ended up getting some quotes for my article." I hadn't had a chance to log into that email account to check whether or not David was lying. That would be a real twist. Not that it meant anything other than he was a bad journalist and didn't deserve his promotion. I wasn't telling Morris until I'd figured it out. There was no use upsetting him for no reason.

"Why do I get the feeling you're not telling us everything?"

Carina nodded. "I get d'at feeling too."

And here I was, thinking I had a good poker face. I normally did when I needed to. "Why do you say that?"

Finn smirked, displaying his luscious dimples. I ignored my stomach's attempt at a double somersault with a one-and-a-half pike. "We know you, Lightning. There's usually more to the story… literally."

"He's right, lovie. We've known you for a while now. So, anyt'ing else you want to tell us?"

It was sweet that they cared. "Nope. Seriously, I just wanted to interview the man."

Finn dropped the smirk. His interrogation face activated—a bit of curiosity and a whole lot of suspicion. "You took a four-hour trip each way and missed an evening with Zeus just for that? Why couldn't you call him?"

Okay, those were good points. Damn him. "I had some confidential information I had to pass on. Bellamy asked me to." If I had a dollar for every lie I told….

Finn turned and shared an "I don't trust her; do you?" stare with Carina. She shook her head and turned her gaze on me. "Is evert'ing okay? Are you in danger?"

"Nope. Not yet, anyway." I gave them a cheesy grin. "Honestly, guys, it's all good so far. I promise." I didn't blame them for worrying—my track record was pretty bad when it came to finding myself in dangerous situations.

"For the record, I don't trust you."

"I'm wit' Finny on d'is one."

I put a hand on my heart. "Oh, how you wound me. But,

seriously, I'm fine. I really want to try to figure it out before Christmas. Give Morris's family some closure, you know?" I gave them my most earnest face. This time, I was all truth.

They looked at each other again, deadpan this time. Finn looked at me. "Fine, but we're watching you." He did the two fingers at the eyes, then at me, except he used both hands because one lot was for Carina staring at me too. "Are we on for dinner tonight?"

"For sure."

"Good, because Zeus missed you."

The way he looked at me made me think that maybe Zeus wasn't the only one. Or was that my delulu thinking? "I missed him too." I smiled. Yep, I meant Finn as well, but only I knew that. He would never find out.

"Is five thirty good?"

I nodded. "Perfect." I didn't miss Carina's smug little face. She waggled her eyebrows at me, and I shook my head, giving her a "you should be ashamed" face. She just grinned. "Right, now that's sorted, I need to get back to work."

"Ditto." Finn turned back to his screen.

I decided to get started on the article for Morris since this morning's interview was useless. This article was about the man and his accomplishments. Once I'd done a first draft, I was going to visit Bellamy. I doubted I could break into that email since emails had two-factor authentication these days. David hadn't said anything about any issues about breaking into it, so I figured he had the means. Their company would have a great IT department, just like the police did, which was why I wanted their help. I also wanted to keep sifting through the box on Everly. Now that I knew a bit more, maybe something would jump out at me.

With a few tweaks, my first draft took about forty-five

minutes. I'd let it sit until this afternoon, then go over it again. Once that was done, I'd hand it to Julian—he could make any changes and add to it because he knew the man far better than I did. Actually, I could even get Morris to read it and make suggestions. Too funny.

I called the two leads Julian had given me and lined up interviews for tomorrow. I asked and made sure there were no toenails involved. *Gag.* Then I threw my stuff in my bag and put my coat on. "I'll see you guys later. I'm off to see Sergeant Bellamy." Thought they'd like to know I wasn't going anywhere dangerous.

"Have fun." Carina smiled.

"See you tonight," Finn said with a quick chin tip before he stared at his screen again. He was in the work groove.

It had stopped raining, so the drive to Cramptonbury wasn't as bad as it could've been. Imagine that... something went right today. I greeted the police officer at the front desk, and he buzzed me in. Even the police I didn't know well knew who I was and let me in, no questions asked. This had become my second place of work. Since they paid me on a contract basis, I supposed I had two jobs. How did that even happen? I wondered what they'd put me down as. Could Bellamy even say I was a psychic, or was I a researcher or profiler? Profilers usually had degrees, so I knew I wasn't qualified at all, but how did Bellamy manage to get me into their system, and why had I never asked about this before?

I made my way to Bellamy's office. Patel was at his desk but on the phone. He gave me a smile, and I reciprocated. Fiona was at the desk next to his, and she waved. "Hey, Aves. How are you?"

"Great. And you?"

"Getting there. Paperwork is the devil."

I chuckled. "Better you than me."

She rolled her eyes and shook her head. I gave a wave and headed to Bellamy's door, which was half open, so I peeked in. He was alone and working. I went in and shut the door. "Hello, Sergeant. Sergeant Fox." I gave the ghost next to Bellamy's chair a nod.

Sergeant Bellamy said, "Hello, Winters."

Sergeant Fox said, "Hello, Miss Winters." So much more polite, not that I cared. It was a sign of the times he'd lived, and if his massive sideburn/moustache combo weren't a dead giveaway, his super politeness would've been.

"Where's Charles?"

Bellamy frowned. "How the hell am I supposed to know?"

"Oops, sorry." I redirected my gaze to Fox.

"I sent him to spy on one of those suspects. He's at Ivan Novikov's bar in Exeter. I overheard Bellamy ordering surveillance on it yesterday, so I figured we could get the inside running. He's going to return when he has something to report."

"That could be ages."

Fox gave me a stern look. "So? Difficulties must be surmounted. He's a ghost—it doesn't matter to him. Besides, if you want him, you can call."

"Right. Fine." I looked at Bellamy, who'd continued working. He knew I'd recap when I was ready, which I did.

"Oh, that's good." He looked at the space next to him and made sure to angle his gaze upwards. I smirked. "Thank you, Sergeant."

"My pleasure, Sergeant."

"He said it's his pleasure. He also said he's glad you didn't talk to his crotch again."

Fox jerked straight, hitting me with a pinched-lipped, spiky-eyed look. Someone wasn't amused. I chuckled.

Bellamy cleared his throat. "Ah, yeah. Won't be making that mistake again."

Fox shook his head. "You're a troublemaker."

I smiled at the dead sergeant. "I know. It's one of my best qualities."

"That's debatable."

My eyes went back to Bellamy. "I was wondering if you can get someone to hack into an email. I have the address and password, but I don't know how to get past two-factor authentication."

The lines on his forehead deepened. "That depends on what it's for. And we'd need a warrant."

I told him about Morris's concerns. "But it could also be relevant to this case. When I went to see David after Morris asked me, he seemed okay, but when I was leaving, I overheard Morris's good friend arguing with someone about giving David a promotion. He said he couldn't trust him. Do you think David might've had something to do with Morris's death?"

"Did you go from point C to point D via Z? What would his motive be? If Morris recommended him for a promotion, why would he want him killed?"

"I don't know. But, well, things don't necessarily add up, which was why I wanted to get into that email account. Maybe he's trying to take the company down?"

"Again, motive." He stood. "Why don't we wait and see if that article comes out, hmm? We have enough suspects without adding someone I think can be ignored at this stage. And, in case I'm not being clear, the answer is no."

I growled, and Bellamy raised his brows. "Fine. Hopefully you'll say yes to my other request, which is to keep looking through Everly's files. I've come across some new information. I have the first names and descriptions of two young women he killed at his rooms in London. I think they've passed on though, so I didn't get a firsthand account."

He stared down at me. "Write up those details for me, please. And, yes, you may have a look through those files. They're here." He bent to his right and lifted the box up, then came to me, placing it carefully on my lap. "Knock yourself out. I'm going to get a coffee." He walked out.

"Thanks for offering to make me a coffee, Sergeant. I appreciate it," I called after him. Patel sniggered. The sergeant ignored me, which was pretty much what I expected. I didn't really think he'd make me a coffee. I was just in a mood and needed to cheer myself up. Fox shook his head again. I shrugged. "Yeah, I know. I'm a troublemaker. It helps me get through the day."

"You are being rather bothersome."

"Why, thank you." I smiled. "Lucky for you and Bellamy, I have work to do, so I've run out of spare time."

He smoothed his moustache. "Thank the lord for small mercies. I'm going to check on Charles. I'll see you later."

"Bye."

He disappeared, and I gripped the box handles and stood. There was always a spare desk I could use as the officers were in and out all the time. I found a vacant desk and plonked the box on it. Digging through it, I found a few folders I hadn't yet investigated. I placed them on the desk and sat.

"Come on, clue," I whispered, "show yourself."

Three hours later, I wasn't any closer to proving anything. I rubbed my temples to ward off the hovering headache. Bellamy had been out for an hour, but he'd just returned and now stood in front of my desk. "I don't need to ask, do I."

"No. Nothing. If only they had the kind of forensics back then that they do now." I sucked in a breath. Why was I so stupid? I was the dumbest person on the face of the earth right now. I couldn't believe I didn't think of this before.

"What is it?" Bellamy had his unflappable police face on.

I looked at the two officers at their desks. One had someone in.... Client was the wrong word. A member of the public complaining about something. The other officer was quietly doing his job, typing something up. I stood. "Can we talk in your office?"

"Yes, but pack that up and bring it with you. I'm not one for leaving evidence lying around." I did as asked, then joined him in his office. He was already in his chair. Fox hadn't returned either. Maybe he and Charles were getting somewhere with Morris's case?

I shut the door, but I didn't sit because I was full of energy. "If we had remains, wouldn't it be easier?"

"Of course." His brows drew down. "Are you saying she knows where she's buried?"

"Yes! At least, I think so. She wouldn't tell me last time I asked, so I think I mentally threw that question away. Also, when she brought up who her killer was, I was so shocked that I didn't think to ask—I asked other questions, but not that one. I'm assuming she knows." I wasn't sure if I'd explained the "rules" to Bellamy, but they were worth repeating. "When we die, if we stay here, we're tied in some way to the place we lived and the place we died. I thought maybe she'd been buried somewhere in the forest near my place, but your guys did ground scans and came up empty. Right?"

"Yes. I didn't even think of that. We've both been asleep on the job." He pulled a face, indicating he couldn't believe what an idiot he was. *You and me both.* To be fair, we had a lot on our plates, and dealing with ghosts took some adjustments. It wasn't a normal question you could ask a dead victim.... Well, you could, but you wouldn't expect them to answer. "If she could tell us where she was buried, that would open a whole new avenue. Can you get her here now?"

"I'll try." I did my usual and gazed at the ceiling. "Everly, can you come here? Everly?" I waited a minute. "Everly, it's Avery. The sergeant and I need to talk to you. Hello?" I sat and looked at Bellamy. "She might be in the middle of something. She counsels other ghosts."

His eyebrows rose a smidge. "Now I've heard everything. Do they have ghost lawyers and doctors?"

I gave him an "are you kidding?" look. "Um, why would they need those? There's no money, you can't contain a ghost in a jail, and they can't get sick."

That was the first time I'd ever seen him blush, spots of crimson giving him a pinched-cheek look. "Right. Of course." He mumbled something I couldn't catch. I would've asked him to repeat it—it was fun seeing him unsettled because he usually had his crap together—but Everly chose that moment to pop in.

She stood just inside the closed door, gave the room a once over, then turned to me. "I was in the middle of a discussion with my friend, sorry. What do you want?"

"She's here, Sergeant." His answer was a harrumph. I held in my smirk. Poor man was still annoyed with me. "Do you want to sit?"

"No thanks."

"Okay, will you please sit? I'm going to get a sore neck looking up at you."

"Well, you should've said." She walked right through me to the other chair— making me shudder—and sat, giving me a face full of smug amusement.

My eyes shot daggers at her. "What is it with you ghosts lately? Everyone's a comedian." Thank God that Charles wasn't here to do something equally as annoying to "enhance" the "joke." I didn't miss Bellamy's bright eyes and smiley mouth. I turned my dagger eyes to him.

"It's nice when the tables turn."

I gave Bellamy and then Everly another annoyed look.

She laughed. "Riling you up is so much fun. Remember when I tried to scare you when you first arrived?"

I thought back to when she appeared, bloody wound and all, in our apartment. "Yes, but you didn't succeed. I remember how disappointed you were."

"True. You were a fun sponge. Finally, someone could see me, yet I couldn't scare them. So disappointing." She rested her arms on the chair arms and gently slapped them with one hand and then the other in a fastish rhythm that I couldn't hear. "So, why am I here?"

I was taking it as a good sign that she wasn't skittish, especially as she must suspect I'd called her here because of her case. "We need to ask you something about your murder. Sorry."

Wariness appeared in her eyes, but it was there and gone in a flash. She sighed. "I figured as much. But it's okay. Ask whatever you want. I've come to terms with what we're doing. I don't feel guilty or scared any more." Fire ignited in her gaze. "I want to catch that murdering, rotting fish head."

I smiled. "Great! I want to catch him too. ASAP. I might touch you for the next bit so that Bellamy can hear you. Is that okay? Also, we might need to do it in stages because I get too cold."

Her mouth dropped open. "He'll be able to hear me?"

Adrenaline warmed my chest, and my throat felt tight as I realised what this would mean. "Yes." I knew what her next question would be before she opened her mouth.

Her breaths—I still didn't know why they breathed—came quickly, and her eyes sparkled like a lake on a sunny day. "Can I speak to my mum?"

If I did that for her, I would risk Mrs Crabby accusing me of being a charlatan. But if she did believe me, she might out me to everyone, especially our neighbours… i.e., Finn. Although, her telling everyone I was trying to fool her would make me look worse. What kind of evil person did that to someone else?

But how could I say no?

I didn't want Everly to hate me, and it could be the thing that brought them both peace if Mrs Crabby deigned to believe it wasn't an elaborate ruse. Could I risk it? I didn't think so. But should I? I knew the answer to that.

I swallowed my apprehension. "Yes, but can we wait until we solve the murder? I don't want her causing problems. Besides, she's more likely to believe it's you and not me trying to hurt her if I can tell her that you helped us find your body and solve this. We'd have proof of who and when." I couldn't imagine being outed and having to leave in the middle of trying to figure this out, not to mention solving Morris's case. I had to consider that I might have to leave Manesbury. I ignored the pain lancing my chest at that potential. Something to worry about if and when it happened.

Don't invite bad vibes, Avery.

She was smiling. "Yes, of course." She slapped her hands on her thighs and wriggled her bottom. "I'm so excited!"

How could I say no to that? "I'm glad. You've suffered enough." The risk was worth it. I looked at Bellamy. "She's going to tell us."

"I gathered that. I also gathered that you're going to take a risk for her."

My joy at Everly's reaction sobered. "Yes. Mrs Collins could make trouble for me. But…." I shrugged and gave him a "what can you do?" face.

"I understand. That's very noble of you, Winters. I know what you stand to lose."

He probably didn't quite understand—how could he? But I appreciated his attempt and empathy. "Thanks. So, why don't we get this show on the road?" Nothing like a good cliché for calming everything down.

"I'll record this." Bellamy unlocked his phone and pressed the screen. "Let's go." He picked up a pen and opened his diary. I guessed he probably didn't want this on the computer and in the system, so to speak. How could he explain it? We'd have to find what we found and figure out how to work backwards so we had a legit reason for going and looking wherever her body was.

I braced my abs and reached out, touching her arm. "Where did Andrew Crumps put your body?"

Her voice, young but quiet, filled the room as she straightened and fortified herself. Bellamy stared raptly at her seat. "After I passed out in the car, I woke up in a small cottage with decorations from the thirties. But my body didn't wake up. I was standing there watching Andrew and… me." She shuddered.

My hand burned with the cold, and I involuntarily snatched it back. I sucked in air and buried my hand under my armpit. "I'm sorry. I'll be right in a minute."

Everly gave me a sympathetic look, and Bellamy nodded and pressed Stop on the recording. He replayed it. "That was incredible. I don't think I'll ever get used to that."

My ghostly friend grinned at him. "I can't believe someone else can hear me! This is amazing. If I didn't have to talk about that night, I'd be enjoying this more."

I repeated what she said. Bellamy's sigh was heavy with disappointment. "I'm sorry he was never caught. You and the other victims deserved so much more."

She held her hand out to me, and I reluctantly gave her mine. This time, I pressed Record on my phone. "I don't blame you or the police. Andrew is a master manipulator, and his family has connections. I was totally smitten, and I sometimes blame myself. But I know that's not right either." I released her hand and went back to warming it under my other arm while Bellamy listened to the recording.

"No, it's not right. It wasn't your fault." He shook his head. "Still… if only we'd done a better job."

Anger edged my voice. "The only person who's to blame is that piece-of-crap, Andrew. And whichever police officer was happy to flub the investigation. We all know that forensics wasn't what it is today."

Bellamy's forehead wrinkled. "But they interviewed Andrew, and historically and now, we all know that men who have a connection to the victim are usually responsible for women going missing in unusual circumstances, and he was the last person to see her alive. At the very least, they didn't try hard enough, dammit." He slapped the table, and I flinched. That was so unlike the unflappable sergeant. I was lucky I stumbled upon such an ethical and caring ally. I could've landed in dodgy-brothers central when I came here, but I hadn't.

We were wasting time. The need to get going on this was like an itch under my skin. "Can you start recording again, Sergeant?"

He nodded and pressed the button.

Realising I didn't need to touch her with my whole hand, I hovered a finger in her arm. *Weird, I know.* My pointer finger screamed it was getting frostbite, but I ignored it. It wasn't black, yet. "Where was that house? What did he do with your body?"

"He…." She took a deep breath, then rushed out the rest, as if she might get stuck if she didn't go fast. "He wrapped me in a body bag and buried me on a large property. It was halfway between Manesbury and his parents' place. It belonged to a great-aunt of his. She left it to him when she died." She gave us the address, and I rescued my finger and stuck it in my mouth to warm it. Bellamy stared at me, eyebrows raised, questioning my manners. I shrugged. As far as I was concerned, there was no etiquette when it came to preventing ghost-induced frostbite. Sheesh.

"Thank you, Ev. You've done the right thing." I gave her an encouraging smile and resisted rubbing her arm in comfort.

"I know. It's still hard. But I'm looking forward to chatting to Mum." Her smile was the golden rays pushing through clouds after a storm.

"Get ready to record again. I need to ask something." Bellamy gave a nod and pressed the button as I reached for Everly. I hovered my finger, waiting until I'd asked the question before I touched her. "I found your locket in the forest near our place. Why did he throw it there?"

She shrugged, and I touched her. "I have no idea. Maybe he wanted to keep it, then thought better of it. Or maybe he was trying to throw the police off."

I shook my hand and stuck my finger in my mouth again as Bellamy listened to her response. When it stopped hurting, I took it out. "But if they'd found it, there might have been DNA on it that they could've used."

She shook her head. "No. He wore gloves when he ripped it off me. It was after he killed me." I repeated that to Bellamy since I hadn't been touching her.

Bellamy frowned. "Interesting."

Everly asked, "So, what happens now?" I passed her question on.

"Now we go through that old evidence again and see if we can tie that place to Andrew. Then we see if we can find the lead police officer on the case. He or she would likely be retired by now."

"If they're even still alive," I added.

Bellamy blew out a breath. He gazed at the seat next to me. "Have you got anything else you think is relevant?"

She shook her head, and I said, "No, Sergeant."

"Right. We need to get to work, then." Again, he turned to the empty chair. "We'll do our best, Everly. I can promise you that."

She rested her ghostly fingers on my arm, and I pressed Record on my phone. "I know, Sergeant. Thank you. I have every faith in both of you."

CHAPTER 18

I was supposed to go undercover at Angelo's club, and fortunately, it was only closed on Sunday nights. My lame disguise was just a fake ID and a brown wig that Bellamy had given me. The plan was to flirt some information out of one of his associates. I'd been researching his inner circle when I had spare time.

For an experienced criminal, he sure was active on social media. Maybe he enjoyed taunting the police? In any case, because he loved to post pics of him living the high life, there were plenty of photos, and the same people seemed to be in many of them. Hopefully one or more of them would be at the club tonight. I'd flirt with the guys and try and make friends with the ladies. I pretended to myself that I wasn't nervous, but I felt like a cat about to run the gauntlet through a yard full of pit bulls.

But first, I had dinner with Finn and Zeus.

I let myself in to Finn's at five thirty. He wasn't home, which was fine. I played with Zeus for a bit, gave him cuddles, and then realised it was six. My phone dinged with a text. *Hey ⚡. Running a bit late. Be there in 30.*

I responded. *I can start dinner if you like. What are we having?*

Can you put a big pot of water on for the pasta? We're having spag bol. Sauce is already done. In fridge.

👍

I was familiar with his kitchen and got out everything I needed, filled the pot with water, added salt, and set it on the stove. I fed Zeus as well. By the time Finn got home and walked into the kitchen, the pasta was almost done. I'd just pulled a strand of spaghetti out to see if it was cooked. Movement out of the corner of my eye caught my gaze. I turned. Finn stood in the doorway, a weird look on his face, like he was figuring out how to feel. Which was weird. He looked sexy in his black turtleneck jumper, and I managed not to sigh.

"It's almost done. Another minute or so on this, and the sauce just dinged in the microwave."

He smiled, warmth shining from his blue eyes. "Great. I'm starving. Sorry you had to cook. I'll set the table."

"Boiling some pasta is hardly a massive effort. At least you'd already made the bolognaise. I've fed Zeus as well." Hearing his name, he trotted over to me and rubbed against my legs, tail high. I bent over and stroked his back. "Love you, kitten."

"Aw, thanks."

I rolled my eyes and straightened. Finn's dimples were showing with his smirky grin. Argh. Stupidly attractive man. "You wish." If he found out I was attracted to him, he'd lose all respect for me. He might even start avoiding me. Yeah, nah. I didn't need that. "Pasta's probably ready." I turned and used the oven mitts to grab the pot handles. I dumped the spaghetti strands into the colander in the sink. Finn, thankfully, decided to stop teasing me and took the sauce out of the microwave.

During dinner, we talked about work stuff and Christmas. Finn was going to see his family. As far as I knew, Meg and Carina were also going to be away. I was staying put with Zeus. I wouldn't miss that time for anything.

"Do you think the Morris case will be solved by then?" Finn asked when we were clearing the table.

"I don't know. I hope so. We have a couple of leads, but nothing definitive. There's no clear single suspect." With a bit of luck, that might change tonight with my little side trip.

"Good luck." We rinsed our bowls and put them into his dishwasher. Then Finn washed the pot and container while I dried. "Want some dessert? I have bread and butter pudding."

"No thanks. Too full." Also, too nervous about later. Would I discover anything helpful? Would they cotton on that I wasn't who I said I was? Although, how could they? Though, they were probably always on the lookout for undercover police. If I were a criminal, I'd be on high alert all the time.

"What's wrong?" Finn peered at me.

"Nothing. Just tired. It's been a long day." Oops. I'd forgotten to set my face into relaxed mode.

He narrowed his eyes. "Are you sure?"

"Positive." If Finn found out what I was doing tonight, he'd insist on coming, and then how could I flirt with anyone? They'd think I was there with my boyfriend. Although, if Bellamy had roped Finn into doing this, he could easily get the ladies talking. Maybe if I failed tonight, I'd suggest it to Bellamy. I headed into the living room, grabbed Zeus, and sat, placing him on my lap.

Finn came in and sat on the other end of the three-seater couch. He put a paramedic show on. I loved those. English

TV had so many reality-type shows, many more than Australia. I loved all the police and medical ones. So good. At nine, I gave Zeus a final squishy hug and kissed his head. I stood. "I'm off. Got an early start tomorrow."

Finn looked at his phone. "It's still early."

"I need lots of sleep. I'm getting up at six tomorrow." I wasn't really, but whatever.

He and Zeus followed me to the door. He picked up the cat before he opened the door. "Goodnight. See you tomorrow."

"Night." I didn't look at him as I slipped past and out the door. We would've been so close, and looking into his eyes at that nearness would've been killer. He would've seen how I felt for sure. The longer I could avoid that happening, the better. And who knew? Maybe I'd get over my little crush in a few weeks. Surely it couldn't last forever.

The freezing air slapped my cheeks as I hurried home. Thank goodness I only lived next door. Problem was, if I was going out, I'd have to wear something sexy, and that meant not much. Why did other women my age have to go out wearing practically nothing in winter? They made it the norm. No guy in a club was going to look twice at me if I wore a warm jacket and jeans.

In twenty minutes, I was ready to roll. I wore a short, tight black skirt, black high-heeled boots that stopped just below my knees, and a tight red halter-neck top that showcased my cleavage. Was it too much? Probably. I felt like I was dressed to make some money on the corner. I put my hair in a hairnet and shoehorned the wig over the top. Once my fake ID was in my purse, I shrugged on my coat and headed out, extra careful not to activate the two squeaky steps. It was nine thirty, and Mrs Crabby would have my hide if I disturbed her.

When I was halfway across our dead-end street, Finn called out, "Lightning?" I stopped and turned. He stood at his front gate, staring at me. "Where are you going? I thought you were having an early night." His expression was hard to make out in the dim streetlights, but his tone of voice was clear—he'd caught me in a lie, and he was proud of himself.

I sighed. "I'm going to a club." I didn't have time to lie and argue. It was too cold to stand here, and I wanted to get this assignment over and done with.

He came out of his gate and joined me in the middle of the lane. He was close enough that I could see his smirk this time. "I knew it! You were acting weird. Early night my arse."

"I have something to do for Sergeant Bellamy, and it's not dangerous. I'm just hanging out at a club."

"It's so safe that you have to wear a wig. I see."

"Just a precaution."

My coat only reached mid-thigh. His gaze stuck to the expanse of skin between the tops of my boots and coat hem for a beat before it returned to my face. "What are you wearing under that coat?"

I sighed. "Normal clubbing clothes." Okay, so they were a bit sexier than I'd usually wear, but I had them because I'd normally pair the top or skirt with something else, so it wasn't "as" sexy. My mother used to tell my sister and me before we went out that if we showed both cleavage and lots of leg, it was cheap and sent the wrong message. I had it drummed into me, but really, shouldn't a woman wear whatever the hell she wanted?

The upshot was that I wasn't normally comfortable showing so much skin, but I was sick of being their daughter, the one who did everything she was told because she was the most pathetic people pleaser, desperate for their love. This was my year of rebellion, even if I was the only one who got to see it.

My sister would be proud, though.

A pang of homesickness hit me. I'd left her there by herself. What a shitty thing to do. But she was always more headstrong than me, and she could handle it. She'd be finished uni soon and would move out. Maybe I could get her to come visit?

"Lighting?"

"Oh, sorry. Um, it's cold, and I'm freezing, so I'd like to get going. Bye." I turned quickly, hoping he'd get the hint.

The crunch of his shoes on the laneway grit and ice made it obvious that he wasn't going to be deterred. "At least let me come with you and sit in the car. If anything happens, you can text, and I'll be straight in there."

I stopped and turned, surprising Finn, who slammed into me. He grabbed my arms to stop me from flying. And I looked into his eyes.

Big mistake.

In the low light, he was all dark pupils and intensity. If I stood on my toes and leaned forward a few inches, I'd be able to kiss him. A horn beeped down on the main road, waking me from my Finn-induced stupor, reminding me that I was making a fool of myself. I took a breath, and I would blame what I said next on the fact that my brain was scrambled from trying not to jump him. "Fine. You can sit in the car. But don't you dare come in and ruin everything. These guys are dangerous, and if any of them think they're being played, things might go south quickly." The moment it was out of my mouth, I knew I'd made a huge tactical error.

His eyes narrowed for a split second before he smiled. "Great. I can do that."

I narrowed my eyes back at him, but I made sure he knew I meant business. "Bellamy will be most displeased if you screw this up. Understand?"

"Of course. I'll wait in the car."

I didn't trust him, but there wasn't much I could do about it now. I gave him one last dirty look and headed for my car.

I parked a minute's walk from the club. I could've let Finn drive and drop me out the front, but that would look weird. Although, he could've been an Uber for all anyone knew. I handed Finn my keys and checked my ID. It was then I realised I should've called Charles to help me. He could listen in to other conversations. It was too late to go through everything with him now, but I could call him before I went in… when Finn wasn't within listening distance.

"Be safe. And if you're not out in two hours, I'm coming in." Surprisingly enough, that was fair. If I hadn't discovered anything by then, I wasn't going to. "And if you need me, text or call. I'll be here waiting."

"Okay. Thanks. I appreciate it. If you need to drive around the block a few times to warm the car up, feel free. It's a bit cold to just sit here with the car off."

"I'll be fine. Just be careful."

"Will do." I opened my door and got out, then took my coat off—my car was too small to wrestle out of it inside. I leaned down and chucked it on the front seat.

Finn's stare was emanating stern vibes. "What's your assignment? Are you trying to pick up?"

"Yes and no. I'm going to flirt information out of someone… hopefully." Not that I thought I was any kind of sex kitten, but I could act any part when I put my journalist hat on.

"You really think that's going to work?"

"Excuse me?"

He cringed. "That's not what I meant."

"Yeah, right. I have a job to do. Bellamy's counting on me." I shivered as the night air ran icy hands up my legs. "Anyway, just because you wouldn't be attracted to me doesn't mean the crims in there won't be." I had to have enough confidence in myself that I didn't need anyone else's. Besides, what did Finn's opinion mean to me? We were friends. It shouldn't matter what he thought.

Ah, the lies we told ourselves.

"I didn't mean—"

I cut him off by slamming the door. "Sorry, Daisy," I whispered as I strutted away, head held high. Just because I was annoyed with Finn, didn't mean I needed to take it out on my car. She'd been good to me.

I should thank Finn for making me angry—it warmed my blood and banished my nerves. His irritating opinion reminded me of my parents. According to them, I should've failed and been back home by now. Despite their attempts to hold me down, I'd succeeded at what I'd set out to do—I had an awesome life here, and I didn't have to rely on anyone, except myself. I was turning out to be the person I'd always wanted. And no man was going to make me feel bad about myself ever again. Brad was the last man I'd give that power to.

By the time I reached the club, I was ready to slay. I slid my phone out of my bag and pretended to be on it. "Charles. Hello, Charles?" In less than a minute, he appeared at my side.

"Whoa, don't you look smokin'." He whistled and grinned.

I laughed. At least one of my friends was encouraging. And I would've bet that Meg and Carina would've had the same reaction. Yep. I wasn't going to let Finn get me down. *Stupid man*. "Thank you." I lowered my voice. "You've been hanging around Bell lately. You get what I'm saying?"

"Oh, the sergeant?"

"Yes."

"You want me to float, see what info I can get?"

"Yes, please. I'll do what I can too."

He rubbed his hands together. "Let's see if we can break this case wide open."

I chuckled. "You're hilarious. Let me know if you hear anything."

"Will do." He walked to the front door and straight through one of the two bouncers standing outside. The towering, beefy, Black man shuddered and gazed around. He wouldn't believe me if I told him.

I put my phone back in my crossbody bag, stepped past some teenage girl smoking a cigarette, and stood behind the three guys and two women waiting to get in. One of the men gave me a once-over and a small smile. He wasn't bad-looking—about my age, five foot ten with sandy-brown hair. He wore jeans and a blue shirt, which was all fine, but his shoes gave me the ick. Neon yellow with green laces. What was he thinking? I gave him a tight smile back. I didn't want to encourage anyone who wasn't on my list of Angelo's nearest and dearest, nor did I want to be rude to anyone. So the thanks-but-no-thanks smile was what he got. Thankfully, he took the hint and turned back around.

When I reached the front of the line, I took my ID out and tried to look friendly but bored, hoping it would hide the fact that my heart was racing. I focussed on my numb-from-the-cold legs. The bouncer didn't even look at my licence. He just gave a nod. "Have a good night." Oh, well, that was easy. It was nothing like Australia. I'd seen fifty-year-olds get asked for ID at my local club.

I smiled. "Thanks. You too."

Woohoo! First hurdle cleared. Relief spun through me like a whirlwind of encouragement as I stepped into the dark room filled with floor-vibrating bass. *I can do this.*

For a weeknight, it was fairly busy. Who were these people who could party all night and still get up for work or study the next morning? Crazy people, that's who. On my walk from the door to the bar, I glanced around, taking it all in.

To my left was a large dance floor, only a handful of dancers grooved to the pop music. Most were alive. Two ghosts dressed in seventies attire were wiggling their hips and flinging their arms around with abandon. I couldn't help smiling. They'd found such freedom and joy, even in death. It would be fun to dance like no one was watching, even in a crowded place.

The bar was straight ahead, on the far wall. Three bartenders—two women and one man—poured drinks and hurried from one customer to the next. There were a few high-top tables with stools around the fringes and three areas with couches, one of those being roped off and elevated a few steps so the VIPs could survey their kingdom.

Careful not to stare, I hovered my gaze momentarily on that area before scanning the dance floor again. There were eight people in the VIP area—five men and three women. It was hard to see clearly, though. Did clubs have to be so dark? I got that it hid most people's imperfections, but did we really need that much help to meet a potential hook-up or partner?

I reached the bar and stood behind a woman who was

being served. The guy next to me gave me a once over and smiled. He didn't look familiar, as in, I hadn't come across his picture while stalking Angelo, Ivan, Jack and their mates on social media. I gave him a lukewarm smile and faced the bar again. This was so awkward. Should I start chatting to just anyone to appear like I wasn't weird? Not that I was weird. Well, maybe I was a bit, but that wasn't the point. Argh, paranoia wasn't fun.

This wasn't as easy as I thought it would be. How was I going to get into that VIP area? I looked that way again. One of the men was standing, chatting, and facing me. I swallowed. It was Angelo. I was sure of it. Talk about hitting the jackpot. There was no way I wasn't going to get onto that stupid roped-off platform.

It was my turn to order my drink. "I'll have a lemonade, thanks." It would look like a vodka and lemonade, most likely.

"Coming right up." The young woman—whose ample cleavage was loud and proud and probably doing its best to attract tips—had my drink poured and on the counter almost faster than I could get my debit card out.

With a drink in hand, I assessed a good spot to eye the VIP section from. I'd like to be in their line of sight. A bit of flirting across the room wouldn't go astray. I'd have to work hard for an invite to their rich-people pontoon that floated above a lake of too much alcohol and future regret. It was still relatively early as far as clubbing went, and a guy and girl were getting steamy on the dance floor. They both looked as messy as a flock of drunk lorikeets.

I found an unoccupied high-top and sat on a stool. Sipping my drink, I scanned around for Charles and found him listening to a group of men, two of whom looked like bikies. I couldn't tell if the men were part of Angelo's posse. The man ruled a group of criminals that were more like the mafia than bikies, though. Unless he had a mixture of "helpers." Those bikie-looking guys might be part of their own organisation, or they could just be guys who liked to ride motorbikes and dress like that. For all I knew, they could be accountants. I chuckled until a tall, young woman appeared next to me. She looked to be eighteen or nineteen and was dressed in modern clothes that were about as skimpy as mine.

But she was a ghost.

Her blue eyes stared at me, bright with what I assumed was excitement. "You can see me."

I smiled and tried not to move my lips much. "Yes."

"Do you know that other ghost too?" She looked over at Charles.

"Mmhmm."

"He's a bit young to be here." Her forehead furrowed.

I put my straw in my mouth and pretended to drink. "It's not like he can drink anything. Besides, he's been dead a long time and seen a lot of things." Even when he was alive. He was older than his years before he died. I ignored the pang of sadness and took a sip of lemonade. The polite thing to do would be to ask her how she came to be here, but I didn't want to risk anyone noticing I was talking to myself… although. I bopped my head to the beat, and thankfully, the music had words rather than just, well, music. I pretended to sing to myself. "Did you die here?"

She sighed, which I could see rather than hear since the music was so loud. "Yes. Someone spiked my drink. I passed out and never woke up. Well, my body didn't wake up. I ended up standing next to myself. I tried to get back in, but it didn't work."

"How long ago?"

"Two months. Time doesn't move the same here, but I look at people's phones regularly, so I know what day it is."

"I'm sorry." Words weren't enough, but sometimes they were all we had. "Did they catch the person who did it?"

She was quick to answer, "No." Her gaze fell on the group in the VIP area. A few more people had entered, and it was becoming quite the crowd.

"Are they there?"

Her lips pressed together, her eyes almost shooting sparks. Someone was angry, and I couldn't blame her. "Yes. He's the son of the guy who owns the club. His name is Ricardo. They call him Ricky. The police pulled video footage from that night, but the video covering that area was conveniently missing. With no other evidence, they had nothing."

"Did they interview any witnesses?"

"A few that I know of… at least that night. I hovered around and listened, but no one knew anything, and his two mates said they had no idea." Well, that went without saying. "There was a girl who videoed it on her phone, though. She looked nervous soon after it happened, so I followed her to the bathrooms, thinking maybe she was involved somehow. I watched her replay the footage. But the police didn't talk to her, and she obviously never contacted them, or that piece of garbage would be in jail."

I was surprised her enraged glare hadn't set everyone in the VIP area on fire yet.

I pulled out my phone and got into my notes app. "Did you get her name?"

"Her friend called her Katie, but that's it."

"What's your name?"

"Mia Whitby. My birthday's the fifth of August… you

know, just in case you need to confirm who I am with the police."

"How often do you come here?"

She bit her bottom lip. "Every night and day. All the time, I suppose. They're shut on Sunday nights, but time is weird here"—she held her arms out and flapped her hands a couple of times, signifying the other dimension in general—"and I don't want to miss a night, so I live here, basically."

"Why?" I could assume that she hadn't come to terms with her death, but maybe it was more than that.

She turned her head and stared at the bar. "I'm trying to work out how to speak to Katie and get her to share her evidence with the police."

There were four guys waiting at the bar and one woman. "Is that her with the pink tube top and blonde hair?"

"Yes. I've tried yelling at her, touching her, and stepping into her body, but nothing works." Mia turned back and stared into my eyes. Divots appeared between her brows. "Please help me. I don't know what else to do. I can't stand the thought of my family never knowing why, and what if they hurt other women?" A tear rolled down her cheek, but her eyes were fiery. She was frustrated as well as upset, and who could blame her?

"I'll help you." I wanted to punch myself in the face because I didn't have time for this. But then again, I didn't have to fix it this minute. "I don't know if I can do anything tonight, but I'm friends with the police sergeant at Crampton-bury. I'll figure something out." I watched Katie as she took two drinks and headed back to her friend. Something occurred to me. "Mia, how well did you know Ricky?"

"We'd been hanging out for a few weeks, but we weren't dating. I thought we were friends. I mean… we flirted, but he was seeing a couple of other girls too. I didn't want to sleep with him unless we were exclusive." Ricky was just as much of a garbage human as his father.

"Did he ever talk about what his dad was up to?"

"Not really. Why?"

"I'm investigating the murder of a journalist. He might be involved."

She sucked in a quick breath, which was weird because she was dead. I was never getting over the ghost vs. breathing thing. "I might've overheard something. Was it recent, like after I died?"

"Yes. It was last weekend." It seemed like a lifetime ago. Had it really happened less than a week ago? That was wild. With all the running around for this and Everly's case, I felt like I'd lived at least six months. And don't get me started on Zeus. Maybe this was how one aged faster than they were supposed to. I probably looked six months older tonight than I had last week.

"I hover around their group sometimes to see if he's even a bit sorry that I died." Her eyes dulled with sadness as she watched the VIP group. "News flash: he's not. He hasn't said anything, at least not while I've been there." Her chest rose and fell with a heaving breath.

"I'm sorry. He's a psychopath, just like his father. They're experts at reeling people in. We'll make him pay for what he did. I promise." Argh, there I went, making promises I had to keep. Would I live long enough to fulfil every promise I'd made to the dead?

She looked at me and gave up a sad smile. "At least I didn't sleep with him. Piece of sh—"

"He sure is, and I'm glad you didn't have that to regret." I slurped the last of my drink. Time for another one. I took one last look at the VIP area. Interesting. Ricky had spotted me and was staring. Not sure if he liked what he saw or if he was picking up on me checking them out. After being with Brad for so long, my flirting game was non-existent. It was hard to tell if a guy was interested—one never wanted to assume. I turned away from the VIP area so they couldn't see my face. "I'm going to grab another drink and see if I can talk my way into the VIP area."

"Before you go, I haven't told you about what I heard… about the bombing."

I blinked, doing my best to keep my expression in check. Looking shocked for no reason would just be weird. "Tell me as I get a drink. I probably won't be able to answer you, though."

"Okay."

I started towards the bar, Mia following.

"They were talking about it on Saturday night. Someone mentioned a journalist getting blown up, and Angelo turned to his bodyguard, laughed, and said it was a job well done. Then him and the bodyguard high-fived. It's the one up there with him now, the tall, blonde-haired guy with the buzz cut." I glanced over. Hmm, I wasn't sure because of the dim lighting, but he did bear a resemblance to the army guy Bellamy was going to question—Jack Noonan.

I put my hand in front of my mouth as I lined up at the bar. "Is that it?"

"Yes. He didn't admit to having anything to do with it, but that was kind of a weird comment and reaction, don't you think?"

"Yes." I bit my bottom lip, thinking. It was imperative that I got into that stupid VIP area. And if I thought this was a risky assignment before, it was doubly so now. Although, if I wasn't obvious with my questions, there was no reason to be afraid.

It was my turn at the bar. I got another lemonade and made a mental note to go for a longer than normal run tomorrow. All this sugar wasn't a good thing. It was a shame they didn't serve coffee here. Now, *that* was an idea I could get behind—cappuccinos at the club. They could offer Irish coffee too.

Drink in hand and ghost by my side, I turned and wandered close to the VIP area, my gaze pinned on Ricky. I swayed to the beat, the music vibrating up through my feet. I didn't overdo it, though. If I tried to look sexy, I'd probably look constipated or something. I'd spent my working life being as unsexy as possible to gain respect among my colleagues, and let's not forget Brad once commenting that I was showing some cleavage and I should do my buttons up almost to my throat, and my days of dressing even slightly sexily had disappeared. So even though I was dressed more skimpily than ever, I did not have the moves to go with it.

I pushed away the bolt of anger that speared me with the reminder of another thing Brad had done. He wasn't in my life, and I wasn't going to give him any power over me. He could never make me feel bad again.

Ricky finally looked at me, and I did my best to hold his stare. When I was sure he'd stared at me long enough that it meant he liked what he saw, I smiled as seductively as I could. Hopefully my internal shudder didn't show. The guy was fairly attractive in a dark-haired Italian way, but knowing what he'd done and who his father was gave me the heebie-jeebies.

When was he going to take the bait? Maybe he wasn't, and I'd misinterpreted his stare. This called for more firepower. I convinced myself I wasn't going to look stupid and wiggled my arse to the music. Argh, who even was I? At least no one I knew could see me.

Laughing came from next to me.

I turned, breaking Ricky's stare. Charles. Of course I'd spoken too soon, even if it was in my head. I narrowed my eyes and gave him a dirty look—dirty as in cranky, not a look that supported my butt-shaking.

"Sorry. You don't look funny… well, not hilarious. I'm just not used to you behaving so… fun."

My mouth dropped open. I quickly shut it and held my drink up to my face to hide my mouth as I danced. "Thanks for nothing, shrimp."

"Hey, that's not fair! I didn't get a chance to grow up."

I was hitting new lows, offending a ghost. Who would've thought it possible? "If you don't want me to snap at you, don't start it. Sorry. I'm just stressed and doing my best. Okay?"

He smiled and play punched my arm, his small fist like a bag of ice cubes against my skin. "I was just joshing ya." If I could've screamed, I would have. *Deep breaths, Avery. He's just a kid… kind of.* I turned my brain from the path of "was he the same age as when he died, or was he as old as his total existence" because it wasn't time to have a mental breakdown. I had a job to do, a very important one.

"Now, I have work to do. Maybe you could hang out in that VIP area after I leave, see if they talk about the case. Okay?"

He bobbed his head up and down to the beat. "Yeah, sure." He glanced at the two ghosts still dancing. "I might go and have a dance until then. I don't know why I've never hung out at a nightclub before. This is fun!"

I shut my eyes for a moment. *God, give me strength.* I opened my eyes again. "See you later." I turned to face the VIP area and let out a little squeal. I slapped my hand over my heart at the surprise of a six-foot-five mountain of a man standing about a foot away, staring at me.

He leaned closer, probably so I could hear him over the music. "Your presence is requested in the VIP area. Follow me." Wow, no request, just an order. At least it was to the point. I resisted the strong urge to tell him where he could shove his order—I loved the person I was becoming—but this was what I wanted, so let him think I was pliable.

I smiled. "Lead the way."

He threaded through the crowd, which had thickened in the last ten minutes, and I bumped into several people as we went. Was it wrong of me to be pleased that I'd succeeded in attracting Ricky, even if he was a disgusting human? At least I'd proven Brad and my parents wrong. They always said I was lucky to have Brad and that I was punching above my weight by dating him. Brad always made a point to tell me that if we broke up, I'd be single forever because I was annoying and not very pretty. I once asked him why he was dating me if I was so terrible. He said he initially felt sorry for me, but when he got to know me, I grew on him.

What in heavens had I been thinking? I guessed I hadn't been, because no one using their brain would've copped that and stayed. My parents had cultivated that garden since I was born, so I supposed I was ripe for the picking when Brad came along.

I shook off the memories and climbed the few steps to the golden rope. The bouncer guy unclipped it and waved me through. Ricky came forward to meet me, bending his tallish frame so he could speak in my ear. Thankfully, it was so loud in here, he was oblivious to my thundering heart. He might not've killed Morris, but he killed Mia. I gripped my glass tighter.

"Hello, gorgeous. I'm Ricky. Welcome to my club."

Ha ha, yeah, "your" club. I resisted the urge to roll my eyes. "Thanks. I've heard good things. Great beats." The music was actually okay, so I wasn't totally lying.

"Only the best here." He eyed my drink. "What are you having? Can I get you another one?"

I swallowed and resisted the urge to text Finn. "Vodka and lemonade." Might as well let him think I was on the way to being a bit drunk. The more he underestimated me, the better.

He grinned. Evil piece of crap. If it wouldn't potentially get me killed, I would punch him in his smug face and scream at him. How dare he kill Mia. How dare he drug women. How. Dare. He. "Anything for you, beautiful. Also, is that an Australian accent I detect?"

"Yeah. I'm on holiday. Gap year between uni and work. Thought a solo trip around England would be fun before I got stuck into being an adult." I gave him a dopey smile. Argh, I was annoying myself with this act of impressed, naïve, too-trusting tourist. In this day and age, accepting a drink from a strange man was one of the riskier things you could do. My thoughts drifted to Everly—not that what happened to her was because of a drink… or a stranger. I forced the smile to stay on my face. Why were there so many predators out there?

He held his arm up, and a waitress appeared. Since when did they have waitresses at the average club? Oh, yeah, since the owners were thugs and expected everyone to be at their beck and call. She bent, and he spoke directly into her ear. I could only hear snatches of what he said, but it was obviously the drink order. She turned and forced her way through the crowd to the bar. Surely she wouldn't drug my drink. Unless he had something over on her or she was brainwashed. I was expecting he would be the one to spike it. *If* he spiked my drink this time. Although, what if I didn't accept a second drink? He'd probably take his chance while he had it.

I took a tiny sip of my drink—I'd make it last the longest time ever. It was time to get some information. Ignoring the nervous flip of my stomach, I leaned towards him. "So, how long have you had this club?"

He stroked the thick gold chain around his neck as if trying to remind me how fabulously rich and wonderful he was. "Two years. Pretty sick, huh?"

"Yeah, totally." I giggled. *Kill me now.* "Is this your only business, or are you amazing at other things?" Oops, I'd given him innuendo, which I hadn't meant to.

He licked his lips. "Yeah, baby. If you're lucky, you'll find out later." How was it that some men didn't know the difference between sexy and creepy?

My drink arrived, saving me from having to agree. I reached for it, but Ricky beat me to it. "I'll mind it for you. Make sure nothing happens to it." He winked. Behind him, the waitress's brow furrowed. Did she know about what he'd done and didn't like it? Hmm....

I touched his forearm. "Thank you! You sure know how to make a girl feel special." If only I could film him to keep an eye on him with my drink. The hairs on the back of my neck stood. Over Ricky's shoulder, I caught someone at the far end of the VIP area staring at me.

Angelo.

My heart skipped and thudded like a rock skidding over water. Had he made me? But how could he? He would have no idea who I was. Maybe he was just protective of who his son hooked up with. Being in his "business" would require a lot of weeding out of people to ensure his secrets stayed private. I would imagine they were wary of undercover cops as well.

I looked away from the father and back to the son. "So, what kinds of things do you do to keep this place running?" I was working up to asking questions about the bombing, but I had to tread carefully. This could take all night. And how long could I put off drinking that drink? *Argh*.

He waved his hand dismissively. "Not much. I have a team of people I order around, and I just *enjoy* the place." He ran his forefinger up and down my arm while staring into my eyes. I took another sip of drink to hide the cringe dying to screw my face up. If I shuddered now, the game was up.

"You're the man, Ricky. I don't think I've ever met anyone so successful. You make it look so easy."

His predatory grin was worse than the sharks' swimming in the waters back home. "I get what I want, baby. People like to please me. What can I say? I have the knack. You'll see." The last was said against my ear, his breath like a wraith's caress against my neck, causing goosebumps to crowd my skin.

It took everything in me to hide the panic and disgust. Angelo was still probably watching, and I wasn't going to give the game away. We needed information. Morris and his family deserved justice.

"Are you okay, Aves?" Charles appeared next to me, and I almost sighed in relief. He couldn't do anything, but it was comforting just having him there.

Mia stood next to him. "I'm watching your drink. I'll let you know if he puts anything in it."

I gave a subtle smile in recognition. I'd been watching the glass this whole time, and so far, he hadn't had a chance to slip anything into it. But even if the waitress had looked at him weirdly, I couldn't be sure she hadn't been forced to drug it.

I turned my subtle smile into something more suggestive as I gave this act everything I had. "Promises, Ricky. Promises."

"I'll show you a good time. Anything you want, baby. I can make it happen."

"I love a man of means who knows how to get things done." The words coming out of my mouth were D-grade-movie horrible. And they weren't the words I needed to say to get him to talk about the bombing. Not that I could be that obvious, but I wasn't getting anything at all. It felt like I was wasting time. "There's a man over there who keeps staring at us. Is that your bodyguard or something?" Stroke his ego while steering the conversation—*good one, Avery*.

I didn't care if Angelo knew we were talking about him. Because he was still focussed on us, and that was just weird. It would look unusual if I didn't say something.

Ricky turned to see who I was talking about. He looked at his father for a beat before turning back to me. He chuckled. "That's my dad. He's a bit overprotective about who I date. He only wants the best for me." The last was said with a sardonic sneer. Hmm, interesting.

"Of course he wants the best for his son. Are you an only child? I'm wondering if that makes it worse."

"No. I have a younger sister. While she's at Cambridge, I'm here holding down the fort. Dad wants me to take over the family business one day, but not for a long time. He's a control freak." His tone had a sharp edge to it.

At least I could speak from the heart in this moment. "Is he overly critical? Like, I hate my parents. They're always putting me down. Nothing I do is ever good enough. I couldn't wait to get away from them, and I couldn't imagine having to work for them. You poor thing." Giving sympathy to a murderer was not on my list of things I wanted to do today, but here we were.

"Yeah, he's difficult. He wants me to be just like him, but I'm not him. I'm me. He used to beat me when I was a kid. But when I turned sixteen, and I was as big as him, I hit back. He laughed and said that I was finally a man, and he hasn't touched me since, but he likes to remind me that he's the boss." He nuzzled his nose against my cheek, and I took a deep breath. "Whether he approves of you or not, I don't care. I like you."

"Ew, he's gross. Are you okay?" Charles's voice helped calm my hands, which were itching to push Ricky away. Poor Mia was paler than pale as she watched in horror. This must be bringing back nightmare memories of the night she died. How had the night become so complicated? Being undercover was nothing like I'd thought. And it was definitely nothing like interviewing someone as a journalist. I was emotionally wrought, and my nerves were electric currents building, crawling over my skin, waiting to short-circuit and blow up my system.

But I had to hold it in check.

Just a while longer.

Breathe, Avery. Just breathe.

There was an opportunity here, and it was time to take it. He'd fallen for my act. "Does he ever make you do anything you hate? My parents used to make me shoplift for them. Losers couldn't make enough money to feed us properly. Plus, my dad was a gambler." Those were lies; although with my parents, they were bad enough that it wasn't a stretch for it to be true.

"Sometimes." His hand found my waist, and he squeezed

gently. "And he has one of his bodyguards come with me and film it, to make sure I do exactly as he's said."

"And if you don't?"

His harsh laugh grazed my ear. "He might not hit me any more, but it doesn't mean his lapdogs don't. So I make sure I do what I'm told, even if I'd rather not." Was he not as evil as his father?

I reached up and caressed his cheek, about to say something comforting when Charles moved to my line of vision. "Avery, Finn is here. He's talking to some woman by the bar, but he's looking this way, and it's not his happy face." Nooooo. Not yet. I was so close to getting information. Hopefully I could count on him to be in journalist mode and leave me alone because he could see I was working. At least I hoped he would surmise I was working and not enjoying myself.

I blinked once at Charles so he knew I heard, and I caressed creepy Ricky's cheek again. I wasn't game to turn and look towards the bar—it might kill the moment, and I didn't want to do anything that would stop Ricky talking. "That's awful. I'm so sorry. Have you ever thought of going it alone? I bet you'd be amazing as the boss." A little flattery was usually the way to a man's heart… or other places. And since Ricky's dad wasn't dishing it out, he was probably hungry for it. I should thank Angelo for making this easier than it could've been.

"Not only gorgeous but smart too. I have thought about it, but I need to plan it carefully. Maybe in a few years. Besides, Dad reckons he'll hand the business to me when he's had enough. It usually works like that… in our world. But if I get jack of working for him before then, definitely."

I was about to ask another question, but Angelo appeared at his son's side, Jack a menacing bodyguard presence behind him. Angelo didn't bother smiling but gave me a nod. "Who's this, son?"

Ricky stiffened momentarily before relaxing. This guy had daddy issues. From what he'd said so far, it was as if he wasn't fully on board with everything his father did or made him do. But he couldn't be too angelic—Mia had proof he'd drugged her. "This is my new friend…." He jerked his head around to look at my face. "I don't think I caught it."

"Annabelle. Lovely to meet you, Ricky's dad." I smiled as if everything was hunky dory and held out my hand.

Angelo's stern expression didn't change, but I caught a twitch of one eye. He clamped thick fingers over mine and squeezed hard enough to be just the wrong side of uncomfortable. I smiled as if it didn't bother me. "Is that so." His tone suggested it wasn't a question.

He released my now-sweating hand. Did he suspect I wasn't who I said I was? But how? He couldn't know who I was. I hadn't questioned anyone in his circle, and Bellamy was the only one who knew what I was up to, so it couldn't be a leak from the police.

Maybe I was just being paranoid.

I shook off the whisps of dread settling on my shoulders like cobwebs in a haunted-house carnival ride.

Angelo gave his son a stilted nod, then went back to his dark corner. Jack smirked at me before following his boss. What was that about?

Charles's eyes widened. "Ricky just put something in your drink from a small vial. While you were looking at his dad." Mia growled and tried to hit the glass, but her hand went straight through.

"Are you okay?" Ricky asked.

"Ah, yeah, of course. Um… your dad's intense. I totally get

it now." Playing the clueless babe was getting old. I was ready to go home, but I still had nothing on Morris's murder.

"He is. He Who Must be Obeyed." Anger tightened his jaw. Getting himself under control, he relaxed his features. He held up the drink he'd gotten me. "Here. Drink this before it gets warm. Besides, I'm sick of holding it." He laughed.

"But I still haven't finished mine." I held up my half-empty glass.

He took it. "It's warm. Here." He put the tainted vessel in my hand. Well, hadn't I made that easy? The urge to roll my eyes at myself was strong. *Note to self: don't go undercover ever again.*

"Mmm, it is cooler. Thanks."

"Are you going to try and drop it?" Mia frowned.

I blinked once, hoping she got the yes in it. Hmm… that could be a great way to communicate with ghosts when humans were around. I'd tell Charles that later. It was about time we had a secret code. Dumb me was sometimes slow on the uptake.

Ricky stared at me. "Are you going to drink it? I'll be sad if you don't." Yeah, real sad that you can't drug and probably rape me. Jesus. And why did his dad want him doing those things? It hit me that his dad had encouraged him. That look he gave Ricky before he walked off must have been a prompt. Did he record the attacks and put them on the dark web or something?

Acid percolated in my stomach, stripping any semblance of positivity. Anger, painful and scolding, rose through my body.

"Avery, don't. Whatever you're thinking, calm down." Charles, ever the voice of reason. I looked at him—Ricky would think I was looking at the people at the next high-top over.

"Are you okay? Don't like being told what to do, hey? Are you one of those independent girls?" He sniggered as if it was funny. *Yeah, nah.*

"Sorry, flashback to my parents ordering me to do things I didn't want to. I'm so glad I left and became my own person." Could he tell I was having a dig?

He slid his forefinger down my cheek. "I think you should drink the drink I so thoughtfully got for you. You want to get to know me better, don't you? Surely you can let me be a gentleman and provide what you need." Was he talking about the drink or something else? Whatever it was, he was icky as hell. And I was getting nowhere.

How was I going to drop it without being obvious? I glanced at Angelo. Yep, he was focussed on us with the intensity of a lion sizing up a gazelle. Tensed. Waiting. If he had a tail, it would be twitching. His mouth was probably watering.

I looked at the glass, at the condensation slipping down it. Cool to the touch, it could cool all of me permanently like poor Mia.

What would Angelo do if I dropped it?

I glanced across the room. I needed to see Finn and get some reassurance. He was talking to three new women now, but his eyes met mine across the room, and he didn't look happy. He raised his brows as if to say, can we go now?

I wished.

"Before I have my drink, can I just get a selfie with you? I reckon it will be great for my Insta. Me with a hot guy at a banging club."

"How can I say no to a beautiful girl?" Argh with the *girl*. I was pretty sure I wasn't ten years old.

"Thanks." As I went to put my glass on the table, I purposefully misjudged the height and caught the bottom quarter of the glass on the edge. It slammed onto the table and rolled to the side, spilling tainted liquid everywhere. "Oh my God, I'm so sorry!" I turned my face to his, making sure he could see how horrified I was. *Oops*.

"Nice work!" Mia grinned. "Take that, you bastard." I had to hold in the smile at her enthusiasm. It wasn't often that I had a cheer squad standing by.

"Annabelle, you clumsy bitch." He swore again, and Angelo, who I could see out of the corner of my eye, pinched his lips together, then said something to Jack.

Yep, I was in trouble. But surely not as much as if I was unconscious and wholly at their mercy. I also doubted I was getting any information. Tonight was a bust… well, except for being able to help the police solve Mia's murder.

Maybe it was time to leave. As much as it pained me, my gut was screaming that it was time to go. Something wasn't right. "Wow, you're not as nice as I thought. I'm leaving."

He grabbed my upper arm, dug his fingers into my soft skin, and pushed his face into mine so our noses were almost touching. "You don't go until I say so."

Mia and Charles gaped, sparks of panic lighting their eyes. Charles looked around at Finn, but there was no way he was going to be able to get his attention. I didn't know how much that mattered because Finn chose that moment to glance over. I gave him a wide-eyed look.

I could go all hapkido on Ricky, but Angelo's goon had managed to make it to us already, and there was no way I could take him on—he was twice my size and likely had way more experience beating people up, not to mention he'd been in the army. The only thing I had now was the element of surprise, and I'd save it for the perfect moment.

"Let go. I'm leaving."

"But, Avery, what if he targets someone else?" Mia nervously licked her lips. I shook my head. I'd have to get the information to Bellamy ASAP, but there was nothing else I could do here tonight except get hurt.

Blonde chest hairs curling over the edges of his black shirt, the shave-headed hulk gave a nod to Ricky. "I've got this." His voice was calm and cold, like thin ice on a lake, waiting to crack and swallow its victim. I couldn't hear my hammering heart over the pounding music, but I felt it reverberating against my ribs.

I wrenched my arm from Ricky's grip and stood tall. I gave the thug a hard look. "Don't touch me. I'm leaving."

Before he could answer, I turned and pushed through the oblivious VIP patrons to the rope. The bouncer at the rope looked at the monstrous shadow at my back before he unclasped it to let me through.

Each fine hair on my nape jumped into an exclamation mark. I was heading for the front door, but the thick crowd impeded my progress, and before I reached the halfway mark, my minder laid a mammoth hand on my shoulder. I'd lost sight of Finn now that I was at ground level and there were too many taller people blocking my view. Surely Jack wasn't going to do anything to me. I'd managed not to get drugged. That didn't require punishment, did it?

I stopped and pushed back, but he added another hand to my other shoulder and pushed. His warning tone wasn't shouted, but it was nonetheless effective close to my ear. "Keep walking."

I ignored my somersaulting stomach. "Or what? Where are you taking me?" If he got me in a private room somewhere, anything could happen. I had to do whatever it took to stay in public or leave. And again, what the hell was going on? I craned my neck, looking for Finn.

One of Jack's hands came off my shoulder, and before I could say get lost, a silver blade appeared in his hand, pointing at my waist. The coloured strobe lights reflected off its surface, a frenzied kaleidoscope that resembled my panicked thoughts. I swallowed. What the hell? This was nuts. He pushed me towards the back of the club and the toilets.

God, where was Finn?

"It'll be okay, Avery. I'll help." Charles floated alongside us, disappearing into people before popping out again. I didn't say a word to question how he thought he could get me out of this. He was trying to make me feel better, and it wasn't working. There was nothing he could do.

Maybe I could keep Jack talking. "Why are you doing this? Isn't anyone allowed to reject Ricky?"

We were almost at the toilets, but instead of going in them, there was another door at the end of the short hallway. The music still echoed off the walls, but it was a bit quieter. "We don't take kindly to journalists being up in our business, Avery Winters."

Breath rushed into my lungs, scraping my throat and making me cough.

Frilled-neck lizards. I was totally scre—

"I'll get Bellamy!" Charles disappeared. It wasn't logical because he couldn't help me if he stayed, but my stomach dropped at his absence. I tried not to think about the fact that he had no way of alerting the sergeant. My only hope was Finn, but the man mountain held me fast—I couldn't turn and see if he was coming. At least they didn't know I was here with Finn… did they?

And how did they know who I was?

How?

Mia hadn't left my side, but she said nothing, just stared, her big eyes set in a pale face devoid of hope. Great, even she thought I was a goner. Who could blame her, though? She'd died in this club. No one had been here to save her. In a room full of people, I'd never felt so alone.

Looked like if I wanted to survive, it was up to me. I could do this.

"I'm surprised you guys are smart enough to know who I am." I wanted to know how they knew. Maybe he'd tell me before I managed to get away.

Yeah, hold onto that hope, Avery.

His grin revealed a missing canine. "We're smarter than you."

"I doubt that. You just paid off the right person. You know if you hurt me, the police will be all over you. They know I'm here."

"Yeah, right. As if the police care what some two-bit journalist is doing."

I smirked. "If you say so."

His eyes tightened at the corners. He raised the knife between us, settling the point at my ribs, near my heart. Showing fear now would be a bad idea, but it was hard keeping it from my face. My palms sweated. Maybe my idea to get him talking wasn't such a good one. "You're a dead woman, and no one will come looking for you because they don't know where you are." At least that wasn't the case, but even if they knew where to look, dead was dead. Although, should that worry me so much when there was life afterwards? Except would I hang around, go up, or go down?

I wasn't ready to die, dammit! And we were so close to solving Everly's case. I couldn't die and leave it undone. "So, if

I'm so dispensable and you're going to kill me no matter what, who told you about me? That's the least you can do before you end my life. Why did you kill Morris?"

"I didn't kill him, well, not directly." His gap flashed again as he smiled. "But let that serve as a lesson to nosy journalists. We don't appreciate anyone poking into our business. Now shut up." He pressed the knifepoint hard enough to make a tiny hole in my shirt, but he didn't draw blood. "Don't move." He turned slightly away from me—keeping me in his peripheral vision—put his other hand in his jeans pocket and pulled out a key.

I wasn't going to get another chance. If he wanted to kill me, he would have to stab me in front of the whole club. Stuff him.

As he reached for the lock, I pivoted side-on to him, brought the knee of my back leg to my chest, and slammed a side kick to his knee, breaking it easily. In hapkido classes, it was a no-no to kick anyone in the knee in any way, shape, or form. Our instructors always said it was vulnerable. And yes, today I could vouch from experience that it was.

He screamed—his voice blending with the pounding music—and went down, gripping his knee, the knife landing on the ground. Without thinking, I picked it up, turned, and ran.

"Faster, Avery! Faster!" Mia didn't have to tell me twice.

Unfortunately, it was like pushing against an incoming tide, and my progress was slow, especially in these heels. I was likely to break my own neck at speed.

My heart raced as I shoved through the crowd. A couple of people swore at me when I spilled their drinks, but I ignored them.

I still couldn't see Finn. Did they know he was with me? God, I hoped not.

I put the knife in my bag as I brushed against one person after another, then grabbed my phone. I put it next to my mouth. "Hey, Siri, call Sergeant Bellamy." I'd call 999, but it would take too long to explain, and they might not take me seriously. Bellamy would have the troops mustered ASAP, no questions asked.

A hand grabbed my forearm. I spun around, ready to drop my phone and grab the knife.

It was Finn. Thank God.

He took one look at the horror on my face, and his eyebrows shot up. "What happened?"

"We need to get out of here. Now! They know who I am. They're trying to kill me." Wow, that sounded dramatic, but I didn't have time. I put my phone to my ear and headed for the door.

"Winters?"

"Sergeant. I need help. Now!" I quickly shouted what had happened, hoping he could hear me over the background cacophony.

"I'll have officers there soon. Get out of there now. Come straight to the station. I'll be here."

"Okay. Bye." I didn't bother telling him I was doing my best to escape. What, did he think I was finishing a cocktail before I left?

Finn had heard what I shouted at the sergeant, and now he was holding my hand and pulling me along, barging his bigger frame through everyone. His firm, warm grip reassured me.

As we burst into the freezing night, Mia called from the doorway, "Don't forget me, Avery. Please."

I glanced back at her and gave her a nod. One of the two guys on the door held his hand to his ear and frowned, then looked our way.

Bloody hell.

I picked up my pace, careful not to slip in my ridiculous boots, icy air knifing through my throat. There was Daisy, thank God. He pressed the button and unlocked her as we reached her, the flashing blinkers a beacon of safety.

We jumped in, and he locked the doors. I stared out the back window as he started the car. A thump landed on Finn's window. My heart almost shot out of my mouth.

One of the bouncers punched Finn's window again, but the glass held fast. That was going to hurt him tomorrow—hopefully, the goon had broken his knuckles.

"Drive, Finn!" Okay, so I was stating the obvious.

He pulled into the street, his breathing heavy. He glanced at me before staring at the dark street as he accelerated. "What the hell just happened?"

I pulled the knife from my bag and held it up. "This is theirs. They tried to kill me. They knew who I was."

He paled. "How?"

My voice shook with the adrenaline comedown. "That's what I plan on finding out."

CHAPTER 19

By the time Finn and I arrived at Cramptonbury Police Station, the adrenaline had worn off, and I was exhausted but wired. Every time I thought about what they tried to do to me and what they'd done to Mia—and probably many other women—the anger returned anew. Finn parked the car and looked at me. "That's the eighth agro face you've pulled since we left the club. Are you okay?"

I cocked my head to the side. "What do you think?"

"You're angry?"

"Volcanically."

"That's… a lot."

"Yes."

He licked his lips. "So, this would be a bad time to lecture you on keeping out of trouble?" I raised one brow and gave him my best warning look. He grinned. "At least you're safe now. Come on. You can explain to Bellamy."

I hadn't said much on the drive home, and he hadn't

pushed. He'd glanced worriedly at me a few times, but he probably figured I'd talk when I was ready. "Okay."

Winter slapped my face as I hurried to the building. My feet ached—these boots weren't exactly made for running, or walking for that matter. And what a waste of time my "disguise" had been. I could have turned up in my work clothes and sensible shoes and achieved the same outcome. In fact, the wig was itchy, so I ripped it and the hairnet off.

"Hello, Davis." Finn smiled at the redheaded constable behind the desk.

"Hiya, Finnegan. The Sergeant said to send you through as soon as you got here." He gave me a nod and smile, and I smiled back.

The door buzzed. Finn opened it for me, letting me go through first. A reminder of his sweetness. Some woman would be very lucky one day. He cared about his friends, so as much as he wanted to stay a bachelor, as soon as he found his one, he'd treat her right.

"Avery, you're okay!" Charles floated towards me as I navigated the hallway. I gave him a subtle nod and pulled a face to try and say, *Hello, Finn is behind me. Der.* He'd have to wait until we were in Bellamy's office to find out what happened. "I'm sorry I couldn't help. I tried. I really did."

I mouthed, "I know," and gave him a sympathetic look. I couldn't imagine how frustrating it was for him—wanting to make a difference and not being able to do a damned thing was hard enough when people could see you. Imagine everyone ignoring you because, to them, you didn't exist. I blinked my damp eyes.

The open-plan office area was empty. Nights were normally a busy time with stabbings and drunken fights. How many officers had Bellamy sent to the club? Had they found anything? Career criminals were good at evading law enforcement, well, the ones who weren't in jail, and Angelo was out. His son had never done a stint, but he deserved to spend life in there, as did Angelo, as well as that piece of possum poo, Jack.

Bellamy's door was open. As soon as he saw me, he jumped to his feet and came around the table, looking me up and down. "Come in. Are you okay, Winters?"

I looked down at myself, relieved there was no blood, and my boot had survived the knee kicking. A smile broke through my stress. How had I forgotten how I'd gotten away? *Nice one, Avery. Thanks, hapkido.*

Finn frowned. "What are you smiling about?" He looked at Bellamy. "She might be in shock."

I grinned. "I'm not in shock. I was reminiscing. I only got away because I broke Angelo's Neanderthal's knee with a side kick. You should've seen it break. He dropped faster than a flaming bag of poo."

Bellamy's bushy eyebrows rose slowly. "What?"

"Ah… you know. When someone does a knock and run on your door, and they leave a paper bag of poo on fire. Well, they want the person to tread on it to put it out, but some people pick it up to throw it, and when they realise what it is, they, ah, drop it." I shrugged at their stunned looks. "It must be an Aussie thing. Moving right along…."

"You Aussies are something else." I didn't think Finn meant that as a compliment.

Bellamy cleared his throat. "I think you should begin at the beginning. Do you want a cup of something warm before you start?"

"No thanks. I probably won't sleep as it is."

Finn sat on one of the guest chairs. "Hot chocolate won't keep you awake."

I looked at Bellamy. "Is that an option?"

"This isn't a bloomin' café." He shook his head. "Just sit, and I'll take your statement. This is a police matter now."

"Even though I was undercover?"

"You're a contractor, and I didn't fill out any paperwork. This was a fishing expedition. You can state that you're a journalist investigating a crime for an article and because you knew the victims. There will be far less paperwork." He sat behind his desk and rubbed his forehead. "That's the last time you do anything undercover. I didn't see it all going so wrong. We'll stick to you helping with—" He stopped and stared at Finn. Yikes—he'd almost spilled our secret.

I froze, waiting for Finn's reaction.

"...information gathered the usual way."

I let my breath out slowly and quietly—no need to make it sound suspicious. Finn would be wondering why I was so relieved. The man in question leaned forward. "How could you not see it all going wrong? Lightning is a disaster magnet." He turned to me. "No offence."

"Some taken." I pulled a silly face.

"Okay, you two. Let's concentrate." Bellamy's desk phone rang. He huffed, then answered. "Bellamy speaking." He listened for a while. "Are you sure...? Yes.... Okay.... Thanks. Bye." He hung up and focussed on me. "Angelo and his cronies were MIA when the police got there, but they're collecting all video evidence from the security cameras. Hopefully they haven't had the wherewithal or time to delete anything. We can also hope the security system hasn't been disabled."

"You might want to let them know to get as much video as possible... from as far back as they can."

Finn frowned. "Why, because of drug deals?"

"No." I couldn't say anything about Mia in front of Finn, which was irritating, but I could work around it. "They tried to drug me."

Finn's mouth fell open before twisting in anger. He swore… quite a few times until Bellamy intervened. "It's okay, lad. We'll get them." The sergeant nodded at me to continue.

"I already had a drink, and Ricky insisted on getting me another one, and then he kept bugging me to drink it. Either he or Angelo dropped it in. I didn't have my eye on it the whole time." I didn't want to give too many specifics in case the video showed I hadn't seen. Who knew what Finn would be privy to now that he'd become involved? I could elaborate to Bellamy later. "When I 'accidentally'"—I made air quotes—"spilled it, the drama started. I argued with Ricky, and then Angelo's thug—who happens to be Jack Noonan—came and escorted me away from the VIP area. He pulled a knife on me, threatened me, and tried to get me in a locked room near the toilets. As soon as I saw an opportunity, I kicked his knee, breaking it. He told me he knew I was Avery Winters, journalist." I placed Jack's knife on Bellamy's desk and went over everything else that happened until Finn and I were safely driving away. I also told Bellamy about my conversation with Ricky, and everything else Jack said. "I haven't got concrete evidence they were involved in Morris's murder, but Jack hinted at being involved."

Bellamy stopped writing everything, his pen poised above the paper for more. "But you didn't see them drop anything into your drink?"

I gave him a look, hoping he'd understand that someone… some ghost… had seen. "Not me. No."

"But you think someone might have seen?" Finn asked.

"Yes, or the video security footage. They were just acting

too sus. And if they did it to me, they've likely done it to countless other women. That's why I think you need to get as much security video as possible." I pulled my phone out of my bag. "Hang on a sec." I googled Mia's drugging—hopefully there'd been an article. Bingo! "See this. I did some research on the club before I went, and this article came up." I read it aloud. It described Mia's death and that she'd tested positive for a date-rape drug. It also mentioned that the video footage had been conveniently missing. As soon as she'd died, they would've deleted it. They'd had time, and it wasn't something they could hide—someone collapsing and dying there. They were probably counting on me being too scared to tell anyone… maybe. Or maybe they were staking my house out right now, waiting for me to come home so they could finish the job.

Finn's adorable forehead wrinkled. Yes, I was pathetic. "What's wrong?"

"What if they're waiting for me at home? They'd want to shut me up. It's not like I'm a normal person. I'm a journalist. I live for exposing the truth."

Finn swore again. He was doing a lot of that tonight.

Bellamy's calm, protective police face was standing strong. "I was going to say…. I don't think you should stay there until we get this sorted."

I shook my head. This had spiralled fast. "Right. But where am I supposed to stay? And is Finn safe? If they saw him running away with me, they'd be able to find out who he is pretty quickly."

"We have a couple of bunks here. You can stay here tonight. Tomorrow morning, we'll figure something else out. I'll get a couple of officers to take you home to get some essentials and shower, etcetera. Maybe you can come and stay with me and Lynda." He chuckled. "It won't be Finn's first time."

Bellamy was Finn's dad's best mate. He'd probably stayed there a few times over the years.

Finn smiled. "I remember staying with you and Aunty Lynda when dad couldn't take time off work and Mum was in hospital with Hannah. Those were good times… except that Hannah had her appendix out."

"Yes, well, don't expect me to play Monopoly this time or read you a bedtime story." Bellamy gave him a sweet, close-mouthed smile.

"Can I say how disappointed I am?" Finn laughed.

Their cheer was infectious, and I relaxed a bit. There was trouble coming, but they had my back. For the thousandth time, I appreciated how lucky I was to have found these people. Unfortunately, the complication with Angelo and co. might hinder the speed at which I tried to nail Everly's murderer. How restricted would my movement be? They didn't have resources for police to follow me everywhere. Maybe it would be better to sleep and work from the station until this was all over, however impractical it was, and forget staying at the sergeant's house. I didn't want to endanger his wife. "So, what happens now?"

"For a start, I'll put this into evidence and have it dusted for prints." He opened his drawer, took out a plastic bag, put a rubber glove on, and put the knife into the bag. He then spent half an hour outlining everything. Life until we caught Angelo, Jack, and Ricky was going to be difficult. Surely there was enough evidence to put Jack away, but as for Angelo and Ricky…. Unless Jack or the video from the club gave us anything, they would be freer than a kilt-wearing Scotsman's nether regions. I just hoped it would be over by Christmas. If not, had I jeopardised Finn's Christmas with his family?

The answer to that was probably yes. He was right—I was

a disaster magnet. How long would it be until Finn decided he was done with me, even as a friend? I'd miss him when he'd had enough, and I'd have no one to blame but myself. If that wasn't incentive to hurry up and nail Angelo, nothing was.

The red and blue lights on Bellamy's small Christmas tree in the corner of his office reflected off Finn's face as I struggled with my guilt. There was only one way to feel better, and that was to solve Morris's murder once and for all and put Angelo, Jack, and Ricky in jail for all the women they'd hurt.

If anyone could do it, I could. A small voice told me I was delusional, but I wasn't listening. It was Christmastime, a time of miracles, which was great because I was going to need one.

CHAPTER 20

After spending the night trying to ignore the fact that Finn was sleeping in a bunk above me and appreciating that he didn't snore, I was exhausted. Having the night's events running around my head hadn't helped me sleep. It had sunk in how close I'd been to being beaten or killed. If I hadn't known martial arts and been a person who was blessed not to freeze in dangerous situations, I would've ended up in that room and whatever fate that led to.

So, it was with about two hours' sleep that I'd accompanied Finn and two police officers to my house to shower and grab my belongings. Despite arguing with Bellamy, we were going to his place. Regardless of the busy time of year, he was stationing two officers outside his house, and Julian was happy for us not to do any person-to-person interviews. Both my interviews today were okay to swap to phone calls, and they would send me photos to use in the articles.

And so it was that at two in the afternoon, I was sitting at Bellamy's dining table in his 1900s stone cottage, typing up one of the interviews. Of course it was for someone normal, and going to their house would've probably been a pleasant experience. Finn sat opposite, working on his own stuff. Lynda Bellamy was out shopping with her sister, but I'd met her earlier, and she was the sweetest woman, all five foot two of her. She had a big personality, though, and I could've sworn she was taller than me when she laughed—which she did frequently. She'd reassured us that she didn't mind having us there. I'd have to get her a big present when it was time to go.

Zeus had come along, too, and he sat curled in my lap as I worked. This was bliss. I soaked in the feeling while trying not to focus on the fact that my time with him was running out.

I was putting the finishing touches on my piece when my phone rang. Bellamy's name flashed on the screen. "Hey, Sergeant. What's up?"

"I wanted you to know that Patel's been through all the footage from the past week, and he's found two instances of Ricky spiking women's drinks."

"Oh my god, that's fantastic!" Finn looked at me over his laptop screen and raised his brows in question. I held up a finger for just a minute. I'd put Bellamy on speaker, but he might mention Mia—I'd managed five minutes alone with him when Finn had gone to the toilet.

"Not so fast."

"What?"

"We couldn't see anyone put anything in your drink. There were bodies in the way, and it was dark. We were lucky to find the two instances we did. We haven't had time to look at the footage around the time Mia was killed. It means that we have further investigations to carry out before we can tie Ricky or his father to any wrongdoing. We don't even know who those women are. Patel's calling around the other stations and hospitals in that area to see if any reports were made or ambulances called. This might take a while by the time we've gone through weeks of footage."

"And what about Jack Noonan?"

I could hear the smile in his voice. "It wasn't easy to see the knife when he was taking you through the club, but the lighting near the toilets was better, and there was a camera just there, so it's clear that he's holding a knife to your chest, and the fingerprints on the knife are a match. Nice kick, by the way. He was on the ground for at least five minutes until his mates came to help him." Yep, that was a chuckle I heard down the phone. "They took him to the local hospital, and they kept him in. He's just come out of surgery. I'm going up to see him now. We have enough to arrest him, at least."

I couldn't help but smile. *Sucked in*! "It's going to be harder to nail Angelo and Ricky after that, though. They'll be on high alert."

"Not necessarily. Because of what happened to you and the fact we have him on camera, we can confiscate his phone, and all their computers. If they've been sloppy or arrogant, there could be more evidence on there of other crimes, including Morris's murder and the person who warned them about you. I'm keeping it quiet around here in case they have someone on the inside."

"Thanks for everything, Sergeant. Can you let me know how you go? It's hard being stuck here and not out there finding things out… not that I don't appreciate you keeping me safe." He'd gone above and beyond for me and Finn.

"Not a problem, Winters. I'll call you later."

"Bye."

He hung up. Finn had been staring at me the whole time,

obviously curious, so I told him the latest. "That's good news. We might not be here for long."

"Hmm, maybe." Things had a way of becoming complicated, and if anyone knew how to play the system, it was mafia-type criminals. They stuck together, too—it was either that or be murdered. I hoped his phone had plenty of incriminating evidence because there was no way he'd talk. I'd also made a massive enemy. Not only had I thwarted his plans for me, I'd also hurt him badly, and I was just a little nothing of a woman. I was sure he was fuming just for that fact. He would never live it down with his dodgy peers. Funnily enough, that made me smile again. *He-he-he.*

"You're remembering kicking him again, aren't you?"

I giggled. "You betcha. It was one of the most satisfying moments of my life."

"Remind me never to get on your bad side."

"Don't try and kill me, and we won't have a problem."

He cocked his pointer finger at me and winked. "Understood."

After the madness of everything that had happened and then trying to work, I'd forgotten to stress about how they'd found out who I was. And even if they'd known I was a journalist, how did they know I was looking into Morris's murder? Why had they been so afraid of me? Which was the conclusion I'd come to—if I was harmless, they would've just told me nothing and let me go. Had someone asked them to hurt me? My eyes popped wide as that idea sank in.

Finn frowned. "What's wrong?"

"Why were they so heavy-handed with me? And who told them who I was... in advance. Why was I on their radar? Bellamy mentioned on the phone that he wanted to make sure there were no leaks at the station, but if not from there, from where? It wasn't even as if I had concrete evidence they were involved with Morris's murder. I still don't." I knew everyone at Cramptonbury Station, and I couldn't believe any of them were in league with Angelo.

"You think someone outside of their organisation wants you out of the way for their own reasons?"

"Yes, maybe. I mean, I don't know why or who, but maybe it has nothing to do with Morris's case?"

Finn's expression screamed unconvinced. "Bit of a coincidence, though. I mean, who else have you peed off lately?"

I shook my head. "No one that I can think of."

"What articles have you done in the past few weeks?"

I went through all the inane and torturous stories I'd covered. "Nothing." And all the murder cases I'd worked on had been solved and closed. No one had threatened me from jail. David's article came to mind. "There's only one outstanding thing I've done anything about, and that isn't even my case. It's a story being covered by another journalist. I went to see him the other day to tell him he didn't have all the information."

Finn's eyebrow rose. "You're butting into another journalist's case? How did he take it?"

I pondered that. "Well, he wasn't super happy because the article was due, and if my information checked out, he was going to have to pull the story and change it, and it was at a critical time in his career. But he wasn't angry with me. Surely that's not enough to want to have someone killed. It can't be." I needed to speak to Morris. I stood and handed Zeus across the table to Finn. "I need to go to the loo."

"You have my permission." He smirked.

"Ha ha, thanks, Vinegar. Thank goodness I don't need to sit here and wet myself." I rolled my eyes.

"Too far, woman. Too far." He settled Zeus in his lap, my adorable kitty shutting his eyes again. That cat was so chill. The vet taking him was so lucky to be getting such a special cat. Zeus was one in a million.

The family bathroom was in a hallway near three bedrooms, while Bellamy's bedroom and en suite were at the other end of the home. Thankfully, the bathroom was nowhere near the dining room, so Finn wouldn't hear me talking to Morris. I shut the door, sat on the edge of the bath, and whispered, "Morris. Hello, Morris? I'm inviting you into Bellamy's home." I'd never tried inviting a ghost into someone else's house, so I wasn't sure it was possible. I might have to go into the backyard if this didn't work. I spoke in a normal voice in case he couldn't hear me. Yes, that sounded a tad unhinged, even in my own head. "Morris, can you come here, please?"

He materialised in front of me. "What's up? Have you got news?"

I stood and sighed in relief. If I was in here too long, Finn would wonder if I fell in and got stuck. I whispered everything that had happened last night and reminded him about going to see David. "Do you think David wants me dead?"

His chin pulled back into his neck like a surprised chicken. "No! That's absurd. How did you get from telling him his story needed more vetting to attempted murder? It's not like you threatened to tell his boss.... Did you?"

"Of course not. But even Duncan has issues with him."

"What are you talking about?"

I told him what I'd overheard when I was at Change Media. "He called him a con man." Morris stared at nothing for a bit, processing. He pulled his earlobe and looked at me. "Look, even if you think I'm out of line, can you please go and spy on David, see if he has any connection to Angelo?"

His lips pressed together as he aimed a scowl my way. Finally, his face relaxed into thoughtfulness. "I still can't believe David tried to hurt you, which is why I'll do it. I'll be back when I've confirmed things. I think I have an idea. Will you be here?"

"Yes. Until all this is sorted, Bellamy isn't letting us leave, and since it's all my fault, I don't dare go against his orders. If something happens to me, he'll never forgive himself, even if it's my own dumb fault." Despite being a "disaster magnet," as Finn so lovingly put it, there was a line I wouldn't cross. Not only had I put Finn in danger, but Bellamy and his wife were sticking their necks out for me.

"Okay. I'll be back as soon as I know something. Bye." He disappeared. What had he meant by "I have an idea?" What idea was there to have? He just had to spy on David for a while, then return.

I flushed the toilet and washed my hands—just in case Finn was listening—before returning to the dining room. Finn was visible through the large opening to the kitchen. Two cups with teabags hanging over the edges sat on the countertop, and he was standing next to an almost-boiling kettle. "White and one, right?" he asked.

"Yes. Thanks." I sat and leaned back in the chair. If Morris couldn't confirm it was David or confirmed it wasn't him, we were back to the beginning. What had I missed?

The kettle button popped, disconnecting the power, and the hissing echo of heating water faded. Finn poured the water, waited for it to steep, and added milk. He placed mine on the table and sat in his seat, curling his hands around his mug. "You okay? You look a bit… put out."

I scrunched my nose. "I wouldn't say put out, but I'm frustrated. Are we missing something? I just don't get why I'm on Angelo's radar."

"Maybe they think you're after them for their other crimes?"

"But how would they know my name? That would be a massive coincidence. Not to mention, if they hate me for possibly investigating them, surely many other journalists would be on their hit list." I pressed my lips together. "This has to be connected to Morris somehow. Maybe someone I spoke to warned them I was looking into it?" There was that small-time crim, Danny, but why would he tell them? He was legit now… supposedly—unless he owed them a favour or something.

"Sorry I can't help. You really can't think of anyone other than that other journalist?"

"Nope."

Finn's phone rang. He saw the number on the screen and gave me an "I have no idea who it is" look. "Hello, Finnegan Walsh speaking." He listened to the person on the other end, his expression making me think of a cat that's just seen a bird. "Can you tell me now?" The voice wasn't loud enough for me to hear what was being said, but I could tell it was a woman. "Okay, then. Are you willing to meet me at Cramptonbury Police Station?"

His gaze locked with mine, but I had no idea what was going on. Whatever it was, was important, and I was dying to know.

"Thank you so much, Shelly. I'll see you there soon. Bye." Before explaining anything to me, he hung up and then called someone else. "Sergeant, I have a favour to ask. I've just received a call from a woman named Shelly. She said she's got information that will blow Morris's case wide open. She's agreed to meet me at your station soon. She'll only talk to me, apparently, but I thought it would be best if we met there so you didn't have to get one of your men to give me an escort." He listened for a bit and nodded. "Okay. Great. Thanks, Sergeant. See you soon. Bye."

"Well, what happened?" At this point, I didn't care who solved this case. If that Shelly woman had information that would put Angelo and his crew away, that would be extremely helpful—assuming that's who'd killed Morris. If it was someone else, at least we'd know for sure.

"As you heard, that was a woman called Shelly. She has information on who killed Morris, but she won't talk to anyone except me. She sounded scared. I'm just glad she's agreed to meet at the station." He ran a hand through his hair. "I'm sorry it's me who's going. I have no idea why she wants to talk to me and not you."

"Maybe she knows another one of your contacts? Or she might've read your work and thought you would be trustworthy and safe. I don't mind. I just want this done. So many people need closure, Julian included. Go find out. Make sure you let me know ASAP. With a bit of luck, it was Angelo, and the police can go lock him and his cronies up."

"Will you be okay here by yourself?"

"Of course. The police are outside. I'm good." I smiled. I was a tad scared, but I was scared with him here, too, worried he'd be hurt if we were attacked. I had a feeling that he wasn't as much of a target as I was, so maybe he'd be safer if he wasn't anywhere near me. At least, that's what I hoped.

"Call me if you get worried." He was such a sweetheart.

"Will do, but I'll be fine. I have stuff to keep me busy, and it's not like I'll be alone." I nodded at Zeus, who was curled up on the table next to my laptop.

"Okay. Good." He grabbed his laptop bag, packed it, collected his keys, and headed for the hallway and front door. "Stay safe."

"You too." I resisted the urge to hug him. What if something happened to him on the way and this was the last time I saw him? *Stop, Avery! Everyone is going to be fine.*

I followed him down the hall. The front door clicked shut behind him, and I made sure it was locked properly before sitting at the dining table again, then remembered my tea and got up. It was lukewarm, so I heated it in the microwave. Of course, I overheated it to scalding, and now I had to wait for it to cool a bit. *Sigh.* I took it back to the table and sat at my laptop.

It was my phone's turn to ring. There was no number, but I answered it because so many people hid their numbers these days, and it could easily be someone I was trying to tee up for an interview. "Hello, Avery speaking."

"Avery, I'm so glad you answered. It's Duncan."

"I thought I recognised the voice. How are you?" I tried not to feel guilty that I didn't have any firm answers as to who killed Morris. I wasn't willing to say anything—especially to another journalist—before I had total proof.

"I'm okay. Battling along. I was just wondering if I could come and have a chat. If this is a bad time, I can see you another day, but there's some sensitive information I have that I've just come across that I don't want to say over the phone. You never know who's listening."

"About Morris's case?"

"Yes. It's about someone I work with, but I can't be more specific. It might even help with your current situation. He has ties to some of the people we've previously spoken about."

I sucked in a breath. So, it *was* David. And I still hadn't had time to check the private email that Morris had given me the password to that I'd given to David. It might've revealed whether he'd knowingly written that article. At least I'd have a clue whether he was a liar or not. Too late now. I told him I was at Bellamy's and the address. "How far away are you?"

"About ten minutes. Do you mind if I pop over?" He sounded as hopeful as I felt. With a bit of luck, his information would be consistent with that Shelly woman, and they could arrest the people responsible today.

"That's fine. The sooner I get that information, the better. Thanks."

"See you soon, Avery. Bye."

"Bye." I hung up and hurried down the hall to peer out of one of the glass panels beside the door. The police were still sitting across the road in an unmarked car with a clear view of Bellamy's house. The grey sky threatened rain or maybe even sleet with how cold it was. The top temp was close to the bottom temp today, and that was two degrees Celsius. At least there was one benefit to being stuck inside all day—I was toasty warm.

I hurried outside, looked both ways to make sure no suspicious cars were around, and crossed the road. Patel got out of the car. "What are you doing out here?"

"Just letting you know that a journalist is coming to see me soon. Duncan Wilson. He's tall and skinny. I'm not sure what kind of car he drives, but let him in. He might have info on Morris's murder."

He raised his brows. "That sounds promising. Make sure you let the sergeant know as soon as you speak to Mr Wilson. I'll check his ID when he gets here."

"Thanks, PC Patel. I appreciate it." I looked both ways and jogged back to the house. I felt vulnerable out in the open.

Anger sizzled just below the surface as I went back in and locked the door. How dare these lowlifes make me feel like this. Good people didn't deserve to be scared for their life.

While I waited, and to distract myself, I made a phone call to reschedule a phone interview, and the woman was a have-a-chat person. Just as I managed to extricate myself from the conversation, the bell rang. I stared at my tea and felt the cup. Cool again. Right. I hurriedly put it in the microwave and set the timer for a minute and a half. By the time I returned with Duncan, it would be ready. I flicked the switch on the jug as well, just in case my fellow journalist wanted a cuppa.

When I answered the door, a rugged-up Duncan held out his gloved hand. "Hello again, Miss Winters. I've just been okayed by a PC Patel."

I shook his hand and gave a nod to the police across the road, indicating all was good. "Thanks for coming by. I love a good piece of information." I stood aside and gestured him in. He kept his coat on but lowered the hood. "You don't want to hang it up?" I lifted my chin towards the coat hooks on the entry wall.

He rubbed his hands together. "Maybe in five minutes, after I've warmed up. It's bloody freezing out there."

I chuckled. "It is. Would you like a cup of tea?"

He hesitated, then shrugged. "Okay. Thanks." We made our way down the hall and into the living area. "Nice place. How long are you here for?"

I sighed. "I don't know. As long as it takes to put Angelo and his cronies away. Could be a day, could be a month. Although, God forbid. Poor Bellamy will be at his wit's end with me and Finn here for that long." It would also ruin Finn's Christmas, not being able to see his parents and sister. Maybe they'd invite them here, but probably not. If I were him, I wouldn't want my family in danger. In fact, I hoped Bellamy and his wife went somewhere else to stay safe. Hmm, no, I didn't. That would leave me and Finn here… alone. I didn't think I could control myself around him if we couldn't leave the house and no one else was here. Maybe I'd lock myself in my room and watch TV on my laptop.

"You don't look too happy about it."

"I'm not. I'm putting a lot of people out, and I don't want my troubles affecting others. But it's too late." The guilt stung. "But you didn't come here to talk about that." The microwave dinged. "How do you take your tea?" It would be a miracle if I got to drink my tea today. Maybe I should call Finn and get him to bring me a cappuccino.

"Black, no sugar. Thanks." He followed me to the kitchen. "You're here by yourself? Aren't you worried?"

I looked around. "Not really. Finn won't be too long, I don't think. Besides—" The electric kettle clicked off. "Mug or teacup?"

"Either or. So, you think Angelo killed Morris? You must have proof."

I opened the microwave and put my cup on the counter. The handle was hot too. Maybe I'd overdone it. Never mind—it would probably be an hour before I got to drink it if my track record today was any indication. "We're getting there." I didn't want to give him false hope. But even if we didn't get Angelo for Morris's murder right now, we still had him, his son, and Jack on other crimes. I reached up to get a mug out of the cupboard. Before I could manage it, Duncan's hand was over my mouth, stopping me from screaming, and a knife was at my throat. I grabbed his forearms, but I wasn't game to try and dislodge them with that knife where it was, taking into account I'd be lucky to move his arms an inch.

What the hell was happening?

"I'm sorry you wasted your time coming here for protection. Angelo and Jack couldn't do the job properly, so I have to finish it. I should've known they would cock it up. At least they managed to blow Morris up successfully." He laughed. "Stupid old coot. Thinking he can railroad me out of a promotion I've spent years working towards. The number of times I've risked myself for him in some godforsaken war zone, hoping he'd champion me, and this is the thanks I get. Some snot-nosed moron taking my promotion with Morris's blessing. I don't bloody think so. I can't believe I fell for his 'I'm the father you always wanted' act. If it's one thing I've learned in my life, it's to never trust anyone. Betrayal's a bitch, but payback is worse."

My heart was racing so fast, it was a wonder it didn't give out. Also, crap on a cracker. Duncan was behind all this? He'd killed a friend and mentor over a missed promotion and some daddy issues? This was insane.

I considered biting his hand so I could speak, but he was wearing gloves. Also, what would I ask? He'd basically blurted everything out. So now what—I just died?

"Nothing to say? Oh, that's right—you can't speak." He laughed again. "Angelo told me what you did to his man. I'm not risking it, so I don't even get to see the fear on your pretty face as I slice. Sorry you won't get to have Christmas this year. Well, actually, I'm not."

Out of the corner of my eye, I spied Zeus watching from the dining room. If only I'd trained him to attack bad people. He was loyal, though. Would he get involved? What if Duncan hurt him? I couldn't risk it. Did I have a choice? Duncan's grip was solid, and the knife blade gently resting against my throat was a terrifying reminder of my predicament.

If I thought about how to get out of this any harder, my head would explode. I was stuck. I had nothing. I couldn't even throw Duncan because the counter was in my way.

Ooh, hang on.

I dropped one hand, slowly flopped forward, and shook as if I were crying—no sudden movements, or he'd get the wrong idea and slice early.

"Sorry, Avery. It's not personal."

Well, this is.

I grabbed my scalding mug off the counter and jerked my upper body forward to avoid the splash as I threw the hot beverage back, in his face. There were benefits to not drinking your tea on time.

He screamed, dropping me and the knife to lunge for the sink and the cold tap.

"Bitch! You burned me."

I picked up the knife and jumped back—he was stronger than me and likely to claw it off me, so I needed to stay out of range. His face and neck were bright red—he had major burns and was no longer a threat. I ran to the front door and out to the police car while he splashed cold water on his face.

Even through my horror and adrenaline dump, I felt terrible—recovery from burns took a very long time, and he'd be in pain for a week at least. If he had scarring, every time he looked in the mirror, he'd think of me. But then again, he was going to kill me, and he'd killed Morris and his wife, so maybe I shouldn't feel so bad.

PC Patel rolled his window down, his forehead wrinkling. "Avery, what's wrong?" His brows rose. "That's a knife."

"Duncan tried to kill me. He's the one who organised Morris's murder. I threw hot tea in his face and grabbed this off the floor after he dropped it." I handed the weapon to

Patel. He didn't waste time looking at it—he threw it into the footwell of his car and put his hand on the door handle. I moved out of the way, and he flung his door open, calling for backup and an ambulance on his two-way while his colleague followed both of us to Bellamy's at a run.

Duncan was still trying to cool his face when we reached him. Patel approached him, holding out his Taser.

I stood in the living room, out of the way. "Be careful. The floor's slippery." The evidence of my attack was all over the floor. Looked like I still wasn't getting a cup of tea. But that was okay because I got something better.

Morris's killer.

Unfortunately, Morris wasn't going to like who it was.

And I was the one who'd have to break the news.

CHAPTER 21

About ten minutes after they carted Duncan away, Bellamy and Finn showed up, along with two other officers who went straight into the kitchen to take photos and whatever else they did at crime scenes. I was relieved to see Finn because, once I'd processed what happened, I realised that Duncan could've told Angelo to go after Finn while Duncan was "taking care" of me. Although, with Angelo under police scrutiny, I doubted he was going to risk doing something now. I smiled as something occurred to me.

Finn had just walked into the living area. He gave me a weird look. "Why are you smiling? Is it the shock?"

"I second Finn's assessment." Bellamy stood next to the dining table where I was sitting in front of my laptop, although it was closed.

"So, I have what you need to arrest Angelo."

Bellamy sat next to me. "Go on."

I told him everything that happened with the attack and

what Duncan said. "So, there you have it. Angelo killed Morris on Duncan's instruction."

Finn swore and sat opposite me, concern in his azure eyes. "Jeez, Lightning. That was a close call. Are you all right? Also, good work on catching the killer."

"I'm okay. Exhausted after the adrenaline comedown, but nothing I won't shake off by tomorrow."

Bellamy shook his head. "Well, you've certainly had an overabundance of experiences with killers lately. You're an old hand now."

I chuckled. "Funny but not funny. Unfortunately, I am. So, does that mean you can arrest Angelo and co. today?"

Bellamy stood. "Yes. In the meantime, if you could go to the station and give your statement, I'd appreciate it." He stood. "I want to move fast on these arrests. Once Angelo learns of Duncan's arrest, I have no doubt he'll be on the next plane out of here."

"Do you mind if I pass by work on the way? I want to tell Julian the news in person. He's probably going to be a bit upset. He worked with Duncan at some stage. Not that they're best buddies, but still… I think it will be hard for him to digest."

Finn stood. "I'll come with you." Oh dear. That meant I couldn't tell Morris straight away. Or maybe I could. I'd go to the toilet when we got to work. Being the bearer of bad news sucked. Normally I was telling ghosts I'd solved their murders, and that was that.

Bellamy gave a nod. "I'd better get going. We'll need all hands on deck to arrest Angelo and his minions. We're calling in the AFOs for obvious reasons. See you both later."

AFO stood for authorised firearms officers. Things were

about to get even more serious. I gave him a worried look. "Stay safe, Sergeant."

"What Lightning said."

"Will do." With that, Bellamy turned and left.

Finn glanced at the officers in the kitchen, then looked at me. "It's time we updated Julian. I'll call him, make sure he's in." I nodded as he brought up Julian's number on his phone. Once he'd confirmed with Julian, he hung up. "Wanna pack up and hit the road?"

"Sounds good to me." I wrote a heartfelt thank-you note to Mrs Bellamy, packed my few clothes and toiletries into my suitcase, grabbed my laptop, handbag, and Zeus, and got into my car. Finn and I had each brought our own cars—I hadn't wanted to leave mine for Angelo and his cronies to put a bomb in it.

My stomach grumbled all the way to work, and it wasn't from hunger. At least I wasn't telling Julian by myself, which was the usual way. The normal loneliness that came after my thoughts of ghosts and what I saw as my duty didn't assail me. Because I had Bellamy now—I could talk to him about it. And what a godsend he was. Yes, I could chat to my ghost friends, but it wasn't the same. I doubted that Bellamy knew how much it mattered to me that he had accepted my weirdness. Hmm… had he confided in his wife? She didn't look at me funnily, and she was happy to have me live with her, so probably not.

I arrived at Macpherson Media just after Finn. When I ducked into our office, he was chatting to Carina. She jumped up, ran over, and threw her arms around me. "Oh, Avery, are you okay, lovie?" She squeezed me tightly before releasing me and stepping back.

I shut the office door and put Zeus on the floor. "Yeah, I guess so." The adrenaline comedown had made me tired, but at this point, I was more worried about telling Morris what happened. Julian would be upset, no doubt, but he was one step removed compared to Morris. Imagine mentoring someone only to have them kill you when things didn't go their way. I shook my head.

"Avery, what's wrong?" Carina's concern shone in her eyes.

"Oh, nothing. Ah, just worried about telling Julian. You know… because he used to work with the guy who set it all up."

She nodded slowly. "D'at is disgusting! What is wrong wit' people? Do you want me to come wit' you to tell him?"

Finn, who'd picked up Zeus, had joined us near the door. He gave me a gentle smile that melted my heart into a puddle of goo. Stupid insides should know better. "Thanks, but I've got this. She did drag me into it, after all."

Carina shook her finger at me. "Next time, I want in too. I hate knowing you were bot' in danger, and I wasn't d'ere to help."

I gave her an "are you kidding?" look. "I didn't even want Vinegar in on this. He almost got killed too."

He chuckled. "That's an exaggeration. No one touched me."

I folded my arms. "Yes, but after helping me, you were on their hit list for sure. Even Bellamy thought so. I wasn't the only one staying at his place." I gave Carina a stern look. "The last thing I need on my conscience is the death of two of my best friends."

She grinned, looking pleased with herself. "I'll take d'at. I feel very privileged. You're one of my best friends too. Which is why I want to help."

How could I stay annoyed with her and her happy face? I

smiled. "Moving right along. I want to get this over and done with." I looked at Finn. "Ready?"

He handed Zeus to Carina. The cat nudged under her chin, and she gave him a kiss on the head. "Good luck. I'll see you when you're done."

We went up the stairs, and I knocked on Julian's door.

"Come in!"

He gave us a sad smile. Slouched posture and a lack of movement had hijacked his usual high-energy state. "Have a seat, you two. So, you're out of lockup. I understand you have news for me." His ghost of a smile faded away, replaced by a haunted look.

Finn raised his eyebrows as if to ask whether I wanted to talk or if I wanted him to. I gave a nod. "I'm fine to do this. Thanks." I turned to Julian and explained what happened at the club and my suspicions about Angelo. He leaned forward, forearms resting on his desk, riveted. Then I got to the part where Duncan visited.

"Oh, did he have information for you?"

The chuckle that burst out of me was all sarcasm. "Something like that." Finn and I shared a look, and then I kept going. "I was too close to the truth, apparently. Duncan was there to kill me." Julian gasped and slapped the desk with both palms, his eyes wide. When I said, "Then I chucked the hot tea in his face and ran out," he pumped his fist in the air.

"Yes! Great work, Winters!" Julian sat back, his hands on the chair arms, slowly shaking his head over and over. "That's an incredible story." We sat in silence as he digested the information for a couple of minutes. His joyful expression over my triumph disappeared. "I can't believe Duncan was behind all this. How could he? What a rotten sod. Morris loved him like a son. If Morris was still alive, this would just about kill him."

Argh, tell me about it. My victory over the latest murderer soured in my long-suffering stomach. I still had to tell Morris. I stood. "I'm going to grab some coffee. Does anyone want anything?"

Julian said, "I'll have the usual, thanks. But seeing as how you've solved the crime, yet again, this is my treat." He took his wallet out and put money on the table. I was about to say "it's fine" when he put up his hand. "I insist. This is a tiny thank-you from me. You risked your life to investigate this, Winters. You're a top journalist with a good nose and a backbone of steel to go with it."

I wasn't sure what to say, except to downplay it, so I just stared at him. In my past life, all I got was criticism from those closest to me. It was difficult to believe praise, let alone accept it. My cheeks heated, and I managed a quiet "Thanks." If I said anything else, I'd be insulting him, and it would only make him argue the point, which would be even worse. The quicker we got past this awkwardness, the better. I turned to Finn. "The usual?"

Finn stood. "I can come with, help you carry everything."

"Thanks, but that's okay. I wouldn't mind a bit of fresh air and alone time to settle the sympathetic nervous system." Argh, could I sound any more ridiculous? I needed to speak to Morris. The sooner I got that conversation over and done with, the better.

"You sure?" His gentle expression almost had me swooning. He cared about me, even if it was just as a friend, and I desperately wanted to sink into that feeling, but that was dangerous territory.

"Yes, but thanks for offering. And thanks for standing by me during all this craziness. I'm sorry I put your life in danger."

He cocked his head to the side. "I did insist on driving you to the club. Remember? I kind of figured something might happen. This is you we're talking about, Lightning." He laughed.

"Ha ha! Very funny. And that was why I didn't want you involved. If you got hurt or worse, I'd never forgive myself."

He folded his arms. "Well, that's also why I wanted to go with you. I knew you'd need help. Besides, Carina would never forgive me if anything happened to you." He smirked. Argh, he was so frustrating. I held in my sigh, but I let my eyeroll off the leash.

Julian laughed. "Look at you two, bickering like a married couple."

Finn wore the same no-way expression that I made sure was on my face. "I'm going to get the drinks… by myself. Bye." I tried not to run out of there. That was all too close to home, and I would die if Finn even got a hint that I was attracted to him. When would this crush be over? Surely it couldn't last too much longer.

I popped my head into the office and confirmed that Carina wanted a tea, and then I hurried out into the drizzling cold.

I put my phone to my ear as I made my way up the street. "Morris. Hello, Morris…."

The ghost appeared alongside me. "I'm sorry to say that I didn't find anything out at the office. David wasn't there, and I didn't know where else to look for him."

"It's not that. I have big news."

"You know who killed me?" His intense stare felt like too much pressure.

I swallowed. "Yes, and you're not going to like it. I'm sorry, Morris, but it's not good news."

His forehead wrinkles deepened with a frown. "What do you mean?"

"Angelo and his group did the actual bombing, but someone else was behind it."

He reached out and tried to unsuccessfully grab my arm. "Stop."

I stopped and stood against the wall of the Manesbury Meaty Morsels, keeping out of the way of anyone crazy enough to be out in this stupid weather. Ben, the butchery owner, waved at me through the window. I waved back and smiled before turning back towards the street.

Morris stared at my face, determination in his eyes. "Just tell me. I'm ready to know. I need to get back to my wife—I miss her."

I wasn't about to remind him that not everyone got to go where they wanted. And what if the powers that be didn't open that door for him at all? I took a deep breath and stared into the street. I was such a coward. "It was Duncan. He was angry that you didn't recommend him for the promotion. He saw it as a betrayal." His gasp was like a stab to the heart. I steeled myself and met his pained gaze. "I'm sorry. It's such a stupid reason, and I know how close you were."

"He wasted my life and my wife's for that? You can't be serious? Are you sure it was him? I don't believe it."

My voice was barely above a whisper when I explained everything that had happened from the time I arrived at the club. When I finished, I was shivering. It wasn't the day to be standing still outside. My hair, face, and coat were damp, and I couldn't be sure, but there might've been frost on my numb cheeks. When I was sure no portal was opening up for our final goodbye, I said, "I'm going to grab coffees, and I'll be back in a few minutes." That would give him time to absorb.

Maybe he'd be stuck here until he accepted it. Or maybe you didn't get second chances when you said no the first time.

I grabbed the hot beverages and returned to Morris. He joined me for a slow walk back to the office. "You know, I sometimes got the feeling he resented me, but I put it down to the impatience of youth. He was always pushing to have more responsibility than he was ready for. When I edited his articles, he often pushed back, disliking my changes. But would I ever have thought he'd have it in him to order a hit on anyone, let alone me? The answer is no." His laugh was self-deprecating. "My journalist's nose failed me on that one. I've been blind. I keep wondering if there's anything I could've done to see it coming, to save Meredith and myself. This is my fault."

"What—it's your fault Duncan is an unhinged psychopath who kills people when he doesn't get his way? You know it's not your fault. And no reasonable person could've seen this coming. What he did was way beyond anyone's imagination."

"Meredith won't like this. She's cooked him dinner countless times. He's spent more than one Christmas with us. How could he?" His lips pressed together in an angry line. "How dare he!"

"I know. It's horrible. I'm sorry." We were almost at the front door of MacPherson Media, and no portal had opened for Morris. I tried not to worry, but a niggling discomfort writhed in my belly.

"What's wrong? Is my anger too much for you?"

I smiled. "Of course not. Your anger is justified, and I hate to break it to you, but it's not scary. I've experienced a bazillion times worse on multiple occasions. I'm just…." Argh, how do I explain that I'm worried he's missed his chance to spend eternity with his wife? Not that I'd know for sure anyway. "Do you feel like you've got closure, now you know?"

We stopped outside Julian's building. "I'm not sure. I think I need some time. I want to see how my children deal with this. My daughter, in particular, hasn't been coping, especially losing her mum. Ellen is pregnant with our second grandchild, and she was very close to Meredith. I also want to see that scoundrel one more time. See how happy he is to be locked up."

"Ah, okay. I'll chat to you later." I held the tray of beverages up slightly. "I'd better get these inside before they're iced coffees and teas."

"I'll see you soon. And thank you, Avery. You've risked your life to discover who did this, and you have my eternal gratitude."

"My pleasure, Morris. I'm just sorry it wasn't quite the outcome you would've wanted."

He laughed and looked down at himself. "Being dead isn't the outcome I wanted, either, but you learn to play the hand you're dealt. Bye, Avery."

"Bye." Was it my fault he'd decided to stay? If I couldn't see ghosts, he likely would've just followed his wife into their eternity. If he was stuck here forever, would it be because of me?

He disappeared, leaving my heart as cold as the air that plumed white with my breath. I dropped my phone back in my coat pocket, opened the door, and slipped into the place that had become like a second home, hoping the warmth could do more than defrost my icy skin. Unfortunately, it couldn't penetrate where I needed it most.

CHAPTER 22

That night, Carina, Finn, and I had dinner at the pub. I hadn't seen Meg since our last dinner at the pub because they'd been flat out—every man and his dog were having work and group Christmas parties. Meg probably wouldn't get a spare minute until Christmas Day when they were closed. I felt like we were only adding to their workload, but I could clear some tables when I was done eating. I'd worked a waitressing job when I was at uni, so I had some skills in that area.

Meg, a gravy food stain on her shirt and escapees from her bun framing her face, had found a moment to check on us. "Congrats on solving the crime, Aves."

"Thanks. I feel like this one was more luck than skill, though."

Finn grinned. "No, Lightning. You kept digging until you irritated the killer enough to come forward. That takes skill."

Carina laughed, Meg gave him a dirty look, and I rolled my eyes. He was probably right, though. I was putting this one down to luck. And I hadn't forgotten Everly's case either. That sicko was still out there and could attack another woman at any time. At least with Morris's case off the table, I could concentrate on Everly's. "Well, you know, whatever it takes. That's how I roll." I smiled at Meg. "This pork belly is delish, by the way. Please tell the chef."

"My dad will be happy to take the compliment. He, Chloe, and Sid are cooking up a storm back there tonight." She gazed across the room, likely assessing what needed doing. "Anyway, it's good to see you guys, but I'd better get back to it."

We all said goodbye and got back to our food. Just as I finished, my phone rang. I almost didn't hear it with all the chatter around me. I placed the phone to one ear and my hand over the other. "Hey, Sergeant. How's it going?" Finn and Carina stared at me after hearing who was calling.

"Where are you? It's rather noisy."

"Dinner at the pub."

"I'm glad someone's enjoying themselves while I'm slaving away." A lighter tone tempered his words.

"I'm glad you're happy for me. The pork belly is delicious. I highly recommend it. So, what's up?"

"I wanted you to know that we've arrested and processed Duncan, Jack, Angelo, his son, and another of Angelo's thugs. They're all going down for Morris's murder and Angelo and his group for drugging and assaulting the women at the club. We found those videos you were talking about. We've only gone through a few hours of tapes, and we've found three drink-spiking events already where the women were taken into the locked room you almost ended up in and sexually assaulted. We haven't gotten to Katie's recording yet, but we'll keep going till we get there. We're going to have many victims to contact. More work but worth it. I hate thinking this was going on so close to home, and we had no idea."

"It's horrible, but you get to do something about it now. Thank you for believing in me, Sergeant. I couldn't do all this by myself." The early days here when he was wary of me and I couldn't say anything about the ghosts were so much harder. I'd also felt much lonelier, but now I was part of two teams—at work and at the station. It fuzzied up my insides with good feelings.

"And I couldn't do all this by myself either. Thank you, Winters. If you want to write your article about the whole thing, I'd be happy to give you a couple of quotes."

"Ah, you know me so well. Thanks."

"My pleasure. Oh, and there's footage of Duncan partying with Angelo and Ricky in the VIP area." He imparted a few other discoveries and then said, "Now, I'd better go. My wife is expecting me home soon. Night."

"Night, Sergeant." We hung up, and I turned to my eager colleagues. They were like collies waiting for a treat.

"So?" Carina asked. "Don't leave us hanging."

"They've been watching security footage from the club, and so far, they've identified three instances of drink spiking. Angelo, his son, and a couple of their cronies are going down for that, as well as Morris's murder. We've even got footage of Duncan partying with them, and after pulling all their phone records, it's clear they've been in constant contact. There were numerous calls flying back and forth between Angelo and Duncan on the night of Morris's murder." I couldn't help the smile that sprung to my lips.

"Well, dat's fantastic."

Finn held up his pint of beer. "A toast to Lightning and her amazing ability to catch the bad guys." He clinked glasses with

Carina and me and took a sip. "All silliness aside, I'm happy they're locked up. I didn't want to spend the rest of my life cooped up in Bellamy's house."

Carina leaned towards him and bumped his shoulder with hers. "Aw, don't lie, Finny. I bet you loved living with Aves."

As much as I didn't want to think about how much he did or didn't want to live with me, the teasing was funny, and I laughed. "It's not like we had to share a bed. You survived."

His blue eyes met mine. I had no idea what he was thinking, but after a moment, he smiled. "Yeah, I did. And so did you. No murderer can keep you down. Here's to good friends and having nine lives." We cheersed again. "Oh, and you'll get another stellar article out of it. Maybe you can earn us all another bonus."

"Oh, the pressure." I chuckled. "But I'll do my best." I wasn't thinking about the article I was going to finish tomorrow—I needed to hurry and figure out how to solve Everly's case. How could I make it so the police could legally explore Andrew's father's property? Would I do that before they killed someone else?

Even though this was a celebration, a shiver ran down my nape. I couldn't stop the thought that I'd need more of those nine lives Finn proclaimed I had sooner rather than later.

Brushing away my morbid thoughts, I finished my wine and stood. "It's my shout. What do you want?" They gave me their orders, and I went to the bar where Bailey and Mike, the newish American bartender, were doing a great job of hurrying with orders while appearing calm. Patrons crowded along the bar front, so I was in the second row, waiting. Bailey gave me a smile and nod when he saw me. I returned it and made a face as if to say "wow, it's busy." He returned that look with a "don't I know it" one.

"Avery," an urgent voice next to me said. I knew that voice.

I looked to the side and down slightly. Without moving my mouth, I said, "Charles, what is it?" I probably looked constipated to anyone watching.

Worry had scored two divots between his eyebrows. "It's Andrew Crumps. He's got another drugged girl in the car. He's driving to his parents'. You have to do something!"

I had many questions, but I couldn't ask them here. I glanced at our table—Carina and Finn were laughing about something. How was I going to leave without causing a drama? I could feign a stomach ache and hope they bought it. Knowing Finn, he'd follow me home and spy on my front door for twenty minutes to make sure I wasn't lying so I could sneak off.

"Well? Did you hear me?" Charles was staring at me, arms half raised as if he wanted to grab my arms and shake me.

"Yes. You'll have to wait while I get the drinks and make my excuses." Someone's life was about to end, and I was their only hope. I swore under my breath. At least this hadn't happened when I was stuck at the sergeant's place. But this was only marginally better. Possum poo. I slid my phone out of my jacket pocket and called the station, hoping I hadn't missed the sergeant. "Hello, it's Avery Winters. Is Sergeant Bellamy in?" I blocked my other ear so I could hear the person on the other line.

"It's Lizzy here. I'm so sorry, Avery, but he finished a little while ago and went home to sleep. He's back in at seven tomorrow morning." He'd worked past his normal shift because of the whole Duncan and Angelo debacle, and he'd hardly been home in the last few days. It wasn't fair of me to bother him. But then, it wasn't fair another woman was in danger.

Maybe I could go by myself and contact the local police when I got there? But what would I say? I'd have to lie about seeing her fighting him as he dragged her into the house, but if they checked the phone ping things of me and her and even Andrew, they'd work out when she was brought to the house and where I was at the time. That was a complication I didn't need. Was Bellamy even allowed to go to the house in an official capacity out of the blue if he wasn't working in that area?

"Okay, thanks, Lizzy. I guess I'll talk to him tomorrow. Bye."

"Bye."

"You have to call his mobile. You can't do this by yourself. Remember what happened last time, and you had Finn to help you."

Argh! I kept my phone against my ear. "Well, what the hell do you want me to do? He needs sleep. And I doubt he could go there for no reason. We're just going to have to involve the local police."

The line to the bar had thinned, and I was next. I said goodbye for the second time and lowered my phone.

Mike stood in front of me and smiled. "Hey, Aves. What'll it be?"

I gave him Carina's and Finn's orders, sans my drink. I wasn't sure what I was going to do, but I couldn't sit and drink and laugh while some poor woman was being tortured and murdered. If only I could tell Finn and Carina about my secret—then they could help me. I held in my sigh at what could never be as I paid for the drinks.

By the time I returned to the table and placed the drinks down, I'd come up with an excuse. Carina frowned. "Where's your drink?"

I pouted. "I have to go. My sister's got a drama, and she's

texted that she needs to talk to me. We don't often get to chat because of the time difference, but I want to talk to her. I'm worried. And it's too noisy here. It might be a long chat. I'm sorry, but I have to go." The stomach-ache excuse would've made them worry—if they believed me—and it would've cast aspersions on Meg's dad's food.

Carina stood and hugged me. "Well, you get home safely, and I'll see you tomorrow."

Finn didn't stand up or give me a hug. Bummer. "Come by tomorrow morning before work, and we can have a coffee with Zeus."

"I t'ought he was more of a tea drinker." Carina laughed.

I laughed too. "We're trying to get him to drink coffee. It's just easier for everyone." I grabbed my bag and put my phone in it. "I'll see you bright and early tomorrow… well, dark and early, as the case may be." Winter was a literal dark time in England. The sun came up late and went to bed in the afternoon. I wouldn't mind having its sleeping hours. But it wasn't really asleep. It was doing a job on the other side of the international date line. Thank goodness no one could see what I was thinking. Was I going mad? Nah, I was probably there years ago. No sane woman would've stayed with Brad for the amount of time I did.

Finn's gaze held mine with an intensity I was probably imagining. "Drive carefully. I'll see you tomorrow."

I smiled. "Night."

As I walked to the car park, Charles smirked. "I think he likes you."

I almost said, "I wish," but then I'd never hear the end of it. "I think he thinks of me in a more sisterly way. There's no way anything's happening there."

"Whatever you say."

"Yep." I unlocked Daisy and got in, Charles slinking through the door to sit on the front passenger seat. I shuddered. "How many times do I have to ask?" Charles's answer was to give me a cheeky grin. I rolled my eyes and started the car.

Just in case Finn and Carina were spying on me from the pub, I turned left out of the premises instead of right, which would've taken me through Cramptonbury and towards the murder house. There was one problem—when Finn got home, he'd see my car wasn't there. Maybe I could get Bellamy to back me up and say he'd called me to come to the station. Why was my life so complicated?

After reaching the end of the village shops and the laneway leading to my place, I turned around and headed back the way I'd come. Hopefully I could formulate a plan on the way because I had time. "Do you know how far from the house they were when you came to tell me?"

"No. But they were leaving a pub called The Bread and Beagle."

"You guys sure have some crazy pub names."

Charles shrugged. "Not my fault."

"Do you know what village it's in? Also, have you been following him?"

"No, and yes. Ev and I have been taking turns. We thought it would help catch him. She found it hard at first, but now she's just angry, but she still has other stuff to do, so she asked me to help."

I pulled over at a break in some hedges so I could look up where The Bread and Beagle was on my phone. "Why didn't either of you tell me?" Also, why hadn't I thought of it? That was a great idea. Not that I expected Andrew to necessarily be looking for his next victim right now. From what I'd discovered so far—ghosts of his victims wise—he wasn't killing every five minutes, but he might have buried more women near where they lived, and I had no idea. Maybe this victim was a Christmas present to his parents? How sick. If she was a twisted present, had he gifted them one every year? I swallowed a surge of nausea. Please, no. If I let that thought take hold, I'd be sitting here in shock for hours trying to fathom it.

Thankfully, there was only one pub with that name in England. According to the map, it was a forty-five-minute drive from his parents'. It would take me longer to get there, but I might be able to get away with the lie to the police about having seen something. And because these gross humans liked to toy with their catch before disposing of it, I would hopefully get there in time to save her. "Charles, can you go and wait at the house and pop back to me when they get there?"

"Okay. I'll see you later." He waved and disappeared.

I pulled out onto the road and put my foot down.

CHAPTER 23

I drove as fast as I dared on the dark, icy roads, and when Charles popped back, I was still ten minutes from the Crumpses'. Heart thudding a panicked beat, I sped up. It was stupid because if I crashed, no one could help the latest victim, but if I took too long, the police might question my information later. I had no idea if they'd even check my phone for my location because I wasn't doing the wrong thing, but you never knew.

To make matters worse, when I was five minutes away, my phone rang, and Bellamy's name appeared on the screen. Charles looked at me. "You'd better take that, or they'll send out a search party."

He wasn't wrong. There wasn't anywhere to pull over on the narrow country road, but I slowed to ten miles an hour and pressed the button to answer via Bluetooth. "Hello, Sergeant."

"Where are you?"

"I'm almost at the Crumpses' place. Charles came and told

me that Andrew had abducted another woman and was heading there. I'm sorry I didn't call—you've hardly slept the last two days. I'm guessing Finn called you?"

"Yes. As soon as he got home and saw your car wasn't there, he was straight on the blower. That lad knows you too well." There was a beat of silence before he continued. "Please don't tell me you were going to rush in by yourself. You're not that stupid, are you?"

"No. I was going to call the local police when I arrived and pretend I saw him dragging her inside while she was trying to resist. If I sound upset enough, they'll be sure to send someone to investigate."

"Can you sit tight until I get there with one of my men?"

"No. It'll take too long. I have no idea how long they'll torture her before they kill her, and I'd rather she didn't have to suffer one minute more than necessary. Besides, the police will wonder why you're in their territory." We could use the excuse that it was a case Bellamy was already working because of Everly, but could we pretend I'd been following Andrew just in case? But if I did that, by the time it went to trial, the lawyers would probably try to get whatever they could to disprove my validity as a witness, and my friends would put me at the pub at the time Andrew left the restaurant with his victim. And the last time I checked, ghosts giving you a message wasn't a valid reason to know something.

"I'm heading over anyway. Do what you have to. We'll think of something."

"Thanks, Sergeant. I'm almost there."

"Don't go in by yourself—do you hear me?"

I batted away the automatic annoyance that begged me to roll my eyes—he was right—I wasn't equipped to deal with three torturing murderers without so much as a Taser, no matter how much I craved running in there and hapkido-ing everyone. Where were superpowers when you needed them? "Yes, Sergeant. I'll call the police and wait." Argh, it hurt to say that.

"Good. I'll be there with Patel as soon as I can. Stay safe." With that, he was gone.

My phone dinged with a message from Finn, which I read in quick glances while I drove slowly. *Bloody hell, Lightning. I called Bellamy. I'm so going to give it to you when you get back. Carina agrees you're in big trouble. Stop running off to save the world by yourself.* A smile crept onto my face at the double entendre, which I would bet he didn't know he'd made. It was nice that they cared, but I had to forget about all that for now. Focus would get me to where I was going safely.

I increased my speed to forty, which was as fast as I was willing to go in sleety conditions. Charles gave me a side-eye. "You meant what you said?"

"About not going in?"

"Yes."

"Yes. As much as I want to save whoever this woman is, I don't feel like dying today, and even though his parents are old, I don't fancy taking on three people at once. They could have an axe, massive knives, a shotgun…." The reality of my own assessment hit me. They lived in a rural area, so it wouldn't be unusual for them to own a gun or several. And if they were entertaining themselves with a victim, they'd have their torture devices out and at hand. Stupid me. I brought nothing, not that I owned any weapons. And yes, I knew that someone stronger could turn my weapon against me, but still. Maybe I should've learned the dan bong at hapkido—a thick, short stick attached to a small rope. They could do some damage. You could whack bone or choke with it.

"Good." Charles leaned forward. "We're not far now. This is the same way they came."

"You have arrived at your destination."

"Thanks, Siri." I drove down the street a bit and did a U-turn, then stopped across the road and eyed what looked like a white car in the driveway—I needed to be near enough that I could tell the police I saw what happened but far away that no one inside the house noticed I was there. Once my headlights were off, I kept the motor running—it was too cold to sit in an unheated car.

Not that I didn't believe what Charles had seen, but I needed to confirm someone was inside, or I'd look like a right moron when the police arrived. I hopped out of the car and crept towards the driveway. I didn't know whether there were cameras that could see me, so I plastered myself against the damp hedge and ventured close to the driveway without going on it. Heart hammering, I whispered, "Petra, are you around?" Nothing. "Hello, Petra?"

Thankfully, Petra appeared, eternally dressed in her running gear. "Avery, thank God you're here. They have a young woman in there. Andrew told his parents that she's eighteen. Her name's Renae, and she's pretty out of it."

"That's exactly what I needed to know. Have they started hurting her?" I held my breath, my throat not missing the scour of arctic air, waiting for the answer.

"They've undressed her and tied her to a chair in the shower. Andrew is laying out some dental tools, and then he said he's getting changed. His mother was… touching Renae when you called me. Are you coming in to stop it?"

I swore. Hopefully they'd given her a drug that would block her memory of this—although would not knowing what happened make her feel worse? I had no idea, but if it were me, I didn't think I'd want to have that in my head. "Not by myself. I promised I wouldn't. I'm calling the police." I ignored the devastation on Petra's face. "I'm sorry. Can you go back in and come tell me as soon as they start the torture or look like they're going to kill her?"

She shut her eyes, then opened them. "Yes. Okay." She disappeared, and I got back in the warmth of the car and dialled 999. I wasn't sure what I was going to say until I said it. After they put me through to the police, my words came out in a rush. "Hi, I'm Avery Winters. I was on the side of the road looking at my GPS when a car pulled into a driveway across the street. A man dragged a woman out of the front passenger seat. She looked half dead and couldn't walk. He put her over his shoulder. I mean, I don't even know if she's alive. And I heard a scream after they shut the door. Please help!" This story might not be too believable later, when they saw she was drugged, but once they uncovered the Crumpses' depravity, were they really going to nitpick what I'd said? No one could prove me wrong—they could only suspect. I would have to come up with something eventually, though, because once they discovered Sergeant Bellamy was investigating Everly's murder and it was tied to the Crumpses, there would be questions as to how I happened to be here at the right time.

"Can you please repeat that?" The dispatcher didn't sound convinced. It was an out-there scenario—I'd give them that. But I would bet they'd heard so many weird but true things, so why not this? I repeated myself. "And what's your location?"

I gave them the address, and before she could ask, I told her my phone number. "Please send someone quickly. I'm so scared. I have a bad feeling, and I'm thinking about knocking on the door. What if they kill her?" The near-panic in my voice wasn't staged. My stomach clenched, waiting for Petra to appear at any moment. Despite my promises to the contrary, there was no way I was safely doing nothing out here while they killed Renae.

"The police will be with you soon. Please stay where you are and don't approach the house. If you need us in the meantime, please call 999."

"Okay. But please hurry."

"We'll be with you as soon as we can. Like I said, please wait for the officers and call us if you need to." Her calm voice made me want to jump out of my skin. This was urgent. I wasn't sure if she didn't believe me and would send someone in an hour or if she believed me but was trained to remain stoic and placid no matter what. It was probably the latter, but it could even be both.

"Okay.... Bye." I reluctantly hung up. Being connected with someone else, even if it was only by phone, was slightly reassuring. All I could do was stare across the road at the driveway and dark shadow of Andrew's car. I couldn't see the house from where I sat, so I didn't know if any lights were on. I pressed my lips together and put my hand on the door.

Charles eyed me. "Don't do it."

I stared at him. "I just want to see if there are lights on and where. It's dark—no one will see me."

"You promised."

"I promised I wouldn't go inside. I made no such assurances about snooping around outside."

He rolled his eyes. "You're going to get in so much trouble when Bellamy finds out."

"Well, he's not here. No one who can stop this is. Except for me. And I need to know what's going on." Yes, I'd asked Petra to keep me updated, but if I needed to go in and save Renae, maybe there was an easier way than knocking on the door. Maybe they had her somewhere I could sneak into when they weren't with her? Okay, so I was having myself on, but whatever.

I turned the car off. It would be just my luck that someone would come along and steal it. "Can you stay near the car and tell me when the police are coming? That way, I can turn the headlights on to signal to them."

"I'd rather come with you. I can be a lookout. If you're going to be stupid, I can at least help you be less stupid." He folded his arms and hit me with a look of utter disdain.

I huffed out a breath. "Fine." I put my phone on silent and checked the time. Two minutes had passed since I'd gotten off the phone, and there were no signs of police. I doubted there was a station near here. It could be ten miles away for all I knew. This place wasn't near any cities, and any police stations would also have minimal staffing. I didn't like Renae's chances of the police showing up in time.

I put my gloves on, took my keys, and got out but didn't lock the car. I might need to get in it quickly.... Winter in England was so unpleasant if you had to go outside.

I opened the boot and considered what would make the best weapon. It was a choice between my umbrella (too flimsy), the car jack (a weird shape that probably wouldn't do much damage and had terrible reach), and the metal wheel-nut wrench thing. It was thinner and shorter than the ideal weapon, but it would have to do. If I managed to land a blow to a head, face, or kneecap, it would be rather effective.

I shut the boot. Gripping the wrench handle gave me a small amount of reassurance.

In the silence, the dead grass at the side of the road crunched loudly under my shoes. I crossed the road and approached the driveway from the side, edging along the hedges that formed their boundary fence.

I glanced up and down the road. Nope, no one coming. God, I hoped they didn't think my call was a hoax. Surely, legally, they had to respond to every call. I knew the ambulances did. I took a searing breath of frosty air, thankful that Petra hadn't returned to tell me they were killing Renae.

"Wait here while I make sure the coast is clear," Charles said before vanishing into the hedge. Killing two birds with one stone, I jogged on the spot while I waited—good for moderating nervous energy and warming up. After roughly thirty very long seconds, he returned. "There are cameras, but would they have them on to record them bringing their victims in?"

I whispered, "Hmm, it depends how stupid they are. We need to assume there's automatic lights too." If I were them, I'd want my video camera to alert me of movement outside, especially if I was in the middle of torturing someone, but I wouldn't want anything recorded. "I think I have to assume they'll be warned. Can you see if there are any other ways to get onto the property?" Last time I was here, I noticed timber posts and wire fencing down one side boundary. The other had been hedges for the bit near the street, but since it was a big property, it probably wasn't all the way down.

Charles gave me a deadpan look. "Do you need to go to the toilet?"

"No, smarty-pants. I'm trying to keep warm."

He grinned. "Ah, a live-person problem."

"Yes. Could you go now?"

His grin widened, and he disappeared.

My gaze wandered up and down the road. Still nothing.

No lights or sirens on the horizon. Daisy sat silently across the road, beckoning me with her warm, safe interior. I sighed. *Not yet, Avery, but soon... hopefully*.

A slash of breeze engulfed me as it passed, the iciness of it stealing my breath. Just great. All I needed was for the weather to worsen. If it started pouring, I wouldn't last long out here before I froze to death. Was I being dramatic? Probably. Was I going to stop being dramatic? Probably not. Although, I shouldn't be complaining. Renae and every woman who came before her had it worse. Much worse.

I gritted my teeth. I'd do whatever I could and last out here as long as needed to save her. I took one last glimpse into the black distance each way down the A1 and turned my back on Daisy.

Listening for Charles and anyone else, I made my way to the edge of the driveway and knelt. Maybe the security light would miss me if I commando crawled. If I was lucky, they had the sensor set up so it wouldn't catch foxes and other nighttime creatures. And with the car in the driveway, it might block some of my movement.

"I'm back."

I started, turned, and looked up. Charles stood there. Seemed even though I was expecting him, I could still be surprised. At least I hadn't screamed. "And?"

"There's nowhere to get in. Fencing all the way around. You could dig under some of the wire fencing or cut it, but digging would take too long, so that's out, and you don't have wire cutters, so I guess that's out too."

I tried to keep the sarcasm out of my voice, but I failed. "Well, thanks for the suggestions. Big help."

"Testy, aren't we?"

"Yes." I poked my head around the hedge and assessed where I was going to go before I looked back at Charles. "I'm going to commando it."

He sucked in a breath, his eyes wide. "You're going naked?!"

"Oh my God, no! Commando crawl. Jeez, Louise." I shook my head. "It's the only way I'll have any hope of avoiding detection." The only positive so far tonight was that Petra hadn't returned with worse news. "I'm going in."

"Are you sure? You can still go and sit in the car and wait for the police… like you promised… several times." He'd raised an eyebrow and was giving me a very stern-father look, which I'd never seen on him before.

"Yes, *Dad*, I'm sure. I appreciate the concern, but right now, I'm not in any danger, and if they decide to kill Renae soon, the more I know about where she is, the better. The police might take another twenty minutes or more to get here, and Bellamy would still be forty-five minutes away."

"He could be driving fast under lights and sirens. That will knock off some time."

I didn't share his positivity since the roads were icy in places. "Hmm, maybe. In the meantime, it's just you and me. If I were Renae, I know what I'd want us to be doing."

He sighed. "Fine. You're right."

I smiled. "Thank you. Let's do this. Also, you can keep being a lookout. It makes a huge difference."

"You got it."

I dropped to my belly on the hard ground, gripping my weapon in one hand, and crawled forward one arm-leg combination at a time. It was even colder down here, but hopefully, the difficult movement would warm me up.

My stomach tensed as I left the protection of the hedges and moved onto the driveway. As soon as my feet left the safety of my cover, I stopped. The light hadn't turned on… yet. The car was parked about twenty feet away, and a few feet in front of that was the single garage door with the house of horrors attached to my right, looming.

I took a deep breath and inched forward, stopping between each movement, ears straining, adrenaline shooting through my system, waiting for something bad to happen.

Each time I lifted my arm to reach ahead, I held my breath. So far, no light. *Thank you, powers that be.* I was almost at the car. A shiver slunk down my spine. If the light went on now, I'd be exposed. Glancing back over my shoulder, I reassured myself that the street wasn't far away, and I'd beat anyone to my car if they were starting from the house and I was jumping up from here.

Charles strode confidently past the car and to the front door. Oh, to be a ghost and know no one could see you. Okay, so the trade-offs cancelled it out, but still, in this moment, I would've appreciated a bit of invisibility.

The door was solid, and there were no sidelights, but there were three small glass panes above the door, about eight feet from the ground. Charles floated up until he could peer in. He stayed there for a moment, his head turning both ways. I crawled closer and reached the car in time for him to return. He sat on the ground next to me. "I couldn't see much. There's a small vestibule with a staircase on the right and a doorway straight ahead. I couldn't hear anything either."

"We should ask Petra what the layout's like." Why hadn't I thought of that before? Why was I so stupid sometimes? My parents would've answered that with "You've always been stupid, and you never try hard enough." *Right, enough of those negative thoughts. Be gone!* What my parents thought was irrelevant and had no bearing on reality. And if I told myself that enough, I'd 100 per cent believe it.

Healing was a long process.

"That's a good idea."

I pictured her in my mind and whispered, "Petra, are you there? Hello?" I wasn't sure if thinking about her would make my message clearer, but there was no harm in trying since I couldn't speak loudly. I had no idea if the volume of my voice made any difference either. I should test that with Charles.

She appeared next to Charles and stared down at me. "Why are you on the ground? Are you hurt?" She kneeled to get closer to me.

"No. I'm fine. I'm just trying to avoid triggering the lights or any video cameras."

Her eyes narrowed, and her nostrils flared. "No. The evil in that house turned the cameras off so there'd be no evidence of Andrew bringing Renae here. The lights are still going to be triggered, but they won't get any alerts."

My head dropped onto my hands in relief as a smidge of tension left my body. Not that I was calm. If they decided to check outside for any reason, I was still in trouble. I lifted my head. "Great to know. Thanks. How's Renae holding up?"

"She's pretty out of it, like, she can't move much, but her eyes…. She's terrified." Sympathy and sadness embedded lines on her forehead and at the bridge of her nose. "Andrew's mum has been stroking her face, and Andrew's dad sliced up the inside of her arm, but not enough to open it all up. Just enough that the blood is dripping out, and he licked it."

"What the hell?" A couple of choice swear words also came out. "Why didn't you tell me?"

"They're just warming up. I didn't want you to rush in before they were all in the room and occupied. They tend to lose track of things when they're in the middle of it. It's like a shark feeding frenzy."

Charles and I shared a horrified look. What was I planning on diving into? Was I a bait fish, swimming to my slaughter, or was I an orca, ready to rip out their livers with one bite? I was definitely the bait fish, but I'd pretend I was the orca. There was no way I could sit out here while they killed her. I couldn't live with myself. My life wasn't more important than hers, and I'd bet that her family and friends would think the risk was worth it. If anything happened to me, fewer people would miss me. I didn't feel sorry for myself—it was more that I was being logical. Practical. The situation called for it. Anything I could tell myself to make sure I helped despite my fear was necessary. Besides, we might both get out alive.

I was counting on it.

There were still no sirens in the distance. How much longer would they take? "What's the layout like? How do I get to where they have her?"

"It's around the side of the house. There." She faced the house and pointed right. "There's a locked gate you'll have to climb over. And the window is at about your head level. It's not very big either."

I shook my head. "Not going to work. I'd rather sneak in and enter the bathroom via the door. I'd be a sitting duck half in, half out of the window."

"There's a conservatory at the back. You go in there, through the door into the family room and kitchen, then through another door to a hallway, and turn to your left to the bathroom. The conservatory door's always locked, though. But that would be the best way in. Can you pick locks?"

"No." Why had I never learned? Oh, because I'd never needed it. As a normal journalist back in Australia, we didn't tend to break into people's houses. Maybe I'd add lock picking to my repertoire when this was over.

Petra glanced at the house, then back at me. The worry on her face spoke volumes. She was even more helpless than me in this situation, and she had to watch it unfold and deal with all the memories and feelings that brought up. I was in a position to *do* something. It was up to me. "Right. Get back to Renae. I'll figure it out. Don't worry. Just come tell me if anything worse happens. Okay?"

She nodded vigorously and disappeared.

The only thing I worried about as I commando crawled across the frosty grass was where Andrew was. If his parents were in the bathroom, which faced the side of the house, they'd never notice if a light went on out the front. But Andrew could be anywhere in that house, and he was the strong one. His parents, being elderly, weren't nearly as much of a threat to me. I had to be careful.

Progress across the front lawn was snail-like. Staying low was challenging. I was fatiguing as I reached halfway—it was a big front yard—so I stopped and whispered, "Charles, can you check if there are any automatic light sensors near the gate? If I'm going to go over it, I'll be way out in the open." I doubted there was going to be a crawlspace under it big enough for me.

"Can do." He hurried to the gate, which was hidden by the darkness. The front yard was lovely and shadowed. Clouds smothered the stars and moon. The smattering of raindrops, while annoying, were reassuring—there would be no heavenly light revealing my position. He soon returned. "I don't think so. At least, I couldn't see any."

"Thanks." I glanced up at the sensor on the front of the

garage. Hopefully it didn't reach as far as the gate. Placing one arm in front of myself and lifting my opposite leg, I kept going, ears straining for any screams or sirens.

The gate was affixed to the house wall, the latch on a post next to the hedge fence. And it was locked. Not that I expected anything else. I took a deep breath, gripped the tire lever until my fingers hurt, and braced to run as I inched to a sitting position against the hedge.

The light didn't come on.

My head dropped to my chest with an outward breath, and I closed my eyes for a moment, centring myself. Once I was over that six-foot-high gate, I was trapped. There would be no quick getaway if I was discovered—a psyche-up was required. I imagined the innocent woman and how she was feeling: the terror, hopelessness, and pain.

I lifted my head and gave myself a firm nod.

It was time.

The gate was inset a few inches behind the line of the house's front wall, so I jammed myself into that space and slowly stood. Charles was watching the front door while I stared down the side of the house. The space between the building and hedge was dimly lit, the light from the bathroom window sneaking out from what was probably a blind.

Another wave of relief hit me when I was at full height with no illumination.

Climbing required both hands, so I slid my weapon through the bars and dropped it on the ground. The gate was taller than me, consisting of vertical bars that made an arch shape at the top with a couple of horizontal bars for reinforcement—one at the bottom and one halfway up. Unfortunately, those bars were on the other side of the gate.

I reached up and grabbed the top of the bars.

Charles watched from my side of the fence. "You can do it!"

I gave him a tight smile that hopefully conveyed thanks through my nerves. I jumped, placed my feet on the gate, and tried to push off them and upwards. Instead, my feet slid down a few centimetres. I released my grip and landed on the ground. If you don't succeed, try, try again.

You can do five pull-ups in a row, Avery. You got this.

Momentum would be my friend. I couldn't step back too far, though, because the sensor would "see" me. I took one step back, then one more and one more, my stomach tightening, my breaths coming faster. The sense I was pushing my luck made me swallow, and I didn't dare try to go further.

Right, the lights hadn't come on, and I had three steps to gain speed. Not much, but it would have to do. *Ready, set, go*!

One, two, three leaping movements and I flew at the gate. My grip connected with the top bars, and I pushed off with my feet and pulled my body up simultaneously. It took all my strength, but I managed to get enough oomph that I was high enough to fling one leg over. I hung over the top of the gate, breathing hard.

"Woohoo! Nice work!" Charles clapped soundlessly.

This time, my mouth managed more of a smile and less of a grimace. I threw my other leg over and lowered myself before landing cat-like on my feet. Charles drifted through the gate and went ahead, down the strip of walkway leading to the backyard. Ghosts had it so easy.

I picked up the steel rod and crept along the side of the house, staying low. Against every survival instinct, I stopped under the bathroom window, the slash of light like one from any other home, belying the horror unfolding inside. Sometimes, the darkness was safer.

Breathing as quietly as I could, I listened for sounds of distress. Nothing. Being drugged up, she probably couldn't scream. I leaned against the wall. Just on the other side was pure evil and an innocent victim. How many women had come before her? How many times had people passed this property with no idea what went on in its bowels?

I wasn't going to find out anything standing here, and Charles was motioning to me from the end of the house. Within moments, I was next to him. His gaze was on the conservatory, which was attached to the building and stuck out about twelve feet from the rear of the structure. "Over there. That's what Petra was talking about."

A faint glow emanated from the all-glass addition. It looked like referred light from another room. "Can you check and make sure Andrew isn't in there looking out?" I didn't want to make any mistakes. I was so close to being able to help Renae.

While Charles did that, I gazed at the back garden. Shrouded shapes hulked from further down the block—trees that appeared ominous, as if they were lying in wait to maim and kill, just like those inside. I shuddered.

"Avery?"

I jumped and stared at Charles, who was right next to me. I let out a shuddering breath. "Sorry. What's the story?"

"All clear." He gave me a meaningful look. "Are you okay?"

"No, but that's irrelevant right now."

"Be careful."

"I'm trying." There wasn't much else to say on that point, and I couldn't ask him to go inside and look out for me because he was blocked—unless a person living there invited him in, there was no way. And that wasn't about to happen.

I gripped the steel rod with both hands, hefting it as if I

was about to swing and hit. It was abysmally light and thin. I'd have to be super accurate with any conks to the head—if I even got the opportunity—and hope that no one in there was wearing a hat or beanie.

Even in the blackness, I felt like a spotlight was on me, so I stuck close to the wall as I edged towards the conservatory. If anyone came out, my best bet would be to run into the dark yard and hope I didn't fall like in a horror movie and twist my ankle.

Charles was in front of the conservatory, peering in. "No one's in there. You're safe." *For now.*

I reached the conservatory and peered into one of the side glass panels, my nose against the glass—I wasn't about to stand in plain sight next to Charles. Attractive pine furniture—a three-seater lounge and two armchairs—a low glass-and-pine table, and three indoor plants swam in shadows, looking about as sinister as a golden retriever puppy. It was as if they were a normal family, with normal furniture, normal hobbies, normal brains. This conservatory was a lie. Their ability to fake it was how they got away with it.

I sucked in a breath as I remembered what Petra had told me.

I turned and stared into the abyss of the backyard. Where were those other women buried? They could be anywhere. Would they be closer to the house where the sickos could watch them from their everyman conservatory, or did they want them out of sight?

"Avery!"

I jerked back against the bricks, and a small squeal came out. I slammed a hand over my mouth, my wide eyes finding Petra next to me. My ribcage would be bruised after tonight—

my heart was doing its best to thump loud enough to be heard a mile away.

"Oh no. I'm sorry, but, but…." She took a deep breath, as if she was trying to calm herself. "They… they're doing it. They've undressed her, and it's all about to get worse. They…." She was hyperventilating, which shouldn't be possible, but…. "They'll rape and kill her soon. You have to come now!"

Charles and I shared a look, and I blinked tears away. The waterworks were unexpected, but it was probably the adrenaline dump paired with empathy. It also might be because I was potentially about to meet my maker. Hmm, unless.

"Okay. Go back in, and after I smash the glass, come back and tell me what they're doing. I'm about to make a lot of noise."

"Is that wise?" Charles looked like I'd just told him I was putting my head into a lion's mouth.

"I have a plan." And it was just as good as any other plan. As long as it distracted them enough to delay doing the worst to Renae until the police arrived. Surely they had to be close.

"Hurry!" With that, Petra disappeared.

"Here goes nothing." I moved in front of the conservatory glass door. Feet planted, I raised the tire thingy with both hands, drew my arms back as if I were playing baseball, and then swung as hard as I could. Even as the glass shattered in a crash of sound, I went to the next section and smashed that. Hopefully they heard. Rather than me going inside and becoming trapped, I wanted them outside, after me and away from Renae. They would likely split up to chase me, and I could pick them off one by one. Was my confidence misplaced? Possibly, but it was all I had, and I wasn't letting it go.

"Bloody hell!" Charles slammed his hands onto his head, his elbows sticking out at right angles. I'd really gotten his attention. "What are you doing?!" He stared into the mess as I raised the bar again.

"Luring them out." Anger drove my strike, and more panels shattered. If Andrew came along now, I was pumped and ready to hit a bull's-eye.

Petra appeared. "It worked! Andrew and his dad are coming out. They left his mother there. Run, Avery. Run!"

The urge to stay and fight burned through me, but it would be two against one, although it would be one old person. I could probably break that man's bones with one good whack. I backed away. "Do they have a gun?"

"I don't think so."

It was irrelevant because their footsteps echoed from inside.

They were coming.

I jogged further into the backyard, eyes straining for any holes that would trip me. The back light flicked on.

Showtime.

Andrew appeared first, his dad not far behind him. They stopped in the semi-dark threshold between the house and conservatory, assessing the damage. Andrew, taller and bulkier than his elderly father, was the first to find me. He stared, then turned to his father. "Go back to Mother. Finish it. I'll be back to clean up."

I hadn't noticed because I'd been concentrating on the house, but Petra had disappeared. As Andrew's gaze found me again, I shivered, and Petra reappeared. "His mother's bringing him the shotgun."

I swore. I could only save Renae by going back in. "Hey, Andrew, sicko bastard. The police are coming. You and your family will spend the rest of your lives in jail." He drew in a breath, standing straighter, his face tightening with rage and indignation—the facial expression of a true psycho. How dare I call him out and threaten him? The fury burning my insides to ash wasn't just from tonight—it was from a lifetime of being tortured by narcissists. The Crumpses could almost be my family—they were just a couple more steps along the path into depravity. I was speaking up for the child I'd been, for all the children and people living a nightmare. "That's right, you pathetic piece of crap. You're all going down because of me, a woman. Suck on that!"

His fists balled.

"Are you going to let her talk to you that way, Son?"

His words came through gritted teeth. "Of course not." He turned and reached out. His mother was there with the gun. He held it up. "I don't know who you are, but you're in my domain now, and since you seem to know what that means, you know what I'm about to do to you." The glass cracked and crunched their warning from under his feet as he strode through the destruction.

Charles was next to me now. "What are you doing? Run!"

He was right. If I stayed here, he'd shoot me. Andrew was already aiming. I swore again. Hunching over so I was a smaller target, I ran as fast as I dared in the dark. I reached a large tree and ducked right. An explosive crack violated my eardrums. Looked like I'd changed direction just in time. But where to go now? Further into the block—which would be expected—or back towards the house? If I could be quiet enough, I might get away with it. Besides, Renae needed saving now.

I fought my urge to run and stopped. Bending over, I looked for a rock. Finding a fist-sized one, I stayed low, turned, and threw it in the opposite direction of the house. The rock landed, making a noise. Another blast of sound that was unfortunately not a firecracker seared my nerves.

"He's coming." Charles was standing close to where I'd ducked off the main path.

I wanted to run so badly. My eyes watered from the cold and maybe a bit from fear, but I held my ground and stayed as small as I could.

"I'll see if I can help." Charles disappeared.

I gripped my steel bar and strained to hear Andrew's footfalls. Those gunshots had made my hearing worse. I didn't recall him having ear protection. Hopefully he was deafer than me.

There. A noise. He was close to the other side of the trees. I was two trees in. My heart hammered. *Don't move. Don't move. Don't move. Please go past.*

His steps halted.

I swallowed and held on, resisted as a whirlpool of terror tried ripping me from my anchor. But I had to hold fast. To run now would be to die.

How long was he going to stand there for? Was he coming around to look?

My wide eyes fixed on the spot in front of me where I expected him to appear at any moment.

Rustling further down the block. A bird? There it was again, louder, like someone passing through leaves.

Andrew called me a few choice names and moved towards the noise. "Coming, ready or not."

His footsteps faded, and a stick cracked. He was far enough away that I could move. I stood slowly but stayed low and crept towards the house, careful to remain behind the trees, some of which were trunks with spindly, bare branches, but their stingy protection was better than nothing.

I'm coming, Renae. God, I hoped I was in time.

Every few steps, I glanced around, making sure Andrew hadn't snuck up on me. Charles still hadn't returned, but that was okay—I knew he'd be safe.

After what seemed like an eternity, I was almost at the house. Petra hovered just outside the conservatory. "Avery, hurry!"

She didn't need to ask twice. As I hurried, another gunshot desecrated the silence, but it came from way down the back. That was all the permission I needed to run. I crunched over the debris in the conservatory as Petra led me to the bathroom. As we passed the kitchen, I picked up a large chef's knife. Normally, I wouldn't want a knife because it could be taken away and used against me, but these were old people—they wouldn't be stronger than me.

I whispered, "Go back outside, and let me know if Andrew comes back."

"Okay. The bathroom's that door there." She pointed down the hallway to the second door on my left. "Godspeed, Avery."

I nodded rather than risk speaking again.

Now wasn't the time to hesitate. Normally, I wouldn't want to hurt anyone, but these people were viler than anyone I'd ever come across, and I wasn't dying for some misplaced sense of being nice. They deserved anything I gave them and more—not that I'd do anything unnecessary, but I'd at least smash up their legs from the get-go.

Without second-guessing myself, I flung the door open.

Please be alive.

Renae was strapped to a chair in the shower, naked and

covered in blood, with Mr and Mrs Crumps standing on either side of her. Oh, God, was I too late?

"Andrew?" Mrs Crumps turned. As soon as she saw me, she shrieked. "Where's my son?"

Mr Crumps turned and lunged at me. There was nowhere to go in the small space. I didn't want to kill him—I wanted him to suffer in jail, so I whipped the knife out of the way and smashed his kneecap with my wrench. Not bad for a left-handed blow.

He screamed and went down.

Mrs Crumps narrowed her eyes and lashed at me with the small silver implement in her hand. Maybe a dentist's tool?

I deflected the blow with my steel rod, and Mrs Crumps screeched, overbalancing. I couldn't get a clear blow, and I wasn't ready to stab her yet. But Mr Crumps grabbed my leg.

Stop stuffing around, Avery. I was going to get myself killed.

Channelling the evil people's energy, I slashed Andrew's father's arm. The blade sliced cleanly but not too deep. He grabbed the three-inch wound with his other arm and rolled onto his back.

Mrs Crumps glanced at him, then back at me, rage spilling from every wrinkled pore. "You stupid bitch!" She opened her mouth again, but I'd had enough. I raised the bar to hit her over the head. Just as I'd hoped, she put her arms up to protect herself. It gave me a clear target for a front kick to the chest.

She made a satisfying grunt as the air left her lungs. She flew backwards, into the vanity, and her head snapped back, smashing into the mirror. Unconscious, she fell sideways, collapsing onto the ground. Mr Crumps shouted, "Eve!"

Charles and Petra appeared in the doorway. Charles was hopping from foot to foot. "I couldn't fool him any longer. He's coming back! You've got about thirty seconds. Shut the door!"

Renae groaned. At least she was still alive.

I tried to shut the door, but Mr Crumps grabbed the bottom of it. "Now you'll pay."

"I don't think so." I stomped on his hand. The second stomp was the ticket. He released the door, and I shut it. I dragged Mrs Crumps over and put her in front of it. Andrew had the shotgun, but if he thought he could indiscriminately shoot, he was mistaken.

"Do you hear that?" Charles, who was on my side of the door, asked.

My ears were still a bit dodgy after being the duck in a shooting gallery. "What?"

"Sirens. They're coming, Avery. The police are finally coming."

But so was Andrew. The handle turned, but I pushed against it. "Open up! Mum, Dad?"

"She's in here, Son. Shoot!"

"I'm holding your mum in front of the door. Shoot now, and you'll shoot her."

Mr Crumps was annoyingly still able to shout. "She's lying."

"Try, and find out."

Petra, still in the hallway, called out, "He's going to shoot. Duck!"

I fell into a squat and blocked my ears just as the door exploded inwards in a deafening boom. When I looked up, I found him looking down at me, a cruel smile lighting his face. He pointed the gun at me. *Not today, Satan.*

I dropped the wrench and flung my hand up, pushing the barrel out of the way, then lunged forward and stuck the knife in his crotch before pulling it out again. I wasn't giving him a second weapon. Noise spewed from his mouth, something between a screech and a bellow, as he gripped his crotch and collapsed to writhe on the floor. "That's for all the women you've killed. That's for Everly." His shocked gaze flicked to me before his eyes squeezed tight against the pain.

"Nice shot, Avery!" Charles cheered.

Petra's mouth was open. "Yes!" She grinned, but then her face changed. "Avery, watch out!"

I turned. Mr Crumps had a scalpel and was about to stab my calf.

I stepped back, out of reach, and then I heard it.

Sirens.

Charles was right. *Oh. My. Word. Finally.*

Knife poised and my gaze flicking between Andrew and his dad, I went to Renae and checked her pulse. The fast, shallow rise and fall of her chest indicated she was alive, but barely. I wanted to run out and tell the police I was in here, but I daren't leave her.

I opened the blind, slid the window open, and shouted with everything I had. "In here. Help! He has a gun. Help!" For good measure, I opened my mouth wide and screamed as if I were on a rollercoaster or watching a horror movie.

Charles raised his brows. "If that doesn't get their attention, nothing will."

I grinned. "I used to practice when I was a kid."

It seemed like forever, waiting for the police to break the front door down. Yes, I could've helped them, but Renae needed me here. I took my jacket off and placed it over her—she needed it more than me, and I didn't want the police getting an eyeful. She'd suffered enough for a lifetime.

Once I was sure the police were inside, I called out again. "Help. We're in the bathroom. Hello? We're in here." I dropped the bloody knife in the sink—there was no way I wanted the police to mistake me for a threat.

A tall policeman in protective clothing and holding a gun was the first to reach us. His bulk blocked most of the hallway. He took in the scene and quickly grabbed Andrew's shotgun, handing it to the armed policeman behind him. Wow, they'd called the tactical response group in. Normal police didn't carry guns.

Tears burned my eyes. They'd taken me seriously.

Andrew was down but not out. He threw an evil look my way, then stared beseechingly up at the police. "Help! That crazy bitch broke in here and attacked us when we got home. We found her torturing that woman in the chair."

Another policeman was in the hallway now and another behind him, both with guns ready. They all stared at me. Oh crap. This wasn't what was supposed to happen.

Crumps Senior weighed in. "My son's right. You have to help us! Arrest that crazy woman. She attacked us. My wife. Help my wife." Mr Crumps tried to get up, but his newly bunged knee was an issue. He groaned and fell back to the floor. *Good. Stay there.*

The first policeman took in everyone in the bathroom, including Renae. Then his gaze found me. "Are you Avery?"

"Yes. That's the victim. She's not breathing very well. They cut h—."

The policeman stepped forward, his hand up. "What's your full name?"

A policewoman helped move Andrew out of the hallway and back into another room as I answered. "Avery Winters." Surely they weren't going to get away with this?

"Did you break into this house?"

Talk about leading questions. "Yes, but only af—"

"Put your hands out. You're under arrest."

My mouth dropped open as a vault of unfairness burst open inside me. I felt like I was about to explode. "You can't be serious."

"Are we going to add resisting arrest to the charges here?"

I tried to calm down by reminding myself that Bellamy would be here soon, and it would all get straightened out. Wouldn't it? This was like a movie where everything went wrong or maybe a nightmare.

I put my hands out in front of me. "At least help that woman. They've almost killed her. Her breathing is shallow. Please."

The policeman cuffed me. How I would love to smash that smug look off Mr Crumps's face. "Don't do it, Avery. I know he deserves it, but…." Charles gave me a sympathetic look as the policeman pushed me from the room, his hand on my shoulder. Thankfully, the paramedics had arrived and went straight to Renae. That was something, at least.

"This is nuts. Why am I being arrested? I'm not the serial killer." The policeman ignored me as he shoved me towards the front of the house. "Why would I call you guys if *I* was doing something illegal? Make it make sense. Also, I'm a journalist with the *Manesbury Daily*."

He stopped, yanking me to a halt. He turned me to face him. "Are you threatening me, Miss Winters?"

"No. I'm just saying that this isn't right. You're arresting the wrong person. There are bodies buried out there somewhere. They've killed so many women over the years. The evidence you find in that bathroom will prove me right, and you'll be sorry. I can't imagine you'll get a promotion for letting them go free. Also, Andrew Crumps chased and shot at me in the backyard. I went into the house after that. I only smashed the conservatory to get their attention. It was the only way I could get inside and help the victim." I didn't dare say her name because how was I supposed to explain how I knew it?

He regarded me for a moment. Was I finally getting through? Before he could say anything, I continued, "Sergeant Bellamy from Cramptonbury Station will be here soon. He called me when my friends noticed I was gone. He knows I've been working on this case, and he was worried. I told him what was happening, but he had longer to travel than you. Can you at least wait until he gets here before you cart me away?" His face showed he was wavering, actually listening. "You can call him on my phone. It's in my jacket pocket—the jacket I covered the victim with. I didn't want her to be naked in front of everyone. Does that sound like the act of a torturer?"

A policewoman was coming in from outside. He looked at her. "Can you grab that jacket from the bathroom and bring it here? Also, if they take the occupants to hospital, I want a police escort. Something doesn't add up." *Oh my God. Ya think?* I did my best to stop those thoughts from showing on my face. Provoking him now wasn't going to help. At least I could breathe properly again. The Crumpses weren't getting away… yet.

"Yes, sir."

We waited silently until she returned. There was nothing more for me to say, and he certainly wasn't in a chatty mood.

"Here, sir." She handed him the phone and went back the way she'd come. He held it towards my face to unlock it.

"It's under Sergeant Bellamy."

"So you said." *Argh, what a smart ar—* "Hello, is this Sergeant Bellamy?" He listened for a bit. "This is Police

Sergeant Frazer of the Devon and Cornwall Police. I have an Avery Winters here. She's under arrest but insists I have it wrong." His forehead wrinkled at whatever Bellamy said, and then one eyebrow went up. He turned a serious gaze my way, his lips pressed together. Bellamy's voice reached me—he'd raised it above his normal level. It wasn't quite shouting, but it was his irritated tone. I pressed my lips together to prevent a smile. I loved that man. He was the father I never had. Eventually, Sergeant Frazer cleared his throat. "Well, then. I'll see you when you get here.... Yes.... Thank you." He hung up and stared down at me. "I'm keeping those cuffs on until he gets here, which should be in about five minutes. Once I confirm his identity, we'll go from there."

I still had nothing to say, so I kept my mouth closed as he pushed me towards the living room, gently this time. The paramedics—carrying Renae strapped onto a banana bed—passed us, heading for the front door. Smears of blood marred her pale face—too pale. They'd put an oxygen mask on her, and her eyes were closed. Petra walked along close to the bed, concern on her face. She gave me a worried look, then followed them to the front door.

Another set of paramedics, two police in tow, carried a still unconscious Mrs Crumps past. Following her was Andrew in a wheelchair. A volcano of hate spewed from his face as he passed me. "You'll regret this. Psycho."

I smiled. It was my turn to be smug. "I regret nothing. You and your sick family will never kill another woman again." The paramedic pushing him sent her colleague a shocked look. Andrew tried to jump out of his chair to grab me, but he was strapped in. The chair jerked to the side, and the paramedic almost dropped it. Andrew winced and grabbed his nether region. I smiled. I opened my mouth to goad him further, but Frazer was on the ball.

"That's enough, Miss Winters." What a spoilsport.

This time, I gave him a disappointed shake of my head. "Just wait till you discover everything. You have no idea."

"Winters!" Bellamy squeezed past the serial-killer procession and hurried into the room, Patel on his heels. The tension gripping my shoulders and neck loosened, and tears moistened my eyes. *Argh, do not cry right now, idiot.* I blinked and took a deep breath.

Now wasn't the time to fall apart because I was so relieved to see someone. Instead, I gave him a small smile. "Boy, am I glad to see you."

His gaze found the handcuffs. He looked at Frazer. "Is that necessary?"

Frazer folded his arms. "Yes. Can I see some ID?" Bellamy was wearing his uniform, for the love of chocolate cake.

Bellamy gave him an irritated look and produced his ID. "Happy?"

"Yes. Thank you." Frazer looked at me. "Stand up." When I did, he unlocked my cuffs, but there was no apology. What a surprise. *Not.*

"How many times have I told you not to go on these things alone?" He had his best angry parent face on, and Patel fought a grin.

"I know, but my informant called me. I couldn't wait. If I had, they might've killed their victim."

"What informant?" Frazer asked.

"I can't say. Sorry. He won't help me any more if I reveal who he is. It's a case I've been working on for some time. It started when I found a locket belonging to a missing woman who used to live in the apartment I rent." I filled Frazer in on Everly's story—the bits we could prove. I left out that we were friends and that she told me it was Andrew. How much easier this would be if I could just spill it all. But not today. I held in a sigh.

Once I'd done that, Bellamy asked me to explain everything tonight, from go to whoa. As I spoke, two more police gathered around, their expressions increasing in shock as the tale continued. "And that's when you guys showed up." I rubbed my wrists at the lingering sensation of cuffs.

Frazer, who'd been taking notes the whole time, looked at his colleagues. "I want you out there looking for shells. We're going to need more resources. Call Sergeant Phillips." They gave him a nod and left. He looked at me. "Do you have any idea where they're buried?"

I couldn't exactly say because I had no way of explaining how I'd discovered that. But maybe I could "encourage" them to look in certain places, one being around the incinerator. "I'm not sure, but I'd guess wherever there aren't many trees. The roots would get in the way. And my enquiries indicate there have been a few murders in the past ten years. I don't know if Everly is buried here, but there are a couple of relatively recent missing person's cases that could be linked to the Crumpses." I gave them Petra's name and the name of one of the women she told me about, Emmy. If I had too many details, it might seem weird. "I do know Andrew used to spend time at his great aunt's place. They were close, and he did work around her house for her." I gave them the address of where they'd likely find Everly's body.

"That's closer to us," Bellamy said. "I can get our lot down there if you like; take some of the pressure off."

Frazer peered at Bellamy. "How long have you known about this?"

"A few weeks. Winters came to me when she discovered the locket. But we didn't have much evidence. After searching the area where the locket was found, I couldn't spare any manpower, so she's been researching things in her journalist's capacity with our… support."

"Well, if you're happy to hand over any notes you have, we can collaborate. It will be easier on both of us." Wow, Frazer was being reasonable. Who woulda thunk it?

"Sounds good to me." Bellamy held out his hand, and they shook. "Not trying to step on your toes, Sergeant Frazer, but I'd like Winters to walk us through what happened outside. It will make finding those shells easier."

"Righto, then. Lead the way, Miss Winters."

As we stepped into the ruined conservatory, a ghost I hadn't met before appeared in front of me. I stopped walking, making as if I was surveying the damage. "Wow, I made a mess."

While Bellamy and Frazer agreed with me, the young woman said, "Thank you, thank you, thank you." A tear rolled down her long-dead cheek. "I'm Emmy. Please tell my parents I'm sorry I missed Toby's birthday and their thirtieth anniversary. Also, tell my mum that I'm okay. Don't forget."

"Okay." I'd lost myself for a minute.

Bellamy gave me the side eye, and Frazer said, "Okay, what?"

"Ah, nothing. Just kind of saying, okay, let's continue. The sooner we get this done, the sooner you can notify the families. They've all had a long wait." I gave Emmy a subtle nod and a small smile.

Tears streamed down her face, and she whispered, "I'm finally free."

A circle of blazing illumination appeared behind her,

blinding me. The familiar freight train noise began in the distance, becoming deafening as it hurtled our way. She turned towards it and held her arms out, embracing something she'd likely been waiting for.

Bellamy gave my shoulder a little nudge, startling me out of my trance. Frazer gave me a weird look. I smiled, sad yet hopeful.

It was time to recover those so cruelly lost.

With Emmy leading the way, we all walked into the light.

CHAPTER 24

Three days later, a few grim-faced police, Bellamy, Everly, and I stood in Andrew's aunt's backyard, looking at the pile of timber next to a newly demolished shed. The police contractors had jackhammered a six-by-three-foot concrete slab to pieces and were digging.

The iron sky hung low in the still air. Each breath felt like too much and yet not enough.

Despite my tense stomach—I wasn't sure how Everly and I would react when her remains saw the light of day—I yawned, which set Bellamy off. We'd hardly slept since the night the Crumpses' life went to hell. The police had dug up three bodies from the Crumpses', and their ground-penetrating image thing had located four more suspicious forms. They'd also found many of the dead women's possessions in Mr Crumps's study. Work would be ongoing there for a while, but there was enough evidence to put that family away forever.

I'd written a brief article to break the story, which, on the back of the arrest of Morris's murderers, made Julian happy.

MacPherson Media was getting yet another scoop. My detailed article would come out once all the victims' family members had been notified, which wouldn't be long now. The process had already started. Petra's family was devastated but said they could now grieve her properly and were planning her funeral. She hadn't gone into the light and would also be attending her funeral, hoping her presence would somehow be felt by her family.

"Stop!" One of the three diggers put up his arm. They were using shovels so as to go slow enough to not damage any remains. Bellamy walked over and knelt next to the three-foot-deep hole. He looked back at me in reassurance.

I held my breath, and Everly grabbed my hand, squeezing tight. Bellamy's mouth dropped open. My eyes widened at the solid, warm feel of her, and Everly and I stared at each other. The shock was enough to break the spell, and the realness froze into pain. She drew her hand away, frowning. "I'm sorry."

Bellamy paled… as if he'd just seen a ghost. No one else seemed to notice.

I shook my head, looked down, and whispered, "Don't be." If only I could say more without risking someone thinking I was crazy.

Bellamy shook his head as if to clear it, blinked, then turned to peer into the hole.

Would Everly disappear now her remains had been recovered? She insisted she knew they were hers as she felt a pull towards the bones; plus, "When you know, you know. I can't describe it." I'd have to trust her on that.

I glanced at Everly—someone I could never have imagined would become one of my closest friends. It had taken a while to adjust to the weirdness that my life had become, but now that I'd accepted things, I didn't want anything to change.

Was I about to lose her? I swallowed the scoring heat of tears in my throat.

"I don't want to go."

"You might not," I mumbled, trying not to move my lips.

"But I might. If I do, please tell my mum I love her, that I stayed with her as long as I could, and that it wasn't her fault." Yet another message to a grieving parent. When would it end?

I nodded. "Okay." Even though Mrs Crabby was the last person who would believe me and the first who would whack me over the head with the nearest blunt object if she was displeased, I'd do my duty.

"Thank you."

Bellamy glanced at me and, likely seeing nothing untoward—Everly—turned his attention back to the grave. The policeman in the gruesome hole was bent over, brushing dirt from the discovery. After a couple of minutes of silence, the men looked at each other, and Bellamy nodded. The policeman put something in a plastic bag and handed it to Bellamy, who came over to me. He knew Everly was with me even before we came because I told him she'd be here. He held up the bag containing a silver-coloured ring with a cherry on top, literally. It wasn't made of anything expensive—it was a more kitsch design of two cherries joined by a silver stalk. "Is this Everly's?" he whispered.

Everly reached for the bag, connecting with it and knocking it to the ground. Bellamy stared at the bag, then at me. "Was that her?" She was getting good at solidifying.

"Yes."

The police watching weren't sure what they'd just seen if their expressions were anything to go by, but they hadn't heard our conversation and would likely put it down to a sudden gust of wind, even though the world seemed like it was holding its breath… at least in this backyard.

When Bellamy had retrieved the ring, Everly said, "It brings back so many memories. Mum got it for me when I was thirteen from a shop called Treasure Chest. She got it for me because she'd had a bad knee, and I'd helped her with the housework for a few weeks. I never took it off, and when I got older, my finger was too big for it, so I couldn't get it off, even if I wanted to. If it wasn't for that, Andrew probably would've taken it." He could've chopped her finger off to get it, but I didn't say that. Things were bad enough without going there. I quietly repeated her story to Bellamy.

Everly frowned, her forehead creasing in worry. "I need to go see Mum. I could get sucked away at any moment." She glanced around, fear in her eyes. "But first, I need to see." Her eyes glistened as she stared at me. "Thank you, Avery. In case I don't get to see you again, I want you to know that you've been the best friend I've ever had. You never gave up on me. And please be kind to my mum. I know you guys aren't the best of friends"—I smiled at the understatement—"but she's going to need someone when all this comes out."

"What's going on?" Bellamy whispered.

I bit my lip, then swallowed. "She's saying goodbye… just in case she disappears."

He nodded slowly, understanding.

"I will, Ev. Promise. I'll miss you." I watched Everly as she walked towards her grave, steps slow but determined.

She reached the hole and stared into it. God knew what she was thinking and feeling. After a bit, she disappeared the normal way. The next dimension hadn't claimed her yet, but it probably wouldn't be long. Her unfinished business was with her mother.

I lowered my head and blinked back tears. It had been such a pathetic goodbye compared to how much we'd been through together. I wanted to bawl, but that wasn't appropriate in front of everyone—they'd think I'd gone mad. Instead, I breathed deeply and lifted my head. "So, now what?"

"We'll comb over this place, make sure no one else is buried here. Give me a couple of days to get organised. Once forensics can confirm it's Everly, I'll tell her mother. We took a DNA swab from Mrs Collins when this first started, and we have Everly's dental records."

"Just let me know when you're going to tell her. I might need your support. Everly wanted me to tell her mother a couple of things, and I have no idea how she'll react. I'm not exactly her favourite person."

He chuckled. "I don't think anyone is." His expression softened. "But after losing her daughter, I can't blame her for being a prickly biddy."

"Neither can I. Um, if she kicks me out after this, can I crash at yours till I find something else?" I tried not to smile—I'd never really impose like that, especially after just having invaded their home.

He narrowed his eyes, his scepticism well placed. "Not sure my wife would be in favour of that." His eyes twinkled. We all knew his wife was amazing and kind—she'd never say no. "I know Finn has a spare room."

Thank God for the cold; otherwise, my cheeks would be flaming red. "Very funny."

"Sergeant Bellamy." One of the police at the hole

beckoned him over. He gave a nod to him and turned back to me. "I'll get on with this, and I'll call you tomorrow."

"Thanks. I'm going to take a few photos, but don't worry; I'll okay everything with you before I submit my article. It's going to be a long one. This has been… well… a lot."

"One of the worst serial-killer cases this country has ever seen, so, yes." His serious gaze turned penetrating. "Thank you, Winters. Yet again, you've gone above and beyond. I don't know what we'd do without you." He didn't wait for my soppy reaction. Under a darkening sky, he returned to Everly's bones.

I held in the burning grief long enough to take some photos, but once I got into Daisy, the floodgates opened. It was a shame they couldn't wash away the pain. I knew someone who could, though. I needed to cuddle with Zeus—another soul I was going to miss. This all felt way more torturous than leaving Australia. I didn't care if I never saw my parents again, but Everly and Zeus, it was ripping my heart out.

And the scars would last forever.

CHAPTER 25

Two days later, it was sleeting, the stinging little balls of precipitation matching my mood.

Much to my surprise, Everly hadn't been sucked anywhere… yet. She'd come to see me last night for a chat—we both needed to process everything, and she wanted to hear all about the gotcha moment and all the action leading up to it that night at the Crumpses' house. We also agreed that I wouldn't play a recording of her voice to her mother yet—she'd have enough to deal with. We did make a recording for the future, though, just in case Everly was sucked away before we got a chance.

My body was tense, waiting for the other shoe to drop and for Everly to disappear forever, which might happen once her mother had been told. That, along with Zeus's impending departure, had made me tired and irritable, so I'd been working from home. But this morning, I'd gotten dressed because Bellamy had texted that he was coming to tell Mrs

Crabby they'd found her daughter. He told me to be there at nine, which was in five minutes. Afterwards, I was going to have breakfast at Finn's—he, Meg, and Carina had forgiven me for running off by myself, and they'd joked about getting a tracking chip implanted in my neck, but things were all good after they'd checked me over and made sure I was okay.

I was killing time staring out the living room window, trying to ignore my nerves at a confrontation with Mrs Crabby, when Charles called from just inside my front door. "Avery, hello."

I turned. "Hey. What's up?"

"Morris is looking for you, but he couldn't come in. Can you invite him?"

"Yeah, sure. Morris, this is Avery. You're welcome to come inside my home."

He appeared in the middle of the room. His head turned this way and that, checking out my place. Finally, he looked at me and said, "I wanted to let you know that the article you wrote about my murder was top-notch. Thank you. And thanks again for putting yourself in danger and solving everything. My family is relieved it's all over. Now they can properly grieve my wife and me."

I smiled. "It's my pleasure." I didn't want to state the obvious, but I felt guilty, and I needed to apologise. "So, the light hasn't come for you yet? I'm so sorry. I feel like this is my fault. If it wasn't for me, you probably wouldn't have stayed."

He blinked. "No! Don't be ridiculous. I'm not sure why it hasn't come, but I think it's because my daughter's pregnancy isn't quite going to plan. She's on bedrest so the baby doesn't come early—she's not due for another two months. I wanted to hang around, make sure she's okay. I also wanted to see my new grandson so I can tell Meredith all about him. Once he's out safely, I'll be ready to leave."

I didn't know if I could believe that—it still might be my fault for being able to see him and offering to help solve the crime. But maybe it was his desire to see his grandchild that was keeping him here. "Okay. I'll go with that for now. Come see me when the baby is born, and if I never see you again, I'll assume you've gone on to bigger and better things."

He smiled. "Will do, Avery. Stay safe, and keep writing those articles. I almost envy you. The information you're privy to. If I'd had that in my day…."

"Yes, well, it has its positives and its negatives." I looked at the time on my phone—9:00 a.m. "In fact, one of the negatives is waiting for me now. I have to go see Mrs Collins downstairs. I hope everything goes well for you and your family, Morris. It's been a pleasure."

"And you, Avery. Goodbye." He waved at me and then Charles and disappeared.

"Okay, Charles, I'll see you later."

"Bye, Aves." He disappeared, too, and I went to my front door.

It was time to face Mrs Crabby and hope she believed me.

I took a deep breath as I left my apartment.

I was careful to avoid the creaky parts of the stairs as I descended, but then I remembered Mrs Crabby was expecting me—old habits died hard. Would it be one of the last times I'd have to worry? Getting kicked out after this was a real possibility, but at least I had some savings now. Last night I checked rental listings in the area. There was one three-bedroom house, and it was too expensive. There were also two shared houses, but I didn't want to live with strangers. Hiding who I was to my friends was hard enough, let alone having to have my guard up when I was relaxing at home. Let's not ignore that with my luck, I'd end up living with crazy people. All the interviews I'd done since I'd arrived were a testament to the fact that sanity was in short supply around here.

There were places available in Cramptonbury. Although it was more expensive for what you got, but if that's what happened, so be it. It wasn't ideal because of all the driving, but then again, I spent a fair amount of time at the police station, and maybe I could work from home more often. I pretended that living further from my friends didn't make me sad. Would we drift apart if I couldn't just pop in and see Meg and if I didn't come into the office every day? Maybe. I slapped my own cheek to stop the worry loop. *You're not moving back to Australia, idiot. Stop catastrophising.* I shuddered. Okay, moving to Cramptonbury wasn't that bad.

I knocked on the door. Bellamy answered it. "Ah, there she is."

"Hello." I gave him a quizzical look, as in, why was he answering the door?

He jerked his head towards the living room. I went in, which I'd never done before. It felt like I shouldn't be here, as if I was breaking in. I halted a few steps in. The room was locked in a time warp. The 1970s called and wanted its brown carpet, orange lounges, and heavy green curtains back.

Mrs Crabby sat in one of the lounges, her face paler than normal and set in a frown, as if any other movement would cause her to disintegrate. Her arthritic hands clasped together in her lap, a piece of plastic bag peeping out from between her fingers—Bellamy must've shown her the ring, but as it was evidence, it was still in its bag. She slowly turned her head to look at me. "Avery." The word came out quickly before her mouth snapped shut. There was no malice, just recognition.

Everly was sitting next to her mother. "Bellamy's told her they found me and who did it. She's in shock. I'm worried the news is going to kill her." Everly tried to stroke her mother's hand, but her hand went straight through, and Mrs Crabby shivered.

Bellamy shut the door. "Go on in."

"Why didn't you wait for me before telling her everything?"

His eyebrows raised, and he whispered, "Where is she?"

"Sitting next to her." He knew what I meant. Mrs Crabby was probably too out of it to take in the meaning of our words.

Bellamy motioned for me to sit. "I'm about to make tea for Mrs Collins. Would you like one, Winters?"

"Ah, no thanks." I peered at the couch that was at right angles to the one Mrs Crabby sat on. It was awkward enough without me standing weirdly in the middle of the room, so I sat. Bellamy left to go make tea. Right. Now what? I glanced at Mrs Crabby, then let my gaze wander the room. Five photo frames sat atop the mantle above the fireplace. All were of Everly, from baby Everly to teenager.

Plastic crinkled, and I stared at Mrs Crabby, who was staring into her lap, exploring the ring with gnarled fingers. Everly longingly stared at her mother with glazed eyes. How did I broach this? I wanted so badly to comfort both of them, but I was ill-equipped with the how. It wasn't as if my own parents had been great role models. They hadn't even been average ones. In fact, could someone be a negative role model? If so, they were it.

Everly looked at me. "Say something. Please? Tell her I'm here." I swallowed. Everly smiled, despite the sadness in her eyes. "You look like a deer in headlights. What's the worst that can happen?"

I wanted to answer that she'd think I was nuts and that I was trying to upset her, but I didn't want to frighten the old lady by talking to the space next to her. How had this become my life? I opened my mouth to speak but croaked instead. Mrs Crabby started, then looked at me. "What is it? Have you got something to say?" Ah, she had a bit of spice to her tone. This was more familiar ground.

"Um, yes. I'm very sorry about Everly." Okay, it was a start.

Mrs Crabby stared at me for a bit before her chest rose and fell with a deep breath. "I hear you were instrumental in finding my daughter, that you discovered things the police couldn't."

"Yes."

"And that you put yourself in considerable danger to rescue that other poor lass."

"Yes." Wow, I was really explaining things well. Although, if Bellamy had told her everything, what was there left to say? It was better to say nothing than the wrong thing right now.

Mrs Crabby's expression was less stunned mullet and more alive. "Not very talkative, are you."

Everly bit her lip to stop from smiling. *Yes, so funny.* I managed not to give my friend the withering look that desperately tried to escape.

"No. I have something to tell you, and I don't know how you'll take it."

"Try me." Easier said than done. It was like a tiger asking

you to stick an arm into its cage with the implicit promise it wouldn't take it off at the elbow.

"Go on. You can do it." Everly gave me an encouraging smile.

Where to start? "You're going to have to suspend disbelief and remember that I have nothing to gain from telling you what I'm about to. I also can't tell you what I'm about to unless you promise not to say anything to anyone. The only person who knows my secret is Sergeant Bellamy." I glanced at the door he'd made his getaway through, and he was still nowhere to be seen. Looked like he was giving me privacy for this. Hopefully he was standing by in case Mrs Crabby reacted badly.

"Well, I don't like to promise anything without knowing the facts. If you've done something bad, I'm not keeping it to myself. People must be warned."

I kept my tone even, reminding myself she was experiencing one of the most stressful days of her life. "People?"

She waved one arm around. "People—Finnegan, Josie, Meg…. *People*."

I looked pointedly at Everly and raised my eyebrows as if to say, "see, this is why I can't do this."

"But you have to. Please, Aves. I don't know if I'm going to leave, and I don't want to, but what if this is holding me back, holding me here? I need this to move on—whatever that means—just as much as she does. Please."

I couldn't ignore the desperate look in her eyes. So, even though I might be about to do something to implode my friendships, I parted my lips. "I can see ghosts." The look she gave me contained surprise but not disgust or total disbelief. She hadn't attacked me. Hmm. It was just enough for me to keep going. "Soon after I moved in here, I met Everly. She's still living upstairs, kind of. I mean, she's not alive. Her ghost is there. In fact, she's sitting next to you right now. She's the reason I'm telling you this. We're friends."

Mrs Crabby's mouth fell open. Whatever she was expecting, it wasn't that. She gripped the plastic bag in her lap. "You wouldn't be so cruel as to make that up, would you?"

"No. I know it's a lot to take in, but—"

"Tell me something, then. Tell me something you couldn't possibly know. I've never trusted you. I mean, you came here all the way from Australia. Why? Are you a wanted criminal? And why did it take you this long to catch her killer if she talks to you? Surely she would've told you as soon as you moved in." Mrs Crabby was fully back to her normal self. Oh, the joy.

"Of course I'm not a criminal. Everly did tell me, but not straight away. I had to beg her. She told me she'd been murdered, but she wouldn't tell me by who. Eventually, she said she didn't want you to beat yourself up, that you'd encouraged her to date Andrew. She met another ghost victim of his and decided that she wanted him caught, that as sorry as she was, she would have to risk you being upset."

Mrs Crabby considered my explanation. Some of the fight had slipped from her voice. "She was always so considerate, my Everly. It would be just like her to worry about my feelings."

"I do. I worry about you all the time."

Ah, what the hell. I was in this neck-deep already. Might as well drown myself. "She just said she worries about you all the time."

Mrs Crabby jerked her head this way and that, looking for her daughter. "Where? She's here?"

"She's sitting next to you." I gave a nod to her right. "You felt her touch you earlier, on the hand."

She stared at the spot, her brow wrinkles deepening. "I'm going to state the obvious and say I don't see her."

"Have you ever died and been brought back to life?"

"What a strange question. No."

"If someone's died and come back, they have the potential to see ghosts, at least that's what happened to me…." Other people might be able to see ghosts for other reasons, but I really didn't know much at all, so I kept it to my own experience.

"Well, that's convenient. You still haven't told me anything extraordinary. Anyone from her past could've told you that I encouraged her to see Andrew."

"She told me the story of her cherry ring."

Mrs Crabby stopped fiddling with it. "Go on, then." I repeated what Everly had told me. She frowned. "I don't know anyone who knows that story. Hmm…."

"Mum prays every night. Tell her you know the number."

Mrs Crabby stared at the empty space where her daughter sat.

"What?"

"She says to God that she wants a sign. That sign is three hundred and forty-seven and two-thirds."

I chuckled. "Two-thirds. I'm not surprised she'd be so specific."

The old lady stared at me. "What nonsense are you going on about?"

"Everly just said you pray every night, and you want God to send you a sign, which is three hundred and forty-seven and two-thirds."

"You've heard me! Have you been spying on me?"

"No." I heavy sighed and looked at Everly. "This isn't

working." She had an answer for everything, a reason I was a liar and charlatan. I was so losing my friends over this.

Everly gasped. "I know!" She told me two stories from her childhood that no one could know.

"Everly says that when you used to kiss her goodnight, you always rubbed noses, too, and that you said it was a penguin kiss. She would say it was from the Eskimos, and you'd have a pretend argument."

Finally, she had no answer. Her mouth opened to give one, but then it stayed parted yet mercifully quiet.

"The other story is that one day, you were gardening out the back—you used to have a veggie patch. And when you sat on the grass to take a break, you sat on a bee, and it stung your behind. You were too embarrassed to go to the doctor, so you waited for Everly to come home from school and get the stinger out with tweezers, a pair of blue ones. She was eleven, and you baked her chocolate cupcakes for a month to buy her silence." I couldn't help it, but I chuckled. Looked like some secrets couldn't stay buried forever.

Instead of anger over the reveal, her face relaxed into wonder. If I didn't see what happened next, I never would've believed it. Her eyes shone, and not with malice. Tears gathered in her eyes and spilled over her lashes. She placed one of her hands, with its bent, arthritic fingers, over her mouth and cried.

Even my eyes were filling. Apparently, I could still feel sorry for someone, even if they'd tortured me. Again, old habits died hard. Sigh. One day I'd stop being a sucker, but today wasn't it.

Everly laid her head on her mother's shoulder and shut her eyes. I watched them, waiting for the train noise and light.

But nothing happened.

Would I get to keep my friend?

Bellamy returned with our tea and a tissue box. He handed it to Mrs Crabby. "Well, ladies, how are things going?"

Mrs Crabby sniffled and looked up at him. "Well, thank you." She turned her attention to me. "I'm surprised to be saying this, but Avery has been a big help today. Thank you. Is my daughter happy where she is?"

Everly smiled. "Happier now."

"She's happy. She's a counsellor for other ghosts." I briefly explained what I knew of the afterlife. "I think she still has times when her murder upsets her, but she's been more worried about you. This has made her happy to know that you're okay. She loves you very much, and she's going to stay with you as long as possible."

"This is just so incredible." Mrs Crabby asked a couple more questions, but it became apparent she was tired. I facilitated a short conversation between her and Everly, and then Bellamy stood.

He looked at me, his lips twitching. "I hear you have a breakfast date with Finn."

Everly laughed, and Mrs Crabby gave me a knowing look. "Yesterday, I would've said he's too good for you, but I've changed my mind."

"Um, thanks, I think." I laughed. "We're not dating, though. I'm going there to see Zeus, the cat I rescued when I interviewed someone for the paper. I fell in love with him, and I'm spending as much time with him as I can before he goes to his new home." It didn't matter how many times I was reminded of the fact that I was losing Zeus; it didn't get easier to handle.

She frowned. "Why aren't you taking him?"

I blinked. "Ah, it says no pets in the lease. I didn't think you'd be amenable to it."

She stood and handed the plastic bag with the ring to Bellamy. "Well…." She faced me. "I probably wouldn't have been. But in light of what you've given me today, I think I shall allow it. But you must keep his litter and the apartment clean, and he's not to go into the common areas. If you can stick to those rules, you have my permission. Oh, and while my daughter is still in this realm, I would like a weekly catch-up. I was determined not to like you, Miss Winters, but I fear you've made that impossible. Not that we're going to be best friends or anything. But I don't hate you."

I couldn't help but laugh again. Also, she was letting me keep Zeus? I blinked away the burn of more tears. Everly shook her head. "She's something else."

I nodded. "She sure is."

"What did my daughter say?"

"She said you're something else."

Bellamy chuckled. "Well, isn't this a splendid outcome? It looks as if good deeds breed other good deeds."

"It seems so." Mrs Crabby started towards the door. "Thank you both again for coming to see me and for catching the monster who hurt my precious daughter. You've brought me peace I haven't felt since Everly went missing. I have a lot to think about."

"Please let me know if you need anything." As much as we weren't best friends, I owed it to Everly to be nice to her mother. Also, the lady was letting me keep Zeus. How could I hate her? Maybe I'd have to retire the Mrs Crabby nickname.

"Thank you, Miss Winters. I will. Now, I think you have a cat to collect." She smiled… actually smiled. Maybe the apocalypse was coming.

"I do indeed. Thank you." Did I bawl and laugh all the way to Finn's? You bet. When I set out to solve Everly's murder, I did it for her *and* because I couldn't stand that someone so evil was out there enjoying their life. But I'd received so much more than I'd ever imagined through the process. Life could bring the worst things ever, but good things could happen to good people.

Zeus was finally coming home to where he belonged.

With me.

Thank you so much for reading Avery's series. If you've enjoyed this series and haven't tried my witch mystery series set in Westerham, England—Paranormal Investigation Bureau—visit my website and checkout my discounted book bundles! https://dionnelisterauthor.com/

ALSO BY DIONNE LISTER

Paranormal Investigation Bureau

Witchnapped in Westerham #1

Witch Swindled in Westerham #2

Witch Undercover in Westerham #3

Witchslapped in Westerham #4

Witch Silenced in Westerham #5

Killer Witch in Westerham #6

Witch Haunted in Westerham #7

Witch Oracle in Westerham #8

Witchbotched in Westerham #9

Witch Cursed in Westerham #10

Witch Heist in Westerham #11

Witch Burglar in Westerham #12

Vampire Witch in Westerham #13

Witch War in Westerham #14

Westerham Witches and a Venetian Vendetta #15

Witch Nemesis in Westerham #16

Witch Catastrophe in Westerham #17

Witch Karma in Westerham Book #18

Witch Showdown in Westerham Book #19

Westerham Witches and an Aussie Misadventure Book #20

Witch Smuggled in Westerham Book #21

Christmissing in Westerham (Christmas novella)

Haunting Avery Winters

(Paranormal Cosy Mystery)

A Killer Welcome #1

A Regrettable Roast #2

A Fallow Grave #3

A Frozen Stiff #4

A Deadly Drive-by #5

A Caffeine Fix #6

An Explosive Ending #7

A Santa Slaying (Christmas Novella)

The Circle of Talia

(YA Epic Fantasy)

Shadows of the Realm

A Time of Darkness

Realm of Blood and Fire

The Rose of Nerine

(Epic Fantasy)

Tempering the Rose

Forging the Rose

Printed in Dunstable, United Kingdom

65613095R00194